Hope

'Ben is a fantastic character – flawed, imperfect but **totally believable**'

'Fast-paced and **utterly absorbing**'

'The action keeps you gripped until the last page and has you on the edge of your seat until the very end. Ben Hope is as brilliant as ever'

'**Twists and turns** keep you hooked till the end. Keep them coming Scott'

'I couldn't turn the pages fast enough!'

'**Ben Hope back at his best**'

WITHDRAWN

'One of the best series of our time!'

'Scott **never fails to impress**. Five stars are not enough'

'**A fast-paced thriller** which is impossible to put down'

'The Ben Hope series is back with a bang. **All action, fast paced and slicker than ever,** I just can't get enough!'

'Scott Mariani **seamlessly weaves the history and action** together'

'Scott Mariani never fails to thrill'

THE CASSANDRA SANCTION

Scott Mariani is the author of the worldwide-acclaimed action-adventure thriller series featuring ex-SAS hero Ben Hope, which has sold over a million copies in Scott's native UK alone and is also translated into over 20 languages. His books have been described as 'James Bond meets Jason Bourne, with a historical twist.' The first Ben Hope book, THE ALCHEMIST'S SECRET, spent six straight weeks at #1 on Amazon's Kindle chart, and all the others have been *Sunday Times* bestsellers.

Scott was born in Scotland, studied in Oxford and now lives and writes in a remote setting in rural west Wales. When not writing, he can be found bouncing about the country lanes in an ancient Land Rover, wild camping in the Brecon Beacons or engrossed in his hobbies of astronomy, photography and target shooting (no dead animals involved!).

You can find out more about Scott and his work on his official website:

www.scottmariani.com

By the same author:

Ben Hope series
The Alchemist's Secret
The Mozart Conspiracy
The Doomsday Prophecy
The Heretic's Treasure
The Shadow Project
The Lost Relic
The Sacred Sword
The Armada Legacy
The Nemesis Program
The Forgotten Holocaust
The Martyr's Curse

To find out more visit **www.scottmariani.com**

SCOTT MARIANI

The Cassandra Sanction

avon

AVON

A division of HarperCollins*Publishers*
1 London Bridge Street
London SE1 9GF

www.harpercollins.co.uk

A Paperback Original 2015

1

Copyright © Scott Mariani 2015

Scott Mariani asserts the moral right to
be identified as the author of this work

A catalogue record for this book is
available from the British Library

ISBN-13: 978-0-00-748619-9

Set in Minion by Palimpsest Book Production Limited,
Falkirk, Stirlingshire

Printed and bound in Great Britain by
Clays Ltd, St. Ives plc

THE CASSANDRA SANCTION

'Even in scientific circles, it is not easy to expunge an erroneous conclusion if it has been cited enough times.'

Professor Ronald T. Merril, University of Washington

'A smart man only believes half of what he hears; a wise man knows which half.'

Col. Jeff Cooper, United States Marine Corps

Prologue

Rügen Island,
Baltic coast, northern Germany
16 July

The woman sitting at the wheel of the stationary car was thirty-four years of age but looked at least five years younger. Her hair was long and black. Her face was one that was well known to millions of people. She was as popular for her looks as she was for her intellect, her sharp wit and her professional credentials, and often recognised wherever she ventured out in public.

But she was alone now. She'd driven many miles to be as far away from anybody as she could, on this particular day.

This day, which was to be the last day of her life.

She'd driven the black Porsche Cayenne four-by-four off the coastal track and up a long incline of rough grass, patchy and flattened by the incessant sea wind, to rest stationary just metres from the edge of the chalk cliff. The Baltic Sea was hard and grey, unseasonably cold-looking for the time of year. With the engine shut off, she could hear the rumble and crash of the breakers against the rocks far below. Evening was drawing in, and the rising storm brought strong gusts of salt wind that buffeted the car every few seconds and rocked its body on its suspension. Rain slapped the windscreen and trickled down the glass, like the tears that were running freely down her face as she wept.

She had been sitting there a long time behind the wheel. Reflecting on her life. Picturing in turn the faces of those she was leaving behind, and thinking about how her loss would affect them. One, more than anybody.

She knew how badly she was going to hurt him by doing this. It would have been the same for her, if it had been the other way round.

Catalina Fuentes gazed out at the sea and whispered, 'Forgive me, Raul.'

Then she slowly reached for the ignition and restarted the engine. She put the car into drive and gripped the wheel tightly. She took several deep breaths to steady her pounding heart and deepen her resolve. This was it. The time had come. Now she was ready.

The engine picked up as she touched the gas. The car rolled over the rough grass towards the cliff edge. Past the apex of the incline, the ground sloped downwards before it dropped away sheer, nothing but empty air between it and the rocks a hundred metres below. The Porsche Cayenne bumped down the slope, stones and grit pinging and popping from under its wheels, flattening the coarse shrubs that clung to the weathered cliff top. Gathering speed, rolling faster and faster as the slope steepened; then its front wheels met with nothingness and the car's nose tipped downwards into space.

As the Porsche vaulted off the edge of the chalk cliff and began its long, twisting, somersaulting fall, Catalina Fuentes closed her eyes and bid a last goodbye to the life she'd known and all the people in it.

Chapter One

Ben Hope had been in the bar less than six minutes when the violence kicked off.

His being there in the first place had been purely a chance thing. For a man with nowhere in particular to be at any particular time and under no sort of pressure except to find a cool drink on a warm early October afternoon, the little Andalusian town of Frigiliana offered more than enough choice of watering holes to pick out at random, and the whitewashed bar tucked away in a corner of a square in the Moorish quarter had seemed like the kind of quiet place that appealed.

Pretty soon, it was looking like he'd picked the wrong one, at the wrong time. Of all the joints in all the pueblos of the Sierra Almijara foothills, he'd had to wander into this one.

He'd been picking up the vibe and watching the signs from the moment he walked in. But the beer looked good, and it was too late to change his mind, and he didn't have anything better to do anyway, so he hung around mainly to see whether his guess would turn out right. Which it soon did.

The bar wasn't exactly crowded, but it wasn't empty either. Without consciously counting, he registered the presence of a dozen people in the shady room, not including the owner, a wide little guy in a faded polo shirt, who was lazily tidying

3

up behind the bar and didn't speak as he served Ben a bottle of the local *cerveza*. Ben carried his drink over to a shady corner table, dumped his bag and settled there with his back to the wall, facing the door, away from the other punters, where he could see the window and survey the rest of the room at the same time.

Old habits. Ben Hope was someone who preferred to observe than to be observed. He reclined in his chair and sipped his cool beer. The situation unfolding in front of him was a simple one, following a classic pattern he had witnessed more often and in more places in his life than he cared to count, like an old movie he'd seen so many times before. What was coming was as predictable and inevitable as the fact that he wasn't just going to sit there and let it happen.

On the left side of the room, midway between Ben's corner table and the bar, a guy was sitting alone nursing a half-empty tumbler and a half-empty bottle of Arehucas Carta Oro rum that he looked intent on finishing before he passed out. He was a man around his mid-thirties, obviously a Spaniard, lean-faced, with a thick head of glossy, tousled black hair and skin tanned to the colour of *café con leche*. His expression was grim, his eyes bloodshot. A four-day beard shaded his cheeks and his white shirt was crumpled and grubby, as if he'd been wearing it for a few days and sleeping in it too. But he didn't have the look of a down-and-out or a vagrant. Just of a man who was very obviously upset and working hard to find solace in drink.

Ben knew all about that.

The Spanish guy sitting alone trying to get wrecked wasn't the problem. Nor were the elderly couple at the table in the right corner at the back of the barroom, opposite Ben. The old man must have been about a thousand years old, and the way his withered neck stuck out of his shirt

4

collar made Ben think of a Galapagos tortoise. His wife wasn't much younger, shrivelled to something under five feet with skin like rawhide. The Moorish Sultans had probably still ruled these parts back when they'd started dating. Still together, still in love. Ben thought they looked like a sweet couple, in a wrinkly kind of way.

Nor, again, was any of the potential trouble coming from the man seated at a table by the door. With straw-coloured hair, cropped short and receding, he looked too pale and Nordic to be a local. Maybe a Swedish tourist, Ben thought. Or a Dane. An abstemious one, drinking mineral water while apparently engrossed in a paperback.

No, the source of the problem was right in the middle of the barroom, where two tables had been dragged untidily together to accommodate the noisy crowd of foreigners. It didn't take much to tell they were Brits. Eight of them, all in their twenties, all red-faced from exuberance and the large quantity of local brew they were throwing down their throats. Their T-shirts were loud, their voices louder. Ben had heard their raucous laughter from outside. Their table was a mess of spilled beer and empty bottles, loose change and cigarette packs. To the delight of his mates, one of them clambered up on top of it and tried to do a little dance before he almost toppled the whole thing over and fell back in his chair, roaring like a musketeer. They weren't as rowdy as some gangs of beery squaddies Ben had seen, but they weren't far off it. The barman was casting a nervous eye at them as he weighed up the risks of asking them to leave against what they were spending in the place. Next, they broke into a chanting rendition of *Y Viva España* that was too much for the ancient couple in the right corner. The barman's frown deepened as they made their shuffling exit, but he still didn't say anything.

The Dane never looked up from his paperback, as if the noisy bunch didn't even exist. Maybe he was hard of hearing, Ben thought, or maybe it was just a hell of an interesting book. The yobs gave him a cursory once-over, seemed to decide he wasn't worth bothering with, and then turned their attention on the solitary Spaniard sitting drinking on the left side of the room. The response they'd managed to provoke out of the old folks had whetted their appetite for more. A chorus of faux-Spanish words and calls of 'Hey, Pedro. Cheer up, might never happen' quickly graduated into 'You speaka da English?'; and from there into 'Hey, I'm talking to you. You fucking deaf?'

They didn't seem to notice Ben sitting watching from the shadows. All the better for them.

The lone Spaniard poured more rum and quietly went on drinking as the loutish calls from across the barroom grew louder. He was doing almost as good a job as the Dane of acting as if the yobs were just a mirage that only Ben, the barman and the elderly couple had been able to see. Or else, maybe he was just too drunk to register that the taunting was directed at him. Either way, if he went on ignoring them, there was a chance that the situation might dissipate away to nothing. The eight lads would probably just down a few more beers and then go staggering off down the street in search of a more entertaining venue, or local girls to proposition, or town monuments to urinate on. Just boys enjoying themselves on holiday.

But it didn't happen that way, thanks to the big porker who'd been the first to call out to the Spaniard. He had gingery hair cropped in a bad buzzcut and a T-shirt a size too small for him with the legend EFF YOU SEE KAY OWE EFF EFF in block letters across his flabby chest. He nudged the guy sitting next to him and muttered something Ben didn't catch, then turned his grin on the Spaniard and yelled out, 'The fucking bitch ain't worth it, mate.'

The atmosphere in the room seemed to change, like a sudden drop in pressure. Ben sensed it immediately. He wasn't sure if the English boys had. *Here it comes*, he thought. He watched as the fingers clutching the Spaniard's glass turned white. The Spaniard's lips pursed and his brow creased. One muscle at a time, his face crumpled into a deep frown.

Then the Spaniard stood up. The backs of his legs shoved his chair back with a scraping sound that was as laden with portent as the look on his face. Still clutching his drink, he walked around the edge of his table and crossed the barroom floor towards the English boys. There was a lurch to his step, but he was able to keep a fairly straight line. There was something more than just anger in his eyes. Ben wasn't sure if the English boys could see that, either.

The Dane was still sitting there glued to his book, apparently oblivious. Not like Ben.

They all stared at the Spaniard as he approached. One of them elbowed his friend and said, 'Oooo. Touch a nerve, did we?'

'I'm shitting my pants,' said the big porker in a tremulous voice.

The Spaniard stopped three feet away from their table. The Arehucas Carta Oro was making him sway on his feet, not dramatically, but noticeably. He eyed the eight of them as if they were fresh dogshit, and then his gaze rested on the big porker.

Quietly, and in perfect English, he said, 'My name isn't Pedro. And you're going to apologise for what you just called her.'

An outraged silence fell over the group. Ben was watching the big porker, whose grin had dropped and whose cheeks turned mottled red. The pack leader; and if he wanted to remain so, peer pressure now demanded that he make a good show of responding to this upstart who'd had the monstrous balls to stand up to him in front of his friends.

'My mistake,' the big porker said, meeting the Spaniard's eye. 'I shouldn't have called her a bitch. I should've called her a cheap fucking dago whore slut cocksucker bitch. Because that's what she is. Isn't that right, Pedro?'

For a guy with the better part of a bottle of rum inside him, the Spaniard moved pretty fast. First, he dashed the contents of his tumbler at the big porker. Second, he hurled the empty tumbler against the table, where it burst like a grenade and showered the whole gang with glass. Third, he reached out and scooped up a cigarette lighter from the yobs' table. Without hesitation, he thumbed the flint and tossed it at the big porker, whose T-shirt instantly caught light.

The big porker screamed and started clawing at his burning shirt. The Spaniard snatched a beer from the table and doused him with it. The big porker staggered to his feet and threw a wild punch that came at the Spaniard's head in a wide arc. The Spaniard ducked out of the swing, then stepped back in with surprising speed and jabbed a straight right that caught the big porker full in the centre of his face and sent him crashing violently on his back against the table. Drinks and empty bottles capsized all over the floor.

The Dane still didn't move, react or look up. This kind of thing must happen all the time where he lived.

Then it was just seven against one. The rest of the gang were out of their seats and converging on the Spaniard in a chorus of angry yelling. The barman was banging on the bar and yelling that he was going to call the police, but nobody was listening and the situation was already well out of control. The Spaniard ducked another punch and returned it with another neat jab to the ribs that doubled up his opponent. But the alcohol was telling on him, and he didn't see the next punch coming until it had caught him high on the left cheek and knocked him off his feet.

The six who could still fight closed in on him, kicking him in the stomach and legs as he fought back furiously and tried to get up. One of them grabbed a chair, to slam it down on the Spaniard's head. Raising the chair high in the air, he was about to deliver the blow when it was snatched out of his hands from behind. He turned, just long enough to register the presence of the blond stranger who'd got up from the corner table. Then the chair splintered into pieces over the crown of his skull and he crumpled at the knees and hit the floor like a sandbag.

The English boys stopped kicking the Spaniard and stared at Ben as he tossed away the broken remnant of the chair and stepped over their fallen friend towards them.

'All of you against one guy,' Ben said. 'Doesn't seem fair to me.'

One of them pointed down at the Spaniard, who was struggling to his feet now that the kicking had stopped. 'What you taking his side for?'

Ben shrugged. 'Because I've got nothing better to do.'

'You saw what he did to Stu,' said another.

'Looked to me like Stu had it coming,' Ben said. 'As do the rest of you, unless you do the sensible thing and leave now, while you still have legs under you.'

The Spaniard swayed up to his feet, looking uncertainly at Ben.

'You're going to be sorry, pal.' All remaining five moved towards him. Except for one, whom the Spaniard caught by the collar and dragged to the floor, stamping on his face. The first to reach Ben lashed out with a right hook that was instantly caught and twisted into a lock that put the guy down on his knees. Ben kicked him in the solar plexus, not hard enough to rupture anything internally, but plenty hard enough to put him out of action for a while.

Ben let him flop to the floor, rolling and writhing, as the next one stepped up. Wiry, shaven-headed, this one looked as if he fancied himself as some kind of Krav Maga fighter, judging from the jerky, spastic little moves he was pulling. Ben blamed action films for that one. He let the guy throw a couple of strikes, which he effortlessly blocked. Then hooked the guy's leg with his own and threw him over on his back. A tap to the side of his head with the solid toecap of Ben's boot was enough to make sure he wouldn't be getting up again any time soon.

The fight was over after just ten seconds. The last man standing, obviously smarter than his friends, fled from the bar followed by the one the Spaniard had punched in the ribs, still winded and clutching at his side as he hobbled towards the exit. Six inert shapes on the floor, among the wreckage of broken chairs and glass, were going to need an ambulance out of there. The barman was on the phone, jabbering furiously to the police.

The Dane had slipped out of the door in the middle of the action, as if he'd finally noticed the commotion and decided to continue his reading somewhere less distracting. Ben hadn't seen him leave.

The Spaniard turned to Ben. He was breathing hard and blood was smeared at the corner of his mouth. 'I appreciate your help,' he said in slurred English. He wobbled on his feet and Ben had to grab his arm to stop him from keeling over.

'Just evening up the odds a little,' Ben said. 'You were doing okay until then.'

The Spaniard wiped at his lips with the back of his hand and gazed at the blood. 'I don't know what came over me,' he said, shaking his head. 'I just went crazy.'

'Believe me,' Ben said. 'I've been there.'

The Spaniard looked mournful. 'He shouldn't have said that about her.'

'I think he knows that now.' Ben glanced at the unconscious mound on the floor. That single punch had knocked the big porker out cold. Two hundred pounds of prime gammon, taken down in a single blow by a man fifty pounds lighter. The Spaniard obviously had some hidden talents, when he wasn't drinking himself stupid.

The barman had finished on the phone and was venturing beyond the hatch to inspect the state of his premises and glower at the two men still standing in the ruins. 'Someone's going to pay for this!' he was yelling in Spanish.

'We should leave before the police arrive,' the Spaniard said. 'I live just a couple of minutes from here.' He paled. 'Jesus, I feel terrible.'

'Nothing a couple of pints of strong black coffee can't fix,' Ben said. 'Let's get you home and sobered up.'

Chapter Two

Neither of them spoke much as the Spaniard led the way from the bar and through the narrow, uniformly white-washed streets of Frigiliana's old Moorish quarter. Ben followed a few steps behind, watching as the Spaniard tried to hold a straight line and had to keep steadying himself against walls and railings. Ben thought about all the times he'd walked out of bars and pubs with a skinful of whisky and some other guy's blood on his knuckles, and wondered if he'd been such a sorry sight as this. Never again, he vowed. But it was a vow he'd broken enough times to know he'd probably break it again, some place, some time.

Ben's left arm felt a little tight and sore after his exertions. A few months earlier, he had been shot from behind at close range with a twelve-gauge shotgun. The surgeon who had pieced his shoulder blade back together had done good work, but he still had pain sometimes. In time, he knew, the twinges would fade, even if they never faded away to nothing. It wasn't the first time he'd been shot.

'This is it,' the Spaniard muttered, stopping at an arched doorway on a sloping backstreet. Every inch of the house's exterior was painted pure brilliant white, like every other building they'd passed, bouncing back the light and warmth of the afternoon sun. The Spaniard fumbled in his pocket and found a ring with a heavy old iron key. After a couple of stabs, he managed to get it in the lock and shoved the door open.

Ben followed him inside. He had no intention of staying any longer than it took to make the guy a remedial cup of coffee and see him settled safely out of harm's way. Ben himself had been rescued more than once from the perils of a drunken stupor. The last time it had happened had been in the French Alps; his saviour on that occasion had been a massive Nigerian guy named Omar, who'd brought him home rather than let him get picked up by the local gendarmes. Looking out for the Spaniard was a way for Ben to put something back, make himself feel like he'd done something good.

The Spaniard's home was simply, economically furnished. The walls were white inside as well as out, hung here and there with tasteful art prints. The living room had a single sofa with a low coffee table between it and a TV stand. A large bookcase stood against one wall, heavy with titles on history and philosophy and classical music CDs. It wasn't the typical home of a bar brawler. The Spaniard was evidently a cultivated guy, within a certain budget. Bookish, scholarly even. But from the mess in the place, it was just as evident that for whatever reason Ben had found him drowning his sorrows in the bar, his comfortable little life had lately fallen apart. Clothes lay strewn about the floor. The sofa was rumpled as though it had been slept on a lot recently. Empty beer cans lined up on the coffee table gave off a sour smell of stale booze.

Ben glanced around him. A corner of the room was set aside as a little study area. Above the desk hung a crucifix, to the left of it a framed degree certificate from the University of Madrid, awarded to one Raul Fuentes for

13

achieving first-class honours in English. To the right of the cross, a poster was tacked to the wall depicting a forlorn-looking polar bear cub alone on a melting ice floe that was drifting on unbroken blue water under a bright and sunny sky, with the legend STOP GLOBAL WARMING NOW.

Next to that hung a smaller framed photo of the Spaniard, grinning and laughing on a white-sanded beach somewhere hot, with his arm around the shoulders of a strikingly beautiful dark-haired woman. She was laughing with him, showing perfect white teeth. It was a happy picture, obviously from a happier time not so very long ago.

'Raul Fuentes,' Ben said. 'That would be you?'

The Spaniard nodded. He slumped on the rumpled sofa. Leaned across to pick up one of the beer cans to give it a shake, in case there might be some left inside.

'No beer for you,' Ben said, stepping over to snatch it from his fingers. 'Which way's the kitchen? I presume you have coffee in the place.' Raul Fuentes flopped back against the cushions and sighed, wagged a hand in the direction of a door.

The kitchen was a mess, though Ben could tell it hadn't always been. Copper saucepans hung neatly on little hooks above the worktop, next to a shelf with a collection of cookbooks. An ornamental wine rack was loaded with a selection of decent bottles that Raul hadn't yet got around to emptying down his throat. The ones he had filled the bin and stood around the surfaces, along with more empty beer cans and piles of unwashed dishes. Ben shoved them to one side and set about making coffee.

Raul had a real percolator and real fresh-ground beans. Ben approved. The instant stuff was essentially dehydrated military rations, popularised during successive world wars. You shouldn't have to drink it unless there was no other choice.

14

As he waited for the coffee to bubble up on the stove, Ben thought about the picture on the wall above the desk and wondered whether the woman in it was the reason behind Raul Fuentes' troubles. *She's not worth it, mate.* The yob's words had evidently touched a nerve.

When the coffee came up, he poured the contents into two cups. Straight, black, as it came. Milk and sugar were trivial nonessentials at a time like this. He carried the cups back into the other room and set one down in front of Raul.

'Drink it while it's hot. It'll do you good.'

Raul slurped some, and pulled a face.

'It needs to be strong,' Ben said.

Raul braved another sip. 'I don't even know your name,' he said, looking up.

'Ben,' Ben said.

'You're not from around here.'

'Is it that obvious?'

'You're English.'

'The half of me that isn't Irish.'

'What are you doing here in Frigiliana?' Raul asked. 'Are you on vacation or something?'

Ben wasn't about to reveal to a stranger how he'd been wandering aimlessly through Europe for the last couple of months, never lingering long in one place, staying in cheap hotels to preserve his savings, travelling by public transport wherever whim or random choice took him.

'I wanted to see the castle,' he said.

Which, as far as it went, was true, although Ben hadn't been aware of the existence of the ancient Moorish fortress – whose ruins topped the hill overlooking Frigiliana – until he'd happened to pick up a discarded magazine on the bus from Sevilla, just for something to read. Then, just for something to do, when he'd got off the bus he'd made the long,

15

hot, dusty hike up the hill to visit the lonely ruins that marked the site of the battle of El Peñon de Frigiliana, where in 1569 some six thousand Christian soldiers had stormed the last stronghold of the Moorish empire and spelled the final end of Muslim rule in Spain.

Once he'd got to the top, Ben had wondered why he'd bothered. He'd seen all the battlefields he ever wanted to see in his life, both ancient and modern. The remains of the fortress didn't look much different from crusader ruins he'd observed in the Middle East or the smoking rubble of killing zones in Afghanistan, from back in the day. It was a sad old place, haunted by the same ancient ghosts as all such places inevitably were.

Ben had perched on a crumbled wall and smoked a few cigarettes while looking out over the valley below, then got thirsty and come wandering back down the hill into Frigiliana to find a cool drink. The rest of the story, Raul didn't need telling.

'Well, I'm glad you showed up when you did,' Raul said after another grateful slurp of coffee. It seemed to be reviving him a little already. 'I can't believe the way you went through those idiots. You must be some kind of seventh-dan Aikido master or something.'

'It's just a few simple tricks,' Ben said.

'Tricks.' Raul considered that for a moment. 'Well, whatever, you saved my ass from a serious beating back there. Probably saved my job, too. Respectable schoolteachers aren't supposed to get into drunken fights and turn up at school all bruised up.'

'You teach English?' Ben said, glancing in the direction of the degree certificate.

Raul nodded. 'In a secondary school, just a few kilometres from here.'

'It's the middle of the week. Is there a holiday?'

Raul said quietly, 'No, I . . . I'm taking time off.'

Ben didn't ask why. 'Respectable schoolteachers don't generally have such a useful right jab, in my experience.'

Raul gave a sour laugh. 'I was an amateur boxing champion in my teens. It's been years since I so much as threw a punch. Stupid.' He sat hunched over with his elbows on his knees, toying with his cup and frowning. 'I shouldn't have gone in there in the first place. As if I hadn't already got enough booze in this place to drink myself into a hole in the ground. Maybe I was looking for a fight. Maybe I wanted it to happen.'

'Whatever it was about,' Ben said, 'it's none of my business. I'm going to finish up my coffee and get out of here. Do us both a favour and try not to get yourself killed with a repeat performance, okay? A broken heart's not worth getting beaten to death over. No matter how pretty she is.' Ben pointed back with his thumb at the picture over the desk.

Raul hung his head down so low that it almost touched his knees. He whispered, 'Was. And she was more than that. She was a lot more.'

Ben said nothing.

'See, everything anyone says about her now has to be in the past tense. Even I catch myself doing it. As if she really had gone, as if she were no longer a part of the world. That's what the police would have everyone believe.'

Ben still said nothing.

'And now Klein says it too,' Raul murmured. 'I thought maybe he'd see it differently, but he's just like the others. Nobody but me can see it's just bullshit.' He closed his eyes, held them shut for a few moments. When he opened them, they were bright with wetness. 'And so there it is. Catalina's dead. That's what I'm supposed to believe, too. But I can't. I just can't. So I won't talk about her as if she were. Everyone else can play that game. Not me.' He put the coffee down on the table. 'You were kind to help me. But it's no good. I'm just going to keep drinking. I'm going to drink until I can't think about anything any more. Except another drink.'

'I can't stop you,' Ben said. 'But you're going to have to get off your arse and pour it yourself.'

Raul looked at him. 'Some friend you are.'

'I'm not your friend, Raul.'

Ben looked at Raul and felt the depth of his pain. But Ben also sensed he was in danger of getting drawn in. There was an untold story here, and he didn't want to hear it.

He drank the last of his coffee and stood up. 'I'm sorry your life turned to shit. I'm sorry your girlfriend died.'

Raul Fuentes raised his head from his knees and slowly turned to look at Ben. The muscles in his face looked tight enough to snap.

'Not my girlfriend. My sister. She's my twin sister. Don't you get it? That's how I know they're wrong.'

Chapter Three

Ben felt a brother's grief hit him like a fist to the face. He went silent. Glanced again at the woman's picture over the desk, and now he could see it. The similarity in the eyes, the nose, the cheekbones. The same fine, lean Latin features. He looked back at Raul, feeling suddenly torn between walking away and staying to hear more.

'My sister did not kill herself,' Raul said, with as much absolute rock-solid unflinching certainty as Ben had ever heard in a person's voice. 'My sister is alive.'

Ben made no reply. He hesitated, then sat down again. It was the least he could do for the guy to listen.

'They're saying she drove her car off a cliff into the ocean,' Raul said. 'Just let it roll right off the edge. They say it was suicide.'

Ben could imagine it. The beautiful dark-haired young woman in the picture sitting at the wheel. Her face strained with terror and resolution as she let off the handbrake and let herself trundle towards oblivion. The car falling into space, plummeting down to smash itself to pieces as that fragile body inside it was pummelled and broken. He pictured torn metal and shattered plastic and bloodied glass. But something about the picture was wrong. Something Raul didn't believe. Ben remained silent for a moment longer before he said, 'Are you going to tell me there was no body inside the car when they found it?'

Raul's eyes brightened visibly, the way a prisoner's on death row light up when they tell him about the last-minute stay of execution that's just been granted. 'Exactly. All they pulled out of the water was an empty car. What does that tell you?'

'It tells me the body could have been flung free of the car, Raul.' He hated dashing the guy's hopes like that. But better to face reality than to be tormented by wishful fantasy for the rest of your life.

Raul flinched as if Ben had pulled a gun on him. 'How would you know? How can you assert something like that?'

Ben wished he'd said nothing at all. The thing he'd wanted to avoid was happening. He was getting sucked in. 'Tell me where this happened, Raul.'

Raul calmed a little and replied, 'Germany. Catalina moved there, for her work. She's a scientist. Well, kind of a bit more than that.'

Still resisting speaking about his sister in the past tense, Ben noticed.

'I know this is hard, Raul. But did Catalina have any reason to harm herself?'

'Why should she? She's successful, she's achieved all she ever wanted and more. She's a happy person.'

'People can look happy on the outside,' Ben said.

'While inside they suffer such torment that they want to end it all. I get it. I know. But I know my sister, don't you see? I know her better than anyone in the world and I know she wouldn't have killed herself. She's a happy person. She has everything to live for. When she walks into a room, she fills it up with laughter and smiles. People love her.'

'An accident, then,' Ben said.

'You think I haven't thought about that? Okay, let's say she accidentally drove to the edge of the cliff and then accidentally forgot to stop, and the car went over. Same story. There's the car, but where's she?'

Ben could have told him there were a hundred ways for a corpse to vanish at sea. The tides could draw it miles out, where it would eventually sink to the bottom before the bacteria inside the gut and chest cavity would start to produce enough methane, hydrogen sulphide and carbon dioxide to float it back up to the surface. That process could take days, during which time the cadaver would become an ever more appetising meal to the numerous species of shark and other carnivorous fish that frequented those waters. Such details were best left unmentioned under the circumstances, so he kept his mouth shut.

'I mean,' Raul went on, 'it's been nearly three months. A body would surely have turned up by now.'

Ben looked at him, surprised. 'Three months? I thought this must have only just happened.'

Raul sank back deep into the cushions of the sofa, as if suddenly deflated. 'It was July sixteenth. Eighty-three days ago. A place called Rügen Island. She apparently drove for hours to get there from her home in Munich. She . . .' He closed his eyes for a moment, as if it was too painful to say more. 'The German police closed the case not long afterwards. There was all kinds of bureaucratic bullshit. My parents, they flew out there. Neither of them had ever been on a plane before. Never even left Valdepeñas de Jaén until then.'

'Did you go with them?'

Raul shook his head sadly. 'Couldn't bring myself to go. I felt like a dog about it then and I still do. I just couldn't deal with it. Had to let them go alone. They were there for five days. My father, he looked like a little old man when they got back, with nothing to show but a wad of police reports. Three more weeks went by, still no body. Can't have a funeral without a body, right? So they had a service for her at the church in Valdepeñas de Jaén. Now they won't even speak to me, because I wouldn't attend it. They think it's like I don't care. Like I cut myself away from the whole thing, and from them.'

'They might have needed your support at a time like that,' Ben said.

Raul turned the red-rimmed eyes back on Ben. 'Yes, and that's something else for me to feel like shit about, isn't it? But I didn't want to be there, because to be there would have been like accepting that Catalina was dead. How could I go through the motions of a phony funeral when I was completely certain that my sister was still alive? They'd all given up on her; I hadn't. As they were all gathering to mourn her, I was searching the internet for someone who could help me. That's when I found Klein.'

'You mentioned him before. Who is he?'

'A former police detective who's supposedly the best private investigator in Germany. Certainly the most expensive. I hired him to find out what the police couldn't.'

'And did he?'

Raul sighed. He dug in his jeans pocket and came out with a rumpled, folded envelope that he handed to Ben. 'This came two days ago.'

The postmark on the envelope, stamped MÜNCHEN – FREISTAAT – BAYERN, was five days old. Ben took out the letter and unfolded it. The letterhead on the single sheet said LEONHARD KLEIN, DETEKTEI – NACHRICHTEN, with an address in Munich, email contact and web address. The rest of the letter was written in English. It was brief, stilted and to the point, expressing the investigator's professional opinion that, despite the absence of a body, after extensive researches he had been able to uncover no evidence to disprove the tragic and unavoidable fact that Ms Fuentes was, in fact, deceased as the official reports stated. He was willing to continue working on the case, although he was ethically and professionally bound to instruct his client that such a course of action was inadvisable and that any further investigation was futile at this stage and would only represent a further waste of his time and the client's money, etc., etc. The letter signed off with a couple of short lines of stiff-sounding condolences.

Ben folded it, replaced it in the envelope and handed it back without a word. He understood now that the letter was what had sharpened the torture of what Raul was going through, and made him want to dive inside a bottle.

'It's garbage,' Raul said. With a sudden flash of anger, he tore the letter apart and hurled the pieces away. 'So much for the great detective. There goes five thousand euros cash, for nothing.'

'Should have put it on your credit card,' Ben said. 'Pay it off month by month.'

'I don't have a credit card. I come from a simple family, where we were taught old-fashioned values. I pay cash for things whenever I can, and if I can't afford something, then I don't have it. That five thousand was most of the savings I had.'

Ben didn't know what to say. He stood, paused for a long time and chose his words carefully.

'I'm very sorry for what you're going through, Raul. But I think you're just going to have to accept that your sister's dead.'

Raul stared at him. A muscle twitched under his eye.

'I wish you well,' Ben said. 'Try not to get into any more fights. And don't drink yourself to death.'

He left Raul Fuentes like that and walked back outside into the narrow, sloping backstreet, feeling bad. He shook out a Gauloise and clanged open his Zippo and lit up. Now he could do with a drop or two of the hard stuff himself, but he wasn't going to. Not right now.

It was early evening, and the warmth of the sun was cooling off quickly. He made his way back through the streets of the old Moorish quarter of Frigiliana until he found the bus station where he'd arrived earlier that day. A queue was forming. He joined it, finished his cigarette and lit up another. A woman in front of him in the queue turned around, sniffing the air, and gave him a look as if he was spraying anthrax spores. He ignored her and carried on smoking.

By the time that one was smoked down to the stub, the bus arrived. The passengers filed on board. Most had tickets. Ben didn't, and fanned out some banknotes to the driver without saying anything, like some foreigner on holiday who couldn't speak a word of Spanish. The driver gave him a ticket and change, and Ben wandered up the length of the bus and found an empty window seat towards the rear. He placed his battered old green canvas bag between his feet and leaned back, soaking up the bustle and the snatches of Spanish conversation around him as the bus filled up.

The motion of life. People going places. And he supposed he was one of them.

In truth, he hadn't even bothered to check the destination of the bus before getting on. His personal compass needle was pointing anywhere but here, and anywhere was good enough for him. You keep moving forwards, you don't slow down for anything or anyone. You don't get sidetracked, and that way you stay out of trouble. There'd been enough trouble in this town already to last him a while. The bus was headed somewhere else down the road, and that was good enough for him.

The sticker on the window glass next to him said NO FUMAR, and he didn't particularly want to antagonise his fellow travellers any more than necessary, so he kept his Gauloises and his Zippo in his pockets. In the olden days he'd have been carrying his well-worn hip flask for company, filled with his favourite single malt scotch, but he'd ditched that a long way back. So with nothing much else to pass the time with, he gazed idly out of the window while waiting for the bus to depart.

And that was when he saw her walking down the street. She was with a group of friends, all around the same age, late teens or early twenties. She was blonde and blue-eyed, wearing jeans and a light denim top, her hair most likely dyed and cropped short, a little spiky, a little punkish, giving her an elfin or pixie kind of look that wasn't at all typical for a region where most of the girls were of the classic southern raven-haired, dark-eyed variety like the rest of her friends. She stood out, and for Ben she stood out especially. She could almost have been—

The sight of her brought a powerful surge of memories and thoughts into his mind, some of them many years old, some of them very recent. Some of the memories she evoked were the most painful of his life, worse than the terror of war, worse than getting shot, worse than torture and beatings or the hell on earth that was SAS selection training.

He watched her keenly through the glass until she disappeared behind the NO FUMAR sticker and then out of sight altogether, and he felt his compass needle waver, droop and then slew around in a hundred-and-eighty-degree arc.

'Fuck it,' he muttered under his breath.

That was when he knew he couldn't stay on this bus any longer.

He grabbed his bag and strode back down the aisle to the door before the driver pulled away.

'You just paid for a ticket,' the driver said.

'I changed my mind,' Ben replied in Spanish.

'You want a refund?'

'Keep it.'

The driver shrugged. He stabbed a button on his dash and the door slapped open and Ben stepped out into the evening coolness. He hitched his bag over his shoulder and started walking.

'It's you,' Raul Fuentes said when he opened the door and saw Ben standing there on the step. He was clutching a fresh mug of coffee and looking a good bit more sober. 'Why did you come back?'

'Like I said, I don't have anywhere else to be,' Ben replied. 'And because of what you told me. I know what it's like to lose a sister. I've known it a long time.'

Chapter Four

Morocco
A long time ago

It is the spring of '85 and he has never been to such a place before. Through the shimmering heat and the glare and the insane buzz of dusty cars and motorcycles, they enter the Medina of Marrakech, the ancient walled city within a city. A thousand years old, and at its labyrinthine heart lies the souk.

The street market is like nothing the young Ben has ever seen or imagined, with its dazzling arrays of meats and fish and fruits and exotic spices heaped in baskets; hanging displays of tapestries and rugs and ornate clothing and shoes and scarves and carvings and glittering lamps that seem to go on and on forever. The air is filled with the jabber of vendors and customers haggling and bargaining in a language he does not yet understand; he can have no way of knowing that one day he will speak it fluently. The merchants of the souk are the sharpest salesmen on earth, but the intricacies of buying and selling are concepts that the boy has yet to encounter in his overprotected middle-class life. Men who look like characters from the Bible walk the narrow street, yelling, 'Balak! Balak!' as a warning to get out of their way as they lead their overladen donkeys through the crowd, the animals' flanks swaying with everything from garbage to goods for sale in the souk. All around him Ben sees veiled women in kaftans, bearded men wearing long, embroidered robes and skullcaps.

He will never forget the smell of this place. The garden at home smells of fresh-mown grass and apple blossom. This is another planet, rich with the pungent scents alien to a young boy's nose, intermingled with the heat and dust, the sweat of men and animals.

As well as a new smell that he will soon experience for the very first time in his life. The feral raw-blood smell of fear and desperation and stark despair.

'Ben! Look!'

It's the excited voice of Ben's sister, Ruth. Nine years old, with tumbling hair more golden than his that catches the sun as she beams up at him and tugs at his sleeve while pointing at something. Her eyes are glowing with happiness and as blue as his own, vivid as the ocean. Her older brother smiles down at her and follows the line of her waving arm, to where a legless man in a black tunic sits on an upended bucket in a corner of a crumbling wall. He is playing a crude pipe and is surrounded by six hooded cobras, half-coiled, half-standing to attention and swaying in front of him as though hypnotised by his strange music. To Ben, the otherworldly spectacle of the snake charmer is like one of the scenes from Sinbad the Sailor or The Arabian Nights that fired his imagination in the comfort of his bedroom back home. Such is the cosy world of the sons of circuit judges.

Ruth has no fear of the snakes. 'Can I feed them?' she asks. 'They look hungry.'

Ben thinks the snake charmer looks hungrier. He's never seen people so lean and hard before, with skin like leather burned dark by the sun. 'I don't think we're supposed to feed them,' he tells her. 'They bite.'

'They won't bite me. Can't I go and see them?' she says, disappointed.

'Stay close to me, okay?'

Ben and Ruth aren't alone in this strange and fascinating place. Martina Thomann is a Swiss girl he met at the hotel only yesterday, the second day of the Hope family holiday here in Morocco. Martina's family are leaving tomorrow. Ben is sad that he will probably never see her again after today. She is seventeen, a year older than him, though she seems infinitely mature in all kinds of ways that he finds mysteriously compelling but can't quite express or understand. Girls back home have asked him out from time to time, but he has never met one he was drawn to this way, so strongly he can almost taste it. The first time she reached out to hold his hand, he almost died.

His secret wish is that it could have been just the two of them, without Ruth tagging along. The kid is cramping his style. He feels guilty just for thinking it. He feels guilty, too, for breaking his promise to his parents to stay in the hotel and keep an eye on his little sister while they are off visiting a museum. But the temptation of Martina's company, and her desire to see the souk, were forces too powerful to resist.

He will soon learn what a guilty conscience truly feels like.

When it happens, it is literally in an instant, while his back is turned, distracted by Martina. He looks back . . . and his little sister is gone.

Ruth?

His first thought is that she's simply wandered off. Perhaps back to see the snakes. He lets go of the older girl's hand and starts pushing through the crowd, calling his sister's name. The men in robes seem to press in on him from all directions, hampering his progress. He's calling more loudly now.

'Ruth! Ruth!'

A cry that will echo on in his nightmares for many years to come.

She isn't with the snakes. She isn't anywhere. The realisation stabs him like an icy blade, making his heart pound and his ears ring and his guts writhe as though he had to throw up. There will be time for that later. He sprints through the twisting passages of the souk, shoving people out of his way, constantly expecting to tear around the next corner and see her standing there smiling up at him, saying, 'Here I am, silly. What are you making such a fuss about?' But she's not there. She could have been sucked into another dimension.

Gone. Taken. Swallowed by the crowd, as though she had never existed.

Blinded by panic, he grabs Martina and runs all the way back to the hotel to wait for his parents to return and tell them what happened. He can't cry. He can't be weak.

He knows they will never forgive him, and that he cannot forgive himself, not ever.

And so the nightmare begins.

Within hours, the Marrakech Brigade Touristique and detectives from the regular Morocco police will be scouring the streets, searching for the missing child. Soon afterwards, British embassy officials are joined by envoys from the Foreign Office as the abduction investigation widens.

All for nothing. No trace of little Ruth will be found, either in the city or the surrounding area. Ben's mother Kathleen will be treated for the near-catatonic state of grief that will ultimately claim her life, while Ben's father, Alistair Hope, desperately draws on every shred of official influence his position as a senior legal figure can lend him. But there is no power that can bring her back.

She is gone.

The worst is imagining what is happening to her at the

hands of the men who took her. The young Ben will no longer be able to close his eyes without hearing her screams in the darkness. When things feel darker still, he will secretly wish her dead rather than enduring tortures he cannot imagine. Just as part of him is now dead inside.

That day is the day that will change everything for him. The day that will light the fuse that will destroy his family and set him on a path that dictates the rest of his life. A life he could not have envisaged before now, but is all that remains for him. He will never be weak. He will never turn his back again. He will learn to become stronger than strong, and to devote himself utterly to finding people who are lost. The people who need him. The people you don't turn your back on.

Whatever it takes. Bring it on.

Even if it means losing himself in the process. He doesn't care any more.

Chapter Five

While he was still a young man, Ben had been schooled in the importance of secrecy. Combat-hardened warriors with ferocious glares and strident voices had taught him how to keep his mouth shut even in the face of determined enemy interrogation; and as his instructors quickly discovered, his response to that training was off the charts. In a world of lies where even elected rulers, let alone top military brass, were often kept unaware of the real truth behind political machinations or cloak-and-dagger black ops, it nonetheless behoved a future Special Forces officer to guard such sensitive information as had been confided in him with extreme caution. Once entrusted with a secret, Trooper Hope would let you slice him to pieces before you could extract a single word.

He'd excelled at it from the start, because he had a natural talent for silence. *Observe, listen, learn, don't say more than you have to.* As a child his teachers had found him private and reserved to the point of obstinacy. Likewise, when the Bad Things had begun to happen in his life he'd seldom, if ever, spoken of them to anyone. It had been that way ever since. The story of what had happened that terrible day in Marrakech was a secret he'd confided to only a bare handful of people over the years. It went against his inclinations to talk about it, but he felt he owed it to Raul Fuentes.

Raul listened quietly, staring intently and absorbing every word. Finally he asked, 'Your parents, where are they now?'

'Both dead. They didn't last long after what happened.'

Raul's expression saddened, thinking of his own family. 'And you? What did you do?'

'I went a little nuts,' Ben said. 'Drank too much, wanted to blow up the world, joined the army, put everything I had into it. For a while, anyway.'

Funny how you could crush thirteen years' service and a thousand exploits into so few words.

'Then I left and put what I had into trying to help people who were lost, like Ruth. People who'd been taken. To find them, bring them back.' Ben talked a little about some of what he'd done in those years, what he'd seen, what he'd learned.

Raul was listening and watching him with such intensity in his eyes that he was almost trembling. 'But your sister, you never found her?'

The question hung in the air between them until Ben replied, 'I found her.'

Raul stared at him even harder. 'She was dead?' Just a whisper, as if he dreaded the word and saying it too loudly could make it more of a dark reality.

'She was alive,' Ben said. 'A lot of time had passed. She was grown up by then. It's a long story, Raul. But the point is this. I'd stopped searching for Ruth many years before. I'd stopped believing, in my heart. Whatever faith I'd had that I might ever find her, alive or not, I'd lost it. And it wasn't by design that I found her. It was just chance. One in a billion, just like it was one in a billion that she'd survived. But it happened. And that's when I realised that I should never have lost faith. That was the most painful thing of all.'

Raul said nothing. He nodded slowly, processing what Ben was telling him.

'That's why I came back,' Ben said. 'Because I, of all people, should know better. And because you wouldn't give up on your sister like I did. I admire you for that, Raul. Even if it turns out that you're wrong. I just wanted to tell you that before I moved on.'

Raul closed his eyes for a moment. When he reopened them, he glanced at the crucifix on the wall. Then his gaze returned to Ben, looking at him with something like wonderment. 'I think you must have been sent to me.'

'I'm not an angel from heaven. I'm anything but.'

'I didn't pray for an angel. I prayed for someone who could help me find Catalina, like you found all those other people.'

'It's what I used to do,' Ben said. 'These days I'm just trying to find myself.'

'But you *know* about these things.' Raul bent forward in his seat with his hands clasped in his lap, his eyes large and liquid and full of pleading. 'Look at me. I'm just an ordinary man. A schoolteacher. What have I ever done in my life?' He pulled a face and glanced around him, as if he was disgusted with himself, his world, his whole existence. 'You must, *must* help me. I'm completely certain that my sister didn't do what everyone thinks. But I know she's in terrible danger. I believe she was kidnapped.'

'Your sister disappeared. That doesn't mean she was kidnapped.'

Raul looked at him. 'You don't read the papers, do you? You don't really know who she is.'

34

Ben shook his head, not understanding. Before he could reply, Raul stood up and went over to the bookcase. He lifted out a stack of magazines, came back and dumped them in Ben's arms. Ben had no idea why, until he recognised the woman on the cover of the top magazine in the pile. It was one of those tabloid glossies that always filled the racks nearest the checkouts in stores and supermarkets, offering to spill the latest exclusive scoop or scabrous gossip about fifteen-minute celebrities Ben had never heard of and truly didn't want to. This was the first time he'd ever recognised the face on the cover, as the perfect smile of Catalina Fuentes shone up at him from the glossy page. The tagline next to her picture said: IS THIS THE WORLD'S SEXIEST SCIENTIST?

He frowned up at Raul. 'Your sister is this famous?'

'Turn to page four,' Raul said.

Ben flipped the magazine open to a double-page spread featuring more photos of her. The article began: '*Who says you can't have good looks and brains? Stunning Catalina Fuentes has them both by the bucket load.*'

If Raul was surprised that Ben had never heard of his famous sister, he didn't make a big deal of it. Even the biggest celebrity on the planet would have to be a stranger to someone. Or maybe something about Ben made it obvious that he didn't exactly keep up with current trends.

Ben put the magazine aside and sifted through the rest of the pile. They were in date order, and the latest two had splashed all over their cover the shocking revelation of the suicide of one of the media's best-loved personalities. HOW COULD SHE HAVE DONE IT? one proclaimed, almost indignant in tone. SECRET AGONY OF TRAGIC CATALINA, the other wailed, below an image of a wrecked Porsche Cayenne being winched from the sea at the foot of sheer white cliffs.

'I had no idea,' Ben said. He laid the magazines at his feet. 'You told me she was a scientist.'

'An astronomer,' Raul said. 'I also told you she was a little bit more than that. It was the television show that really started the whole celebrity thing. Until then, she was devoted to her work. She taught astrophysics and cosmology for a year in Madrid, then decided she wanted to broaden her horizons. She always had an incredible talent for languages, and could speak four of them fluently by the time she was twenty-one. She had no problem teaching herself German in six months so she could take the lectureship at the University of Munich. She was always a genius, ever since we were kids. She was chairperson of this science board and that, and wrote all these books on solar physics. Then five years ago she became the youngest ever, and only female, winner of the Kilosky Astrophysics Prize. It's like a more specialised version of the Nobel Prize. Won lots of teaching awards, too. Her students loved her.'

Raul paused sadly for a moment, then went on. 'Anyway, four years ago, a British television producer asked her if she'd present this six-part series on astronomers in history. Not the ones everyone's heard of, like Galileo and Newton. Ones like the female American astronomer Henrietta Leavitt, who have been kind of overstepped and forgotten but are still really important. You know?'

Ben just spread his hands. He knew how to navigate by the constellations when GPS went down, but that was about the sum total of his astronomical knowledge.

'She was young, beautiful, intelligent and as well qualified for the job as anyone, and she thought it was a worthy project to get involved in. She had no idea what great TV it would make and how popular she'd become as a result. She took a sabbatical from her teaching and writing, and travelled all over with the film crew. A year later, the first episode aired on BBC, then RTL in Germany and all around Europe. Suddenly, she was this big media celebrity. It just kind of exploded, not because of the subject matter – I mean, who really cares about a bunch of dead astronomers? It was *her* the people loved. She set the screen on fire. Next thing, she was getting offers from all over the place for more main-stream shows, and had to start cutting her teaching down to part-time just to fit all the work in. You couldn't turn on the TV without seeing her.'

'I haven't watched it in a while,' Ben said truthfully. His last place of residence of any duration had been a monastery in the French Alps, where the monks had barely even heard of TV. His being there was another long story, one he didn't intend to share.

Raul went on, 'And magazines like this one couldn't get enough of her. She was the darling of the media. She used to laugh about it all, this science academic getting to rub shoulders with movie stars and pop singers, like she couldn't take it too seriously and was just enjoying the ride while it lasted. And the money, too.'

'Okay,' Ben said. He was soaking up information fast, but he still didn't understand why Raul Fuentes thought his celebrity sister had been kidnapped. Rich people got kidnapped all the time. The motive was almost invariably financial, which meant the victim's family could generally expect to receive a ransom demand within hours, sometimes within minutes of the abduction. But that hadn't happened in this case.

'She didn't talk much about the dark side of it all,' Raul went on. 'Like all those damn photographers always hanging around, trying to get a shot of her, so many she started having to sneak out of the house in disguise. I think she accepted it, like it just went with the territory. But then the Lukas Geerts thing happened.'

'Lukas Geerts?'

The corners of Raul's mouth downturned and he looked as if he'd just got a whiff of something out of a sewer. 'A Belgian IT consultant and amateur astronomy nerd who'd become fixated on her after watching her on TV. This creep somehow managed to convince himself he was in love with her, and that he could make her love him too, if only he could meet her. He travelled to Munich, hung around the university and followed her home. It was easy for him to find out where she lived, and somehow got her personal mobile number too. Next thing, he was turning up there the whole time. He'd sit outside her place in his car and phone her, ten, twenty times a day. I mean, he had *her face tattooed on his arm*. Can you believe that?'

Ben had once pursued a child abuser and kidnapper who'd tattooed the names of his victims in Gothic script on every part of his own body, including his genitals. Ben could believe more or less anything.

'Catalina was freaked out by him and wouldn't have anything to do with him, of course, but on his Facebook page he was making out that he and she were an item. He created images on Photoshop showing them holding hands. I kept telling her she should report it to the police, but she actually felt sorry for him because he was mentally deranged. Then it got even worse, with the porn stuff he was doctoring to make it look like them together, and putting up online. In the end, she had to get the police involved and there was a restraining order and criminal charges. It was only then it turned out he was guilty of the attempted rape of some poor girl in Zeebrugge a year earlier, and he ended up sentenced to eighteen months behind bars.'

'I understand. So you think Geerts has come back after her, except now he's angry and prepared to go to extremes to make her his.'

Ben wasn't liking the sound of it. Suddenly, the idea of foul play entered the scenario and sounded plausible enough to be a concern. If the motive was about revenge or possession rather than money, a ransom demand became immaterial.

Raul shook his head. 'No, because Geerts is dead. A few months into his sentence, one of his fellow prisoners stuck a shank between his ribs. I wasn't exactly sorry.'

'That would tend to rule him out of the equation,' Ben said.

'Him, but not a hundred others. Who's to say some other lunatic hasn't turned up there in Munich with a delusional fixation about her? There are crazy people everywhere.'

Ben had been expecting a little more substance to Raul's kidnap premise. 'That's it?'

'That's it.'

'Have you mentioned this to the German police? To the investigator, Klein?'

Raul shook his head. 'Not yet. It's a new theory. The only one that makes sense to me.'

'That's not a theory, Raul. It isn't even a hypothesis. It's more like a guess, based on nothing but the emotions you're feeling.'

'That's why I need someone to help me,' Raul said.

'Help you do what?'

'Prove that she's not dead. Find who took her, and get her back. I want you to come with me to Germany. I'll pay for the flight and all expenses. I still have a little bit of savings left over. Whatever we don't spend on the trip, you take as a fee.'

'I don't want your money,' Ben said tersely.

'You have to help me. You're the only person I've met who can.'

Ben took out his cigarettes and Zippo, fished out a Gauloise and bathed its tip in the lazy orange flame of the lighter. He puffed for a few moments as he reflected. Thinking that Germany was a long way away, and that he'd come back here to offer Raul moral support, not to get involved in what was almost certain to be a dead-end undertaking that would only cause further heartache. Raul might soon find himself wishing he'd attended his sister's funeral, after all.

Raul was watching him, worriedly trying to read his thoughts. 'You told me never to give up. You *said* those words to me.'

Ben went on smoking. He thought about the girl he'd seen from the bus. Thought about the real reason he'd come back here. If he was honest with himself, maybe it hadn't been just to offer moral support. Maybe he needed to do more than that, for his own sake as much as that of a stranger he'd met in a bar only that day.

He knew he couldn't turn away, any more than he could have sat back and let Raul take a bad beating in there.

'I don't want you getting your hopes up,' he said. 'You have to be ready for the worst. The odds are slim.'

For the first time since Ben had met him, Raul Fuentes allowed himself a smile of relief. 'One in a billion. But it wouldn't be the first time those odds paid off, would it?'

Ben looked at him.

'So you'll help me?' Raul said.

Chapter Six

Ngari Prefecture
Autonomous Region of Tibet, China
Five months earlier

The man stood at the top of the rise and gazed around him
in an arc thousands of miles wide. The bleak, windswept
wilderness that stretched almost to infinity could have been
part of the Martian landscape, if not for the vast dome of
blue sky above it and the white-capped peaks in the far
distance. On clear days like this, the man imagined that he
could see as far as the Trans-Himalayas that bordered the
Tibetan plateau to the south and west, and the top of holy
Mount Kailash: in the Tibetan language, 'Kangri Rinpoche',
meaning 'Precious Snow Mountain'. For Buddhists, the
sacred Navel of the Universe; for Hindus, the perpetual
abode of Lord Shiva, the destroyer of ignorance and illu-
sion.

What total, utter bollocks. The man did not believe in
such things, and felt only contempt for the poor benighted
suckers who did.

The man's name was Maxwell Grant. He turned to face
north, the wind slapping him in the face and clawing at his
suit. It was an Ermenegildo Zegna three-piece, and far too

good for sitting around in helicopters and getting covered in dust, but it was tailored to hide his bulk well and made him look every bit as important as, in fact, he was.

He smiled as he surveyed the industrious scene in the giant, desolate bowl of rock and earth below. After twenty years in the business, the sight still impressed him. From up here on the rise, it looked like an ants' nest of fantastic proportions as a battalion of labourers in khaki uniform swarmed and toiled around the edges of what looked like a monstrous volcanic crater, or the remnants of a cataclysmic asteroid impact. The hole was hundreds of metres across and went down at least as deep, waiting to swallow up the container loads of drums that were Grant's responsibility to make disappear. The dust from the diggers rose up in huge clouds that were whipped away by the wind and caked the clothes, faces and hair of the workers. What the heavy plant didn't dig out of the hole was hacked and shovelled and dragged out of there by hand by the mass of men, working like slaves in a scene from ancient history. Others scurried back and forth from the trucks, rolling out the cargo and placing it on wooden pallets ready to be lowered into the pit. They were Chinese prisoners brought here aboard the same military train as the cargo itself, and the eighty or more People's Army soldiers standing guard with assault rifles to ensure the job was done. Grant's own private army, mostly ex-military themselves, were there to supervise the soldiers. It was a slick operation that Grant had witnessed many times before, in many parts of the world.

This, Grant believed in. And for good reason. It had made him a very rich man. With a personal net profit close to nine figures over the last year, he was doing even better out of this enterprise than from his other main business interest, the one he could talk about, Grantec Global.

The cargo had been shipped from a location in western Europe aboard a superfreighter called the MV *Charybdis*, under false papers that in no way could be traced either to Grant himself or his anonymous company name, Kester Holdings. On docking at the Chinese port of Shenzhen after its month-long voyage, the containers had been unloaded by crane and placed on military trailer trucks originally designed for transporting tanks. From there, the convoy of trucks had taken it to an army rail depot, where the huge vehicles had rolled up onto the even more massive military train already loaded with troops and prison labourers.

The purpose-built railway stretched many hundreds of miles northwards through China and deep into the mountains of Tibet, the line itself mostly carved out by chain-gangs of convicts. Threat of execution made them the most effective workers, and by definition they were the cheapest. However many dropped dead of exhaustion, were crushed by heavy machinery or shot while trying to escape, fresh reserves were always readily available.

The cargo consisted of 892 drums of high-level nuclear waste. Each drum contained 55 US gallons or 208 litres, and measured 35 inches in height by 24 inches in diameter. Their yellow paint was scored and scuffed from rubbing together in transit, and many of them were already showing signs of corrosion after their long sea voyage. They'd eventually rust through, but by then it wouldn't matter, at least not to Grant. The occasional drum might rupture as it degraded, and if it wasn't buried deeply enough the small explosion could sometimes break the surface, spewing radioactive white foam that resembled whipped cream and would remain lethally radioactive for hundreds of thousands of years.

Grant didn't care much about that, either. They had unlimited space out here. Every time they excavated a new site, it was far enough away from the last one to avoid contaminating too many of the convicts. They were routinely checked for radiation after handling the merchandise. If one of them made the Geigers crackle, the soldiers would just put a bullet in the bugger and toss his body in the pit. It was the cheapest solution to the problem. These communists understood free enterprise better than most nations.

The nuclear waste dumping facilities came courtesy of the Ninth Academy, the most secretive organisation within the whole of China's extensive nuclear programme. It was largely thanks to the Ninth Academy that, in the years since its annexation to the People's Republic in 1951, Tibet had steadily developed into China's Nuclear Central. First they'd ravaged the unspoilt wilds for their plentiful uranium resources, then they'd used the country for conducting nuclear weapons tests, and now it was used as a convenient dumping ground for nuclear waste – not just from the vast territory of China itself, but from all over the planet.

Hey, it all had to go somewhere. Grant had wide experience of offloading nuclear waste in a number of countries. Simply tipping it into the sea was a cost-effective no-brainer, common dumping grounds being the coasts of Italy and Africa. If you couldn't get away with that, burying it was your next best option, though transportation became more of a problem in the kinds of wilderness areas essential to escaping the watchful eye of the environmentalists. Kester Holdings had established nice little niches in Somalia, Kenya and Zaire, but China (despite being so much damned further to travel) was his favourite. The Chinese were excellent to deal with, even if the presence of so many armed troops made Grant edgy at times. While stringently denying any such practice, in reality the Chinese government were more than happy to accept deals from western corporations with large quantities of so-called 'black list' materials to dispose of, as quietly as possible, and equally large quantities of cash to offer in return.

It worked out beautifully for all concerned. The environmentalist NGOs found it difficult to penetrate the country, which meant the little creeps couldn't spy on what he was doing, and he could operate freely. A few years back, a group of Green campaigners from Lhasa had tried to infiltrate the operation but the silly bastards had been caught, imprisoned, tortured and disposed of before they could blow the whistle to the world media.

The Chinese authorities were also highly accommodating when it came to their total non-investigation of the sharp increase in disease rates and birth defects affecting wide areas around the dumping zones. Reports of two-headed babies being born in Tibetan villages, you could generally ignore in the safe knowledge that nobody knew, nobody cared and nothing would ever come of it.

Anyway – as Grant had been known to joke in private to his colleagues – two heads are better than one.

Grant peeled back the sleeve of the Zegna and looked at his Breguet Classique. The watch had cost almost as much as the suit. He nodded to himself. The last of the drums would soon be in the ground and the giant hole filled up with a thousand tons of earth and stone. He was getting cold and bored out here, and decided he didn't need to hang around any longer.

But he'd be back, soon enough. There was always another cargo to deliver, another operation to oversee. Another gigantic pile of money to make.

Free enterprise. Where would we be without it?

He started walking back towards the helicopter.

Chapter Seven

Raul Fuentes emptied a third sachet of sugar into the paper cup of coffee, stirred it in with the little plastic stick, took a sip and screwed up his face, muttering, '*Sabe a mierda.*' He turned to Ben. 'How can you drink it?'

Ben shrugged and went on gazing out of the plane window. If the flight was taking the most direct route, then by his reckoning they were somewhere over Bordeaux. Their destination was Hamburg, Germany's most northerly airport and the nearest to Rügen Island. Before heading all the way south to Munich, Ben first wanted to pay a visit to the cliffs where Catalina Fuentes was said to have killed herself.

Raul poured in a fourth sugar, sipped again and pulled another pained expression.

'Give it to me,' Ben said, grabbed the cup from his hand and swallowed it down in four gulps. It was bad, but once you had tasted army coffee you could drink pretty much anything. As far as Ben was concerned, adaptability was a virtue. Besides, he was tired and needed the caffeine. His night on Raul's couch had been a sleepless one, his mind too full of thoughts and refusing to switch off. If Raul would only shut up a while, he might get some rest before they touched down at Hamburg. But Raul had barely stopped talking since they'd left his Volkswagen in the long-stay parking and hit the departure lounge at the Aeropuerto de Málaga. Ben knew the guy was nervous and upset, and didn't have the heart to tell him to put a sock in it. He turned away from the window and closed his eyes, hoping maybe that would give the Spaniard a hint.

'Your sister,' Raul said. 'Ruth, is that her name?'

Ben opened his eyes. 'What about her?'

'Where is she now?'

Ben looked at him. 'Now?'

'What happened to her? Where does she live? Do you see her? Are you close?' It seemed as if Raul had been plucking up the courage to ask for so long that his questions had all come tumbling out at once. Ben could sense he really needed to know the answers. If one lost sister could be recovered, then maybe so could another. That was the only thought that could offer Raul any solace at this moment.

Except that Ruth Hope hadn't driven her car off a sheer drop into the sea and given every indication of having taken her own life.

'Ruth lives in Switzerland now,' Ben said. 'She has a business there. I haven't seen her in a while, but we speak on the phone.' Ben didn't mention that his sister was no longer talking to him.

'You never told me how you found her.'

'Her kidnappers were Arab white slavers,' Ben said. 'Middlemen. Once they had her, they transported her into the desert, probably to meet with one of their contacts. Money would have changed hands, she'd have been put on a truck and taken to any of a million places in North Africa or the Middle East, and her life would have been as good as finished. But the meeting never happened. A fight broke out between the kidnappers, she escaped, and then a sand-storm separated her from them. She was taken in by a

Bedouin family and lived with them for a while. Then some time later, she was adopted by a rich Swiss couple called the Steiners, who were touring the desert when they happened upon this little blond-haired, blue-eyed European girl living with the Bedu.'

'I don't get it. They never returned her to her proper family?'

'Steiner told her that her real family were dead,' Ben said. 'His story was that we were all killed in a plane crash.'

Raul suddenly looked unsettled. You obviously weren't supposed to talk about plane crashes when you were flying in one. Ben sometimes forgot that violent sudden death was a taboo subject for normal folks.

'But why would he pretend that?' Raul asked.

'Because he wanted to keep her,' Ben said. 'The Steiners had lost a daughter the same age, in a riding accident. He believed that Ruth was a miracle sent to them, and he wasn't going to lose his little girl again. He used his wealth and influence to make her believe his lies for years. I'd left the army and was working in VIP protection when I happened to get involved with a private security team assigned to guard Steiner. That's how I eventually found her again.'

'Wow. What are the odds?'

'I know,' Ben said. 'But that's the way it happened.'

'Never lose faith,' Raul murmured, more to himself than to Ben. Shaking his head in amazement at the story, he settled back in his seat and fell silent for the first time since they'd left Málaga that morning. Ben went back to gazing out of the window, thinking about those times and wondering when he'd ever see Ruth again, and whether you could lose a person twice.

Two hours later, as Ben's Omega Seamaster was reading exactly midday, the aircraft touched down at Hamburg

Flughafen. So many armed cops were standing on guard about the place, in tactical armour with machine carbines cradled across their chests, that it looked as if a state of martial law had been declared. Maybe war had broken out in northern Europe while Ben had been wandering about Andalucía.

Ben had only his battered old green bag for luggage, and Raul had packed a single small holdall. With their bags over their shoulders they stepped out into the drizzle in search of a car rental place. 'Damn, it's cold here,' Raul said, scowling.

'First you won't drink the coffee, now you can't stand the cold,' Ben said. 'Remind me never to take you on a camping trip.' Even he felt the bitter chill in the air after the climate of southern Spain, but he was getting used to it with every passing second. Adaptability.

When they found the Europcar offices, Ben stopped Raul outside the door and said, 'Better keep the paperwork in your name only, okay?' When Raul asked why, Ben replied, 'I'm not their favourite person.'

'Are you blacklisted or something?'

'Not quite. But let's keep this simple, and my name out of it.'

'Sure, I understand,' Raul said, though he didn't. Not yet.

'How about that one?' Ben said as they perused the line of cars a few minutes later. He was pointing at a Golf GTI. Something quick and sporty that would get them where they needed to go without wasting time.

Raul frowned. He had insisted on paying for everything, so it was his decision. 'I don't like that one.'

'Too expensive?'

'And high-performance cars give out unacceptable CO_2 emissions. I won't be a party to that,' Raul said.

Ben remembered the polar bear cub on the melting ice floe. 'You're calling the shots,' he said.

The preferred choice was a little silver Kia hatchback that fitted comfortably with Raul's environmental sensibilities. As long as it had four wheels, an engine and a roof to keep the drizzle off, that was fine by Ben. He did all the talking to the rental agent, but as arranged, his name was left off the hire agreement.

Once they were out of sight of the office, they switched places so that Ben could take the wheel. Raul had never driven in a foreign country before, and couldn't read any of the road signs. 'First Spanish, now German. You certainly seem to speak a lot of languages.'

Ben was considerably more fluent in French and Italian, was conversant in Persian and Arabic, had a working knowledge of Urdu and Hindi, and could get by in Swahili, Somali, Berber, Hausa and Yoruba. 'I don't much care for being a tourist,' he said as he settled in behind the wheel of the cramped little Kia. The last car he'd driven was an H1 Hummer, about the size and weight of an Abrams main battle tank. This thing felt like a shoebox by comparison. The sticker on the dash said BITTE NICHT RAUCHEN, so he fetched out his Gauloises and sparked one up.

'Let's go,' he said.

Chapter Eight

It was two hundred and fifty kilometres from Hamburg to the Pomeranian coast and the Stresalund Crossing that connected the small city of Stralsund on the mainland to Rügen Island. The little car kept up a good pace on the autobahn as the wipers slapped back and forth all the way. They stopped once for fuel and to grab a couple of sandwiches at a Tank & Rast motorway services. Raul said he wanted to stretch his legs. Ben bought another cup of scalding coffee from a machine, and as he sat in the car alone drinking it, he dialled up Google Maps on his phone and spent a few minutes checking the rest of their route and examining the lie of the island. Then he took another look at the pages that Raul had shown him before leaving Spain, taken from the copy of the police report obtained from Leonhard Klein, the private detective. Raul had made vague noises about showing Ben the rest of the report, but hadn't mentioned it again since. Ben wondered why, then decided not to press the issue. There was enough here to be getting on with.

Just after two in the afternoon, as the rainclouds finally drew aside to make way for a half-hearted sun in a pale and washed-out sky, they crossed the Rügen Bridge and followed the single road onto the island. The closer they got to their destination, the quieter Raul became, and seemed to draw into himself with a grim expression that became more and more set as Ben drove. Ben guessed that if he were heading towards the scene of his own sister's apparent suicide, he'd be looking pretty grim himself.

The police report detailed the exact spot on the far side of the island where Catalina Fuentes' Porsche Cayenne had gone off the cliff. Ben turned off the main road and followed a rough track that led to a small car park. Beyond, the track continued for quarter of a mile, running steeply upwards parallel to the coast and steadily narrowing between clumps of bushes that shivered in the sea wind. Raul was hunched up in the passenger seat, looking pallid and about a hundred years old. Ben left him alone and said nothing.

The final stretch of coastal track led to a grassy incline that the police report said Catalina had climbed in her Porsche. The Kia was no four-wheel-drive, but the ground was firm and Ben gunned the little car up the slope at an angle, for better traction, and slowed to a halt on the approach to the cliff edge. Ahead, the coarse windswept grass sloped gently downwards for about twenty metres before it dropped away into nothing. A triangular yellow warning sign showed an outline image of a little matchstick man toppling off the crumbling drop, for those who couldn't read German.

'If you don't mind, I'd rather stay in the car,' Raul said in a tight voice.

Ben nodded and stepped out. The wind was coming sharply off the Baltic, carrying a penetrating cold from the Scandinavian lands across the water to the north. This was a lonely spot. It wasn't surprising that no witness to what had happened that day in July had ever come forward.

Ben walked down the slope towards the edge, scanning

the ground. The police forensic team had identified four contact patches of flattened grass a little way from the edge that corresponded to the long, wide wheelbase of a Porsche Cayenne, suggesting that she had parked for a few minutes before letting the car roll off the cliff. Ben crouched down, then dropped lower on his palms and toes as if he were about to launch into a set of press-ups. He examined the grass from different angles, but time had erased the impressions of the car wheels. A little further down the slope, he found a ghost of a tyre tread in the sandy, chalky dirt, what remained of it smoothed by wind and rain, the rest obliterated by dozens of fading shoe prints that could have been made by the forensic examiners, or perhaps by hordes of broken-hearted fans on a pilgrimage to the spot where Catalina had met her death.

Ben walked slowly to the edge, following the natural line of the tyre tracks through the tufty yellowed grass of the slope. The gradient was steep enough to let a car freewheel down unpowered. The Porsche had suffered such damage in the fall that the investigators had been unable to tell whether the engine had been running when the car went over. Either way, simply slipping it into neutral and disengaging the handbrake would have been enough to get it moving. As it had picked up speed, the tyres had dislodged a few stones and flattened a couple of shallow ruts. Where the slope suddenly dropped away to nothing, the chalky edge had been freshly crumbled as the wheels had passed over it and lurched heavily downwards into empty space.

Ben toed the brink of the drop and looked down. It was one hell of a long way to fall. Most people would have flinched away from the edge, but Ben was as unbothered by the height as he would have been standing on a chair to replace a light bulb. He could see the foam of the surf lashing and boiling white over the rocks hundreds of feet below. He imagined the impact of the falling vehicle, visualised the devastating explosion of crumpling metal and shattering glass as it hit. That was what he'd come here to see, and now that he'd seen it, it was very hard for him to imagine how anyone inside that car could possibly have survived. The fact that the car's interior hadn't been painted with blood when it had been fished out of the sea didn't mean a thing. The salt tide would have washed it clean.

He gazed out across the Baltic for a few moments, watched its implacable heave and listened to the crash of the waves. He could taste the salt in the air, like tears. He loved the sea, but it was a hard and cruel element.

He turned and started back towards the Kia. Raul looked small and shrunken in the passenger seat, watching him with an expression that was half curious, half dreading what Ben might have to tell him.

'There's nothing here for us,' was all Ben said as he slipped into the car. He didn't want to say too much for now. Although he feared it was simply delaying the inevitable, under the circumstances he felt he had to do as thorough a job as he could for Raul's sake.

In the meantime, they had a long road trip ahead of them. They would be traversing Germany north–south, the reverse of Catalina's last journey in her Porsche. Raul said nothing about taking turns at the wheel, and Ben didn't raise the matter either. He was here now, and he had nothing else to do but sit and drive, smoke and think.

It was evening by the time they reached Munich. Raul had stayed quiet for nearly all of the seven-hour drive, as if the nervous energy that had kept him babbling on the flight was now completely expended, leaving only the sombre reality of what he was doing here so far from home.

Catalina Fuentes' apartment was on the top floor of an upscale building in the fashionable district of Glockenbach, off Palmstrasse just a few blocks north of the River Isar. The area was Munich's answer to Greenwich Village, a popular haunt for musicians and artists and writers and other left-leaning individuals of the creative variety who could somehow afford to live there and frequent its bohemian cafés and bars. Raul produced a key as they stepped out of the lift onto a broad landing that smelled of pine air freshener and new carpet, and led Ben to one of only two glossily varnished doors at opposite ends. He paused at the door and looked about to ring the buzzer, then drew back his hand and closed his eyes with a sigh. Then he inserted the key in the lock and pushed open the door as if his own death lay beyond it.

Ben followed Raul inside the apartment, and closed the door behind them. Raul strode along a short hallway with a gleaming parquet floor that opened up into a large modern open-plan space. He took off his jacket and slung it on the back of a white leather armchair, as if he'd done it a hundred times before and was at home in the place. He glanced around the room, and for a second Ben thought he was going to call his sister's name, in case she might suddenly appear, smiling her perfect smile at this unexpected visit and wanting to be introduced to Raul's interesting new friend. But Catalina Fuentes didn't appear, and her brother turned to gaze heavily at Ben.

'My parents want to sell this place, once all the craziness with the lawyers is settled,' he said. 'Can you believe that, so soon? I told them I wouldn't let that happen, no way. It's still her home, you know?' He shivered. 'It's cold in here. You'd think the building manager would keep the heat on.' Going over to a panel on the wall, he flipped open a cover

56

and prodded small buttons. Ben couldn't see radiators or pipes anywhere. Without them, the lines of the room looked clean and elegant. Electric heating, magically hidden under the gleaming wood floor.

Raul gazed around the big living room with a wistful frown. 'It all looks just the way I remember it.'

'When were you last here?' Ben asked.

'I know the exact number of days,' Raul said. 'Too many. It was last autumn. Our birthday, November third. I stayed here for a week.' He thought for a few moments then added in an undertone, 'In fact I hardly saw much of her. She was so busy with her work, some new thing she was working on that she was terribly excited about. I didn't even ask her what it was.'

Raul's voice trailed off as he lost himself in memories of the last time he'd seen his sister alive. In one corner, a gleaming classical guitar rested on a stand. He went over to it, gazed at the instrument for a moment and then softly drew his fingers across its six strings. Its sound was deep and sonorous. 'Catalina's guitar,' he murmured.

Feeling he should say something, Ben was about to ask, 'Did she play well?' Too much past tense, he decided. Against his instincts, and to avoid hurting Raul, he said instead, 'Does she play well?'

Raul smiled sadly. 'I suppose so. She took it up years ago. But I never heard her play. She always kept it to herself.'

Too much past tense. Raul had snagged the emotional tripwire that Ben had managed to avoid. He began to droop as if his limbs and his head weighed nine hundred pounds, and lowered himself into the nearest armchair with his elbows on his knees, forehead cupped in both hands and his eyes screwed tight.

Ben walked slowly around the room. It was an elegant

blend of modern and old that spoke of good taste and a fine eye. He paused at a heavy sideboard, brushed his fingertips along wood that felt like oiled silk, and snicked open one of its doors. His guess had been right: drinks cabinet. Catalina's good taste extended to single malt scotch, nothing less than a fifteen-year-old Glenfiddich. He grabbed the bottle and two cut-crystal glasses, set them on the top and glugged out two generous measures. One for him, after the long drive. One for Raul, to take the raw edge off what he was feeling. Sooner or later they'd have to think about food, having eaten nothing since their sandwich before Rügen Island. Scotch would substitute fine for the moment.

Ben held out Raul's drink. Raul opened one eye, then the other, reached out for the glass and downed most of its contents as if he could happily chug through the whole bottle that night. Ben didn't intend to let him, not after what had happened last time.

'Mind if I look around?' he asked.

Raul just waved a hand at him. Ben thought he could trust him alone with the bottle for a few minutes while he had a quick reconnaissance of the apartment, sipping his whisky as he went from room to room. The kitchen was large and modern, spotless and gleaming and equipped with all the right accessories for someone who probably ate out most of the time but liked her kitchen to look the part. Ben checked the fridge and found two bottles of chilled 2011 vintage Chablis nestling on a rack inside. A couple of thin-crust pepperoni and anchovy pizzas were stacked in the freezer compartment above. Dinner was sorted, at least.

From the kitchen, he wandered down another passage to what looked like a home office, although it had to be the neatest and least-used home office in the world, entirely clutter-free and a few neat rows of abstruse-looking astrophysics and cosmology titles arrayed on the shelves. One wall displayed a blown-up framed still of Catalina pictured against the backdrop of an astonishingly resplendent Milky Way. Her face was aglow with enthusiasm, those big brown eyes as incandescent as the heavens. Ben presumed it must be an image from her TV astronomy series. Looking at it, it wasn't hard to see what her public had loved in her. He gazed at it for a moment, then went on examining the room.

According to the police report, Catalina's personal computer had been checked for suspicious emails or anything that could provide leads to contradict the suicide motive. Nothing having been found, the computer had been replaced, unplugged from the monitor on the desk. Ben was confident that the contents of drawers, her address book, phone records and general paperwork would have all been routinely examined, too, but he had a riffle through the desk just in case anything jumped out at him. It didn't, although he wasn't particularly sure what he was looking for. Sometimes you just had to go by instinct. And so far, his instincts weren't feeding much back to him.

Of the three bedrooms in the big apartment, the first he looked into was a guest room with a huge empty wardrobe and a timber-framed bed piled high with silk cushions. The second was stripped bare and in the middle of being redecorated, a stepladder against one wall, paint pots, plastic sheeting on the floor. He found that potentially interesting. Suicidal people didn't tend to care much about the state of their home decor. Then again, it wasn't much to base a theory on.

The third bedroom was Catalina's, the largest of the three with Gustav Klimt on the walls and a broad expanse of glass overlooking Glockenbach district. Her bed was an antique Louis XI kind of affair the size of a Cadillac Fleetwood. Old and modern side by side, the same elegant blending of styles. Ben did a five-minute search of her wardrobe and drawers, feeling as if he was prying. Finding nothing out of the ordinary, he walked into the ensuite.

Despite his experience of domestic life with his ex-fiancée Brooke Marcel, a woman's bathroom nonetheless remained a world of mystery to someone of Ben's ingrained spartan ways. Automatic halogen spotlights caught him by surprise as he entered, and he could see about twenty of himself reflected from all angles in the blaze of mirrors covering every vertical surface. A thick sheepskin rug stretched over the floor near the walk-in shower. Fluffy towels draped thickly over a chrome rail. The biggest vanity unit he'd ever seen held a collection of cosmetics and perfumes and creams and lotions and feminine paraphernalia that could have stocked a small pharmacy. Tools of her trade, he guessed. He had no doubt that being the world's sexiest scientist must be hard graft.

A walk-in wardrobe led off the ensuite, a whole other room in itself. Ben stepped into it, gazing around him for clues the police might have missed, like a pair of bathroom scissors lying in a red pool on the floor, or a cryptic message daubed in blood by the kidnapper.

What he found instead, he stared at for ten long seconds and then hurried back through the apartment with to show Raul.

Chapter Nine

Raul hadn't moved from his position on the armchair, and barely glanced up as Ben walked into the room.

'What's this?' Ben said, striding up to him.

'What's what?'

'This.' Ben tossed it in Raul's lap. Raul picked it up and gazed at it.

'It's fluoxetine,' Ben said. 'Any ideas why I might have found a whole stash of it sitting on a shelf in your sister's walk-in wardrobe?' He was trying to keep the anger out of his voice, but it wasn't easy. His discovery had left him feeling betrayed and made a fool of.

Raul slowly examined the small amber bottle of pills, then turned a blank expression on Ben and shrugged. 'I don't understand.'

'They're antidepressants,' Ben said. 'And they've got your sister's name on the label. And I want to know why.'

'Anyone can take medicine.' A flare of defensiveness lit up in Raul's eyes as he said it.

'Fine. If her doctor put her on pills for migraine headaches or a dust allergy, that would be one thing, wouldn't it? But this is something else.'

Raul said nothing. He stared at the bottle in his hand as if he could will it to change into something else.

'You told me she was a happy person,' Ben said. 'You said she loved her life and filled every room she walked into with laughter and smiles.'

'She did,' Raul said quietly.

'As long as the drugs were doing what they were supposed to do?' Ben said, pointing at the bottle. 'And what about the rest of the time?'

Raul fell silent. He closed his eyes. Maybe he thought that by shutting out the light, all his problems would vanish in the darkness. Ben glared at him, wanting to grab him by the neck and shake him.

'Answer me, Raul. Did you know about the pills?'

'Yes!' Raul burst out. 'I knew, all right? She went through a phase of feeling anxious and low when she was in her teens, and was on medication for it then. She was mostly fine, then every now and then she'd have a relapse when there was too much stress in her life. It happened again when that whoreson Austin Keller broke her heart. It hit her hard and she needed medical help to get over it.'

Ben didn't bother to ask who Austin Keller was. He shook his head in disbelief at what he was hearing. 'She was prone to depression and you knew about it all along, but you didn't see fit to mention it?'

'But it doesn't mean anything,' Raul insisted. 'That was all in the past. She got over it. She always has.'

'Read the label, you idiot. Look at the date. What does it say?'

Raul read it and sighed. 'It says July eleventh.'

'This year. Not last year, or the year before. It says she was prescribed this latest treatment five days before her car went over the cliff. And more than a third of them are gone. In less than a week? She must have been popping them like sweets.' Ben could hear his voice getting tighter with anger.

His stomach felt knotted and there was a beating in his temples that was growing into a dull ache. He took a deep breath to try to settle his pulse.

Raul waved his arms in frustration. 'Fine. All right. But if she was taking them, then she wasn't depressed, was she? Isn't that the whole idea of antidepressants?'

'Happy pills don't always work that way, Raul. Sometimes they take away sadness and replace it with rage and hatred and all kinds of other emotions instead. They can make a perfectly ordinary, gentle person with mild anxiety decide to take an axe to their family. Or take a jump off a high building, whichever way the brain chemistry happens to lead them. There have been thousands of proven cases. They call it the paradoxical effect. I call it mind-altering garbage that screws people's heads up.'

Raul frowned, a line appearing between his brows. 'How come you know so much about it?'

Ben pointed again at the bottle. 'Because my mother was prescribed some kind of crap just like that the year after Ruth disappeared, to help her cope with the loss. Over the next few months my father and I saw her degenerate into a total stranger. One day when I was eighteen years old, she wandered like a zombie into her bedroom, locked the door, lay on the bed and swallowed a jar of sleeping pills and never woke up. *That's* how I know so much about it, okay? Because I made it my business to find out what those things can do to a person.'

The breathing control wasn't working. The thumping in his temples was amping up into a full-blown headache. He'd never told anyone that much about his mother's suicide before, and he didn't enjoy revisiting the feelings it raised up in him.

Raul lowered his eyes and said nothing.

'Look at me, Raul. Tell me the truth. You knew Catalina was still on these drugs, didn't you? But you hid it from me, because of how I might react. That's why you didn't show me the full copy of the police report, because her antidepressant use would have been mentioned there as corroborative evidence to back up the coroner's suicide verdict. You removed those pages so I wouldn't see them.'

Raul's face twitched as he stared hotly at Ben, like a child caught with its fingers in the pie. 'Okay, I admit it. I did know, and you're right, it was in the police report. It came out at the inquest that she'd gone to her doctor not long before her disappearance, worried she was slipping back into depression, because of work-related stress and other private matters. The lawyers pulled strings to keep the details out of the media, but that's what happened. There. I've said it. I should have known you'd find those pills in her things, but my head's been so fuzzy with all this nightmare that I didn't think about it. I should have told you the truth. I screwed up. Are you satisfied now?'

Ben glowered at him. 'No, I'm not, Raul. Don't you see how this changes things?'

Raul paused, then pursed his lips as a new thought seemed to come to him. 'It would . . . if it was for real.'

'What? How can it not be for real?'

'It could all be part of the set-up. Kind of makes sense, actually.'

Ben couldn't believe what kind of wildly twisted logic Raul was throwing at him. 'Let's think about that for a moment, shall we? The kidnapper made her go to her own doctor for antidepressants, so that they could then plant them here in her apartment as phony evidence that she killed herself.'

Raul spread his hands. 'Does that sound so crazy?'

'Yes, Raul, it does. It makes it sound as if you're doing everything you can to deny the truth about what happened to Catalina.'

Raul's face paled to an ashen grey, as if Ben had punched him. 'What are you telling me, that now you believe all that bullshit story about her killing herself? I thought you were on my side.'

'There's no other way to see it, not now.'

'Listen. Ben. I know how it looks, you finding the pills, me lying to you.'

'Good. Then you understand why I'm thinking you brought me here on false pretences.'

'Yes. And I know you're thinking you want to walk away from all of it. I'm begging you, don't. I need your help. Never give up hope, remember? That's what you said, remember?'

'There's faith, Raul, and then there's self-delusion.' Ben turned away from him and went to the window, stood there for a moment looking down at the street. Night had fallen and the drizzle had returned, spitting diagonally from a charcoal sky and haloed in the street lamps. One of them was flickering intermittently. Further down on the opposite side, light flooded across the slick pavement from the windows of a café-restaurant. The street was empty apart from the parked vehicles that lined the kerbs and the occasional passing car.

'Please,' said Raul's voice behind him.

Ben went on gazing out of the window for a while. His jaw was wound so tight that his teeth hurt. But under all his anger was a thread of sympathy for Raul that he couldn't so easily let go of. He knew he should, and he knew he was being stupid and weak, but there it was.

He turned from the window to face Raul and said, 'All

right. One more chance. But I'm warning you. Any more surprises, and you're on your own. I mean it.'

'There won't be,' Raul said, brightening. 'Thank you. From my heart.' He gave a weak smile.

Ben grunted and did not return the smile. 'In the morning we'll go and talk to Klein. Now let's eat.'

Down in the street below, bathed in the intermittent glow from the flickering street lamp, the watcher sat perfectly still inside the plain black Fiat panel van with an easy view of the apartment windows. He had been sitting there since not long after the silver Kia had parked at the opposite kerb outside the apartment building and its two occupants had disappeared inside. The van's smoked glass hid him from passersby and allowed him to use the compact but powerful Canon 8x25 image-stabilising mini-binocs that were part of his kit. Another part was the Walther PPX nine-millimetre handgun nestling in its Kydex concealment holster on his belt. Those weren't all that he had brought with him.

Seeing a figure appear at one of the apartment's windows that overlooked the street, he picked up the binocs. The man at the window was the blond one who'd hooked up with Raul Fuentes over the last couple of days. They knew all about him, his name, his former occupation, his level of expertise. Hence the Walther PPX. What they didn't yet know, and were keen to discover, was how and why he'd suddenly appeared in the picture.

The watcher went on watching. Ben Hope was half-silhouetted in the light from the apartment, but enough showed of his face to make out his grim expression through the image-stabilised field of view. His hair was a little longer than in the photograph in the file the watcher had been shown. After a few moments, Ben Hope turned away from the window and his lips moved as though he were speaking, then he disappeared from sight. He could only have been talking to Fuentes. That would be confirmed by the watcher's teammates who were monitoring the bugged conversation back at base.

The watcher lowered his binoculars, satisfied that neither of the men inside the apartment was about to emerge to disturb the next phase of the operation.

He zippered up his black nylon jacket and pulled the woollen beanie hat tight down over his ears, partly to keep the rain off, partly to hide his features. Picking up a small black backpack from the passenger seat, he opened the van door and stepped quietly out. A quick upwards glance at the apartment windows to ensure nobody was watching him; then he moved quickly and silently across the street and slipped between the silver Kia and the Audi parked behind it. He took the small unit from the backpack and knelt beside the Kia as if he needed to tie a loose shoelace.

The unit clamped without a sound to the inside of the car's rear wheel arch. The watcher checked that it was secure, then continued walking down the street until he was out of sight of the building. He crossed the road and doubled back on himself, hands in pockets, shoulders hunched, like an ordinary pedestrian walking fast to get out of the rain.

When he returned to the van, he made his call. Soon afterwards, he started up the van and drove away into the night.

Chapter Ten

The private investigations offices of Leonhard Klein were situated to the north of the Glockenbach district, in an area called Maxverstadt close to the heart of Munich. After hustling through early morning traffic under a blanket of drifting rain, Ben and Raul arrived there shortly before nine. The nondescript cream-coloured modern building off Schellingstrasse stood back from the road, with a small cordoned parking area in front and a polished steel sign above the door that said L. KLEIN, DETEKTEI – NACHRICHTEN as on his official letterhead. Two cars were parked outside, a bright green VW Polo and a big black S-Class Mercedes. It wasn't hard to tell which belonged to the man himself, Klein.

The building was warm inside and smelled of flowers and fresh paint. A short hallway led to a tastefully appointed reception area, where a middle-aged woman with bobbed platinum hair was fiddling around behind the desk. Her handbag and a set of car keys with a Volkswagen fob were lying on the desktop next to her, as if she'd only just arrived for work. She peered over her spectacles as Ben and Raul approached, arched her eyebrows and glanced at the clock.

'You have an appointment?' she asked in German, in a tone that made it clear she knew perfectly well they didn't.

'He's a client,' Ben replied in German, jerking a thumb at Raul. Switching back to English he said to Raul, 'That's his office. Follow me,' and pointed at a door to the right. Raul nodded.

The receptionist scurried out from behind the desk as Ben moved towards the door. 'You can't go in there. Herr Klein is in a meeting.'

Ben ignored her, opened the door and stepped inside. It was a large, comfortable office, thickly carpeted, nicely furnished. Leonhard Klein was alone behind a broad desk that was empty apart from a cordless phone and the newspaper he was reading. He looked quickly up as Ben entered the office, then his expression of surprise turned to one of wary recognition as Raul stepped into the room at Ben's shoulder.

The detective closed the newspaper and stood up behind his desk. He was a tall, thin man with grey hair carefully combed over a freckled scalp and close-set eyes the same washed-out, warmthless colour of the ocean off Rügen Island. His nose and cheeks were florid with broken veins. Behind him on the wall hung a framed photo of a much younger version of himself, mean and moody in the uniform of the old West German Bundespolizei, peaked cap pulled low, a pistol riding on his hip and sergeant's stripes on his sleeve.

Klein smiled, but it was a thin smile and his eyes were narrowed with suspicion. Ben could have spotted the ex-cop in the man even without being told. Klein didn't look like someone you could slip too much past.

'Herr Fuentes. To what do I owe this unexpected visit?'

'I got your letter,' Raul said. 'I have a few questions.'

'I see.' The pale eyes turned towards Ben, shrewdly looking him up and down and obviously wondering who he was and what he was doing there.

Raul said, 'This is my associate, Mr Hope. He's aware of all the details of my sister's case.'

'I'm sure that it was unnecessary for you and your, ah, associate to travel all this way to discuss your questions in person,' Klein said. 'I only have a very few minutes before I'm due to see a client.'

A client. Not *another* client, Ben noticed. As if to say, *your case is yesterday's news.* 'This won't take long, Herr Klein,' Ben said, reverting back to German. The detective's eyes grew smaller and one eyebrow twitched in surprise.

'Very well. Please, take a seat.' He guided them to a pair of handsomely upholstered chairs facing the desk, waited until they were seated and then sat in his own plush leather swivel. He slid open a drawer of his desk and took out a notepad and a pen. 'Is there anything in my letter that was unclear to you?'

Ben leaned back and let Raul do the talking.

'Mr Klein, I still believe that my sister is alive,' Raul said, cutting straight to the chase.

A small ripple passed over Klein's face and his lips tightened. He seemed about to protest, then just spread his hands and said, 'Go on.'

'I'm here to ask you whether it's possible, with all respect to your professionalism, that you might have missed something.'

Klein began tapping the pen on the desk. 'I've been in this business a long time, Herr Fuentes.'

'I appreciate that. But please listen to me. I now believe she might have been abducted.'

Klein looked at him unwaveringly. 'Have you heard from the kidnapper?'

'No. No contact, no ransom demand, nothing like that.'

'Then may I ask what makes you think this is the case?'

Ben was inwardly cringing, knowing what Raul was going to say next. He badly wanted to be somewhere else.

'I have no evidence,' Raul said. 'Not yet. That's why I'm here.'

Klein went on tapping the pen on the desk, the way a cat switches its tail back and forth when irritated. 'To find evidence?'

'To find Catalina,' Raul replied firmly. 'And to ask you to think very hard about what could have been overlooked. There's something we've missed. I know there is.'

'We?'

'You. And me. Both of us.'

Klein's face was hardening. Something flickered in those cold eyes. Tap. Tap. Tap. He glanced again at Ben. 'And does your associate share your belief that Fräulein Fuentes is the victim of an elaborate and cleverly disguised kidnap plot?'

'Mr Hope has extensive experience in the field,' Raul said.

Ben cringed even more. Great, Raul. Thanks.

Klein gave Ben a long, searching look. Then he dropped the pen and reclined in his chair. 'I find it somewhat insulting, Herr Fuentes, to have my professional capabilities brought into question in this way, especially in front of a third party. I have done everything that is possible with your sister's case, both here in Munich and at the scene of the incident, where I spent two entire days scouting the location and speaking with local residents as well as the police. I have spent a great many hours investigating the matter, and my conclusions are definitive. I'm afraid there is simply no doubt, in my mind or in fact, that Fräulein Fuentes was a deeply unhappy young woman who tragically took her own life. Her history of mental instability and her ongoing treatment for severe depression are compelling evidence in themselves. The lack of a body was the only reason I agreed to take your case on in the first place, which I now must say I regret. If you and your *associate* can do a better job, then I wish you the very best of luck, gentlemen.'

Klein stood up, leaning his knuckles on the desktop. 'Now, Herr Fuentes, I have much better things to occupy my time. At this point our business is terminated, and I must ask you to leave my office.'

'You didn't say a word,' Raul muttered as he and Ben stepped out of the building and walked back towards the Kia. The rain was falling harder. 'Not a single damn word to back me up in there.'

Ben remained silent as they got into the car. He was still smarting from embarrassment, angry with Raul for dragging him into this and even angrier with himself to have allowed it to come this far.

So wrapped up in his own dark thoughts that he failed to sense the eyes watching his back and the metallic grey BMW that followed at a distance as he pulled the Kia out into the traffic.

Chapter Eleven

By the time they were nearing Glockenbach district, the rain had worsened into a deluge and Ben had made the decision to walk away from the whole situation. He could have been sitting on a beautiful lonely hilltop in southern Spain at this moment. Climbing in the Sierra Nevada or trekking along the Costa de Almeria in search of a deserted white-sand beach or cove where he could maybe rent a little place next to the sea and spend a while figuring out where his life was going. Not hacking through dirty traffic on a cold wet day in a city he had little love for and no longer any reason for remaining in.

'Klein's right,' Ben said at last.

'I knew you were going to say that,' Raul muttered.

'I'm sorry.'

'What are you going to do?'

Ben shrugged. 'What can I do?'

'I need a drink,' Raul said.

'Yeah, why not,' Ben agreed. One for the road. Then he was out of here. Maybe by train or bus, back down south to where it was warmer. Maybe to Italy. He had friends there. He could drop in and see his old army comrade Boonzie McCulloch, the most ferocious grizzled wardog of a sergeant the SAS had ever unleashed upon the world, now retired to a cosy life growing tomatoes and basil with his Neapolitan wife Mirella in their tranquil smallholding up in the hills near Campo Basso.

'There's a place up ahead,' Raul said sullenly, pointing through the rain-spattered windscreen. 'Pull up here. I can't face going back to the apartment yet.'

They hurried from the car and went inside. It was one of those kinds of upmarket café-wine-bars that Ben found a little too precious for his tastes, the sort of place they charged three times the going rate for a measure of ordinary scotch, just for the privilege of planting your arse on one of their dainty chairs and being served by some disdainful prick with an attitude problem. They took a table at the back and Raul ordered a stein of beer that came in a litre tankard shaped like a jackboot. Hello, Bavaria. Ben bypassed the local traditions and asked for a double whisky, straight, no ice. The waiter was a malnourished-looking guy in his twenties, stooped and bald-headed and brusque in his ways, at least with Ben and Raul. Maybe he disapproved of whisky drinkers at ten in the morning.

Neither of them had much to say. Ben was okay with that. Enough had been said already, and now they were at the end of the road, there seemed little point in prolonging the pain. They sat and worked quietly on their drinks, drawing one or two looks from people at other tables. They obviously disapproved, too. Ben was toying with lighting up a cigarette, just to scandalise the clientele even more. Then again, in Germany you could probably be clapped in irons or flogged in the town square for public smoking offences, so he decided to leave it.

Raul had the same look on his face that he'd had in Frigiliana when Ben had first seen him. He clutched the ridiculous boot with both hands and had already worked his way down to near the ankle when the woman walked in.

Ben had no reason to take much notice of her. Like most of the bar's customers she was well dressed, middle class, affluent looking. If he'd given her a second glance he would have put her age around fifty-eight. She had a mouth like a razor slash. Blond hair turning to iron, scraped severely back and heaped and pinned up on her head like a Pickelhaube helmet. She draped her rain-spotted Burberry coat over the back of her chair, settled her ample frame down, and when the bald-headed waiter scurried over to take her order, all smiles and fawning, she asked for some kind of wild berry tea that arrived a few moments later in a tall chintzy pot with a matching cup and saucer.

Ben quickly forgot she existed. He cradled his drink and was back to thinking about how soon he could be out of Munich when he noticed that Raul was staring at the woman as if she'd sprouted horns.

Ben glanced over. She hadn't sprouted horns. She was sitting demurely sipping her tea and studying what looked like an art exhibition brochure.

'What?' Ben said, but Raul made no reply and went on staring fixedly for twenty more seconds before he slid his jackboot stein away from him and stood up.

'Raul,' Ben said, warning him with his eyes. 'What are you doing?'

But for reasons best known to himself, Raul was on a mission and didn't seem to hear. He skirted their table and stalked intently across the room to where the woman was sitting. It was like watching a replay of the fight in the bar in Frigiliana, except this time Raul didn't set fire to anybody. Not yet.

Raul stopped at the woman's table and stood over her with his fists balled at his sides. '¿*Dónde encontraste eso?*' he demanded loudly, then remembered where he was and repeated it in English, the only language he knew that she might understand. 'Where did you get that? Tell me!'

Ben had sprung up from his chair and was immediately right behind him with his hand on the Spaniard's shoulder. 'What the hell are you at?'

The woman was gaping up at him. Her gash of a mouth opened an inch and quavered in bewilderment.

Raul turned to Ben. 'Ask her in German. Go on, ask. I want to know where she got that.'

'Got what?'

'That.'

Raul pointed at the woman's chest.

Ben stared, baffled, until he realised that Raul was talking about the piece of jewellery that was hanging around her neck. The pendant caught the light and sparkled against the black cashmere polo-neck she was wearing: a glittering cluster of fine-cut white and coloured stones arranged in a spiral pattern about three inches in diameter. Ben was no jeweller. The stones could have been any old cut glass, or they could have rivalled the Koh-I-Noor diamond for value. Either way, Ben was more interested in what had got into Raul Fuentes.

Ben wasn't the only one who was perplexed by Raul's sudden outburst. The bald waiter had spotted trouble and was quickly threading his way through the tables towards them. The woman's eyes were wide open with terror. She backed away from the table and stumbled out of her seat to retreat from this crazy person who was accosting her.

Raul lunged forward and grabbed her wrist. She let out a yelp. People were turning to stare. The waiter was running faster towards the table.

'For Christ's sake, Raul,' Ben said. 'Let her go.'

Raul shook his head and held onto the struggling woman's arm. 'She's not going anywhere. She could be one of them.'

'Enough. Have you lost your mind?'

'That's Catalina's necklace,' Raul said through gritted teeth. 'She's not going anywhere until I get an answer.'

The waiter had reached them and was waving his hands frantically. 'You, back off,' Ben warned him in German, aiming a finger at his chest.

'*Ich werde die Polizei anrufen,*' the waiter said, drawing back a step as if Ben's pointed finger were a pistol.

Raul picked up on the word 'Polizei' and said, 'That's right, you go right ahead and call them.' He aimed a finger at the terrified woman. 'We've got a kidnapper here.'

Ben turned away from the waiter and snatched Raul's hand. He dug a thumb into the nerve point in Raul's wrist. Just a little pressure was enough to make the muscles spasm and let go.

'I said, enough,' Ben told him seriously. 'Look at her. She's going to have a heart attack.'

The woman was bawling now, her face bright purple and wisps of hair coming loose from her pinned-up helmet. Most of the good citizens in the place had turned to gape in alarm. Two or three other men were half out of their seats, hesitating to weigh in. If enough of them rushed forwards at once, things could get messy. The waiter had raced back behind the bar to grab a phone and call the cops.

Raul's eyes bugged. 'I'm telling you, this bitch is wearing my sister's necklace.'

'It's just a necklace,' Ben said.

'No, it's not just a necklace, Ben. It's *her* necklace. There's no other like it in the world. It's a diamond and sapphire spiral galaxy made just for her by a top jewellery designer. It was a gift from that bastard Austin Keller.'

Austin Keller again. 'The one who broke her heart, I remember.'

'She stopped wearing the necklace when they split up. It's engraved on the back, *All my love, A.J.K.*'

'It is mine!' the woman shouted in heavily accented English, speaking for the first time. She clutched protectively at the spiral pendant with both hands, as if you'd have to break all her fingers to take it from her.

'Ah, so she does understand,' Raul sneered at her. 'Fine. So you can tell that to the police.'

'We're not waiting for them,' Ben said. 'Let's go.' He grabbed Raul's arm again, but this time Raul was ready for him and elbowed him sharply backwards in the ribs before tearing free of Ben, lunging after the woman a second time. Raul knocked her hands out of the way and clawed the pendant from her neck. The woman let out a cry as the flimsy silver chain snapped.

Raul clutched the diamond cluster in his fist, turned it over to examine the shiny silver mounting plate on the back and let out a 'Ha!' of satisfaction. 'There. I knew it! I told you! Look!'

Raul turned triumphantly to Ben and showed him. Up close, the exquisite craftsmanship of the piece was unmissable. It was a beautiful thing. The glittering white diamonds radiated in an elliptical spiral from the bluer stones in the centre, the outer jewels delicately mounted on tiny silver arms to give the impression that they were floating freely in space. You could almost see the galaxy slowly rotating on its axis.

As Raul flipped the piece over on the palm of his hand, Ben could clearly see the fancy engraved lettering on the backplate.

All my love
A.J.K.

Ben looked sharply up at Raul. The Spaniard was grinning a nasty grin and his eyes were glittering almost as brightly as the stones. 'How did I know that, hmm? How did I know that? This bitch took it from her, that's how.' He wheeled back to glare at the woman.

Unless Raul Fuentes was clairvoyant, Ben couldn't see any other explanation either. In the blink of an eye, the situation had totally reversed.

Two men from nearby tables had eased from their seats and were slowly advancing. Ben gave them another warning stare and said in German, 'Easy. Nobody's getting hurt here.'

Raul was still questioning the woman. Now that she realised she wasn't about to be murdered, she was coming out more freely with answers.

'*Ich habe es mir gerade gekauft* . . . I – I buy it!'

'When?' Raul demanded.

'She says recently,' Ben said. She looked too frightened to be lying. In a gentler tone than Raul's, he asked her in German to tell him exactly when and where she had purchased the piece of jewellery.

'Not long ago . . . I think three weeks. I saw it in a window for sale . . . A pawnshop. I wouldn't normally go into those places but it was so beautiful I—'

Ben said to Raul, 'She says she bought it from a pawnshop three weeks ago.'

'Bullshit!' Raul spat, enraged. 'Now, listen, you—'

'Cool it, Raul.' Ben was still holding up a hand to warn away the heroes from the nearby tables. It wasn't easy to smile reassuringly in that position, but he needed to put the woman at her ease. 'Please, Fräulein, tell me the name of the shop where you found it.'

The woman gave an address, and Ben repeated it back to her twice. She was crying, partly from shock and fear, and probably also partly because she thought she'd lost her precious pendant.

'Let her have it,' Ben said.

'No way she's getting it back. It's Catalina's.'

'You can't steal it from her. She's telling the truth. For Christ's sake, look at her. She's scared to death.' Ben held out his hand. Reluctantly, after a beat, Raul dropped the pendant into his palm. Ben returned it to the woman. 'There. Everything's fine. Please sit down and finish your tea. We're leaving.' He repeated it more loudly for the rest of the room to hear. 'Okay? No problems here. We're going now.' He pulled a few euros from his pocket to pay for their drinks and left them on an empty table as they retreated towards the door. Then they spilled back out into the rainy street and ran for the car before the police arrived.

'This is getting to be a habit since I met you,' Ben said as he accelerated the Kia up the street.

Chapter Twelve

Around the corner, Ben squealed the car sharply into the kerbside and punched the address the woman had given him into the on-board satnav.

'I was right,' Raul was saying over and over. 'I was right. Something happened to her.'

'Let's take this one step at a time, okay?' Ben said.

Raul turned to face him with liquid eyes. 'You see I was right, don't you?'

'About the diamonds,' Ben said. 'That's all we know for now. Stay calm.'

'How can I stay calm, damn it? A *pawnshop*. Can't you see? It proves she was kidnapped. Whoever took her sold the jewels for some quick cash. Bastards!' Raul punched the dash so hard that he cracked the plastic and left a smear of blood.

'Don't wreck the car,' Ben said.

The address was just a few blocks away. If the woman lived in the area, it increased the chances of her frequenting both the shop and the café. Which meant it wasn't the impossible coincidence Ben had first thought. How Catalina Fuentes' pendant had ended up there, and what this turn of events signified, were questions still to be answered.

As they pulled up outside ten minutes later, Ben could

see why a respectable middle-class denizen of Munich might not readily admit to shopping in the place. He'd seen shabbier pawnshops, but he really couldn't remember when.

'Are you coming in?' he said to Raul.

'Are you joking with me?'

'Fine. Then try not to beat the guy up, all right? I'll handle it.'

A bell tinkled as Ben pushed open the door, and a hanging sign saying GEÖFFNET slapped against the glass. There were no other customers. The pawnshop smelled stuffy inside, and there was so much clutter in the windows that it blocked much of what little light the grey sky was throwing down. Ben wondered if the murky ambiance was also meant to camouflage the crappy quality of most of what was on sale in the place. The usual assortment of golf clubs and hockey sticks and electric guitars and saxophones and exercise machines and dinner sets and racks of clothing and air rifles and a thousand other dingy-looking items traded for ready cash by their former owners stood, hung or were stuffed inside crowded shelves around the walls. A closed office door marked PRIVÄT lay behind the counter, which housed a glass-topped display cabinet that constituted the pawnshop's jewellery wares not displayed in the window, consisting mainly of watches, along with a few brooches and earrings, bracelets and strings of fake pearls nestling in velvety little presentation boxes.

Whoever Catalina Fuentes' ex-boyfriend Austin J. Keller was, Ben thought, he'd have to be pretty seriously rich to be able to afford a bobby dazzler like the spiral galaxy pendant. All the weirder, then, that it should have ended up in a dump like this, sitting among a pile of third-rate trinkets. Either Catalina must have hated the guy so much after they split up that she didn't give a damn, or else she had to be desperate. Desperation oozed from every crack of this place.

Ben was gazing at the jewellery when the office door opened and a squat man with a scrappy beard, a flowery shirt and a pronounced leg length discrepancy limped through it.

Ben decided to skip the preliminaries. '*Sprechen Sie Englisch?*'

The guy shrugged, like saying, 'So-so.'

Switching from German, Ben asked him, 'Are you the owner?'

The guy's eyes narrowed to slits. 'I am the proprietor. What is this concerning?'

'We're here to inquire about an item of jewellery you sold about three weeks ago. A pendant made of diamonds, shaped in a spiral, blue at the centre, about so big, with a silver mount. Very distinctive. I think you know the one I mean.'

The guy made a big deal of trying to remember, but Ben could tell he knew exactly what piece he was talking about. '*Ja.* What about it?'

'We'd like to know who sold it to you.'

'Are you cops?'

Ben shook his head.

The guy pulled a face. He probably would have spat on the floor if he hadn't been in his own premises. 'Then is none of your fucking business who sold it to me. I do not remember anyway. Now I have business to run. You are not here to buy, the door is that way.'

Ben nodded. 'Fine,' he said. He turned and walked towards the door.

Raul stared at him. 'Just like that?'

Ben said nothing. He reached the door, flipped the open sign around so that it read GESCHLOSSEN, then popped the latch. Then he walked back to the counter and said, 'Your business is now closed until we say it isn't. *Ist das klar, mein dicker Freund?*

Three shades paler, the pawnshop owner raised his hands. 'I want no trouble.'

'That's good,' Ben said. 'Because my associate here has a tendency to get extremely violent when people piss him off. Once he starts, I can't stop him. The last person who pissed him off, he—'

'Okay, okay.' The guy glanced nervously at Raul, suddenly all eager to help.

'What's your name?' Ben asked.

'Mattias. Mattias Braunschweiger.'

'Okay, Mattias. Now let's rack our brains and see if we can't remember who sold us that diamond cluster. I don't believe pieces like that come your way every week.'

'A woman sold it to me.'

Raul and Ben exchanged looks.

'Description,' Ben said.

'Very beautiful woman. Dark. She looked familiar to me. I think afterwards, she is a movie star. Or singer.'

Ben smiled. The pawnshop had 'haunt of the rich and famous' written all over it. 'Would you remember her face?'

'You would not forget her,' Braunschweiger said, showing yellow and grey teeth.

'Is this her?' Raul asked. He took a photo from his wallet. It was a duplicate of the one framed over his desk at home, showing himself and Catalina on a sandy beach. He'd folded it in half so that only she was visible.

Braunschweiger squinted at the picture and nodded. '*Ja.* That is the woman.' His eyes darted back up at Ben and Raul. 'You are not cops?'

'Just tell us about the woman.'

'She had lot of things to sell. Very good stuff. I show you.'

He limped back through the door that said PRIVÄT. Ben watched him in case he tried to run, though he wouldn't have got far on that leg. Braunschweiger reappeared a moment later, carrying a tray that glittered even in the dingy light. There was a delicate gold watch with a tiny rectangular case, several pairs of diamond earrings and a bracelet studded with small emeralds. The stuff was on a different planet to the trash in the display cabinet.

'I have to revalue,' he explained. 'I think after I sell the other, price is too small.'

Braunschweiger laid the tray on the counter, and Raul stepped close with a deep frown on his face to examine the things on it. He recognised them immediately. 'This is Catalina's,' he said, holding up the small gold watch. Its rectangular face was studded with minute diamonds.

'You're sure?' Ben said.

'No question. It's hers. A Cartier Tank Américaine. She'd always wanted one. I was with her when she bought it. And these earrings. You can see them in a lot of photos of her. And this bracelet—'

'All right,' Ben said, convinced. He turned to Braunschweiger. 'When exactly did she bring you these things?'

'Exactly? You want date?' Braunschweiger considered for a moment, then grabbed a thick, well-thumbed ledger from beneath the counter and started flicking back through its pages, which were covered in entries: description of goods, date of transaction, price paid. After a few moments he tapped a page with his thick finger. 'I find it. She come here *Zwölftel Juli*.'

July twelfth. Just four days before Catalina's car had gone over the cliff. Ben and Raul exchanged glances. Raul's brows were knitted and his jaw was clenched. 'Are you certain this is right?' Ben asked Braunschweiger.

'You want see security recording? This prove it, *ja*?'

'Get to it,' Ben said.

The German led them behind the counter into his office, a poky room that smelled of stale body odour and was choked with clutter and stacked paperwork. On a scarred pine table that served as a desk was Braunschweiger's grimy computer, hooked up to wires that ran up the wall, attached by duct tape, and disappeared through a hole to connect up to the security camera Ben had noticed in the corner of the ceiling overlooking the counter.

Braunschweiger cleared away piles of mess with a sweep of his arm and scraped up a chair. Air seemed to hiss out of him as he sat. 'For insurance I must keep video footage one hundred days,' he explained, pointing at an external hard drive that was plugged into the machine. 'Then I delete.'

Catalina Fuentes' car had gone over the cliff eighty-seven days ago. According to the entry on the ledger, the recording of her visit to the pawnshop should still be here.

Ben and Raul stood flanking Braunschweiger's chair as he turned on the computer and spent a couple of moments dithering about searching for the hard drive icon on his busy desktop. Finding it at last, he clicked with his grubby-looking mouse and a window flashed up showing a menu of video files arranged by month. He scrolled back to July and clicked again, and a list of thirty-one separate files appeared with individual dates. Braunschweiger ran his cursor back to the twelfth of the month, clicked once more, and the screen dissolved to black, then flicked back into life with a wide-angle view of the counter and shop as seen from the raised perspective of the security camera. The light was so dim, it was hard to make anything out. A time readout in the bottom corner of the screen showed that the footage commenced at midnight.

'I fast-forward,' Braunschweiger said, and clicked a couple of keys on his keyboard. The image onscreen remained fixed, but the clock started to race ahead with an hour elapsing every few seconds. As dawn approached, the image quickly began to brighten in time-lapse sequence. The clock had hit eight thirty a.m. when the shop's front door seemed to fly open and a crazily speeded-up Braunschweiger came waddling into the premises, looking as if he could limp for Germany in the Olympics. For a few instants he ricocheted around the shop like a steel bearing in a pinball machine, then shot out of sight. The time readout raced on. Nine a.m. Nine thirty. Nothing happened. The image was completely static.

Then the door flew open again and another figure hurtled into the shop.

'There,' Raul said.

Braunschweiger tapped the keys and the image reverted back to normal speed. The time readout said 09:42.

Raul leaned closer to the screen, and swallowed. 'That's her.'

Chapter Thirteen

The image was poorly defined, but there was no question that they were looking at Catalina Fuentes. At normal speed, the nervousness in her step was obvious even to a stranger like Ben. Raul was fixed intently on the screen, breathing heavily through his nose.

July twelfth. The last known images of her. Four days before her purported suicide. The day after getting the antidepressants from the doctor.

Catalina looked tense and edgy.

They watched as she walked up to the counter. She was wearing jeans and a light top. Her hair was tied back under a plain black baseball cap and a large pair of sunglasses covered her eyes. She was carrying a shoulder bag, which she unslung and rested on the counter. The figure of Braunschweiger appeared in the corner, just within view of the camera's range. They seemed to be talking.

'Is there no sound?' Ben asked.

Braunschweiger shook his head. 'Insurance company does not ask for this, so why should I pay for expensive system?'

Onscreen, Catalina was opening up her bag and taking out the items to show him. He was examining each one in turn.

'What did she say to you?'

'That these were things from her grandmother. Old woman has died and she does not want them.'

Raul shook his head in disbelief. 'Why would she say that? Our grandmothers have both been dead for years.'

'What else did she say?' Ben asked Braunschweiger.

'Nothing. That she needs the money fast. My offer is twenty thousand, for all.' Braunschweiger made a grasping motion that was probably unconscious.

'Cash?'

Braunschweiger turned away from the screen with a worried frown, as if it had just occurred to him that if he admitted to carrying such large sums of cash on the premises, these two guys would surely beat him up and rob him.

Raul looked ready to punch him in the face. 'I hate crooks like you who take advantage of people. That's a fraction of what this stuff was worth. You're lucky we don't burn this place to the ground.'

Ben looked at Raul and could see the fury in his eyes. He put a hand on his arm to steady him. He asked Braunschweiger, 'And she didn't give any clue why she needed the cash in such a rush?'

'*Nein*, she spoke hardly a word. She did not try to argue price. I offer the money, she nods okay, and that is it. I fetch the cash from safe, count it before her and she takes and puts it in the bag, as you see.' The events were happening on the screen as Braunschweiger narrated them. A few moments later, the transaction was over and Catalina Fuentes left the pawnshop looking just as nervy and tense as she had before. She seemed to pause at the entrance, as if peeking through the door to check the coast was clear. Then she was gone.

Raul kept staring at the empty shop as if waiting for her to return. His face was etched with sadness.

'You want that I should burn to disc?' Braunschweiger offered. Maybe he thought that if he was generous, these two wouldn't beat him up and rob him after all.

'Do it,' Ben said.

Braunschweiger delved in a box and came out with a sealed pack of DVD-ROMs. He tore open the packaging and slotted one into the computer, hit a few keys and clicked here and there, and a minute later the file was burned onto it. Ben pocketed the disc, then stepped over to the counter and picked the gold Cartier from the tray. 'We'll take this, too.'

'Ten thousand,' Braunschweiger said. Generosity had its limits.

Ben shook his head.

'Seven, then.'

Ben took out his Zippo, clanged it open and thumbed the striker. Braunschweiger stared at the flickering flame, got the message and swallowed. 'No charge,' he said. 'What the hell, I make enough on the necklace.'

'You're a credit to your profession,' Ben said, flicking the lighter shut. He gave the watch to Raul. Raul clutched it tightly in his fist, looking at Braunschweiger as if he would like to make him eat it.

They left the pawnshop and returned to the car. The rainclouds had drawn back like a curtain, and the sunshine was peeping timidly through the gap but it didn't feel any warmer.

Raul was so worked up that his hands were shaking. Ben didn't start the engine. He cracked the window open just an inch, so the rain couldn't get through, and lit a Gauloise. With all the pieces of the puzzle up in the air like confetti spiralling in a wind, it was time to do some serious thinking.

Raul kept staring at his sister's gold watch. 'I'm more sure than ever. Who would cash in their precious valuables to raise twenty thousand euros when they're planning to kill themselves four days later?'

'Tell me,' Ben said. 'Was your sister the kind of person who spent everything she earned on fancy stuff and high living?'

Raul looked at him. 'Don't keep talking about her in the past tense. And no, that has never been her way.'

'Then there's still plenty in the bank?'

'She left behind over six hundred thousand euros in her account.'

'Where's the money now?'

'My parents refused to accept it, even though legally it passes to them. Said they wanted to donate it all to their church.'

'And nobody's called in any big debts that you know about?' Ben asked.

'No debts. If she'd been worried about money, I'd have known about it. She'd have told me.' Raul narrowed his eyes at Ben, as if he could see where he was going with this line of thinking. 'You're wondering why she didn't just withdraw the money from her account, if she needed it.'

Ben nodded. 'There's always a reason why people do the things they do. A cash withdrawal would have left a paper trail. This looks like a deliberate attempt to cover her tracks. She was nervous, edgy. Something was frightening her.'

Raul pursed his lips and wrinkled his brow. He was silent for a while, thinking so hard that Ben could almost hear his brain grinding. 'I know what happened. The bastard was extorting money out of her. Blackmail, for something.'

Ben had already considered that idea. 'For what?'

'I don't know. But it would explain why she needed money without leaving a trace.' Raul worked it over for a few moments longer, then shook his head. 'No. Why would someone blackmail her for twenty thousand euros when she was worth so much more? And why would she have to disappear afterwards? The blackmailer suddenly turns kidnapper? That doesn't make sense either. If they'd simply kidnapped her in the first place, they could have asked whatever ransom they wanted.'

'Or,' Ben said.

Raul looked at him again, pale with worry. 'Or what?'

'There's another possibility, Raul. One you need to be ready for.'

'I'm ready.'

Ben took a long draw on the cigarette, and flicked ash out of the crack in the window. 'Suppose you're right and there's some weirdo extorting money from her for some reason we don't know yet. She doesn't want anyone to know, and selling her jewellery is the only way she can think of to raise the money quickly and quietly, without leaving a trail. She can't go to a respectable jeweller, either, not if she wants to avoid any kind of paperwork, records, receipts, official evaluations. That's why she ends up having to go to a piece of shit like Braunschweiger, even though she knows she'll get a fraction of what the items are worth. She's willing to take the loss. So, she gets the twenty thousand cash, passes it straight over to the blackmailer, in the hope that it'll all go away, but then it turns out the twenty thousand was just the start. Maybe he starts pressuring her for twenty more, or fifty, or a hundred. She refuses.'

Raul stared at him. 'And?'

'There's a confrontation. Maybe he threatens her. She's defiant. It gets violent. Maybe he never intended to hurt her, but he kills her in the struggle. He makes it look like suicide.'

'I keep telling you, she's alive,' Raul said. 'She's in danger, but she's alive.'

Ben took another draw on the cigarette and blew smoke. 'That's what you believe, or what you want to believe?'

'It's neither. It's what I know.'

Ben shrugged. 'Fine. Then let's take that as our bottom line. She's alive, and she's scared and in danger.'

'Yes.'

'Then consider this alternative scenario,' Ben said. 'Maybe she didn't need the money to pay off someone else. Maybe she needed it for herself. We could be getting this all wrong. Imagine the situation from another angle.'

Raul blinked. 'What other angle?'

'Stalkers are cowards. They're also delusional enough to believe that they might actually have a chance of scoring with the person they're obsessed about. If some creep was hanging around, it's more than likely he'd have been making a nuisance of himself for a while. Typically, these types of people will try to insinuate themselves into the victim's life in all kinds of ways before all the rejections, warnings, and finally court exclusion orders, cause them to build up enough rage and resentment to resort to anything as drastic as abduction. If he found out her private email address, he might have bombarded her with messages. Or written her letters. The police found nothing like that. Now, that could mean they weren't looking thoroughly enough, or it could actually mean they were right. There's no evidence that she was being stalked. None at all, just like we have no body. The only thing driving that idea is your fear that some nutjob is holding your sister captive in a cellar somewhere.'

'What are you trying to say?'

'Go where the evidence points,' Ben said. 'Take the stalker out of the equation. What if there *is* no kidnapper? What if she was just running from something, or someone, who had her so scared that she faked her own suicide?'

'Like what? Like who?'

'I don't know. But that would explain why she couldn't withdraw cash from the bank. Like you said, money's not on a suicidal person's priority list. You can't take it with you. And twenty thousand euros isn't exactly a fortune, especially not by Catalina's standards. But for someone on the run, someone scared and desperate, someone who's mentally switched to survival mode and thinking only in the short term, it's plenty to be getting on with.'

All kinds of thoughts and emotions were playing behind Raul's eyes, which were jacked wide open and staring into the middle distance.

'If she's alive, she didn't just drop off the face of the planet,' Ben said. 'Where would she go? Where would *you* go?'

Raul shook his head.

'I know where I'd go,' Ben said. 'To ground, somewhere wild and remote where nobody could find me. Where I could stay hidden for as long as necessary to figure out my options and decide on my next move. I could live in a dugout burrow in the woods if I had to. I'd be able to make a habitable shelter in a cave, hunt my own food, live on nothing, disappear so completely that not even a professional could ever track me down. Because that's who I am, and that's what I was trained to do. But I'm not Catalina. You know her better than anyone. So think.'

Raul was silent for a long minute. Then a dawning light appeared in his eyes and the tension seemed to drop from his face.

'There's one place she could have gone,' he said.

Chapter Fourteen

'I'm on them. Looking at them right now,' said the man behind the wheel of the dark grey BMW 6-Series Gran Coupé that was parked down the street. From where he was sitting, he had an oblique view of the pawnshop doorway through the rain-splatted windscreen, and he could see the two targets inside the silver Kia. The one called Hope was in the driver's seat as before. The watcher could see intermittent wisps of cigarette smoke drifting from the inch-wide crack in the window.

Cars hissed past on the wet road. Some workers from nearby offices were out on their eleven-o'clock break, munching pastries in the street and trying to soak up what anaemic rays of sunshine were struggling to reach down from the damp sky.

The watcher and his colleagues had been monitoring the targets' movements all that morning, ever since before nine when they'd left the apartment and driven north through the city to see the private investigator, Leonhard Klein. That visit hadn't taken long. From Klein's, a different car had shadowed them back to the bar on the edge of Glockenbach district and then reported back to base when, not long after, Fuentes and Hope had come running out of the place as if they were onto something.

When Hope had suddenly veered to the side, for an anxious moment the watchers had thought they were blown. They knew he was good; very, very good; but they were experts and extra-careful about constantly switching between the three cars in the chase, keeping in constant contact via their mobile phone conference network that worked like unlimited-range two-way radio and also allowed them to keep the Boss informed of their movements. Nobody was that good. After that false alarm, they'd dropped back and followed the silver Kia straight here. The two men in the grey BMW watched from a distance as Fuentes and Hope entered the pawnshop.

'Are they still inside?' asked the Boss on the phone.

'Negative. They're out and back in their car. Engine's off. Just sitting talking. Fuentes looks agitated.'

'They know something,' the Boss said.

That was how it looked to the watchers, too.

'Time to make a move.'

'Negative,' the watcher said, eyeing the office workers. Another car hissed past. 'It's too public here.'

'First chance you get. Take them down as planned.'

'Roger that,' the watcher said. 'Hold it. They're on the move again.' He'd seen fumes spurt from the Kia's exhaust as its engine started. Its indicator started flashing to pull out into the traffic.

'Stay with them,' the Boss said. 'Hacker, Ruddock, move into position.'

'We're on it,' said Hacker's voice.

'Copy,' Ruddock came in. 'We're circling the area.'

Cook, the driver of the BMW, checked his mirror as he waited for a yellow minivan to pass, then pulled out. The silver Kia was two cars ahead, moving as if Hope was eager to press on. Cook followed, with the dogged, flat-eyed look of a man just doing his job. The tools of his trade were in a case on the back seat. He'd be using them soon enough, but the thought didn't leave him much moved.

Some men fixed cars for a living. Others paid their bills by frying their brains sitting behind computer terminals all day. Cook and his colleagues hurt and killed people. It was no big deal. Today would be no different, except it meant they could get out of this German shit hole. Fucking Germans. Cook hated the food, hated the language, hated the people. Then again, Cook hated just about everything, and his employer most of all.

The BMW stayed with the Kia for three kilometres with Cook hanging carefully back and Lewis in the passenger seat maintaining phone contact. They peeled off as Ruddock and Dean in the black Fiat panel van took over for a stretch, Ruddock driving, Dean on the phone. Ideally, they'd have air backup and a couple of motorcycles to fill out the surveillance team. It wasn't as if their employer couldn't afford them. But his resources were scattered elsewhere in pursuit of this mission, and in any case six on two was considered ample to get the job done. Which Cook had to agree it was, more or less.

Cook followed a parallel course as Dean reported the Kia's progress. It was clear that Hope was returning to Catalina Fuentes' apartment. The strike could take place there.

As the Kia hit Glockenbach, Nicholson and Hacker in the Opel Insignia picked up the chase. When the Kia parked outside Fuentes' building, Hacker pulled up fifty metres down the street, and Nicholson phoned in to say that Hope and Raul Fuentes had gone inside.

The Boss said, 'Do it.'

The six-man team closed in from three directions and positioned their vehicles close to the building with the Fiat panel van parked near the entrance, two spaces behind the silver Kia where the frontage of the building blocked its view from the apartment windows. Cook and Lewis left the BMW and joined Hacker and Nicholson, and the four of them stepped quickly into the back of the van, where Ruddock and Dean had already opened up the kit bags and started laying things out.

They togged up in silence. Body armour under black nylon jackets, thin gloves. The ski-masks would go on at the last minute, before the assault. Lastly, they checked their weapons. Pistols only, for this kind of urban work. The hollow shell of the van resonated to the metallic noises of magazines being snicked home, actions being jacked, locked and loaded. None of them had a problem with doing a job like this in a busy city environment. They'd done it plenty of times before, for this employer and others in the past. If there was any tension in the air, it was because all six of them knew what they were going in against.

If Fuentes had been on his own, this would have been an easy one, straight in, get it done, clear out and gone. It wasn't going to be so simple. Even unarmed and caught off guard, Hope was dangerous. Whatever his involvement, his presence made Fuentes a hard target. For that reason, the team had come doubly prepared.

Cook clipped his pistol into its concealed holster, zipped up his jacket and stuffed the ski-mask into a hip pocket ready for use. He scanned the five serious faces and said, 'Okay?' Nods and grunts all round. Nicholson leaned over the front seats so he could peer out of the passenger window at the entrance of the building.

'We're clear,' Nicholson said.

Cook picked up the phone and said, 'Moving in.' He signalled to Hacker. Hacker went to open the back doors. Once they committed themselves, speed was going to be everything.

'Wait,' Nicholson said from the front, raising a hand. 'Hold it. They're out.'

Cook shoved Nicholson out of the way to look out of the window, just in time to see Hope and Fuentes stepping out of the building and walking fast to the silver Kia. Fuentes was carrying a holdall, Hope had a green canvas bag slung over his shoulder, old-spec British military issue. The two climbed into the Kia, Hope taking the wheel once more.

They hadn't been inside the apartment five minutes. Cook noticed the way Fuentes looked jumpy and on edge. This could be it.

Cook reached again for the phone. 'Standing down. Targets are in motion. Looks like something's happening, for sure.'

'Stay with them,' said the Boss. 'Do not bugger this up.'

Cook snapped off the phone.

The silver Kia started up and pulled out sharply and moved off fast into the traffic. Cook waited three seconds, watching the car disappear into the distance, then he and Lewis burst out into the street and raced for their BMW and Nicholson and Hacker ran to the Opel while Ruddock and Dean clambered into the front of the van.

The BMW took the lead, chasing fast up the street in the direction the Kia had gone. The targets were out of sight by now, but they wouldn't get away. Strategically, Cook faced a decision whether to concentrate all his forces on going after Hope and Fuentes or to send Nicholson and Hacker to check out the pawnshop connection.

He decided to leave that for later. If the hit went smoothly, they could forget about the pawnshop. And for now, they needed the numbers to take down Ben Hope.

Chapter Fifteen

Motorways radiated from the city of Munich like the arms of a starfish, E52 to the northwest towards Augsburg, E53 to the northeast in the direction of the Czech border, E54 to the west heading to Landsberg and the River Lech, and E45 and E533, forking southwards in opposite directions east and west for Liechtenstein and Austria. The location punched into the Kia's satnav lay two and a half hours' drive to the west, in the Alpine foothills on the Bavarian side of Lake Constance.

'I was one of the only people who even knew about the place,' Raul was saying as they left Munich behind. 'The last thing she wanted was a bunch of reporters showing up there, or fans. She bought it under a company name and only told people she absolutely knew she could trust. It was like a hideaway for her. She used to stay there often.'

'You said it was an observatory.'

Raul nodded. 'Yes, with a small house attached. Not much more than a cottage, together with a few other buildings. It's out in the middle of nowhere, about five kilometres from the nearest village, so it was ideal for privacy as well as astronomy. No light pollution. Although she did a lot of observing during the day, too.'

Ben looked at him. 'What kind of telescope can see the stars during the daytime?'

'Just the one kind, and just the one star,' Raul said. '*Our* star. The sun, viewed through a solar scope. Catalina is a specialist in solar physics. That has always been the biggest part of her work. Have you ever seen the sun up close?'

'Not that I can recall,' Ben said.

'The one time I went to visit her observatory, she took me into the dome and let me look through the solar telescope. Some piece of equipment, I can tell you. I've never seen anything so amazing in my life as this giant ball of fire, more huge and powerful than we can even imagine.'

Giant balls of fire were something Ben could take or leave. Even the small ones he'd come into contact with, usually in the form of enemy incendiary devices, had been more than hot enough for him. 'So this place of hers is out in the middle of nowhere and you've been there only the once?' he said to Raul. 'What are the chances you can find it again?'

'I'll find it.'

'Why didn't you tell anyone about this place before?' Ben asked him. 'Why not the police? Why not Klein?'

Raul shook his head. 'Everything has changed since then. Before, I wasn't thinking she might have gone back there. I wasn't really thinking at all. I only knew she was alive, and that while she was alive I was betraying her trust in me if I told her secret. I kept telling myself that one day, everything was going to be normal again, and her life would go on as it had before. Then later, when I started to think she'd been kidnapped, I never thought about the place. She wouldn't be there, she'd be in some place the person had taken her. I imagined the worst places. A cellar, full of rats and filth. A box buried deep under the ground with just an air hose to breathe through. All these awful images in my head. I couldn't stop thinking about her trapped, frightened, calling for help.'

He stared ahead, his eyes fixed on the road as if he could reel in the horizon and bring them instantly to their destination. 'But she *is* there. I know that's where we're going to find her. Frightened, and in terrible trouble. But safe and unharmed. I *know* it.'

'Maybe,' Ben said.

Raul glanced at him sharply. 'Yes, maybe. But maybe is good enough for me right now. Maybe is all I have. Faith, remember?'

'Faith,' Ben repeated. They were still over two hours from finding out whether that faith would be justified or not.

The long road carried them westwards past towns and lakes. Landsberg, Buchloe, Mindelheim, Memmingen. Some time during the drive, it occurred to Ben that this must be the most miles he'd ever clocked up on a rental car without being personally responsible for getting it destroyed, pulverised, burned, blown up or shot to pieces in the process. *Touch wood*, he thought, and looked around the Kia's plastic interior for anything resembling wood.

When he couldn't see any, he abandoned such weak-minded superstitious notions, lit another of his dwindling pack of Gauloises instead and went back to thinking about Catalina Fuentes. Whichever way he tried to arrange the pieces of the puzzle in his head, he couldn't make any sense of what was going on. Something crucial was missing from the picture, and if they didn't find Catalina lying low in her astronomical bolthole in the mountains, they'd have to hope they dug up more to go on – or else Ben had no idea where they could turn to next.

He hated it when the success or failure of the mission

depended on just a single scrap of a lead. Funny how it never seemed to be any other way.

The first half of the afternoon had ticked past by the time they finally reached Catalina Fuentes' observatory in the Alpine foothills, two hundred and forty kilometres west of Munich. The motorway was far behind them, the road having grown progressively narrower and quieter as they neared their destination near the small town of Klosterkirche. Raul's memory proved just a little less precise than he'd given Ben to believe, and it was only after getting lost three times in the forest roads bordering Lake Constance that they finally stumbled on the right path and Raul started to recognise the landmarks. 'This is it, I'm certain,' he said.

After turning off the road onto a stony trail that looked like no more than a farm track, they wound and snaked uphill for nearly ten minutes through empty hillside before the place came into view at the top of a rise. The first thing that caught Ben's eye was the white fifty-foot dome that stood like a temple overlooking the forested valley below and the blue lake waters in the distance, seventy kilometres from end to end and smudging the boundaries of three countries. Adjoining the dome was a rambling single-storey cottage. Nothing ostentatious, just a simple stone building with ivy trailing up its whitewashed walls and small, cottagey windows. It looked clean and maintained, but the message was clear: all the money had gone into the dome. The dwelling itself was secondary, like a bunkhouse.

A cluster of smaller buildings stood behind the house, looking like old storerooms and animal pens converted from their original use. The property was fronted by a beaten-earth yard that ran off to patchy grass and then to a wooden fence that ringed the perimeter. Faded grass and the last wildflowers of the year waved in the breeze. As the land sloped up towards the hills the terrain became rougher, strewn with rocks. There were stumps where trees had been cut down. Trees being, Ben supposed, the universal bane of astronomers everywhere.

So this was where Catalina Fuentes had been in the habit of escaping to from the pressures of celebrity. Now they were about to find out whether her remote hideout was an escape from something else.

There was no lock on the wooden gate, despite the sign that said in German, PRIVATE PROPERTY – KEEP OUT. Raul got out of the car to open it, and Ben drove through. He paused for Raul to dive back into the passenger seat, then bumped up the rest of the uneven track, which widened out into the dirt yard in front of the house. There were no other vehicles in sight, but one of the buildings could have been a garage.

'Pull up here,' Raul said urgently, thirty yards short of the house. 'I don't want to scare her.'

Ben was concerned that Raul was taking a little too much for granted, but he said nothing and stopped the car. Raul kicked open his door and almost fell out in his eagerness. He ran towards the house, waving his arms and calling out in Spanish.

Ben killed the engine and stepped out of the Kia. The air was crisp and fresh, the view magnificent and unbroken in a sweeping vista that didn't stop until it reached the faraway peaks of Switzerland. He could see why a person would choose this spot to admire the heavens. He lit a cigarette and began walking towards the house.

Raul had already reached the door and found it unlocked, pushing his way inside still calling out in Spanish to his sister. 'Catalina, it's me, Raul. It's okay. I'm here.'

Ben followed, still saying nothing. The doorway was set

deep into the thick stone walls and the lintel was low, cottage-style. He had to duck an inch to walk inside. The front entrance opened straight into a small, beamed living room that was simply furnished and very different in style from the apartment in Munich. To his left was a pine slat door. Straight ahead, another door that Raul had already gone through, into a kitchen.

'She's here,' he said, turning back towards Ben and pointing at a small pine table, on which rested a china mug and a plate with the remnants of a sandwich. Raul felt the mug, and his face glowed excitedly. 'Still warm. See? Didn't I tell you?'

He burst out of the kitchen and hurried to the other door. It led through to a small office, from whose far side climbed a flight of wooden steps that Ben realised was the entrance to the observatory dome. The office was even less like Catalina's apartment: not a penny spent on designer chic, as functional and utilitarian as any military HQ Ben had ever seen. The view from the window was of the unpretty storage buildings outside. Metal shelving lined the walls, heavy with files and textbooks and heaps of paperwork. More of the same cluttered the little desk space that wasn't taken up with her computer.

Ben was sensing a very different Catalina Fuentes from the party-going, bejewelled and fashion-conscious celebrity whose walk-in wardrobe in the city was bigger than a lot of people's homes. This was the real her, the serious hard-grinding scholar she'd been before the circus of fame and fortune had entered her life. The place was the nerve centre of her work. No frills, just science.

Raul stepped quickly through the room and called up the stairs, 'Catalina! It's me, Raul!' Glancing back at Ben, he said, 'She could be in the dome.'

Ben followed him through the door into a bare-block, concrete-floored space about a dozen metres square, its main feature a massive steel pillar bolted to the floor via a thick circular plate and disappearing up through the ceiling, the height of the roof of the house it was attached to. Raul was clattering up a metal staircase that coiled around the pillar, leading to a circular hatch through to the level above. Ben climbed the steps after him.

The observatory was dark inside, sealed off from the sunlight with the roof closed. Raul found a light switch near the hatch entrance and flipped it on. Now Ben saw that the dome consisted of sections bolted together like the segments of an orange sliced into a hemisphere, insulated on the inside with some kind of space-age silver material. The dome stretched the same dozen metres across at its widest point, a dozen more from its rubberised floor to the apex of its arched ceiling.

The space was filled with a bewildering array of rack-mounted electronics, computers and optical equipment that was dwarfed by the pair of giant white aluminium telescopes that stood in the centre of the circular floor. They were mounted on a massive pivot atop the steel pillar and trained upwards in parallel like twin artillery pieces. Ben wondered why she needed two, then remembered what Raul had said about his sister's solar observations. One scope for night, the other for day. Each more than twelve feet long and hooked up to a spaghetti of curly multi-coloured wiring for motor drives and banks of digital readouts at whose function Ben could only guess, their bulk was steadied by a counterbalance weight like an Olympic powerlifter's barbell, on which was mounted a padded operator's chair. Just the thing for those long hours spent gazing into space, Ben thought.

The dome ceiling curved smoothly above the upward-pointing twin telescopes. Noticing a complex arrangement of cables and pulleys connected between the centre of the roof and a large electric motor with a control panel, Ben realised that a whole section of the dome could be opened up at the flick of a lever to expose a vast expanse of sky. A separate motorised system allowed the upper section of the dome to rotate, running on tracks like the gun turret of a tank, so that the telescopes could be swivelled around to cover the entire firmament in a three-hundred-and-sixty-degree circle over the tops of the racks of electronics and computer equipment.

The inside of the dome was an impressive sight. It was also empty. No sign of Catalina Fuentes, or of anybody else.

Refusing to admit defeat, Raul headed back for the spiral stairs, switching off the light as he went. He clattered back down the steps, and again Ben followed. They returned inside the house, which seemed strangely rustic now in comparison to the high-tech wizardry of the observatory. Raul was calling 'Catalina! Come on out, it's me! It's Raul!'

As Ben wandered back through the study towards the living room, he was thinking that the still-warm coffee mug on the table downstairs had to belong to someone.

Then he stopped. Stepped back a pace, looked out of the study window overlooking the back of the house, and realised he hadn't imagined the sudden, furtive movement he'd glimpsed out of the corner of his eye.

There was a man outside.

Chapter Sixteen

The man was young, dark, and thin; Ben didn't get a clear look at him as he made a break from one of the smaller buildings and darted out of sight around the corner, throwing a glance at the parked-up Kia as he went. One thing was for sure. Whoever he was, he hadn't been expecting company, and he wasn't happy about the unexpected arrival of two strangers.

Ben froze, but what seemed to him like a hesitant pause before he exploded into action was less than three-quarters of a second. Before another second had gone by, he was already racing out of the study and sprinting for the door. As he burst outside, the layout of the property was burned into his mind and he was locked on and calculating the quickest route to his target. He turned left from the doorway, skirted the length of the house, turned again and the outbuildings came into view ahead. He ran faster, dust and gravel flying from his feet. He couldn't see the man. He chased around the corner of the outbuilding.

Then, suddenly, there he was. This time, Ben got a better look at him. He was maybe twenty-four or -five, with the black hair and olive complexion that could have made him anything from Spanish to southern Italian to Middle Eastern. He was wearing faded jeans and a scuffed old leather jacket.

A motorcycle was parked around the back of the building. It was old and had seen better times, with peeling chrome and red paintwork and a big metal TRIUMPH badge on the tank. The man was grappling it off its sidestand by both handlebars as he desperately stamped on the kickstart lever to fire up the engine.

Ben ran straight for him.

The bike coughed and failed to start. The man lashed at it again with his foot, but this time the lever kicked back with the compression of the piston and he let out a grunt of pain as it jolted up and raked his shin.

By then, Ben was six fast strides away from him and closing. The man let the bike go and it fell over on its side. He took off as if a pack of pitbulls were snapping at his heels. Ben hurdled the fallen motorcycle and chased him, running hard. The man was young and fast, but Ben had been faster at that age, and he was still just as fast now.

Where the guy was heading, Ben had no idea. But it was clear there was no escape. He seemed to be aiming for the rocks, as if he thought he could scramble up the hillside like a goat, and away. He hammered over the long grass and hit the boulder-strewn incline at a bounding sprint. His toe caught the edge of a rock and he stumbled, and Ben came up behind him and jerked him backwards off his feet in a choke-hold that cut off the carotid artery feeding the brain.

The guy struggled hard for three seconds, but it was chaotic and untrained struggling that did him no good at all in Ben's iron grip. By the count of five, he was as limp as a sack of clothes.

Ben lowered him to the ground, rolled him on his back and checked him for weapons. He was unarmed. Finding a slim wallet in the inside pocket of his jacket, Ben counted thirty-five euros in cash. There was no driver's licence or other form of identification, not even a bank card. Ben had frisked the pockets of dozens of dead or unconscious bad guys, and nearly all of them had had that much in common with this one. Bad guys didn't turn up ID, unless it was fake, or unless they were incredibly stupid, or it had been planted on them for a reason – usually after they were dead.

Except this one didn't appear to be a bad guy, in any real sense. He didn't look like a particularly threatening individual, and he certainly was less of a fighter than he was a runner.

Ben thought about the still-warm coffee Raul had found in the kitchen. Bad guys didn't sit around drinking coffee in a victim's home, least of all unarmed when they couldn't handle themselves with their bare hands. And they especially didn't turn up on prehistoric 1970s Triumph Daytonas with old-fashioned carbs you had to tickle and an engine you couldn't fire up without jumping up and down on a kickstart lever.

So who was he, and what was he doing in Catalina's secret sanctuary?

Ben grabbed the collar of the leather jacket and dragged the guy back to the house. He didn't weigh too much. Raul stood in the doorway, watching anxiously.

'What's happening? Who is he? Where's Catalina?'

'That's what we're going to find out.' Ben hauled him through the entrance into the living room and dumped him on the floor. 'Grab an arm, will you?' he said to Raul, and together they heaved the guy up into a chair. By now, Ben already knew that the man wasn't a threat. But he was scared enough to run, and sometimes to make a scared man talk you had to scare him a little more.

'I'll watch him. Go and see if you can find something to tie him up with.'

Raul nodded and hurried off. Ben heard him rooting about in the kitchen, then a few moments later he returned with a roll of silver duct tape. One of the most useful and versatile household items ever conceived, with applications most honest, law-abiding citizens could never begin to dream of. 'Found this under the sink,' Raul said.

Ben nodded. 'Perfect.'

Two minutes later, the prisoner was securely trussed up and going nowhere, his head lolling forwards with his chin on his chest. Ben slapped him softly across the cheek a few times to waken him.

The man's eyes opened slowly, unfocused, then suddenly snapped wide open as he registered Ben. He began to struggle again, straining against the tape that held his wrists and ankles to the chair, his head twisting from side to side in panic as he poured out a stream of words.

Raul stared at him in incomprehension, but Ben knew the language. Farsi was the same thing as Persian, spoken across a wide-ranging area covering Iraq, Iran, Afghanistan, Tajikistan, Uzbekistan, Azerbaijan and parts of Russia. Ben had worked in a lot of those places. He snapped out a command in the man's language, a very vulgar expression meaning 'Be quiet'. Along with a warning glare and a raised finger, it had the desired effect. The guy stopped thrashing in the chair, and looked up at Ben like a beaten dog.

'Are you going to behave yourself?' Ben asked him in Farsi.

The man nodded.

Still in Farsi, Ben asked, 'What are you doing here? Where are you from?'

The man seemed surprised that Ben didn't already know. 'I am from Tehran,' he blurted. 'I came to Germany for work.' They were making progress, but Ben was still wondering why they'd come here looking for a Spanish female scientist and found an Iranian man in her place.

'Please,' the Iranian muttered, his mouth half numb with fear. 'Don't send me back. I can't go back.'

'I'm not here to send you back,' Ben said.

Chapter Seventeen

The Iranian's eyes widened even more and he turned a shade paler. 'You're not from the BAMF?'

BAMF was the Bundesamt für Migration und Flüchtlinge, Germany's federal office for immigrants and refugees. Now Ben was understanding a little more about why the man had run from him.

Ben shook his head. 'I don't work for the government.'

That should have been good news for the Iranian, but it seemed to frighten him ten times more. Sweat was beading on his brow and he began to shake. 'Then you're here to k-kill me,' he stammered. 'Please! I'm not a threat to you!'

'What's he talking about?' Raul asked, impatient that they were still speaking Farsi and he couldn't follow a word of the conversation.

Ben explained, 'He's an illegal immigrant from Iran, and he thinks we're here to kill him.'

When the Iranian heard his captors speaking English, it seemed to terrify him still further. 'I swear to you that I know nothing!' he blurted out, switching now to English himself. 'Do not hurt me! I am begging you!'

'Oh, you'll beg us,' Raul snarled at him, making a fist. 'You'll beg for a bullet, if you don't tell us what we want to know.'

Beg for a bullet. Ben looked at Raul and raised a hand. 'Please,' he said. 'I'm handling this, all right?'

Turning back to their prisoner, he softened his tone and asked in English, 'What's your name?'

'I am Kazem Behzadi. I work here. Please do not—'

'Just answer the questions,' Ben said.

Raul's eyes narrowed and he chewed his lip as if remembering something. He nudged Ben's arm and beckoned him aside to say quietly, 'She told me about a Kazem.'

Ben turned and walked to the kitchen. He came back holding a large chef's knife from the block on the worktop. Kazem's eyes popped at the sight of the blade, and he began to gibber in fear as Ben stepped around behind the chair.

'Who's your employer, Kazem?' Ben asked.

'Catalina! Catalina Fuentes! Don't kill me!'

Ben believed him, and holding the guy prisoner made no more sense. Ben quickly slashed the tape holding Kazem's wrists to the chair, careful not to cut him, then did the same for his ankles. Realising that Ben wasn't about to saw his head off, Kazem stopped panicking and sat quietly in the chair, rubbing his wrists. His eyes followed the knife as Ben laid it down on a side table with the point turned towards the wall. Now that he understood that these two men were here neither to deport him nor to murder him, he looked bewildered. 'Catalina Fuentes,' he repeated softly, and then his eyes clouded. 'But I do not work for her any more. She is dead.'

'I'm her brother,' Raul said. 'Raul Fuentes.'

Kazem peered at Raul, and through the dissipating fog of his terror a look of recognition dawned as he took in the physical resemblance. 'Yes, yes, she talk about you all the time.' Then his face fell again, etched deep with sadness. 'I am so sorry she is gone.'

Raul looked down and said nothing.

'How did you come to be here?' Ben asked.

Stumbling over his English, Kazem explained that while working as a lab technician back home in Tehran, he'd been involved with a group of anti-government campaigners and been drawn into the protests of 2011 and 2012 in which social unrest had sparked off violent rioting in the city. Amid the subsequent brutal clampdown by the Iranian authorities, in which thousands of people had been arrested, beaten and even killed by police, Kazem had fled the country. Like many other political refugees from the east he'd ended up in Germany, where, managing to obtain a temporary visa and residence permit to allow him to work, he'd bummed about from one casual job to another until eventually finding suitable employment as a science lab tech at the University of Munich.

He'd been happy there, until two things had happened to shake his world. First, the expiry of his work visa, which slipped by him and also went unnoticed by the university personnel department. Second, the retirement of his kindly supervisor and his replacement with a by-the-book hardass racist bigot who'd made it his business to harass and persecute Kazem at every turn. When his hated new supervisor had discovered that Kazem had outstayed his work visa, he'd gleefully threatened to denounce him to the immigration authorities.

Terrified that he was about to be deported back to Iran, where many of his friends were still in jail, Kazem had been at a loss until Catalina Fuentes stepped in to rescue him. He explained how he'd often met her at work, and how pleasant and friendly she'd always been to him, helping him with his German and encouraging him to study towards a science degree, unlike many of the other academic staff who treated the techs like non-humans. When his visa crisis had threatened to ruin everything, Catalina had offered him private employment, for better pay, as her personal assistant and live-in caretaker out here at the observatory. He'd been only too happy to move out of his shitty digs in the city and move here, where he had his own mini-apartment in a converted outbuilding, and a peaceful life working for someone he liked.

That had been nearly eleven months ago, during which time they'd become friends. He was learning more about astronomy, maths and physics, studying German, English and even a little Spanish, and impressing her with his appetite for advancement through study. She'd bought him a motorbike to run errands on, as he didn't drive a car. She had been a wonderful, warm, generous person.

Then it had all come crashing down.

Kazem almost wept when he talked about her suicide. He was broken-hearted over it, as well as worried about his own future. He'd taken a part-time job washing dishes in a hotel nearby, still living here in the knowledge that he couldn't remain forever, and in fear that the immigration people would come to whisk him away in the night. Sooner or later, he knew, this would all be over.

As he talked, a large black cat appeared through the gap in the entrance door. It hovered there for a second, scrutinising the humans inside with suspicious green eyes, then stalked into the room, the tip of its tail switching to signal its displeasure.

'That is Herschel,' Kazem said. 'He is kind of wild. He turn up here one day, and make this his home. Catalina name him after her favourite astronomer.'

Ignoring the three of them, the cat wandered nonchalantly through into the kitchen, hopped onto the table and started chewing at the remains of the leftover sandwich.

'Herschel, *hör auf damit, du blöde Katze*,' Kazem called after him, then jumped up and went to scoop it up in his arms and march it back to the door. The cat wriggled and twisted as Kazem put it outside and closed the door. 'He always stealing my food,' he explained to Ben and Raul. 'I speak to him in German and he understand, but he never learn.'

Ben looked at Kazem Behzadi and saw a sincere, good-natured and completely guileless young guy in whom Catalina had obviously placed a great deal of trust. He felt bad about having treated him roughly before. But there was still one thing Kazem had said that perplexed him.

'Why did you think we were here to kill you, Kazem?' Ben asked him.

Kazem shifted uncomfortably, hesitated a moment and then replied, 'When you tell me you are not with the BAMF, then I think you have come to steal. Is lot of expensive equipment here. Is much crime in Germany. I am sorry,' he added. 'I should not have run.'

Ben reflected for a moment and said, 'I'm sorry too. We didn't mean to alarm you. If I damaged your motorcycle, I'll help you fix it up, okay?'

Raul hadn't spoken during Kazem's account. Now he leaned closer to the Iranian and said, 'Let me tell you why we're here. I believe that my sister is still alive. I came from Spain to find her. You were her friend. If you know anything, anything at all, that can help me find out what really happened and where she is, I need to know. I don't have a lot of money but I will pay you, and help you in whatever way I can.'

Kazem stared at Raul for the longest time. Then he shook his head. 'No, she is dead. She has driven her car into sea. Nobody survive this. She not want to survive. I think she have a sad heart.' He pressed a hand to his own chest.

'They never found the body,' Raul said.

Kazem went on shaking his head and looking deeply uncomfortable. 'No,' he repeated. 'This is not possible she is alive. She is gone and she is not coming back. I am sorry. Like you, I miss her very much. She look after me, help me in so many ways. I think perhaps one day I can study and become something in my life. If this can happen, it will be because of your sister. She was honourable person.' His eyes had become moist as he talked. He quickly reached up and dabbed at them.

Herschel the cat had stalked around to the window outside and jumped up onto the ledge, where it curled up with its legs tucked underneath its body and green eyes narrowed to slits.

'Kazem, when was the last time you saw Catalina?' Ben asked.

Kazem frowned and thought for a moment. 'It was just some days before she kill herself. She come here to use the Lunt.'

'The Lunt?'

'The solar scope,' Kazem explained, motioning towards the observatory. 'Lunt is its name. She want to observe a solar filament she very interested in. I help her set it up. Afterwards she cook dinner for us, then she stay the night and drive back to Munich the next morning. That is last time I see her or speak to her.'

Ben didn't bother asking what a solar filament was. 'How did she seem to you? Considering what happened a few days later?'

Kazem shrugged. 'She seem normal to me. I did not think anything is wrong. Her pain, she was hiding it very well.'

Ben glanced at Raul, who was staring down at the floor and chewing his lip. 'I'd like you to think really carefully,

120

Kazem. Did she say anything to you that made you think she was frightened?'

Kazem frowned, and shook his head slowly. 'I cannot think. Frightened of what?'

'We don't know yet,' Raul said.

'Did she need money? Was she in trouble? Was somebody threatening her?' Ben knew that this line of questioning was going to run out soon, and he couldn't think of anything more to ask Kazem.

'I do not understand,' Kazem said, shaking his head faster. 'What is this you are talking about?'

It looked to Ben as if they were drawing a blank here. He turned away in frustration and walked to the window. He stood there as if looking out at the view, but his gaze was turned mostly inwards as he thought hard about the situation and what to do next. The window pane had a thin layer of dust on it. The other side of the glass, the black cat was still nestled on the ledge.

Suddenly, the cat went rigid and sprang to its feet. The green eyes flared. A ridge of hair bristled up down its spine and its tail became rigid and spiked.

The cat sensed danger.

Chapter Eighteen

The BMW Gran Coupé coasted the last few metres with its engine switched off, small stones pinging from under its tyres. It ground to a halt on the track, followed by the blue Opel, then the black Fiat van. The very top of the white observatory dome was visible over the rise, but they couldn't be seen from the house.

Cook, Lewis, Nicholson and Hacker got out of the two cars. The back doors of the van swung open and the four gathered around. Patiently, calmly, they went back through the same motions as they had in Munich, though the equipment was different this time. With no need to conceal their light body armour under their normal clothing, each man put on a tactical vest with pouches for ammunition. And out here in the sticks where the ear-shattering noise of heavy armament wasn't going to draw a thousand police and land them in a siege situation, they could afford to relegate their pistols to backup status and bring on board some serious firepower. Ruddock and Dean were assigned a pair of black Benelli semiautomatic shotguns, Nicholson and Lewis a brace of their tried-and-trusted workhorse MP5 submachine guns, the A3 version with the collapsible shoulder stock. Thirty-round magazines. They were old, worn but reliable weapons that had served them on assignments all over the world.

Just in case those weren't enough, Cook had something extra. Unzipping a padded gun slip he pulled out an HK 417 battle rifle in sniper configuration, set up by him personally with the twenty-inch accurized barrel and telescopic sight and accurate at eight hundred metres. He slapped in a magazine loaded with twenty gleaming bottlenecked 7.62mm NATO rounds, racked the bolt and set the selector lever to safe. Flipped open his scope lens covers. Ready to rock.

Between them, they had enough hardware to take on a platoon. Nobody was leaving anything to chance. This wasn't some fatboy Mafia hood or drug-addled Somali militiaman they were going up against today.

The six donned their black ski-masks and then fitted their earbud headsets with miniature condenser mikes that would keep them in touch by phone. Cook had already notified the Boss of their arrival, and the Boss was listening and waiting in anticipation of a rapidly and successfully executed mission.

They left the vehicles blocking the track and stalked up towards the house on foot. As the roofline came into view, they split up and spread out, moving cautiously and keeping their heads low so as not to be spotted. The silver Kia was parked thirty yards from the house. They were bang on target. No other vehicles were in sight. It was probably just Hope and Fuentes in the place. If there was someone else inside, then too bad for them.

Nicholson, Ruddock and Lewis took a wide, circuitous route around the right side of the property while the other three cut around the left. Hacker and Dean positioned themselves prone in the long grass beyond the fence over-looking the front of the house and awaited their orders. Short minutes later, Nicholson's whisper in their earpieces told them that the three were successfully infiltrated among the outbuildings to the rear.

The Boss was eagerly listening in. The six could sense his presence there, silent and commanding and full of expectation.

Cook split himself off from the others and made his way slowly and carefully up and around behind the rocky rise, unseen from the windows, to a point on the hillside where he was roughly level with the roofline of the house, with a perfect view of the yard and front entrance. Finding a spot between two rocks, he laid himself prone behind his rifle. Planted the HK's bipod legs on the uneven ground and steadied the gun so that it was solidly mounted against the triangular support of his shoulder and his elbows. The left arm crooked with his hand resting loosely on his right bicep. His right hand not too tight on the pistol grip of the weapon's synthetic stock. His body at a slight angle behind the rifle, legs splayed, the right knee cocked for maximum stability. The classic sniper position that he'd been taught over twenty years earlier in the British army. His right cheek was pressed against the stock, with exactly the correct amount of eye relief for the scope. The optics mounted on the gun were Swiss, top quality and worth twice as much as the rifle itself. The magnified image was pin-sharp, over-laid by the tactical mil-dot reticle of the crosshairs. The dots looked like tiny black beads threaded on a silk strand. Their purpose was to offer different aiming points to compensate for the bullet's trajectory at long range, when the inevitable forces of gravity began to suck it towards the earth.

At this distance, though, no compensation was necessary. He aligned the exact centre of the crosshairs on target. The scope's inbuilt laser rangefinder told him the house was eighty-two yards away from his firing position. Eighty-two yards was like point blank range for a rifleman of his experience, armed with a high-velocity precision tool like the HK.

'Cook, in position,' he said into his headset microphone, and imagined the Boss smiling to himself and thinking this was already in the bag. Six on two, no witnesses, no distractions, nowhere to run.

Easy.

Cook lingered on the front entrance, then slowly panned a few degrees right, the rifle muzzle moving imperceptibly as he scanned his target. Seeing nothing in the window on the right side of the entrance, he swivelled the rifle gently in the other direction. His reticle flashed by the image of the doorway and found the window to its left.

The glass was dusty, but there was no mistaking the figure of a man standing at the window gazing out. Five-eleven, blond hair. His features were easily clear enough through the optics for rapid identification.

Hope.

Cook felt the familiar stab of satisfaction. *Ping.* Target acquired.

He eased the selector switch to fire. His finger stayed off the trigger, resting against the curve of the trigger guard.

He muttered into his mike, 'Cook. I have a clear shot at Number Two. Awaiting instruction.'

That was directed not at the other team members, but at the Boss himself.

The Boss replied immediately, 'Take the shot.'

Cook moved his finger to the trigger. The target remained

steady in his crosshairs. He slowed his breathing to settle his heartbeat. Drew in a breath, let it half out. Felt the trigger mechanism break like a glass rod under the pressure of his finger.

The gun boomed and recoiled against his shoulder.

Chapter Nineteen

The cat is a wild predator. Fundamentally untameable, a force of nature, governed by a feral instinct informed by a million generations of wild predators before it. And Ben Hope was as close as it was possible to get to that in human form. He'd spent so much of his life so close to violence, come within a whisker of sudden violent death on so many occasions, that it took only the tiniest stimulus to instantly strip away the veneer of the ordinary man and reveal the primordial creature hiding under his skin.

In the split-second the cat reacted to whatever unseen danger it had sensed, Ben reacted too. Why he flinched away from the window at that precise moment was not an impulse that ever reached his conscious mind. Pure instinct. He simply was, and he simply acted, without thought, without hesitation.

In the next instant, the window exploded.

Ben spun back into the corner as the storm of broken glass blew into the house. His conscious mind was still disengaged. He didn't have time to think about what was happening, or why. He didn't have time to be surprised.

There was a momentary pause, just long for him to make eye contact with the frozen, aghast faces of Raul and Kazem and yell 'Get down!'

Then they were under heavy fire from both sides at once. The other front window burst into a million shards and splintered holes punched through the door, while the kitchen windows shattered and more bullets hammered into the walls from the opposite direction. Ben could tell that the crossfire was angled and calculated by an unseen enemy who had a pretty good idea of what they were doing, firing from both sides without endangering one another. Who they were, and what they were doing here, were questions that could be addressed later.

Raul had thrown himself to the floor as bullets zipped overhead and smacked into the walls. A table lamp blew apart, showering him with china fragments. The chair Kazem had been taped to caught a violent impact that split its backrest and toppled it over.

Kazem didn't move. He stood pinned to the spot, paralysed by shock at the suddenness of the attack.

From where he was pressed into the angle of the thick walls, Ben shouted 'DOWN!' Kazem stared at him with huge bewildered eyes. Then his shirt seemed to ripple and pucker and a spray of red flowered from his neck, below the corner of his right jaw. He staggered a half-turn and his knees buckled under him and he hit the floor, hard. He lay there on his belly, his face turned towards Ben. His mouth was opening and closing, like a landed fish. His eyes were distant and glassy. The blood was pumping fast from his neck and chest wounds and spreading over the floor.

The gunfire continued in sporadic bursts. Ben chanced a glimpse out of the shattered window next to him and saw two men in black ski-masks and tactical vests strafing the silver Kia with submachine guns. Its screen and windows blew in and silver-ringed holes patterned its bodywork. The men dumped their magazines and slammed in fresh ones as they ran onwards from the car to the house.

Ben reckoned on at least three more round the back. Five men, not counting the sniper who'd come pretty damn near to tagging him at the window.

Kazem looked in a bad way. And Ben and Raul were seconds from joining him, if they didn't do something. Ben scrambled from the corner. Kept his head down and crossed the floor in a half-bounding, half-crawling gait that took him through the blood pool in the middle of the room. Raul was pressed down tight behind the side table, as if flimsy wooden legs could protect him from a bullet. The moment the attackers invaded, they'd shoot him where he cowered. They'd finish Kazem off with a shot to the head, and then they'd do the same to Ben. No questions, no mercy. Simple execution. These men were here to do business, and it was not a situation in which Ben liked to be unarmed and utterly defenceless.

Ben got to Raul and reached up and over the table. His fingers closed on the hilt of the chef's knife he'd used to slash Kazem's tape bonds, and managed to pull it down off the tabletop without getting his arm shot to pieces. His hand was slick with Kazem's blood after splashing through the spreading mess of it. He wiped it on his jeans and gripped the knife. The blade was a slim triangle, seven inches from tang to tip. It had been sharpened recently. The steel was shiny, stamped SOLINGEN – ROSTFREI at its base. Solingen was in Germany's Rhineland and was known as the 'City of Blades'. They'd been making swords there since medieval times.

Almost defenceless. But not quite.

More bullets pounded through the front door, tearing splinters from its ripped slats. A brief lull, then the door smashed inwards as a heavy boot kicked it open. The shape of a large man in black paramilitary kit was framed in the low doorway. He was wide and bulky in armour and vest, and he was an inch or so taller than Ben, which meant he had to duck his head two inches to clear the lintel. Ducking cost him somewhere just short of a second, and in that second Ben had him.

The knife whipped hard through the air. To the man in the ski-mask, it was nothing more than a blur that crossed the distance between him and his targets faster than he could react. He hadn't even got his gun raised before he was staggering backwards with the first four inches of sharp Solingen steel embedded in his right eye socket and punched through bone deep into his frontal lobe. He was brain dead before the message reached his legs to crumple under him. His trigger finger went into an involuntary spasm that loosed off a burst of rounds in a sweeping arc which stitched a jagged line of holes in the floorboards.

Ben was right behind the knife. He caught the man's weight before it crashed lifelessly to the floor. Kicked out and slammed the door shut in the face of the second attacker who was running towards it. Shots slammed through the wood and punched into the dead man's back. His MP5 was attached to a single-point sling looped around his neck and shoulder, made of bungee cord material that was elastic enough for Ben to twist it round under the dead man's armpit and rattle off a burst of fire through the door to discourage anyone from following.

Up close, the noise of the gunshots was ear-numbingly loud, but not so loud that Ben didn't hear Raul's yell. He half saw, half sensed the men running into the house from the back door, into the kitchen. Ben let go of the submachine gun and heaved the dead guy's weight around to use as a body-armoured human shield as the attackers from the rear opened fire. Two of them were armed with military shotguns. The blast was twice as loud as the rip-snort of the nine-millimetres. Ben made himself small behind his shield of dead human flesh and thanked God for sending him a big guy. The impacts from the shotguns were hard and heavy. Solid slug rounds, one-ounce lead ingots travelling over the speed of sound.

Ben reached down to the dead man's hip and tore the pistol he was carrying from its holster. In the world of generic modern polymer-framed, striker-fired combat pistols, they all pretty much operated the same way: just point and squeeze. Ben punched the weapon out from behind the dead man's side and loosed off three, four, five rounds as fast as he could mash the trigger, BLAMBLAMBLAMBLAMBLAM, before he felt the weight of the corpse start to fall away from him and he couldn't hold him up any longer. But by then, one of the attackers was on the floor and the other two were falling back through the kitchen and out of the back door.

Ben let the dead man flop to the floor and stepped quickly over to Raul, grabbed his arm and hauled him out of the crisscrossed lines of fire that could start coming from either side of the house at any moment. Raul was trying to speak, but couldn't make the words. Ben popped the pistol's magazine release to check his ammo. It was a high-capacity Walther PPQ, and a full mag minus five left him with ten, one up the spout and nine in store. He replaced the mag and shoved the pistol in his pocket, bent quickly over the dead man and unclipped the MP5 from its quick-detach sling mounting. The submachine gun was nearly empty, but there was a spare mag nestling in the guy's vest pouch. Ben slipped it out, making the change as slickly as anyone who'd done it ten or fifteen thousand times before. The MP5 was to him what a fork or a toothbrush was to an ordinary citizen.

Working fast, Ben yanked the chef's knife from the dead man's eye socket. It came free with a sucking sound and liquid oozed from the punctured eyeball. Ben wiped the blade clean on the guy's trousers and thrust the knife in his own belt. He glanced down at Kazem. He seemed still to be breathing, but only weakly, and there was a lot of blood. Ben felt bad for him, but there wasn't time to do much to help him at this moment. He had no idea how many of them might still be out there. He only knew that another wave could move in at any moment, and he couldn't hold off a sustained assault from both sides at once.

He stepped over to the second dead man and snatched the identical Walther PPQ nine-millimetre from his pocket. A pistol was safer to entrust to a novice than a semiauto shotgun that could blow your foot off if you swung it around carelessly. He thrust the Walther into Raul's hand. 'It's easy to work it. Just aim and pull.'

'What's happening?' Raul managed to groan.

'We're surviving this, is what,' Ben said.

Chapter Twenty

Ben pointed through the study, towards the door that led through to the base of the dome. 'That way,' he said, and hurried Raul through into the bare block-built square that supported Catalina's observatory. There was no other way in or out and no windows, making it invasion-proof as long as Ben had the door covered. Or as long as the ammunition held out. It was the best tactical retreat he could come up with, in the circumstances.

He told Raul to stay still while he ran back into the living room and grabbed Kazem's prone body by the collar. Kazem was still alive. Ben couldn't say how long for, but he wasn't going to leave him alone out there. He snatched the roll of tape they'd used to bind him up earlier. Then dragged the young guy through the doorway, slammed and bolted the door securely behind them and propped him against the big round steel pillar in the middle of the space.

The blood trail across the floor was thick and shiny. Kazem's clothes were black with it. More blood spurted from his lips when he tried to speak and began to cough. The wound in his neck was drawing air with a terrible wheezing noise as he fought to breathe. Raul stared at the blood and looked about to throw up.

Ben used the kitchen knife to slash material from Kazem's

shirt, and stuffed it into the wounds to try to stem the bleeding. 'Put pressure on here,' he told Raul, pointing to the chest wound. Ben did the same for Kazem's throat wound, trying not to choke him. Blood welled up between his fingers and soaked the shirt material. Ben pressed a thicker wad of it against the wound, tore off a strip of tape and fastened it into place, but the tape wouldn't adhere to the blood-slicked skin. It was hopeless.

The gunfire had stopped. Either the bad guys had packed up and left in defeat, or they were just regrouping. Ben didn't think they'd gone. 'You're going to be okay,' he lied to Kazem. 'Hold on. Keep looking at me. Listen to my voice.'

Kazem blinked and tried to focus, but his eyes kept fading. His head lolled. Blood bubbled out of his mouth and ran down his chin. Ben glanced back towards the door. Still nothing happening outside. It wouldn't remain that way for long. That was for sure.

'Stay with me, Kazem. You're going to make it through this.'

The Iranian slowly raised his head and looked at Ben. His red, glistening lips moved a fraction and he managed to rasp some indistinct words out that took Ben a couple of seconds to understand.

'She . . . is . . . alive.'

Raul jumped as if he'd been shocked with a cattle prod. 'Have you seen her? Where is she?'

Kazem managed to shake his head that he didn't know, but it seemed to cost him almost all his remaining strength. He mustered up what was left to croak a few more words, crimson bubbles forming at the corners of his mouth.

'I . . . am . . . sorry . . . I . . . lied . . . to . . . you . . . She . . . tell . . . me to . . .'

'She told you to lie,' Raul said.

Kazem nodded weakly, then coughed and spat another gout of blood. It was bright red. Arterial. Not good.

'*She . . . knew . . . they . . . come . . . for . . . her . . . She . . . have . . . to . . . dis . . .*'

'Disappear?' Raul said. He turned to Ben. 'She was running from them. It's what we thought.'

Now Ben understood the real reason why Kazem had taken flight when he'd seen the two of them arrive earlier. He'd mistaken them for whoever was after his former employer, believing they'd come for him too.

But that was all he had time to think before he heard the fast steps on the other side of the door. The men were back.

Gunfire exploded from the living room and splinters burst from the inside of the door. The attackers knew where they were hiding, and they were intending to shoot the door down. A few shotgun blasts, and it would separate into firewood. Then they'd be inside.

Ben ran to the door and pressed himself flat against the wall next to it. Thick, solid stone, impenetrable to any kind of small arms fire short of a big fifty-calibre. He reached out to his side and jammed his pistol against the splintered wood and squeezed the trigger, then again and again until his ears were ringing badly and the gun muzzle was smoking hot and the wood was smouldering.

The gunfire fell silent again. He seemed to have driven the attackers back for now, but it had cost him every round in his pistol. Ben tossed it. All he had now was the submachine gun with one magazine. Thirty rounds wasn't as much as it sounded in a weapon that spat out thirteen of them every second.

Kazem coughed more blood. Raul was right beside him, clutching his hand. His trousers were soaked red to the knee.

'What do these people want?' Raul was asking. His tone

was urgent but he seemed oblivious of the shooting and the danger. He seemed hardly to notice the blood any more. Kazem was slipping fast, and what he knew was everything that mattered to Raul at this moment. 'Kazem, talk to me. Why is she in trouble?'

Kazem raised a bloody arm and extended his finger towards the dome above. He was pointing at the observatory.

Ben understood Kazem was trying to say that it had to do with Catalina's work. But that was impossible. Her work was studying space. By definition, there was no less worldly occupation. Detached from all human concerns, from politics, from money, from religion, from everything.

Kazem bubbled red from the mouth and a croak came from his lips that to Ben's ringing ears sounded like 'core sheet'.

Then Ben realised that Kazem had reverted to his native tongue as his life ebbed away. It wasn't 'core sheet'. It was the Persian word 'khorshīd'.

Khorshīd was Persian for the sun.

The sun, which had been the main focus of Catalina's work. Kazem's fluttering, bloody hand was pointing up at the dome where he'd helped her carry out her solar observation work through the specialist Lunt solar telescope.

But how could that be?

Ben wanted to ask him. He didn't know if the dying man could reply, but he opened his mouth to ask him anyway.

His question was drowned out by the shotgun blast that exploded like a grenade the other side of the door. Wood shards blew into the room and a hole the size of a grapefruit appeared in the shattered planks. Then another, and the hole elongated and the door came loose at its top hinge.

Raul threw himself behind the steel pillar for cover. Ben spun towards the attackers and hosed a stream of automatic fire at the door, turning what was left of it into a colander of nine-millimetre holes. Thirteen rounds a second. Ben kept his finger on the trigger maybe a second and a half. Long enough to drive the enemy back again. Long enough to deplete most of his only magazine.

Now there was little left to fight with, and only one place to run. Up into the dome.

Cornered.

Chapter Twenty-One

The air was acrid with gunsmoke and the stink of cordite. Ben crushed empty cartridge cases underfoot as he hurried over to Kazem, thinking he'd have to carry the injured man over his shoulder.

But Kazem was already dead. His eyes were a glassy stare and the hole in his neck had stopped sucking air.

'Leave him,' Ben said to Raul, who was gaping at the dead man who'd been his sister's assistant and possibly the last person to speak to her. Ben grabbed Raul's arm and shoved him towards the spiral steps.

Behind them, the door crashed in and tore off its second hinge and came apart as it hit the floor. One, two, three men in black ski-masks burst through the doorway.

Ben shoved Raul's back, urging him to go faster. Their racing steps clattered on the metal staircase. Shots cracked out. A bullet whanged off the steel pillar a few inches from Ben's head. Another sparked off the metalwork at his feet. Raul stumbled and for an instant Ben thought he'd been shot. Raul's gun fell from his hand as he grabbed the rail to steady himself. The weapon clattered and bounced past Ben on its way down the steps. No time to try to go back for it. He pushed Raul harder. Raul kept moving. He plunged up through the hatch. Ben was right behind.

Now they were inside the dark, shady interior of the astronomical dome, and Ben knew that his tactical retreat had turned into a bad mistake. They were trapped in a dead end. You could defend it, if you had enough ammunition. Which they didn't have. But either way, with the enemy occupying the only exit, you couldn't escape from it.

Already, he could hear the voices below as the gunmen took control of the room beneath them. One of them sounded as if he was talking into a radio or phone. Ben caught the words 'They're in the tower'.

Speaking English. London accent.

Ben didn't have time to wonder why. He checked his weapon. Three rounds in the magazine, plus one in the chamber. Not good. Not good at all.

The darkness inside the dome was their only friend. Ben found the light switch on the wall near the hatch, but he didn't turn it on. He hit it hard with the butt of the submachine gun, felt the plastic crunch and hit it twice more until the switch was in pieces and dangling uselessly from its wires. He grabbed Raul's arm again and urged him into the shadows.

Now there were footsteps ringing on the staircase as the three men headed up towards them. Ben and Raul drew back behind the hulking forms of the telescopes. Ben wondered why the attackers didn't just fire up through the floor with twelve-gauge slug rounds, or just pop a grenade or two up through the hatch. It was what he'd have done. And these people didn't seem short of hardware. It wouldn't take much more firepower than they'd already demonstrated to blast the whole dome and everything in it to pieces. But there was something reticent about their tactics. Almost as if . . . The first man emerged through the hatchway. Just a dark outline, dimly illuminated by the daylight shining up from below. Followed by the second, then the third. In turn, each vanished into the shadows. Ben could no longer see them, but he could sense them splitting up and circling the dome, guns ready. He could picture their relative positions from the tread of their footsteps on the spongy rubber floor. He didn't dare fire, because the muzzle flash would only give away his position and invite an overwhelming reply of superior force. He quietly transferred the gun to his left hand and drew the knife from his belt. Nudged Raul as if to say, 'Stay close to me.'

Ben listened hard in the dark, visualising what his ears told him. One man had moved to the left, one to the right, stalking around the circumference of the dome in opposite directions to flush out their prey. The third man was cutting across the middle, stealthily approaching the telescope mounting in the centre of the floor. Not stealthily enough. His rubber soles creaking on the rubber floor, under the weight of a large man weighed down with body armour and weaponry and ammunition. He stepped forward another metre, then another. He was close now, close enough that Ben could hear him breathing.

Ben waited, perfectly immobile in the shadow of the telescopes. He silently placed the gun down by his feet. Laid a hand on Raul's arm, telling him to hold steady. Three more seconds. Then five. *Creak. Creak.* He could smell the guy's sweat.

Then Ben struck, with the speed and surprise of an attacking leopard when it explodes out of deep cover to take down an unsuspecting gazelle.

Except that Ben's enemy was no gazelle. He was a dangerous predator in his own right, and Ben had to put him down hard and fast. He knocked him sprawling backwards into the operator's chair attached to the rear of the twin telescope mounting, and used the knife. It was brutal, and it was merciless, and it was exactly what Ben had been trained to do many years earlier.

As the man twitched his last in the chair, Ben was already retreating back into the depth of the shadows, clutching the bloodied blade. He picked up his near-empty weapon. There hadn't been time to snatch the man's gun. The other two, fanned out at opposite sides of the dome, had heard the muffled commotion and come rushing to the centre to investigate, and he'd had to withdraw quickly. Ben heard the rustle of clothing as one of them crouched down to check their fallen companion. It didn't take them long to tell there was nothing they could do for him. They quickly split up again.

Ben and Raul pulled deeper into the darkness. Ben felt the edge of one of the racks of high-tech astronomical equipment against his elbow and slowly, silently moved around the back of it.

A mechanical click caught his ear. Followed by the hum and whirr of an electric motor, the taut jerk of a steel cable taking up slack, the sound of wheels turning, pulleys rolling.

One of the men had found the controls for the dome. The whole upper section was rotating on its base, like some kind of gigantic artillery emplacement or a missile silo bearing towards the direction of its target. There was a muted rumble that resonated through the whole dome as the huge fibreglass construction swivelled around on roller tracks inset into the rim of the perimeter. The rumbling continued for several seconds, then it stopped.

What was he doing?

Then Ben heard another click, and he knew the answer. *Shit.*

The man had activated the control to open the roof. The

electric motor kicked in again, and this time the mechanical sounds came from directly overhead as the cables and pulleys bore on the sliding section of ceiling that could be pulled right back for observing the sky. A bright crack of daylight appeared, three metres in length and growing quickly wider. The pale afternoon sunlight flooded the inside of the dome, dazzling in its suddenness.

The cover of darkness was suddenly gone. Ben blinked, feeling as naked and exposed as a fugitive caught in a search beam.

Then it got worse.

Chapter Twenty-Two

Cook had listened to the whole thing unfolding through his headset, but he hadn't moved from his vantage point in the rocks overlooking the front of the house.

Their opponent, this Hope guy, had proved even tougher to kill than they'd anticipated. The Boss was tearing his hair out and ready for an apoplexy on the other end of the phone. Hope had first taken out Ruddock, then Nicholson. Now, as the dome opened like the top of a giant egg and filled with light, Cook could see through his rifle scope the bloodied corpse of Phil Dean sprawled in a chair that was part of the astronomical telescope mounting. Three men down. Half their force. But now the show was over, because nothing could compete with what he was about to bring to the deal. His field of fire was laid wide open. A sniper's delight.

Cook panned the rifle to the left and his crosshairs picked out the fleeting shape of a man who wasn't one of his team, and wasn't Raul Fuentes. Hope.

Cook didn't need to call it in this time. As fast as he locked his sights on target, he squeezed the trigger.

Ben felt the shockwave of the incoming rifle bullet before he heard the thunderous crack of its report. It missed him, but not by much as it slammed past and punched a clean round hole through the fibreglass wall behind him. Ben caught a momentary glimpse of the sniper eighty metres away among the rocks, about level with the roof of the house and angling his rifle up at the dome.

As another shot cracked out, Ben was already diving out of the line of fire. Moments ago, he'd been groping about in darkness. Now every detail of the dome was lit up bright and clear. He retreated behind a metal table covered in computer equipment. He had lost sight of Raul, and that worried him. What worried him even more were the sniper outside, and the two enemies still in the house. Four rounds left. He could afford a single miss. The rest had to count, one for one.

A deafening blast came from inside the dome. A spread of twelve-gauge buckshot blew the computers on the table to pieces and showered Ben with debris. The masked man holding the shotgun was hunkered down behind the telescope mounting, and Ben didn't have a clear shot at him. He inched around the side of the table. Too late, he saw that the sniper in the rocks had moved position, climbing higher so he could command a better view into the dome.

There was nothing reticent about their tactics now. Ben scrambled away as the sniper opened up with fully automatic fire and the high-velocity rounds chewed through the metal table as if it were made of cheese. Whatever kind of battle rifle the guy was equipped with, it could shred the whole dome apart in no time.

But the sniper could only climb so high, and the bottom sill of the dome's aperture was higher. Which meant that as long as Ben stayed pressed down close enough to the floor, he couldn't be seen. That couldn't prevent him from being seen by the two heavily armed men left inside the dome, though. He wedged himself as far as he could into the side of the observatory, behind a latticework of metal struts that supported the weight of the roof. He was pinned, and he couldn't move, and he still couldn't see Raul.

Ben heard a harsh voice say, 'We got your mate here. Lose the weapon and come on out.'

Ben peered out from his hiding place, and saw them. In the middle of the floor, one masked man was standing behind Raul with a pistol to his temple. The other had a shotgun.

'Three seconds, Hope. Then we kill'm. Give yourself up, it's over.'

Ben gritted his teeth. He had only one alternative. It was down to the wire now, kill or be killed.

Four rounds left.

He broke cover. Keeping his head down so the sniper couldn't get him and moving too fast for the guy with the shotgun, he dived across the floor and landed on his shoulder and rolled and fired all at once. The guy with the shotgun staggered back and went down.

Three rounds left.

The other guy still had his pistol pressed hard up against Raul's head, but he didn't shoot. He aimed at Ben instead, but Ben came out of his roll in a low crouch and fired first, and the guy's face burst red and he fell away from Raul and collapsed sideways.

Two rounds left.

Raul swayed on his feet. One side of his face was misted with blood. He gazed down at the body of the man who'd been holding the gun to his head.

Now Ben knew why the guy hadn't shot Raul. It was for the same reason the sniper eighty metres away in the rocks didn't blow Raul's brains all over the inside of the observatory when he was standing there in full view.

Ben sprang up out of his low crouch and ran straight at Raul. He spun him around towards the opening in the dome with one arm clamped around his chest, pinning Raul's body tightly against his own. Raul struggled with surprising strength, but Ben clamped him harder.

Eighty metres away, the sniper shifted his aim and then went very still. Ready to fire the instant he got a clear shot at Ben.

Ben pointed the MP5 single-handed over Raul's shoulder. The submachine gun was no target pistol, and eighty metres was a very long shot with a nine-millimetre even if Ben hadn't been trying to hold still a struggling man who was nearly as strong as he was. Ben fired and saw his shot skip off the rocks with a puff of dust eighteen inches from the sniper's position.

The magazine was empty now. All he had left was that one round in the chamber.

Before Ben could pull the trigger, the sniper fired back. Maybe he'd rushed the shot, or maybe he was being over careful not to hit the wrong man. The bullet whipped past him and perforated the polished aluminium tube of the solar telescope. More than twice the velocity of Ben's gun in metres per second. Nearly four times the muzzle energy in foot pounds. Capable of punching through a concrete block at ten times this distance. And Ben was guessing the guy had a lot more than a single round left.

Ben shoved Raul aside, leaned on the edge of the dome, held his breath and lined up his sights, said his prayer and squeezed off his last shot.

The gun cracked and jolted in his hand, and the bolt locked back empty.

He was off to the right, but it wasn't a miss. The right side of the sniper's head dissolved into a pink mist and he slumped across his rifle.

Ben lowered the gun, able to breathe again.

Then his vision exploded in a white flash and he felt himself falling.

Chapter Twenty-Three

He hit the floor on his back, looked up and saw Raul standing over him with a clenched fist.

'You crazy English bastard!' Raul yelled at him.

Stars were swimming in front of Ben's eyes. He shook his head to clear them, and touched his fingers to his jaw where Raul had hit him. He blinked a couple of times, then through the haze he saw a black shape rise up behind Raul with something long in its hands.

The man with the shotgun staggered to his feet. Ben's bullet had caught him too low and hit the body armour, only stunning him. He was bruised, but he was very much alive. He clamped the shotgun's butt into his shoulder and advanced on Ben.

Ben knew the man had him cold. There wasn't a thing he could do, lying on his back still dizzy from the punch. This was it. He saw death coming.

Raul spun around, saw the man with the shotgun and shouted something Ben didn't understand. The man came on another step, trying to elbow Raul out of the way to get a shot at Ben. The shotgun muzzle came up, the big black O pointed right at Ben's face.

Raul punched him in the neck. The man staggered and fought to keep his balance. The gun went off line. Then Raul hit him again, this time with a monster uppercut that caught him square under the jaw, almost lifted him off his feet and sent him sprawling backwards towards the edge of the dome opening. The man dropped his gun and hit the edge with the backs of his legs and went over backwards with a short scream, disappearing from sight as he fell. There was a frantic slithering as he slid down the curve of the smooth fibreglass. Then a muffled *crump* as he hit the ground below. Then, nothing.

Ben struggled to his feet and went to the edge, looked down and saw the twisted body lying in the yard in front of the house. His neck looked broken. Ben looked up at the hillside. The sniper was immobile across his rifle, leaking blood over the rocks.

'Think I broke a knuckle,' Raul said.

Ben rubbed his jaw. It was tender and beginning to swell. 'On him, or on me?'

'You were going to let them shoot me, you bastard. I can't believe you would do that.' Raul was ashen and his voice sounded like that of a man who had just woken up, badly shaken, from a horrible nightmare.

'No,' Ben said. 'That wasn't going to happen.'

'How can you say that? You can't know that.'

Ben said nothing. He picked up the fallen pistol and stuck it in his belt, then checked its former owner. The dead man had voided his bowels. The stench mingled with the smell of the blood pooling over the floor and trickling between the cracks in the rubber matting. Ben knelt beside him and searched him for ID, found only a phone that he switched off and pocketed. He removed the guy's mask and studied his face. Then went and did the same with the body of the man who'd been holding the pistol to Raul's head, and again with the dead guy in the observation chair. He found two more phones. Switched them off, like the first, and slipped them in his pocket. Aside from that, zero. All three men were nameless, with anonymous faces. They could have been anyone.

Ben listened hard and could hear no sounds from down below. Just the ringing in his ears, the thud of his heart and the exaggerated silence that comes in the aftermath of battle.

'It's over,' Raul said, leaning against his sister's ruined solar telescope. He looked weak and faint. Shock was kicking in, in the aftermath of the adrenalin rush. Ben had seen it happen a thousand times before.

Ben shook his head. 'It's only just beginning.'

'I killed a man.'

'You saved me, you saved yourself. Now it's time to go and save Catalina.' He took Raul's arm and found that Raul was shaking. Ben led him back to the hatch and down the steps.

Raul paused to gaze sadly at Kazem's body, while Ben went through to the living room and checked the two dead bodies there. He wasn't surprised to find that they had no ID either. Two more phones, making five. He switched them off, like the first three, and added them to the collection in his pockets. He was pretty certain that the headsets the men had all been wearing were keeping them in touch on an open line with whoever had sent them here. Who that might be, he had no idea.

He stepped outside and lit a cigarette. His jaw was aching and he had his own nerves to settle in the aftermath of the fight. He looked at the wrecked Kia, then headed up the slope to where the sniper's body lay.

Like the others, the sniper had been carrying no ID, just a thick roll of banknotes in his back pocket, and his phone. Number six for Ben's collection. It was identical to the others, apart from a small dent in the casing where Ben's first shot had kicked up a stone that had bounced off it. But something about the man was different; the dissimilarity became obvious the moment Ben plucked the ski-mask off his head and saw his face. Even with half his skull blown away by Ben's last shot.

A few moments later, Raul walked outside, looking stricken. Ben called him over. 'Come and see this.'

Raul walked reluctantly up the slope and then peered at the corpse with a disgusted frown. At first he didn't understand what it was Ben had summoned him over to see. Then he got it.

'I think I know him. Haven't I seen him before somewhere?'

'Yes, you have, and so have I,' Ben said.

The sniper had pale features and receding straw-coloured hair. He was the book-reading stranger from the bar in Frigiliana that Ben had thought looked Danish.

'They've been following you all along,' Ben told Raul. 'Since before you left Spain, since before I even met you.'

'I don't understand.'

'Nor me, not yet.'

Ben walked back to the Kia and ran his eye along its bullet-riddled bodywork, thinking. He dropped flat on the ground and peered underneath the car. Then reached under a torn wheel arch, feeling around in the recesses. He walked around the car and tried the other three. There it was. 'Damn. I should have known,' he muttered to himself.

'What are you looking for?' Raul asked, joining him and looking even more baffled.

'This,' Ben said, showing him the small black box he'd found clamped under the wheel arch. 'It's a GPS homing tracker. They must have tagged us with it last night, while the car was parked outside Catalina's place.'

'They followed us from Spain, to Munich, to here?'

'Without breaking a sweat,' Ben said. 'These boys were professionals. We didn't spot them behind us on the road, because with this thing they could hang right back out of visual range and still know our exact position to within a metre.'

'So where's their car?' Raul asked.

Ben turned and gazed down the track, then started walking. The vehicles were parked just out of sight around the corner. A metallic grey BMW 6-Series, a blue Opel Insignia and a black Fiat van. All three vehicles still had the keys in their ignitions. All three had German registration plates. Very likely stolen. Ben checked the two saloons first, but the interesting stuff was what he found inside a zippered bag in the back of the van.

'That makes sense,' he said.

'What do you mean?' Raul asked, trying to see inside the bag.

'I mean that there's a hell of a lot more to this than either of us thought,' Ben said. 'First, it suggests they know who I am. Nobody sends out a hit team so well kitted up to take down one man, unless they've reason to believe he might give them their money's worth.'

'One man? There's two of us.'

Ben showed him the contents of the bag. 'Three rolls of duct tape and a bottle of chloroform. I told you they weren't going to shoot you. It was obvious from the way they attacked us that they were under strict orders not to harm you. The guns were for my benefit only, to put me out of the way so they could get to their real target.'

'Their real target?'

'You, Raul. They were planning on taking you alive.'

Chapter Twenty-Four

Raul blanched. '*Madre.* Why?'

Ben replied, 'Why do you think? Did you piss off the wrong people back in Spain? Do you owe money to the mob?'

'No. None of that. Of course not.'

'I didn't think so. Then there's only one possible reason. They want you because they believe you probably have information about Catalina's whereabouts. Twin siblings are about as close as it gets. They must reckon if she's in contact with anybody, it's you.'

'You're saying—'

Ben nodded. 'It pretty much proves that Kazem was telling the truth. Your sister's still alive and we're not the only ones looking for her.'

Raul thought about it and realised what it must mean. A glow of hope, intermingled with anxiety, spread over his face. 'Then . . . they don't know where she is either?'

Ben shook his head. 'But they're very committed to finding out. Whoever sent these guys after you wants her pretty badly.'

'If they don't know where she's gone, if they haven't found her . . . it means she must be safe. She's okay.'

'Maybe,' Ben said. 'For the moment, at least. But only if we find her before someone else does.'

'What will they do to her? No. I don't even want to think about it.'

'You should think about it,' Ben said. 'That's what makes it so important you get to her first.'

'Who are these people? What do they want with my sister?'

'They're not celebrity stalkers, that's for sure,' Ben said. 'But that's not the only question. Think about it the other way around. Who is she to them? What is it about her that they're so interested in?'

'The same thing that made her run from them,' Raul said.

'Right. And according to Kazem, she believed it was connected with her work on the sun.'

'That's insane,' Raul said. 'It's just, I mean, it's just . . . *the sun*.' He looked up and spread his hands out at it, just a pale orb giving out little warmth on that cool afternoon, and gradually sinking into the clouds.

Ben had no reply to offer Raul, because as far as he was concerned, it was insane too. To them, but evidently not to everyone. He walked to the lead vehicle, the dark metallic grey BMW, and climbed behind the wheel. He fired up the engine, leaned over and pushed open the passenger door and called to Raul, 'Get in.'

Back up at the house, Ben retrieved his green bag from the Kia. It had been nestling down low in the space behind the seats, and had only taken a couple of bullet holes. It had had worse in its time. He slung it over his shoulder and walked into the house, overstepping the dead man with the red hole where his eye used to be, and went into Catalina's study. While the living room and the observatory either side of it were badly wrecked, the study had been barely disturbed in the attack.

Ben looked around the room, at the desk, at the shelves and the bookcase. Somewhere in here could be evidence, even just the smallest clue to guide them. Without it, and with Kazem gone, they were nowhere. He had no idea what to look for or where to start, so he decided he'd take everything he could find that looked even remotely connected to Catalina's solar research.

He packed what he could into his bag – her laptop, the external hard drive hooked up to the desktop Mac, and as many storage discs and paper files as he could cram inside the straining canvas. Catalina was precise in her ways. Each file and container was carefully labelled in neat writing, done with a thin marker pen. Anything referring to solar research was potentially interesting. As Ben searched the shelves for more, a file fell open, scattering papers over the floor. Swearing, he crouched to gather them up. He noticed that in place of all the usual dense and incomprehensible scientific charts and graphs, the papers in the file were low on hard technical data and mostly consisted of written English. It looked like notes written for an essay, containing quotations and references dated from the mid-nineteenth century. It seemed completely out of place with the rest of the stuff.

Ben was about to leave the pages where they'd fallen, when he saw that the cover of the file was labelled HERSCHEL / SUN. Underlined in heavy bold, as if to highlight its importance.

Herschel. Ben remembered that was what she'd called the cat, named after her favourite astronomer. Who the human Herschel had been, or what singled him out as so special, he hadn't the faintest idea. But if it was important to Catalina, then maybe it should be important to Ben, too. He shuffled the papers back inside the file and crammed them into the bag.

When he had everything he could find, Ben left the study and found Raul still outside in the yard.

'What happens now? Do we call the police?' Raul asked.

Ben lit another Gauloise. He only had four left after this one, which annoyed him. He blew smoke and said, 'What for?'

Raul nodded. 'That's what I thought you were going to say. Then we have to bury Kazem. He was her friend. We can't just leave him here.'

They found a shovel in the toolshed. It was old, and not up to much more than shovelling snow. By the time they'd finished digging a shallow grave in the hard ground, the blade was badly buckled. They carried Kazem out of the house and laid him in the grave. Raul folded the Iranian's arms across his chest.

'Muslims wash the body of the dead before burial,' Ben said. 'To cleanse the deceased of impurities ready for the next world.'

Raul looked down at Kazem and nodded. 'We should respect that. It would be a sin not to. I'll do it.'

They did it together, using jugs of water from the kitchen. As best they could, they laid Kazem's body to rest. Infidel prayers seemed inappropriate to the occasion, either Raul's Catholic ones or Ben's half-remembered Anglican ones. They simply bowed their heads for a moment and then shovelled the dirt back over him and piled stones over the fresh earth.

'That's all we can do for him,' Ben said. His jaw was tender. He worked it from side to side a couple of times. No clicks or catches. Nothing seemed to be broken in there. He worked his tongue around his teeth and didn't feel anything loose, either.

'I'm sorry I punched you,' Raul said.

'You certainly pack a wallop.'

'I didn't mean—'

'It's okay,' Ben said. 'You had your reasons this time. But if it happens again, I'll shoot you. Deal?'

Raul gave a weak smile. He was silent for a moment, then asked, 'What about Herschel?'

Ben realised he meant the cat. Herschel was nowhere to be seen. 'He's a hunter. He'll survive and feed himself fine out here alone.'

Raul nodded. 'What about the other bodies? Shouldn't we bury them as well?'

Ben looked at him. 'Rats have to eat too. You want to be here all day?'

'No, we should probably get out of here,' Raul said. 'Not in that thing, though,' he added, pointing at the Kia. 'What's left of it. I've never seen a car in a state like this.'

'I've seen plenty,' Ben said morosely.

Raul forced his smile a little wider. 'Now I know why you're blacklisted by the rental companies.'

Chapter Twenty-Five

Four months earlier

'Ladies and gentlemen,' the Master of Ceremonies said over the PA system, 'it's my great pleasure to welcome to the stage a true legend. Chief Executive of Grantec Global, ranked among Europe's top five leaders in renewable energy technology. Founder and Director of our very own ISACC. Voted Green Entrepreneur of the Year for the last two years running. A tireless champion for environmentalism and all-round saviour of the planet: Mr Maxwell Grant.'

Amid the upbeat music cue and noisy applause from the audience gathered in the grand lecture hall of the Edmonton House Conference Centre in London for the International Society for Action on Climate Change annual symposium, Maxwell Grant shook the emcee's hand and stepped up to the podium with a broad smile. He hadn't even said a word yet, and he had the crowd in his pocket, just as expected. Not exactly a hard guess, considering that there wasn't a single delegate out of over three hundred in the packed lecture hall who wasn't already a staunch convert. Nor was it unrealistic to predict that he would receive a rousing ovation at the end of his twenty-minute talk. They'd bring the roof down with rapturous applause when they got a load of the big announcement he was here to make.

The big screen behind him flashed up the Grantec Global company logo with the slogan A CLEAR SOLUTION FOR CLIMATE CHANGE in bold green script. After thanking them one and all for attending this vitally important event, Grant launched into his earnest and well-prepared speech. The onscreen PowerPoint slide show reinforced his words with slick graphics and images. 'It's been my honour and my life's passion to watch the company I founded, and nurtured from such humble origins, rise up to become the major driving force for environmental change that it is today. Grantec Global is recognised worldwide as one of the pioneers of the movement for renewable energy, and we're as proud of that record as we are of the cutting-edge turbine technology we've developed, making us a world leader in offshore wind farm energy production. No fuel. No water pollution. No air pollution. No toxic damage to the environment. Providing sustainable and protected new habitats for marine life. Most vitally of all, making a priceless contribution to the reduction of the greenhouse gases that are dangerously warming our planet. We *are* the future.'

More applause. Grant smiled and waited for it to abate, then went on, never droning, never verbose, never too technical. He was relaxed, witty and among friends. The audience hung on every word as the minutes ticked smoothly by.

'By 2020, we can confidently project that an entire quarter of Europe's energy requirements will be produced offshore, drawing global investment in the tens of billions of dollars and creating vast employment opportunities for the rapidly growing environmental workforce. In order to help achieve our critically important climate change target to reduce human-generated CO_2 emissions by between eighty and ninety percent by 2030, we are determined that in coming years over half of worldwide energy will ultimately be provided by wind, from a projected 3.8 million large turbines across the world, between them creating a footprint of less than fifty square kilometres. You could barely fit the island of Manhattan into it.' Laughs from the audience. 'And Grantec Global will be the spearhead of that development. Europe is already leading the way in wind energy, and the UK already hosts some of the largest offshore wind farms – up to a hundred and seventy-five turbines, such as our installation off the Kent coast. Ladies and gentlemen, I'm delighted to announce that, as of today, Grantec Global is set to push those incredible achievements to the next level, with the official go-ahead to build what will, comprising over five hundred turbines off the coast of Wales, be the largest offshore wind farm *ever in the world*, fulfilling up to four percent of the UK's energy requirements. Onwards and upwards.'

The news got exactly the wild reaction from the audience that Grant had anticipated. By the time he'd finished speaking ten minutes later, they were moved to joy, even to tears. It was a wonderful moment, especially for Maxwell Grant. He left the podium and was instantly surrounded by a sea of hands. He gripped and grinned like a visiting dignitary, received dozens of hearty pats on the back and even a couple of kisses from adoring female delegates, and finally managed to beat a path through them and back to his dressing room.

'Stupid fuckers,' he said when he was alone. But he was smiling as he said it.

Grant was still smiling to himself as he emerged from the modern steel-and-glass entrance of the Edmonton House Conference Centre and stepped out into the early evening air, expecting the car with his usual driver and bodyguard to be there to pick him up to take him back to the townhouse in Mayfair. But there was no sign of them. Grant's smile fell.

At that moment, a black Jaguar saloon with darkened windows hissed to a halt at the kerbside, and a well-dressed man in his forties whom Grant had never seen before got out of the front passenger seat and approached him. 'Mr Maxwell Grant?'

'And you are?'

The man opened the back door of the Jaguar and motioned sombrely inside. 'If you please, sir.'

'I think I'll take a cab, if you don't mind.'

The man gazed at him, deadpan. 'I will have to insist that you get in the car, sir.'

'Now look here—' Grant began, but the look in the man's eye stifled his objection. He got into the back of the car and found himself sitting beside another well-dressed stranger. The first man climbed in after him, so that Grant was sandwiched between them. The door shut. Without a word, the driver accelerated smoothly and briskly away. Grant didn't like what was happening. He was going to say something when the man to his left produced a small handgun, and the man to his right took out something that looked like a black cotton balaclava, except that it had no eye holes. It was a hood.

'Just slip this on for me, would you, sir,' the man said. It was the pistol that persuaded Grant to comply.

The rest of the evening unrolled like a surreal nightmare. The fast car journey lasted for the best part of an hour. When it stopped, they hauled him gently but firmly out of the back and started marching him along. Blind, stumbling and frightened, he was convinced they had brought him to

161

this unseen place to shoot him and dispose of his body. He knew who his enemies were. He'd long been afraid they would get to him eventually. They'd tried often enough.

The men led him into a building, and through it to a room where he was made to sit on a hard wooden chair. Only then did the hood come off. Apart from a plain table placed next to his chair, the room was bare. A closed cardboard file lay on the table, cover down. The only light was a powerful lamp that was shining right into his face from the far side, dazzling him and making him blink. He thought he could discern dark silhouettes behind the light, the shapes of a row of men sitting opposite him. Four of them, he thought. He couldn't see them clearly or make out their faces.

'Mr Grant,' said one of the silhouettes behind the dazzling light. 'The file you are about to be shown is eyes-only. Do we need to explain what that means?'

'No, you don't need to explain,' Grant replied in a shaky voice. He was confused. What the hell was happening here?

'Then you may turn it over and read.'

Grant picked up the file in a trembling hand. The front cover was plain, except for a simple printed label that bore a single word. It was the name CASSANDRA.

Grant opened the file and frowned as he took in the first page of text, then the second. Photographs were clipped to the pages. The face on the pictures was a familiar one. 'This can't be real,' he said out loud.

'It is very real indeed,' said the silhouette. 'And we would urge you to take it seriously. As you can see, the subject in question is a threat to our interests, and to yours.'

'I don't know what you're talking about,' Grant began.

'Please, let's not waste time. We are perfectly aware of the nature and scope of your business dealings. By which we mean not only your legitimate activities with Grantec Global, but also your more lucrative dealings under the anonymous banner of Kester Holdings.'

'How do you know about—'

'Silence, please. We estimate that in the last financial year, Kester Holdings personally netted you in the region of eighty-two million pounds, approximately twice what you received from your stake in Grantec Global. We also know exactly how that money was earned. Kester Holdings illegally transports and disposes of nuclear waste in several countries across the world. Having been monitoring your activities for some time, we have gathered enough evidence to send you to prison for the rest of your life.'

Grant thought he was going to throw up. So that was what this was, a shakedown. There seemed no point in denying it. They knew everything.

'However,' the silhouette went on, 'we aren't interested in prosecuting you for your crimes. In fact, we are more than happy for you to continue to operate as you have been doing. Yours is a valuable service that our friends in the nuclear industry wish to retain.'

'Who are you people?' Grant demanded.

'But we can't promise to persist in our willingness to turn a blind eye if you fail to cooperate with us on this matter. As you'll be aware, the contents of the file are as much an issue for you as they are to us, albeit for slightly different reasons. The situation is, potentially, highly dangerous. In the medium to long term, you stand to lose a great deal, as do we.'

'What do you want from me?'

'We require you to resolve the problem on our behalf, Mr Grant. All the necessary resources will be placed at your disposal, in addition to those you already control.'

'Resolve the problem . . . how exactly?'

'Quietly. Discreetly. Permanently.'

'No, no, no. You're talking to the wrong person. I'm a businessman, nothing more.'

'It is the nature of your business that qualifies you for the task,' said the silhouette. 'In the more illicit circles in which you move, you have made a good many enemies. Notably, organised crime gangs such as your main competitors, the Italian Ndrangheta mafia syndicate, who have been involved in illegal nuclear waste dumping for some time. We know about the three attempts made on your life in the last five years, as we also know about the group of former private military contractors whom you employ to shield you from further assassination attempts. And to carry out certain dirty work to protect your business interests. You may not have pulled any triggers personally, but you are a murderer. We can prove that, too.'

Grant said nothing.

'In return for your cooperation in the resolution of our mutual problem,' the silhouette went on, 'we will exert the necessary pressure to ensure that your competitors are kept at bay. That, along with our willingness to show discretion and tolerance regarding the activities of Kester Holdings, will be your recompense for accepting the responsibility for carrying out this sanction, fully and to the letter. Do you agree to the terms of the arrangement?'

Grant looked at the CASSANDRA file and sighed. He knew there was only one possible response he could give.

'Very well,' he said. 'It'll be taken care of.'

Chapter Twenty-Six

Ben looped the BMW around in the yard and they headed back down the track. As they left the observatory behind, Raul cast a last wistful glance out of the window. Reaching the bend, Ben slowed and steered to the left a little with two wheels on the grass so that he could edge around the side of the blue Opel and the black Fiat van. When he was past them, he hit the gas and the BMW's tyres bit down hard into the dirt as they sped away down the track about twice as quickly as they'd come.

Seven minutes later, they reached the road and Ben steered left, picking up the route they would have followed earlier if they hadn't turned into the track. As to where they were going, he had no clear idea yet, only three basic objectives.

One, because the BMW was most likely hot, he wanted to stay away from major roads and traffic cameras that might automatically flag the registration to a central computer. Two, and for much the same reason, he generally wanted to avoid any kind of police entanglements. He and law enforcement officials tended not to mix well. He'd never really understood why. Something to do with his consistent inability to remain, for any length of time, the kind of peaceful, passive, docile civilian they liked being able to control. He considered that to be their problem, as long as it didn't become his. When the cops did eventually turn up at the scene, as well as all the bodies to bag up there was going to be a wealth of forensic evidence lying around all over the property for them to get their teeth into. Some of which could potentially lead them to Raul and himself – but there was nothing Ben could do about that.

His third and most important objective was to put as much space between themselves and the scene of the attack as possible, as quickly as possible. They had work to do, and Ben wanted to do it somewhere he could be assured nobody, either cops or anyone else, could find them.

He drove fast, too concentrated on the road to speak to Raul. They met with no screeching convoys of response vehicles, which meant that nobody had heard or reported any distant gunfire. And they met with no reinforcements of bad guys, which meant that whomever the six had been communicating with by phone either didn't know what had happened to them, or hadn't had time to organise themselves. Alternatively, it could mean that the half dozen corpses scattered around the observatory represented the enemy's total force, now spent. Ben would have liked to believe that, but hard experience had taught him to veer towards the pessimistic side of cautious. Hope for the best, expect the worst and be ready for something worse still.

They skirted westwards, contouring the German side of Lake Constance along twisty and half-empty roads that lost themselves in thick woodland for long periods, then emerged into the open to offer flashes of the great lake and the little towns clustered around its shores. After a dozen kilometres, Ben spotted a layby flashing up on the right, and he braked and pulled in.

Raul woke from the brown study he'd lapsed into, looked out of the window and saw there was nothing around them except grass and shrubs and trees and the empty stretch of road running by, then turned to Ben with his eyebrows raised. 'Why are we stopping?'

Ben cut the engine. His trouser pockets were bulging. Three phones in the left, another three in the right. He fished out all six and laid them in a row along the top of his thigh. 'If they could track the car, they can easily track these phones. I want to check them over, but I'm not doing it wherever we hole up for the night. We don't want any unexpected visitors.'

All six phones were identical in make, model, colour and condition, which was shiny and virtually brand new, apart from the small ricochet dent in the one Ben had taken from the sniper. He activated each in turn, scrolled through its menus and call records, and found exactly the same thing in all six cases. The phones were devoid of any records whatsoever, except for a list of calls made over the last few days, all to the same sole number, at the same times and for the same duration.

Whoever they'd been calling was the boss man. One rank down and immediately answerable to him would be the team leader, and Ben was fairly sure the sniper had been it. Back in the day, Ben had been the kind of team leader who led from the front, right there in the thick of it with his men and first in line to take a bullet. There was also the kind who preferred to hang back from the action and send the others in first while they watched from a safe position. Evidently, the sniper had been one of those. Not that it had done the man much good, in the end.

Ben picked up the sniper's phone and redialled the number. He relaxed back in the driver's seat with the phone to his ear as the dial tone rang twice, three times.

The man picked up on the fourth ring.

'I've been wondering why you didn't call me sooner, Cook. Update me.'

A deep voice, rich and sonorous. He was English, like his crew, but where Ben had heard them talking in rougher, more working-class London accents, this man spoke with what Ben had heard termed the RP accent. Received Pronunciation, the formalised dialect of the cultivated, the privately educated, the moneyed, the prestigious. He sounded cold, remote and fully in control. He sounded unquestion-ably like the boss. Someone who coordinated strategies and outcomes from afar, and wasn't happy when he wasn't kept abreast of all developments. Someone who expected results, and had most certainly paid a lot of money to obtain them.

Ben could play this in two basic ways. He could take a gamble and pretend to be one of the dead gunmen, copying their way of speaking, and hope he could fake the man out long enough to get him to reveal useful information. His name, his location, ideally both. Depending on whom Ben was dealing with, that could have been the right strategy. But not with this one. Ben sensed from the man's tone that trickery wouldn't get him far. He knew nothing about his enemy, except that he was far too clever to fall for such an obvious ploy.

So Ben decided on the straight approach.

He said, 'I'm afraid Cook isn't available. Not any more. Not unless you're a spirit medium and can communicate with the other side.'

There was a silence on the phone. Ben said nothing and rode it out.

After ten long seconds the voice said, 'I see. Then to whom am I speaking?' Cool, unruffled, unfazed.

'I'm the guy who made him unavailable,' Ben said. 'His friends too. You won't be hearing from any of them again.

Which puts you six men down and at something of a disadvantage. The element of surprise is a valuable thing. Lose it, and you stand to lose entirely.'

'I know who you are,' said the voice after another pause.

'I know you do. That's why you know to take very seriously what I'm about to say.'

The silence on the other end of the line seemed to intensify. Ben could feel the man listening intently, still composed but tensing up. Gripping the phone tightly, pressing it hard against his ear and his clenched jaw. The strategic mind hard at work.

'I'm calling to make you a deal,' Ben said. 'And to give you a chance. You gave it your best today, and you came away with nothing. Less than nothing. You failed badly. If you try again, you'll fail worse. Now it's time to back off and leave these people alone. If you do that, you might live a long and happy life and never hear from me again. If you don't, this is going to end very badly for you. That's a promise. A guarantee. I will come for you. If you know who I am, you know what that means.'

'Are you finished?' the voice said. Calm and smooth as a millpond on a lazy summer's afternoon.

'I haven't even begun,' Ben replied.

'I appreciate your offer,' the voice said. 'Regrettably, I must decline. That is to say, regrettably for you, Major Hope. It's you who needs to back off and walk away, while you still can. Forget these people. You have no idea what you have become involved in.'

'I never walk away,' Ben said.

'Then too bad for you if you get under my feet,' said the voice. And the man hung up.

Chapter Twenty-Seven

Ben redialled the number, but as expected all he got was a generic answering service. It would be the last time that number was ever used, and the other guy's phone was probably already trash. Dead and gone.

Raul's face was flushed. 'That was great. Just fantastic. You didn't get his name, you found out nothing, and all you did was antagonise him.'

'He sent six professional gunmen to kill me and kidnap you, presumably with a view to torturing you to extract information on the whereabouts of your sister, whom he also most likely wants to eliminate. I'd say he's already as antagonised as it's possible for a person to be.' Ben looked at Raul. 'Face it. There was no way I was going to get much out of him. What matters is that I got the measure of the kind of person we're dealing with here. I learned that he's serious, and that he's unconcerned enough about the loss of six men to mean he has plenty more at his disposal. He won't give up. He's going to keep trying until he finds her, one way or another.'

'Then we have to find her first,' Raul said tersely. 'Which isn't going to happen while we're sitting here looking at the countryside.'

Ben started the car again and they took off. He pushed

the BMW hard for another seventy kilometres, still avoiding major roads as they threaded through pasture land and forest, villages and small towns. Afternoon was wearing into evening, and the sun was climbing down fast. They passed plenty of places where they could have stopped for the night, but Ben kept going. He could still hear the calm, collected voice resonating inside his head.

The landscape became more rugged and the woodland thickened as they pressed deeper into the Black Forest with the hills and limestone escarpments of the Swabian Jura visible now and then through the gaps in the trees. Eventually, the woods opened up and the road dipped into a valley and a small village that felt right and safe to Ben. The streets were narrow and filled with black and white wood-framed houses. Over a stone bridge that crossed a river, they found a traditional inn that probably looked exactly the way it had three centuries ago.

They parked around the back and climbed out into the falling dusk. Raul grabbed his holdall from the back, and Ben scooped up his bag. It was a good deal heavier now, stuffed with the combined weight of Catalina's computer, her notes, and a salvaged MP5 along with a pistol and half a dozen assorted magazines bombed up with nine-millimetre full metal jackets.

The dour, unsmiling old guy who ran the inn looked as if he'd been there when it was built. Ben did the talking, and asked for a pair of rooms for the night. Either the old guy had had problems with guests running off without paying, or maybe he was generally of a suspicious disposition, because he insisted on money up front. Ben shelled out some notes from the roll he'd taken from the dead sniper's pocket. The old guy didn't balk at the sight of good old-fashioned hard cash, and he didn't seem interested in seeing their passports either. That must have been the way, back in the 1700s. It was fine by Ben. The less record of their movements, the better.

The old man hobbled and dragged his way up an ancient wooden staircase to the first floor, and showed them their rooms. Ben's overlooked the narrow street, with a little railed balcony made of black-painted wood. It had a quilted single bed and a threadbare rug, a chair and a table and a couple of lamps. By Ben's standards, it was wildly opulent luxury. Raul's looked out into a small garden out back, where a stream wound its way between a stand of trees on its way to feed into the main river. It was a cosy, pleasant kind of place. A little dusty, a little creaky, but safe. Alone in his room, Ben dumped his bag on the single bed, unbuckled the worn leather straps and took out both firearms, which he loaded and made safe and tucked away out of sight underneath the pillow. You could never be quite safe enough. Then he kicked off his shoes and lay down and stared at the ceiling.

He hadn't been staring at it long when Raul knocked once at his door and came in, shut the door behind him and immediately started pacing the floor.

'Happy with the accommodation?' Ben asked.

'No, of course I'm not happy. I mean, the room is fine. But how long are we going to stay here?'

'Just long enough to do what we need to do,' Ben said. 'We'll grab some rest, get some food inside us, then we'll see what we've got and figure out our next move.'

'I've been thinking that I should phone my parents. I need to tell them that I think Catalina's still alive.'

Ben sat up on the bed. 'That's a bad idea,' he said.

Raul stopped pacing and looked at him. 'You don't think they have a right to know?'

'As far as they're concerned, they've buried their daughter. You're only going to stir all those emotions up again. Let them be in peace.'

Raul knitted his brow and looked flustered. 'Hmm. Maybe you're right. I shouldn't call them until we find her.'

'Still a bad idea,' Ben said.

Raul's frown became a scowl. 'What are you talking about – I can't even call them to say I found their daughter they thought was dead? I can't tell them this terrible nightmare that has torn our family apart is over, and they're going to see her again? How can I keep something like this from them?'

'We're up against people who have a long reach,' Ben said. 'We should proceed with caution.'

'I know what you're thinking,' Raul said defiantly. 'Cell phone tracking, right? You're worried they can pinpoint where the call came from?' He took out his phone and waved it. 'See? It's just a cheap prepaid one. I don't have a contract or anything. I told you I always pay cash for things. I bought it for cash, top up the minutes with cash. It can't be traced to me.'

'That's fine,' Ben said. 'But that wasn't what I was thinking. I'd say there's a very good chance that your parents' phone is tapped. They might even be under observation, the way you were. It would make sense to have surveillance on anyone Catalina might contact. Family, friends, former colleagues. Not to mention keeping tabs on her apartment in Munich. They'd have been onto this place too, if she hadn't managed to keep it secret so well. It was just a fluke that they weren't already waiting there for us.'

Ben was aware of another reason why Raul shouldn't tell his parents Catalina was alive, but it wasn't one he could bring himself to express out loud.

It was that she might not still be alive by the time they found her. If they ever did. It would just be cruelty for Raul to wipe away his parents' grief at a stroke, only to redouble it again when he had to tell them she was dead after all. He would have tormented them for nothing, broken their spirit completely. And if they were the kind of principled, dignified and traditionally minded people Raul had painted them to be, Ben was pretty sure they would never forgive their son for it. What little they had left as a family would be irreversibly destroyed.

Raul had no clue as to Ben's thoughts. He was still focused on the immediate threat, and he looked bewildered by what Ben was telling him. 'Can they really be so well organised?' he asked.

'They could be even more organised than we think,' Ben said. 'Maybe they knew the moment we'd landed in Germany. They could have had someone sitting right behind us on the plane. Basically, we have no way of knowing how big an operation this could be. Therefore, no way of knowing what kinds of financial backing and other resources they might have at their disposal. Therefore, we need to proceed with extreme caution. If we're going to stay under the radar, that means no calls. Okay?'

Raul digested the information, then grunted his acceptance of Ben's point. 'Okay, I understand.'

Ben stood up from the bed and walked over to him, holding out his hand. 'May I see that phone for a minute?'

Raul shrugged, and held it out. Ben snatched it and dropped it in his own pocket.

'Hey, what are you doing? I thought you just wanted to see it.'

'Why would I?' Ben said. 'You've seen one phone, you've seen them all.'

'Then let me have it back.'

Ben shook his head. 'Consider it a gesture of kindness and friendship. Sparing you from the evils of temptation.'

'You don't trust me one little bit, do you?'

Ben said, 'Let's get something to eat.'

Chapter Twenty-Eight

The inn's dining room was a more recent add-on to the ancient building, housed in a conservatory overlooking the little garden that was visible from Raul's window above. Except that now it was dark outside, and all that could be seen in the glass were the reflections of the few diners scattered about the little restaurant's mostly empty tables.

Ben automatically scanned each face and assessed the threat. He wasn't going to be caught out the way he had been in Frigiliana. A solitary middle-aged man in a wrinkled suit who looked like a stressed-out salesman or low-flying business executive stopping over for the night on his way somewhere bigger and more important: threat level, zero. A young couple, maybe newly-weds, all rapt and dewy-eyed with adoration for one another. Threat level, ditto.

Ben relaxed, smelled the cooking aromas wafting through from the kitchen and realised how hungry he was. When the waitress appeared, he ordered the biggest sirloin steak on the menu and a bottle of red wine. Raul opted for grilled fish in a butter and parsley sauce, and a glass of good Riesling.

'Just a glass?' Ben said.

'I don't like to drink too much.'

'If you were always this sober, I would never have got to know you,' Ben said.

'Anyway, it's too expensive by the bottle.'

'We're not paying,' Ben said, patting his pocket where the roll of cash nestled. 'Like the rooms, this meal is all on our generous departed acquaintances. Spoils of war.'

Raul frowned. 'Thanks. I was trying to forget about today, and now you have to remind me about this nightmare. Maybe you're right. One glass of wine isn't enough.'

'You can always have some of my red,' Ben said.

'It wouldn't be appropriate, not with fish.'

'That's the difference between you and me,' Ben said. 'If I want to drink, I'll drink. If I don't, then I don't.'

'You don't worry about much, do you?' Raul said.

'Not those kinds of things,' Ben said.

'What about the kinds of things we did today?'

'I don't worry about those, either,' Ben said. 'You do what you have to do. Then you forget it and move on with a clear conscience.'

'You've done it a lot, haven't you?'

Ben looked at Raul. Anyone listening in to this conversation would have found it very odd indeed.

'I've done my fair share. More than some, less than others.'

'And that's okay with you?' Raul asked.

Ben shrugged. 'There have been times when it wasn't okay. Times when I was under orders to do things I didn't agree with. But other times, it was plenty okay. Today being one of them. Today was one of those days when I wouldn't think twice.'

'It seems so simple to you.'

'Some things in life are,' Ben said.

'Not for me. I'm just a teacher. I live in a different world from yours.'

'That's where you're wrong,' Ben said. 'We all live in exactly the same world, because we're all human beings, and the human condition we created for ourselves is fundamentally a cruel, violent and brutal state of affairs that shapes the world accordingly. Some of us are used to dealing with the reality of that. While others hide behind the veil, insulate themselves from reality and try very hard to fool themselves with high ideas about civilisation and progress in the kind of safe, cosy modern society they want to believe protects them from all the bad and dark things they'd rather not think about. I don't blame them, in principle. But now and then they get a peek through the veil, like you did today, and it's a shock to the system. More than most people can handle. All you can do is keep telling yourself that you came through it. You survived. You get to move on to the next stage. Which is to find your sister. Or die trying.'

Raul sighed. 'Damn it. I *am* going to get drunk.'

'No, you're not,' Ben said. 'You're doing a pretty good job of holding it together so far, and you're going to keep it that way. Suck it up. Deal with it. We're going to find Catalina.'

'Thank you,' Raul said after a beat, looking straight into Ben's eyes.

'For what?'

'For sticking with me. For being here.'

Ben shrugged. 'What else have I got to do?'

The food arrived, and Ben stopped talking and occupied himself with eating and drinking. The steak was tender and rare in the middle and served with green salad and sautéed potatoes. The wine was a three-year-old Côtes du Rhône called *Plan de Dieu*. God's Plan. After studying theology on and off for half his life Ben still had no idea what God's plan was. His own was simply to polish off the rest of this excellent food and then get on with the task in hand. Which was to get back up to his room and lay out

Catalina Fuentes' stuff and try to figure out exactly what the hell she'd got herself mixed up in. He'd devoured most of the steak and nearly half the wine when he looked up and saw that Raul was sitting staring at an untouched plate.

'I don't think I can eat.'

'Force yourself,' Ben said. 'I can't have you running on empty. You and I have work to do.'

Ben finished his wine while Raul picked at the fish. By the end of the bottle Ben still wasn't any the wiser about God's plan, but the muscular tension in his neck and shoulders had unknotted itself, and he felt mentally loose enough for what promised to be a long session of combing for whatever clues it might be possible to unearth when neither of them had the first idea what they were looking for.

The night was still young, just before nine o'clock. Ben paid the bill from the roll of notes. Then they left the dining room and returned upstairs.

Chapter Twenty-Nine

Back in his room, Ben emptied all the stuff out of his bag that he'd taken from Catalina Fuentes' study. He laid the paper files in a stack on the bed, with the laptop next to them.

'You know anything about computers?' Raul asked.

'I know how to turn them on,' Ben said. 'I can do the basics of internet searches and such. Beyond that, not really.'

'I'll see what I can do.' Raul picked up the laptop and carried it over to the little table, pulled up the room's single chair and flipped open the screen and sat hunched over the keys like a pianist about to launch into a concerto.

Ben let him get on with it, and focused on the files. He found a cheap ballpoint and stuck it in his mouth like a cigarette, ready to make notes. Sitting on the bed, he made himself comfortable and then opened the cover of the first file in the stack, a thick and heavy one labelled SOLAR VARIATIONS TO 2015. It was a random choice, the equivalent of closing his eyes and sticking a pin in a map. When you didn't know where you were going, one road was as good as another.

The top page was penned in the same neat, feminine handwriting as the label on the cover. Ben spent a moment looking at it, then turned that page and stared at the next one.

He swallowed. This might actually be less easy than he'd imagined.

Because there was an awful lot of science. In fact, there was nothing but science. The pages were black with it, and his brain was instantly swimming.

Ben was modestly aware of the fact that he wasn't an entirely uneducated or unintelligent person. His academic record was well above average. At age eighteen he'd burned out his brain sitting in Oxford's Bodleian Library poring over swathes of ancient Greek and Hebrew texts. Years later in the army, he'd laboured over the complexities of battlefield forensics. Struggled with the complicated concepts of classical mechanics involved in understanding the forces governing projectile trajectories. Crammed his head with Stokes' drag and Newtonian drag and gravity and inertia and momentum and the categories of internal and transitional and external and terminal ballistics that described the flight of a missile from muzzle to target; and all kinds of other initially baffling technical information that had ultimately helped him to become that little bit better at his job of destroying buildings, materiel and human lives, all in the name of Queen and country.

In short, without getting too big-headed about it, and all moral considerations aside, he'd learned that he could grasp pretty much anything he turned his mind to.

But this here was on another level entirely. It would take him fifteen years of study to even begin to get to grips with the brain-numbing forest of numbers and graphs and charts and equations that seemed to cover every page from top to bottom. Even where the damn stuff was presented in actual words, he could seldom go a quarter of a line without ramming headlong into a wall of specialised terminology that might as well have been the native language of alien creatures on some far-distant planet in another galaxy that humans would never know existed.

In other places, meanings suggested themselves to him, but only in the vaguest possible terms:

> _2001_
> _Solar wind velocity = 454.7 km/s_
> _Density = 6.0 protons/cm³_
> _2014_
> _Solar wind velocity = 412.8 km/s_
> _Density = 2.1 protons/cm³_

Which definitely looked like a comparison of data for different years, telling him that something had decreased during that time period. Something, being solar wind velocity and density, but that was as far as he could follow it.

Ben ploughed on, or tried to. He spent a few moments trying to decipher a graph that looked a little less complex than some of the others. It was headed X-RAY FLUX (1 – MINUTE DATA), FEB 2014 150000 UTC. Its left axis was graduated in meaningless power numbers in watts m⁻², and down its right side was written GOES 13 0.5 – 4.0 A / GOES 15 1.0 – 8.0 A. The graph showed a slightly squiggly red line that was almost flat, and another beneath it in blue that was jagged and wild with peaks and troughs.

Nice colours.

Time to move on.

Here and there, Ben saw disparate words and phrases he was able to latch onto, in the hope they might yield something comprehensible. Comprehensible, being the first step to significant, being the first step to important. On one page of notes he found a line standing proud of the rest, which read:

1980 54 Piscium mag activity slumped

Which was the only place so far in Catalina Fuentes' files he'd found as many as four words in consecutive order creating anything like a meaningful phrase. The only question was, what did it mean? 1980 was clearly – or was it? – a date, but apart from the fact that it had been the year in which John Lennon had been shot, and the year of the Iranian Embassy siege in London that had catapulted his future regiment, 22 SAS, to massive (and generally unwelcome) international media stardom, in this context it meant nothing to him.

Raul appeared to be busy on the laptop and Ben didn't want to disturb him, so he reached for his smartphone and started dialling up an internet search.

'Hey,' Raul said, noticing what Ben was doing. 'I thought we had to be careful about those things.'

'Relax,' Ben told him. 'This phone can't be traced to me.'

'I don't even want to know,' Raul said.

'Then don't bother me with useless questions,' Ben replied. He keyed in '54 Piscium'. A few moments later, he learned that it was the name of a star in the constellation Pisces. More correctly, an orange dwarf.

Orange dwarf. Ben blinked away the surreal image that threw up in his mind, and tried to focus: 54 Piscium was approximately thirty-six light years away, his internet source informed him. Thirty-six years of travel in the fastest space-craft never invented. Return journey, virtually a whole human lifetime. At that moment, he felt about that far away from understanding. What was 'mag activity'? To do with magnitude?

Ben put the phone down and returned to Catalina's papers. A little further down the same page was another name, Tau Ceti. Ben had never heard of Tau Ceti before, but he could hazard a guess that it was the name of another star. Looking that one up as well, he discovered he'd been absolutely right. Constellation of Cetus, twelve light years from Earth. Barely a hop and a skip away. A rather large star, as far as he could gather, comprising something like seventy-eight percent of the mass of the sun. Magnitude again. However million times that made it bigger than the puny little planet he was sitting on at this moment, Ben had no idea. He now felt as insignificantly minute as he did utterly clueless.

Flick, flick. Page after page, graph after graph. Ben chewed his pen. His heart was sinking faster than a burning Zeppelin.

Now he came to a page containing only a vertical list of hastily scribbled figures that looked like someone working out their thought processes on paper. The figures were all four digits long. There was nothing there to explain what they were, but to Ben's eye they could have been dates. If they were, most were long gone in history, apart from the last.

1010
1280
1460
1645
1790
2016 - ?

Okay, he told himself. Here was something he could potentially grasp. If they were dates, they were spaced out – albeit loosely – at rough intervals that averaged just under a couple of centuries. And if they were dates, the last one with its question suggested some kind of relevance to modern times. But the concept of relevance could only be understood if you had at least two variables to play with: such as the relevance of *a* to *b* or *x* to *y*, whether those were miles to kilometres or apples to oranges. Or clever to stupid. With nothing at all to go on, the whole number sequence fell flat, meaningless and worthless.

The question mark after the last date stood out. Like a reference to the unknown future, a note of uncertainty in the midst of all the inflexible hard data. Or maybe it just stood out because it echoed the giant question mark in his own mind that made him ask himself why he was even bothering with this stuff.

Ben sighed and closed the file. Forget it. There was no point in this. No point at all.

He laid the file to one side and went on sifting through the stack. More random choices, more roads leading nowhere.

Until he came back across the file that said HERSCHEL / SUN.

Chapter Thirty

Prior to that moment, all Ben had ever known about the astronomer called Herschel was that Catalina Fuentes had named her pet moggy after him. As he opened the file and began to scan the first page, he saw he was about to learn some more about the man.

The contents of the file were distinctly unlike the rest of the papers Ben had taken from the observatory. The first difference was that, to his relief, they were written in language he could understand, free of dense number equations and technical graphs and charts. The second was that the text was typed up and printed off, rather than handwritten, although it was heavily edited in green pencil, with crossings out and underlinings and asterisks scattered liberally everywhere. The margins were crammed with rephrasings and insertions, and arrows pointing here and there to indicate how certain lines and paragraphs should be reordered. It looked like an essay, or a first draft of an article written by a self-critical author striving to get the wording exactly right. With the corrections in place, the first paragraph began:

In the history of astronomy, few characters are as colourful and diverse as the German-born English astronomer William Herschel (1738–1822). A true polymath who seemed capable of turning his talents in whatever direction he chose, Herschel was a pioneer of the study of binary stars and nebulae, the discoverer of infrared radiation in sunlight, a skilled mathematician, optical lens grinder and telescope maker, a ground-breaking naturalist and a prolific classical composer, to name just some of his achievements. His discovery of the planet Uranus in 1781, as well as two of its moons and two more moons of Saturn, garnered him fame, acclaim and a place in astronomical history. However, not all of Herschel's scientific work was equally well received, and not all his discoveries are as well known today.

Ben paused reading and thought about the tone of the piece. For a start, he was struck by the fact that he could understand it at all. Which clearly meant it wasn't intended to be a serious piece of academic writing, but accessible to be read by a wider audience.

Audience. That sparked off another thought in Ben's head. Maybe the text wasn't intended to be read at all. It had a certain kind of ring to it that suggested to his ear that maybe it was intended to be *heard.*

'How's it going?' Ben called over to Raul, who was still at the table, hunched over the laptop as if he could will it to yield its secrets by staring hard enough at it.

'Like shit,' Raul said.

Which Ben didn't want to get into at that precise moment. He had something else on his mind. 'Listen, did you say she presented an episode of her series all about this guy Herschel?'

'William Herschel? Yes, that's right,' Raul replied distractedly, without turning away from the screen. 'She did lots of research into his work. Said it was incredible and revolutionary. Why, what have you found?'

'I don't know yet,' Ben muttered, and fell silent again as he went back to reading what he now understood was an early version of what had later become a television script.

One of Herschel's key areas of study, and a subject of great fascination for him, was those stars that seemed to change their brightness: what we now call variable stars; and he was responsible for much of the progress made in the understanding of these distant suns. His son, John Frederick Herschel, wrote in the 1833 A Treatise on Astronomy *that, thanks to his father's catalogue of brightness of the stars in each constellation, 'amateurs of the science with only good eyes, or moderate equipment, might employ their time to excellent advantage'.*

In today's science, we know why variable stars vary in brightness. But in Herschel's time, this was still a source of some mystery. As he sought to understand why these stars appeared to change, he attempted to correlate the phenomenon with another that he had studied extensively, namely the existence of sunspots on our own planet's nearest star. Herschel posed the hypothesis that these more distant suns might also possess spots, which perhaps were the cause of their vacillation from brightness to dimness. Just two centuries after Galileo had proposed that sunspots were dark clouds floating about in the solar atmosphere, Herschel shared the contemporary scientific view that the greater the number of spots on the sun, the more these would block out the light energy radiated to Earth: hence, the 'spottier' a variable star, the less bright it would appear from Earth.

Spurred on by the fact that he had perfected a telescope that gave him a view of the sun whose clarity was unprecedented at the time, Herschel deepened his study of sunspots, and this led him to form a new and radical notion: **the**

possibility of a correlation between the number of sunspots and Earth's climate.

He had noticed that, between July 1795 and February 1800, there had been a number of days when there had been no sunspot activity at all. Then, they had suddenly returned in abundance. He wrote: 'It appears to me . . . that our Sun has for some time past been labouring under a disposition, from which it is now in a fair way of recovering.' In 1801 he presented a paper to the Royal Society entitled 'The Nature of the Sun', in which he wrote:

'I am now much inclined to believe that openings [sunspots] with great shallows, ridges, nodules and corrugations, instead of small indentation, may lead us to expect a copious emission of heat, and therefore mild seasons . . . A constant observation of the sun with this view, and a proper information respecting the general mildness or severity of the seasons, in all parts of the world, may bring this theory to perfection or refute it if it be not well founded.'

But how was Herschel to back up his hypothesis?

Hampered by the lack of precise meteorological records by which to test his theory, he persevered by lateral thinking. Given the effects of lesser or greater quantities of sunshine on vegetation, it struck him that records of good or bad harvests might provide him with the data he needed. Any correlation between these and periods of many or few sunspots would theoretically support his argument.

Using as his source Adam Smith's famous 1776 book on economics, The Wealth of Nations, Herschel was able to single out five periods when, due to poor harvests, the price of wheat in England had been particularly high. Comparing these records to those of sunspot activity during those periods, he discovered to his surprise a clear correlation between poorer wheat harvests and a relative lack of sunspot activity.

Contrary to what had been thought until then, the presence of sunspots did not reduce the amount of heat from the sun, **the opposite was true***: greater sunspot activity corresponded to good weather and lower wheat prices, while a lack of sunspots corresponded to high wheat prices, which implied less favourable weather.*

'It seems probable', he wrote, 'that some temporary scarcity or defect of the vegetation has taken place when the sun has been without those appearances which we surmise to be the symptoms of a copious emission of light and heat.'

As we now know, the sun emits greater ultraviolet radiation, causing more heating of the Earth's atmosphere, during periods of greater sunspot activity, or Solar Maximum. But in Herschel's time this was a revolutionary idea – and the apparent correlation with Earth's climate made it more revolutionary still.

Excited by his findings, Herschel urged his scientific colleagues to examine solar activity in more detail. Sadly, far from praising his discovery, his peers responded with scepticism and even ridicule. A piece in The Edinburgh Review *lambasted his 'erroneous theory concerning the influence of the solar spots and the price of grain' as a 'grand absurdity'.*

Clearly, the world was not ready to accept such stuff. For once in his illustrious career, the great William Herschel had fallen flat and his attempt to wake the scientific community to his radical idea had failed.

At which point Ben decided he'd read enough, and gave up.

Okay, he thought, so he'd learned about some bygone astronomer's claimed, and apparently debunked, connection between these sunspots and the price of wheat in nineteenth-century England. Riveting, no doubt, for those who were interested in such titbits of science history. But to someone trying to figure out why a modern-day solar scientist was in the firing line of dangerous people, somewhat less so. What might have seemed revolutionary over two hundred years ago was hardly about to set the world on fire now, less still get anyone into trouble for researching or writing about it. And even if some deranged villain took exception to what Catalina had said about Herschel's wheat theory, the time to do anything about it was four years ago, when the TV programme had aired. Not now.

Ben had absolutely no doubt by then that he was wasting his time.

He slipped the papers back inside the file and closed it, with no intention of ever reading more. The agricultural economic history of 1800s England would just have to manage without him.

He stood up and walked over to Raul's table, where he quickly realised things hadn't been going much better. Raul turned to Ben with a defeated look. 'Anything?'

'Not exactly what you'd call anything useful to us,' Ben said. 'You?'

'The same,' Raul said. He motioned at the screen. It was filled with a more or less blank window that said 'Documents'. Ben looked. He couldn't see any.

'I thought there might be all kinds of document files here,' Raul explained. 'But I've searched everywhere in both the laptop's own drive and the external hard drive, and they're each virtually empty apart from the default programs and stuff already stored in them. It's as if she never used the machine at all.'

Ben was no expert, but the laptop didn't look to him like a brand-new item freshly unwrapped from its factory packaging. It bore the typical marks and scratches of a machine that had been in occasional, if not everyday, use for maybe a year or more. It had to have been used for something.

'Or else she deleted whatever documents were stored on there,' he said. 'Alternatively, she could have called Kazem from Munich and told him to do it.'

'We can't exactly confirm that with him either way, though, can we?' Raul said unhappily.

Ben thought for a moment, then pointed at the screen. 'You've checked the recycle bin? Deleted items could still be stored there.'

'I'm not an idiot. Of course I've checked it. And backup files, and everything else. I'm telling you there's nothing here.'

Ben rubbed his chin. 'What about emails?'

'There's a shortcut on the desktop that takes you to a webmail service she could have accessed from anywhere,' Raul said. 'Here, I'll show you.' He clicked out of the files menu he was in, and the desktop appeared. Catalina had replaced the default image with one that looked like the curved edge of a blazing golden disk set against a black backdrop. Ben realised it was a close-up of the sun. It was a stunning image that he could almost feel the heat from.

Raul moved the little white arrow cursor over the sun's face to double-click on a desktop icon. The sun disappeared abruptly and was replaced by a blank window with a blinking cursor that asked for the access password. He said, 'I'm scared it will shut itself down if we get too many wrong guesses.'

'How many have you tried so far?'

'Five. First I tried "Amigo". That was the name of the little mongrel dog we had when we were children. She loved that dog. Then I tried "Marisol", the name of our maternal grandmother, who Catalina was closest to out of all the family. Then I tried—'

'I get the picture,' Ben said.

'I can't think what else she might have used. I mean, it could be absolutely anything.'

'Try "Herschel",' Ben said. It was the first thing that came into his head, but it had as much chance of being correct as anything else they might come up with.

Raul looked at him. 'Come on. Based on what?'

'Just try it.'

Raul shrugged. 'Okay. It's on you if the program closes down and shuts us out forever.' He used one finger to prod out the letters H-E-R-S-C-H-E-L, and then hit Enter.

'I don't believe it,' Raul muttered as the email program opened up and a new window appeared in front of them.

'Told you,' Ben said.

The website flashed up on the screen, with a 'welcome back' message. In the top corner was a little red icon labelled WEBMAIL. Raul clicked on it, and a box appeared with the heading MY TODAY PAGE, with the current date. Down the left side was a vertical menu for Inbox, Sent Messages, Deleted Messages, Drafts and Trash. Over to the right was a subheading that said UNREAD MESSAGES (0). Beneath that was CALENDAR, which had no entries, then LATEST RSS ITEMS, of which there were none, then right at the bottom, DATE LAST ACCESSED.

Proof that the last time Catalina had visited her webmail account was July twelfth. The same day she went to the pawnshop. Four days before her car plummeted into the Baltic.

'Let's see what we have,' Raul said, and flashed the cursor over to click open the Inbox.

There weren't just no unread messages. There were no messages at all.

'Damn.' Raul tried Sent Items.

Empty.

He clicked on Deleted Items, then on Drafts, then on Trash.

Same result each time. The folders were all completely blank.

'It's just like what we found before,' Raul muttered. 'She must have deleted everything.'

'She wouldn't have needed to call Kazem to do it, either,' Ben said. 'She could have erased the emails herself back in Munich, from her desk at work, or at home, or anywhere.'

It was bad news. Raul stared sullenly at the screen. He looked as if he wanted to punch it. 'This leaves us with nothing. Zero. No way even to tell who she was in touch with, let alone what about or why.'

'One thing we do know,' Ben said. 'She didn't give this email address out to many people. Only to a closed circle, or else the inbox would have been flooded with messages since her last visit.'

'A very closed circle,' Raul said bitterly. 'And we're closed right out of it.'

'Hold on,' Ben said. He reached past Raul's shoulder and went to place his finger on the laptop's touchpad.

'What are you doing?'

'We can assume that the last time she logged onto her webmail is the same day she deleted whatever messages were on here,' Ben said. 'Yes?'

Raul shrugged, nodded. 'That sounds logical.'

'And we know that was the same day she visited Braunschweiger. You remember how edgy she looked on the security video. She was anxious and had a lot on her mind, with a whole list of things to take care of before she disappeared, and not much time.'

'Yes. So?'

'So people running scared and looking over their shoulder don't always remember to tidy up every loose end,' Ben said. 'That's usually how they get caught. Even someone as organised and methodical as your sister can miss something under pressure.' His finger on the touchpad, he steered the cursor back up to the inbox and clicked it open. CREATE NEW MESSAGE. Click. The new message appeared, a blank sheet with an empty space inviting him to enter the address he wanted to email. But Ben had no intention of writing anyone a message. In the top corner of the message box, there now appeared the thing he'd been hoping to find.

The address book.

Ben clicked again, and smiled as a drop-down list of names opened up on the screen. In her haste, Catalina had been too flustered to remember to delete them.

'Loose ends,' he said.

Chapter Thirty-One

It was everything they had, but it wasn't much. Only four names had been entered into the webmail address book. A closed circle, all right. All four were men. Their names were listed alphabetically by first name: Dougal Sinclair, James Lockhart, Mike McCauley and Steve Ellis.

'Who are they?' Raul said.

'Obviously, people whose correspondence was important enough for your sister to want to erase every last word,' Ben replied. 'Now all we have to do is figure out what that correspondence was.'

'And how do we do that?'

'We could always email these four blokes and ask them straight out.'

'You think that would work?'

'Maybe.' Ben slid the cursor up to the top name on the list. The small white arrow morphed into a small white pointing hand as it touched, and the alchemy of software conjured up another little box that showed the corresponding email address. Ben grabbed his pen and snatched a file from the bed, and wrote both the name and email down on the back of the cover.

The suffix of the email address puzzled him a moment or two before he understood what it signified. It wasn't a regular

@joebloggs.com or *.co.uk*. It was *ed.ac.uk*. Odd, until Ben realised that he'd seen similar in the past. As a mature student returning to finish his theology degree at Oxford – an undertaking that had been cut short in typical fashion by the kinds of events that governed his life – his primary contact there had been a don with the memorable name of Vaughn Goss-Custard, whose email address was *v.goss-custard@ox.ac.uk*: *ox*, for Oxford; *ac*, for academia.

Ox, ed. Oxford, Edinburgh. Which made Dougal Sinclair some kind of lecturer or professor at Edinburgh University.

Ben did the same thing with the second name on the list, James Lockhart. This time, the email suffix that popped up at the touch of the cursor was *auckland.ac.nz*. University of Auckland.

Germany, Scotland, New Zealand. Three academics, three countries. It might have meant nothing, or maybe it meant everything.

The pattern broke at the third name in the list. Mike McCauley had a regular email with one of the big providers in the United Kingdom. Which at least narrowed the field down to a specific country, but didn't tell Ben anything more. Steve Ellis, the fourth name on the list, was another Brit with another generic email.

'That's a start,' Ben said to Raul as he wrote it down with the others. 'Now let's refine what we know.'

Ben went back to sit on the edge of the bed, picked up his phone again and used it to jump back online and run a search on each of the four men, starting again from the top of the list. Raul sat backwards on the chair to face him, resting his chin on his forearms along its backrest and watching Ben intently as he worked.

It didn't take Ben long to start finding information. But what he found wasn't good.

Dougal Sinclair had been born in the Scottish town of Kirkcaldy in 1972, and earned his PhD in climatology in 1999. After a two-year stint as a senior researcher at the National Oceanic and Atmospheric Administration Science Center in Silver Springs, Maryland, Sinclair had quit NOAA to return to his native Scotland, joining the faculty at Edinburgh University's School of Geosciences. He had published various books and papers and won a number of academic awards for his research work.

'But I don't think he'll be winning too many more of them,' Ben said.

Raul asked, 'Why?'

'Because he's dead.'

Ben passed the phone over to Raul, who reached out an arm to grab it. The news item hadn't taken a lot of digging to find online, given its recency. According to BBC News Scotland, the tragic accident had occurred somewhere over northern Greenland on July eighth, when the light Piper aircraft chartered by the independent R.I.C.R. Reykjavik Ice Core Research science expedition, had lost control and flown into a glacier. All four people on board had been killed, including the pilot, the expedition leader Dr Sinclair himself, and his two research assistants, Kerry Holder and Mark Linton, both graduate students at Edinburgh.

Ben watched Raul's face darken as he read. Raul handed the phone back. 'July eighth,' he muttered.

Ben said nothing, but they were both thinking the same thing. The dates were clustering together like bullet holes in the ten ring of a marksman's target. Returning to his search engine, this time Ben entered the name James Lockhart.

'Here we go,' he said a few moments later when the search had thrown up its results. 'Professor James F. Lockhart, departmental head at the Faculty of Earth Sciences, University of Auckland.'

'New Zealand,' Raul said. 'That fits with the email address.'

'Looks like our man, all right. Says here he's a leading oceanography expert and authority on Antarctic climate conditions, and a former advisor to the New Zealand government on environmental issues.'

Raul buried his face deeper into his arms and frowned. 'Ice core research, meteorology, climate. I get the connection between these people. But what's that all got to do with a solar astronomer like Catalina?'

'William Herschel,' Ben said. 'That's what links her to them. The reason she was interested in his work. Something to do with the sun, solar energy and Earth weather.'

'Solar power? Clean energy resources? Is that what this is all about?'

'I don't know,' Ben said. 'This Herschel stuff is two centuries old. I don't think people were too worried about green issues back then.' He scrolled a little further down his search results, then stopped. His shoulders felt suddenly heavy, and a pain started biting into the muscles of his neck.

'Shit,' he said.

'What? What did you find?' Raul asked, jerking his chin up off the back of the chair.

This was getting worse. Ben heaved a sigh. 'From a website called "stuff.co.nz". Listen to this. "A man who suffered gunshot wounds during what police believe was a serious aggravated burglary at his home in Tamaki Drive, Auckland, has been identified as university lecturer Professor James Lockhart, 53. He was found unconscious following the incident, and despite the efforts of paramedics who attempted CPR for twenty minutes, he died at the scene. A woman named as the victim's wife, Mrs Patricia Lockhart, 46, was taken to hospital with severe head trauma. Today a police cordon remains at the scene as detectives continue to investigate Professor Lockhart's death. Tributes are being paid . . ." etc., etc.'

Raul had gone rigid and pale. 'Oh, my God. When did this happen?'

'July tenth,' Ben said. 'This year.'

'But that's—'

'A very big coincidence, that's for sure,' Ben said, nodding. 'Two deaths, two days apart, both victims in email contact with your sister, who deleted their correspondence just four days before she apparently killed herself.'

'It's not possible these were unrelated incidents, is it?'

'It's possible,' Ben said. 'But I wouldn't put money on it.'

Raul jumped up from his chair and started pacing up and down the room, teeth clenched, burning up with nervous energy. 'It's unbelievable. It's just incredible. My God, it's so obvious. Completely transparent. They're not even trying to hide it. How could anyone not see what's going on here?'

'It's only obvious if you know what connects them,' Ben said. 'Catalina's email is the common denominator. Without that, it just looks like random incidents, scattered across the world. Shit happens all the time. Planes crash, people get murdered, folks kill themselves, every second of every day. No particular reason why anyone should ever put it together.'

'How many names left on the list?' Raul asked.

'We're two down. Literally. With two to go. Steve Ellis and Mike McCauley.'

'Two more scientists, do you suppose?'

'It would fit the pattern,' Ben said.

Raul grunted. 'Yeah. And what are the chances they're dead as well?'

Ben said nothing, but he was willing to bet that Raul was right, and that the next two searches would turn up two more corpses. Accidental drowning, maybe. Food poisoning. Chemical asphyxiation. Falling asleep drunk on a railway line. Anything was possible.

But as it turned out, Ben and Raul were both wrong.

Chapter Thirty-Two

The university email addresses for the first two had made them simple to identify. Numbers three and four wouldn't be so easy, with generic email providers and common names that would throw up a million false results. Ben ditched the search on Lockhart and keyed in 'Steve Ellis scientist', which he decided might even the odds in his favour.

It did.

If he was the same guy Catalina had been in contact with, Steve Ellis was indeed a scientist – albeit a retired one, as Ben discovered from the man's personal website. Images there showed him as much older than Sinclair and Lockhart, pushing seventy with a snow-white beard that looked as if he'd been growing it since around the time Ben had left school. According to the short résumé on the site, he'd been an astronomer like Catalina back in the day. Quite a celebrated one, too – having, at the tender age of twenty-eight, won the 1975 Copley Medal for his research on solar physics: a highly prestigious award, as far as Ben could make out. After going on to teach at several different universities Ellis had taken early retirement in 1997, and now supported himself by making custom-built astronomical telescopes for private clients in his own workshop in Brecon in the Welsh borders, not far from where Ben had once upon a time endured the hell of 22 SAS selection training.

The website displayed images of Ellis's telescopes, which looked to be of extremely fine quality. Ben wondered whether maybe Ellis had built equipment for Catalina's observatory. Why else might they have known each other?

'So? Is the guy dead or what?' Raul asked tersely from the other end of the room, where he was still pacing up and down.

Ben saw there was a news page, and navigated to it in case he might find anything of note there, such as a helpful recent entry saying 'I am dead' or an announcement from a distraught relative saying that Steve had suffered a bizarre accident in his workshop. He found neither. Instead, right at the bottom of the webpage, was a paragraph in large block font declaring:

**JULY 10TH: DUE TO A CHANGE IN PERSONAL CIRCUMSTANCES, I REGRET THAT I AM NO LONGER TAKING ORDERS FOR THE FORESEEABLE FUTURE. ALL OPEN ORDERS WILL BE REFUNDED IN FULL.
I WILL BE UNAVAILABLE TO CONTACT UNTIL FURTHER NOTICE.**

'Ellis is alive,' Ben said. 'Or was, when he suddenly closed up his business in a real hurry. July tenth.'

Raul froze mid-pace. 'The same day as Lockhart was killed.'

Ben nodded. 'Another coincidence?'

'No way,' Raul said. 'This makes it certain.'

'And it tells us that they all knew each other,' Ben said. 'Catalina and the other four. They were like some kind of group.'

'Friends?'

'Or associates,' Ben said. 'Two astronomers, two climatologists. That can't be a coincidence.' He paused to think for a moment. 'New Zealand is thirteen hours ahead of the UK. So news of Lockhart's death on the evening of the tenth could have reached Ellis the same day in Wales. On receiving the news, Ellis immediately suspends his business and goes off the radar indefinitely. At exactly the same time, your sister is putting together her own contingency plans. They were hitting the panic button.'

'Panic over what? What could they have been into?'

'You tell me,' Ben said.

'Do you think there's any possibility of contacting this Ellis?'

'I doubt he's even within fifty miles of home,' Ben said. 'That's if they haven't already got to him.'

They were silent for a moment. Both thinking the same thing: that their options were running dangerously thin again.

'Just one name left on the list,' Raul said. 'McCauley. Another scientist, you can be sure.'

'Only one way to find out,' Ben said, and returned to his phone to start searching.

There were Mike McCauleys all over the internet. A platinum-selling country and western singer from Tennessee who'd developed Tourette's Syndrome. The managing director of a Scottish pipe fitting firm based in Inverness. An Australian arsonist who'd attempted to burn down a government building in New South Wales as a protest over shark culling. None of those seemed especially likely candidates. Nor did the fourth, or the fifth, or the sixth Mike McCauley Ben checked out.

Ben finally scored on the seventh. 'Got him,' he said to

Raul once he was certain. 'This is our guy. Lives in London. He has a webpage and the email address is the same as the one Catalina was using.'

'Let me see,' Raul said, grabbing the phone and scrutinising the screen for a second or two before he looked up at Ben in surprise. If he'd been expecting to find another esteemed professor of astronomy, his expectations had been wildly off the mark.

'He's a reporter for some independent British newspaper called *The Probe*.'

'He's a little more than that,' Ben said.

'I see it,' Raul said, reading. 'Voted by the Press Gazette as the top investigative journalist of 2010 for his work unmasking corporate corruption in the wake of the BP Macando Prospect oil spill disaster. Then again in 2012, for being the first to expose a hundred-and-sixty-billion-dollar money-laundering scam involving four major British banks. It says here, "Heroic and unstoppable, Mike McCauley's relentless lone crusade as the scourge of greedy capitalist fatcats and rogue bureaucracies everywhere marks a return to the 1970s glory days of investigative journalism and is living proof that not everyone in his profession is fixated by the private lives of media stars and footballers."'

'Definitely not a fellow scientist, then,' Ben said.

Raul blinked. 'Why would my sister be in contact with a man like this?'

'Not to give him the scoop on the latest celebrity gossip, presumably.' Ben took the phone back from Raul and glanced at his watch. They'd been at it for two hours. 'We're done for tonight. You should get back to your room and catch some sleep, because we'll have an early start in the morning.'

'Why? Where are we going?'

'First flight we can grab to London,' Ben said.

'On a plane? With these people following us everywhere we go?'

'Then we'll have to stay one step ahead of them,' Ben said.

'They could be a step ahead of us already, like before. I mean, they could already know about this McCauley. They could be waiting for us there. We could be walking right into a trap.'

'Could be,' Ben said. 'But this time we won't be surprised.'

Chapter Thirty-Three

Late that night, long after Raul had gone to bed, Ben stood out on the little wooden balcony overlooking the quiet street below, looked across the sleepy rooftops and up at the stars, and spent a while wondering about the depths of space that scholars like Catalina Fuentes devoted their lives to studying. Ben was no astronomer, but even his meagre knowledge of just how vast that big dark sky out there was left him shaking his head.

There was an awful lot of space out there, that was for certain. No wonder that astronomers had to specialise in just one limited area, or else they'd only end up spending their whole careers skimming the surface.

He thought about Catalina's celestial body of preference, that vastly gigantic nuclear blast furnace at the centre of the solar system, and the insignificantly minuscule little planet called Earth that was spinning round and round it. To him, the sun was, had always been, just the sun. To be sure, there had been times when he'd cursed it, often when he'd found himself baking inside the infernal pizza oven of an SAS Land Rover in the roiling heat of a desert somewhere. Just as there had been plenty of other times he'd craved to feel just a tiny touch of its warmth, when he'd been freezing his arse off trudging over some mountain, numb as deadwood inside his boots with the weight of pack and rifle threatening to drag him down into the snow.

But hate it or love it, it occurred to him how little he really knew about it. Which was strange, when he stopped to consider how vital to life that big old fireball up there in the sky actually was. Its eternal cycle was the hub of all things for every warm-blooded creature that had ever lived, and ever would. And billions of people just took it every bit as much for granted as the blood in their veins and the air in their lungs, while only a minute fraction of the world's population ever bothered to take the time to try to understand how it worked, what made it keep on ticking, and the future of its relationship with the trillions of life forms under its fiery dominion.

As Ben's contemplations slowly descended back to earth, he leaned on the balcony rail and lit up the first of his last four cigarettes to help him think. Raul might be right about walking into a trap. That was a potential worry, but Ben was almost equally worried about the possibility of not finding Mike McCauley in London. Guys in that line of work, especially of the hungry lone-wolf variety such as McCauley obviously was, tended to spend most of their time out in the field chasing down stories. He could be in Papua New Guinea for the next two months, for all Ben knew. Or, like Sinclair and Lockhart and possibly Ellis too, he could already be a dead man.

The fourth-last cigarette didn't seem to last long, so Ben lit up the third-last. By the time that one was smoked to its stub, it was after two in the morning and he was fairly sure he wasn't going to get a lot of sleep that night. He walked back through the dark room to sit on the bed, and pulled out the phone he'd taken from Raul earlier. Paid for in cash, no traces. He dialled a familiar number and waited. After five rings, a sleepy-sounding voice answered, 'Hello?'

It had been a while since they'd spoken. The last time hadn't been pleasant.

'Hello, sister,' he said.

Ruth treasured her privacy almost as much as her elder brother did. Maybe it was a Hope family trait. Her personal mobile number was known to barely four people in the world; Ben reckoned that if the bad guys were tapping her phone, it would be the company line.

'*Ben?*'

'I know it's late,' Ben said.

'My God. Where *are* you?'

Ben heard a rustling sound on the line as Ruth propped herself up against the pillow. The sleepiness was quickly disappearing from her voice.

'I was thinking of you the last few days,' he said. 'Felt like talking.'

'I was thinking of you, too. I haven't heard from you for so long. What are you doing now?'

'Now, I'm sitting on a hotel bed waiting for the morning to come.'

'Right. I meant generally.'

'Walking, eating, sleeping. The usual things.' He decided it was time to change the subject, before she started asking difficult questions. 'How's life for you? I heard that Steiner Industries was bidding for a buyout of the Lufthansa Group.'

She laughed. 'That'll be the day. Maybe we'll start with Swiss Global and work up to it. Shouldn't take more than about twenty years to clinch the deal.'

'That's your whole problem,' Ben said. 'No ambition.'

'Have you spoken to Brooke?' Ruth cut in, with typical directness. Good old Ruth. Straight to the point.

Ben was silent. *Here come the difficult questions*, he thought.

Hearing Brooke's name spoken out loud brought a wash of uncomfortable emotions.

'I spoke to her a couple of months ago,' Ruth said. 'She told me you never call her.'

'Why would I call her?' he said. He heard the cold detachment in his own voice, and wondered if it sounded as artificial to Ruth as it did to him.

'I think she'd like you to. She misses you.'

'You know what happened between us,' he said stiffly. 'There's nothing left to miss.'

'As a friend, then.'

Ben said nothing.

Ruth said, 'Nobody knows where you are or what you're doing. You worry people.'

'Did Brooke say she was worried about me?'

'She didn't *have* to say. You could be dead, and we wouldn't even know.'

'We?'

'There are people who care about you, Ben.' Ruth paused for a few moments and Ben could hear her moving about, plumping up the pillow, sitting up in bed.

'I'm sorry I woke you. Maybe I shouldn't have called.'

'It's okay, I'm alone anyway.'

'I won't ask.'

'It wouldn't do you much good if you did,' she said. 'Listen, have you talked to Jude? Your son. Remember him?'

Ben ignored the sarcasm. 'Not lately.'

'He and Brooke keep in contact. She said he's quit university.'

'I thought he might.'

'And how hard did you try to talk him out of it?'

'I can't force him to do what he doesn't want to do,' Ben said. 'Once his mind's made up, that's it.'

'Sounds like someone else I know,' Ruth said.

'Did she say what he's doing now?' *She.* It hurt him to say Brooke's name.

'Not much, apparently. Sounds like he's kind of drifting. He needs direction in his life, Ben. He needs a father to guide him.'

'I don't think I'm much of that,' Ben said, then fell silent. He wanted to ask what Brooke was doing now, but didn't.

'Where are you?' Ruth asked again.

'I told you. I'm in a hotel. Actually it's more of an inn.'

'That tells me a lot. You could be anywhere from Albuquerque to Znamensk.'

'Germany. Somewhere near Freiburg, I think.'

'You're kidding me. Then you're almost in Switzerland. Just a hop over the border. Why don't you come and see me here in Zurich? Spend some time?'

'I'm sure you're busy running your corporate empire.'

'Never too busy for my big brother, you know that.'

'You've forgiven me for crashing your plane in that lake in Indonesia?'

'Hey, these things happen. I bought a new one. Don't change the subject. Are you coming to see me, or what?'

'Some time, I will. I'm in the middle of things at the moment.'

'Business?'

'I'm retired from business.'

Ruth's tone grew firm. 'Ben, are you in trouble again?'

'Somebody is,' he said, after a beat.

'Somebody's always in trouble, Ben. You can't help them all.'

'That's the only thing I'm afraid of,' he said.

'What are you afraid of?'

'Not getting the job done,' he said.

'I don't think you need to worry about that, brother. You always get the job done.'

'Thanks.'

'You be careful.'

'As ever,' he said.

'And safe.'

'As houses.'

'Call me more often, okay?'

'Soon,' he said, and put down the phone.

He lay back on the bed and closed his eyes, sorry that the call had ended without him finding the courage to ask after Brooke. Instead he'd let himself sound like a cold-hearted bastard. Maybe he *was* a cold-hearted bastard. Or if he wasn't, maybe he should try harder to become one. Cold-hearted bastards didn't get sleepless nights reliving bad moments over and over, or feel gnawed by guilt and regret over words and actions that couldn't ever be undone.

Ben tried to visualise Brooke's face in his mind, but others kept intruding and clouding his imagination. Roberta Ryder. Silvie Valois.

He snapped open his eyes and looked at the luminous dial of his watch in the darkness. Still not three o'clock. Dawn was a long way off, but he felt more restless than ever.

Maybe calling Ruth hadn't been such a great idea after all.

Ben closed his eyes again, buried his head in the pillow and tried to shut out the unsettling images and voices in his head.

Chapter Thirty-Four

Welcome to Britain. London was every bit as wet and cold as Hamburg had been.

The longest part of the journey had been getting from the sleepy Black Forest village to the nearest decent-sized airport, which had been a choice between Strasbourg over the French border to the north, Zurich to the south and Basel to the west. After a bit of calling around, in the end Basel had offered the earliest direct flight to Heathrow, and the cheapest for Raul, who insisted on paying for both one-way tickets. Ben had left the BMW in long-term parking at the airport, where it would be unlikely to be flagged up to the police for days, if not weeks. When the police did eventually find the stolen car, they'd get an extra surprise when they discovered the weapons in the boot. Ben didn't like leaving them behind, and felt naked the whole time they were sitting in the departure lounge and on the flight, in case they were being followed.

But he'd spotted nobody suspicious among his fellow travellers, and they'd reached Heathrow without a single shot fired. Once they'd breezed through arrivals and exchanged a few hundred of their euros for pounds sterling to have some walking-around money, they jumped on a Piccadilly Line train direct from their terminal. Just under an hour later, they were experiencing the joys of a rainy afternoon in central London. Huddled crowds moving fast in all directions, noise and traffic fumes and confusion and roadworks and slippery pavements. Even to Ben's hardened sensibilities, the place was a shock after the rural serenity of the Black Forest village they'd woken up in that morning. It was Raul's first visit to London, and his verdict as they clambered into a taxicab and sped through the city was, 'It's, how would you say? An armpit.'

Raul was even less impressed with the district where Ben had the taxi driver drop them, in a backstreet off Pretoria Road in the dingy, crime-rotted heart of Tottenham. Even the cabbie seemed cagey about letting them off there. To Ben's mind, it was the perfect setting for the next stage in his strategy.

'Where have you brought us?' Raul said, staring around him as he hunched his shoulders against the rain. Graffiti and boarded-up windows, windswept litter and remnants of drunks' vomit gurgling down the gutters weren't everyday sights back home in Frigiliana.

'They call this area Little Russia,' Ben said. 'It was a ghetto for immigrant refugees after the 1917 revolution and became one of the most notorious dens of iniquity in London. You could hardly walk the streets without getting stabbed or shot. It's gone downhill since then.'

'Thank you for the history lesson. I'm still unclear as to what we're doing here.'

Ben shrugged. 'There's so much gang and drug crime in the place, nobody even cares any more. The police just let them get on with it. Which makes it the best place I know of to nick a car.'

Raul frowned. 'Nick? You mean *steal*?'

Ben looked at him. 'You have scruples about taking a

car? After punching a guy off a roof and breaking his neck?'

'I'm not a murderer,' Raul said. 'I'm not a thief, either.'

'If it makes you feel better, around here the chances are it'll already be stolen,' Ben said. 'Anyway, we won't need it long. We're just borrowing it, so to speak.'

Within ten minutes, Ben had found a seven-year-old Renault Laguna estate far enough out of sight of any surveillance cameras to spark his interest. Judging by the damage to the door locks, this wasn't the first time it had been broken into. The rest was easy. Less than a minute later, they were driving away. There was an empty hole where the radio used to be, and the suspension knocked badly, probably from being joyridden over too many speed humps. But the motor ran smoothly, there was enough fuel in the tank to get them where they needed to go, and the Laguna had no faulty lights or worn tyres that might attract unwanted police attention. Ben tossed his smartphone into Raul's lap. 'Now dial up the GPS on that and find me the offices of *The Probe.*'

'I hope for their sakes they're based in a nicer part of London than this *puta letrina,*' Raul muttered. 'This car stinks as if someone has pissed in it,' he added, and wound down the window only to receive a faceful of rainwater spray as Ben went hammering through a puddle.

'I didn't realise you were so sensitive,' Ben said.

Raul stared at him. '*Besa me culo.*'

The Probe was one of a group of independent publications privately operated under the corporate banner of Trinity Media Ltd, based in Hammersmith a few miles to the southwest. Trinity House turned out to be a converted Georgian three-storey tucked away among a cluster of office buildings near the banks of the Thames, where Ben found a parking spot that allowed them a view of the entrance.

'Now what?' Raul said.

'Now we sit, and hope that our guy's in there, and wait for him to show his face,' Ben replied. The image on McCauley's website showed a lean-faced man somewhere in his mid-fifties, with round wire-framed glasses, thinning hair and a scraggy beard turning grey about the chin. As Ben imagined him, he could have been a lecturer at a former polytechnic, the kind of guy who would wear open-toed sandals and sew leather patches onto the elbows of his corduroy jackets. The whole vegetarian look. Unless he'd shaved off the beard, he shouldn't be too hard to spot.

Ben checked his watch. It was 3.17 p.m. 'If McCauley keeps regular nine-to-five office hours, it shouldn't be that long a wait.'

'Someone like that, he could be at his desk until midnight,' Raul said. 'If he's even at work. We could have come all this way for nothing. We should have phoned in advance to find out if he would be here.'

'I didn't want him to know we were coming,' Ben said. 'If he has any inkling of what's going on, he might have got the strangest idea that bad guys were gunning for him, too.'

'Fine. Then we sit and breathe stale piss for the next however many hours. Could you not have stolen a better-smelling car?'

Ben looked at him. 'If it's fresh air you want, you can take a stroll to that newsagent's we passed back there, and grab us a couple of sandwiches. Get me some cigarettes, too.'

Grumbling, Raul hurried off through the rain in search

of the newsagent's while Ben sat alone in the dank car and watched the building. Trickles of rain snaked through the dirt on the windscreen. Now that they were here in London, his worries about not finding McCauley so easily had returned in full force to haunt him.

Raul returned a few minutes later with two floppy sandwiches, a couple of Mars Bars and a pack of Mayfair Superkings. Ben stared at the cigarettes. 'What's this you've bought? I can't smoke this crap.'

'I'm pleased to hear it,' Raul said. 'Then I won't have to choke on your fumes on top of the stench in this car. Why can't you vape e-cigarettes like all the other addicts these days?'

'Maybe because sucking pure liquid nicotine is like shooting poison directly into your system,' Ben said. 'That stuff'll kill you.'

'Not me. I respect my body.'

'Oh, I noticed that, first time I laid eyes on you.'

Ben left the Mayfairs unopened. He wasn't that desperate. He'd just have to smoke twice as much to catch up, when he eventually got hold of some real cigarettes again. For now, he contented himself with the sugar rush from the chocolate.

Time passed. They didn't speak, partly because of the nervous tension Ben could sense coming from Raul, and partly just because there was nothing new to say. Four o'clock came and went. Now and then, a vehicle pulled up in the little car park to the side of the offices, and someone would go in. Three people emerged from the building, but none of them looked like Mike McCauley, with or without a beard. Ben lapsed into the still, watchful, disembodied state that had seen him through a hundred stakeouts and military missions. He could sit for hours, days, silent and immobile.

That was a talent Raul lacked, and after the first hour he was becoming more and more restless.

Four thirty passed. Quarter to five. Traffic was building in the street, as well as through the entrance of Trinity House as office staff started leaving. Still no McCauley. Five fifteen. Half past the hour ticked on by, and they watched in silence as the building slowly emptied. Some people departed on foot, some in groups, some alone, some on bicycles, wearing pointy helmets that made them look like extraterrestrials. Green London. A less ecologically concerned minority got into their cars and drove off, until only a beige Smart car, a Ford Transit and a motor scooter remained in the little car park. Raul could hardly sit still any longer as the stress of waiting got to him. Ben was aware of his own neck and shoulders gradually stiffening as his apprehension grew.

'So what's the story with this guy Austin Keller?' Ben asked.

Raul grimaced. 'You already know the story. He broke her heart. Before that, nobody on the outside even knew about the relationship, because they wanted to keep it secret to protect their privacy. What do you want to know about him for?'

'I was thinking that if this McCauley lead falls through, we might need to go and talk to him next.'

Raul looked at him. 'Why, you think it will?'

Ben shrugged. 'Anything's possible.'

'Forget it,' Raul said. 'Not even you could find that one. He's . . . how would you say it in English? A *bicho raro*.'

'An oddball,' Ben said. 'A weirdo.'

Raul nodded. 'That's it. A very rich weirdo. If he's not sailing around the middle of some ocean in his yacht, he's hiding like a hermit in one of his many secluded properties all over the world. He's paranoid. Hates being seen in public, can't stand to be photographed or anything like that. It was what finished things between him and Catalina. She was getting more noticed and beginning to go places, and he wouldn't give up his reclusive lifestyle. He tried to put pressure on her to quit and come and live with him. Everything had to be his way, the selfish prick. She loved him, but she wouldn't let him ruin her career. So she refused, and in the end they split up.'

'How did they meet?'

'Baxter Burnett introduced them. The movie star? You must have heard of him.'

Ben shook his head.

'You live in a monastery or something?'

'I did,' Ben said. 'For a while.'

Raul raised a dubious eyebrow. 'Hmm. Anyway, a bunch of film and TV people got together one summer for a weekend party at Burnett's place on the Italian Riviera. Keller made a brief appearance. Apparently he dabbles in movie producing from time to time, not that he needs to work. For some reason I never understood, my sister apparently took a . . . what's the expression?'

'A shine,' Ben said.

'A shine to him. Like I said, he has his head so far up his own ass that he wouldn't be worth talking to even if we could find him.'

'It was just a thought,' Ben said.

They fell back into silence. More time dragged by.

Then, as the hands on Ben's watch were closing in on ten to six, the door of Trinity House swung open and a casually dressed man with round wire-framed spectacles, thinning hair and a scraggy beard walked out of the building, carrying a battered leather satchel on a strap. He wasn't wearing open-toed sandals, but there was little doubt as to his identity. He paused to pull a key ring from the pocket of his jeans, then headed for the beige Smart car.

'McCauley,' Raul said, straightening up in his seat and going as stiff as a gundog tracing a scent.

Ben was already reaching for the ignition.

Chapter Thirty-Five

Ben waited for McCauley to turn out of the car park and drive fifty metres up the street before he fired up the Renault, hit the lights and windscreen wipers and pulled out in pursuit. He hung back, allowing two other cars to slot in between.

'Don't lose him,' Raul said, eyes glued to the rear of the Smart car as it weaved through the traffic.

'As if,' Ben replied calmly.

Not much bigger than a shoebox, the Smart car was quick and nimble through the London traffic. Ben had to spur the wallowing Laguna hard to keep up as they cut westwards over Hammersmith Bridge and into Barnes. Twice, Ben had to jump a red light. Raul was leaning intently forwards in his seat and gripping the door handle as if urging the car to go faster. The wipers slapped their relentless back-and-forth rhythm. Taillights and brake lights flared like angry red stars in the dirty windscreen.

McCauley led them onwards through Barnes, until they reached a quiet residential street and the Smart car's left indicator came on before it pulled into a driveway. Following fifty metres behind, Ben slowed as they passed the house. It was a small and unexceptional semi-detached 1960s property that, in this part of London, had to be worth a couple of million. Given what McCauley probably earned in his crusade against the world, the house was probably a family hand-me-down. Ben cruised a little way further down the street, and pulled up at the kerb.

'Let's go,' Raul said, reaching for the door latch.

'Not yet,' Ben told him. He angled the rearview mirror so he could see the house. Sat still behind the wheel and watched as McCauley got out of the Smart car carrying his satchel, bleeped the locks and walked up a little path to the front door. No Mrs McCauley came to greet him. McCauley opened the door and disappeared inside.

Ben counted to a hundred.

'Okay,' he said to Raul. '*Now* let's go.'

Ben grabbed his bag from the back seat, and they left the car and walked quickly through McCauley's front gate. The garden was overgrown and unkempt, and the woodwork on the house needed painting. Too busy battling injustice and corruption to have time for basic maintenance, obviously. The brass surround of the Yale lock was tarnished and weather-stained.

'Do we knock, or do we smash the door in?' Raul asked.

'Neither,' Ben said, taking out his wallet. He unzipped a little compartment that he seldom needed to open. It was where he kept a set of bump keys that could open any standard Yale lock, especially an old one like this, made before manufacturers had got wise to the ease with which burglars could bypass their security. Ben quickly found the right key, inserted it into the lock, and three seconds later they were in. Ben put his finger to his lips to shush an astonished Raul as they slipped through the small entrance hall into an open-plan living room.

The room was empty, and smelled vaguely of incense and spices. McCauley's decor was heavy on the ethnic style, with

222

a mix of African, Indian and South American furnishings and sculptures and wall hangings. There was a giant framed picture of Nelson Mandela over the fireplace. Next to an open-tread staircase hung a poster showing a caricature of an obese banker with multiple chins, a sleazy grin and a giant Havana, bearing the caption 'YOU SAY "GREEDY CAPITALIST PIG" LIKE IT'S A BAD THING'. On the wall opposite was a large glass-framed print of the classic Pulitzer prize-winning photo of the 1968 execution of a Viet Cong guerrilla. Ben had seen that harrowing image a hundred times before, and seeing it again now was all the proof he needed that there was unlikely to be a Mrs McCauley living in the house. Ben hadn't met a woman yet, not even the redoubtable Commander Darcey Kane of the National Crime Agency, who would tolerate a glossy 16x20 of a terrified man about to get his brains blown out with a .38 Smith & Wesson snubnose hanging pride of place in her living room.

The leather satchel was lying on an armchair where McCauley must have carelessly tossed it as he came in. Ben stepped over to it and undid the clasp to check the contents. A notebook and pen, a mobile, an iPad, a spare pair of glasses. Ben closed the bag, then moved to the stairs and heard the muted patter of the shower coming from above. He nodded to Raul, and they climbed the open treads. Thick polished wood, no doubt from a sustainably managed forestry source. The staircase walls were lined with framed photos of McCauley in his journalistic exploits all over the world, posing surrounded by smiling African children in one, standing on an oil-slicked beach in another, all spruced up and receiving his Press Gazette award in another.

Upstairs, the bathroom door was ajar and the sound of splashing water was louder. Ben peeked through another door, saw it was a bedroom, and led Raul through it. The bedroom was small and orderly, with a wardrobe and a bed and little else. Ben and Raul positioned themselves by the window and waited. Soon afterwards, the water stopped. They could hear McCauley mooching about in the bathroom. Then he stepped out, skin rosy from the hot water and wearing nothing but a short towel around his waist, and strolled nonchalantly into the bedroom. He was in surprisingly good shape, with the lean muscularity of a man who needed to keep himself fit and strong for challenging assignments in sometimes dangerous places. So much for the whole vegetarian open-toed sandal thing, Ben thought. Maybe McCauley was more than he seemed at first glance.

The journalist's hair and beard were still wet from the shower, and his glasses were steamed up with condensation. He removed them, wiped the lenses on a corner of his towel, put them back on, and his eyes opened wide in alarm as he saw his unexpected visitors standing there. He froze, and said, 'Whoa.'

'Keep the towel on,' Ben said. 'We've seen enough unpleasant sights lately.'

McCauley took a step back. His fists were clenched. He was more outraged than frightened. 'Who the fuck are you?'

'Relax, Mike,' Ben said. 'We're here to talk to you, that's all.' He motioned to the bed. 'Take a seat.'

McCauley hesitated. Flicking his gaze warily from Ben to Raul, he stepped to the bed and sat. The muscles in his shoulders were bunched tight, and his face had flushed scarlet. 'I said, who the fuck are you? What are you doing in my home?'

'This is Raul Fuentes,' Ben said. 'We have reason to believe you're acquainted with his sister.'

McCauley stared up at Raul, his anger subsiding, confusion taking its place. 'Catalina? You're Catalina's brother?'

Raul tore his passport out of his pocket and tossed it into McCauley's lap. 'There's the proof. Look at my name. Look at the birth date. We're twins.'

'No,' McCauley said, still peering closely at Raul as if studying his face. 'No. I don't need to. The family resemblance is obvious, now that I think of it. But what—?'

'What am I doing here?' Raul said. 'What do you think? I'm looking for her.'

'I . . . I have no idea what you're talking about,' McCauley said. 'That's insane.'

'I apologise for the rude entry,' Ben said. 'You'll appreciate that it needed to be a surprise, under the circumstances. There are some bad people looking for her, too. But you already know that as well, don't you? Come on, Mike. We came a long way to talk to you. Don't be a disappointment.'

'But I don't understand,' McCauley said. 'You're mistaken. Catalina Fuentes died. Her car went over a cliff. It was all over the news . . . I mean, surely you must know that? Her brother, of all people?'

He stared at them both with such an earnest look of absolute blank stupefaction that Ben was rattled by it. In that moment, the awful thought struck him that McCauley genuinely knew nothing. Or, even worse, that it was true, and that Kazem had been wrong, or lying.

'She's alive!' Raul snarled, and stepped towards McCauley as if he was going to hit him.

Ben put a hand on Raul's shoulder. McCauley might actually hit back, and that wasn't going to help their situation much. 'You were in contact with her,' he said to McCauley.

The journalist frowned, playing it cagey. 'What makes you think I was in contact with her?'

'There isn't time to play games,' Ben said. 'Your email

225

address was on her private computer. The messages themselves were deleted. We need to know what that correspondence was about.'

'And that's why you broke into my house, to find out about a bunch of emails?'

'We didn't break in,' Ben said.

'The door was locked.'

'It still is,' Ben said. 'Nothing got broken. Therefore, technically, not a break-in.'

'You've got the look,' McCauley said. 'Ex-military. It's virtually written on your forehead. Think I haven't met people like you before?'

Ben said nothing.

McCauley pointed at Raul. 'Okay, so he's Catalina Fuentes' brother. Do you have a name?'

'You can call me Ben.'

'He's just a friend,' Raul said.

McCauley gave a grunt. 'Peculiar kind of friend to have. One who can get through locked doors and slip into people's houses like some kind of fucking ninja assassin. Did you follow me here from the office? Have you been watching me?'

'You can trust us,' Raul said.

McCauley paused, narrowing his eyes and scrutinising Ben and Raul with the thoughtful, cautious look of a seasoned investigator. 'Then you need to let me get some clothes on,' he said. 'We'll go downstairs and discuss this like civilised human beings, and I'll tell you what I know.'

Chapter Thirty-Six

'All right,' McCauley said a few minutes later when the three of them were sitting around the table in his tiny kitchen, by a sliding glass door that looked out onto his even smaller million-pound back garden. McCauley's hair was combed and he'd put on a denim shirt and a pair of baggy green chinos. The kitchen table had the look of being handcarved by indigenous people of somewhere or other. The coffee was Fairtrade stuff from Guatemala, served in stoneware mugs. McCauley had fouled his with soya milk. Raul hadn't wanted any. He was already wound up enough. Ben took it black. It tasted pretty good.

McCauley took a deep breath and looked at Raul. 'On July sixth, a woman calling herself Carmen Hernandez called the *Probe* offices and said she wanted to speak to me. When she was put through to my personal line, she apologised for the deception and said that her real name was Catalina Fuentes. Naturally, due to her celebrity, I already knew who she was. It's not unheard of for famous people to go by false names now and then, but I was surprised that she had contacted me. I was even more surprised when she said she wanted to meet, somewhere we could talk confidentially. She said she was aware of the kind of journalism I did, had been following my work and so on and so forth, and that she had something to tell me that would be of great interest to me. I could tell right away that something odd was going on, and that she was deeply afraid.'

'So you met with her?' Raul asked.

McCauley nodded. 'In Munich, three days later, on July ninth. She set the whole thing up, paid my travel expenses by wire transfer. A car turned up to collect me from the airport, drove me to a dingy hotel in a less salubrious part of town, and dropped me off with instructions to go to room 22. A little weird. Not exactly what I'd expected.' McCauley gave a tight smile. 'As you might imagine, unorthodox and clandestine meetings are hardly unusual in my line of work. But those are normally with crooks, whistleblowers or informants, not with glamorous television stars. After I'd been waiting alone in the room for ten minutes, wondering what the hell this was about, she arrived. I wouldn't have recognised her. She was wearing a blond wig and dark glasses. That's when I knew she really was serious. And scared out of her wits.'

Ben sipped coffee. 'Go on.'

'It took her a while to compose herself. I got the impression that she was nervous of me, at first. I mean, here she was meeting this total stranger in a seedy hotel room. Evidently not the kind of thing she was used to. I could sense that she was having second thoughts about the meeting, and was verging on running off at any moment. I did my best to put her at her ease, and after a few minutes she began to open up to me.'

'What did she say?' Raul asked.

'First, she apologised for having made me come all the way to Germany. Said it wasn't because she considered herself so important that people had to come to her, but rather that she was nervous about coming to London to see me because she believed she was being followed, and she didn't want to implicate me. She was convinced that someone was trying to do her harm, because of something she'd become involved in through her work.'

'Her scientific work?' Ben said. 'Solar physics?' His green bag was propped against his feet, full of Catalina's solar research notes and the William Herschel file. He'd been half hoping that McCauley could shed some light on this stuff.

'I don't know anything about it,' McCauley said, killing Ben's optimism at a stroke. 'She didn't elaborate, and it was a short meeting. Nor did she reveal to me specifically who was apparently threatening her, or what reason they might have had for doing so. A very cautious woman.'

'Didn't she tell you anything at all?' Ben asked.

McCauley shrugged. 'Like I say, we didn't talk for long. I think she just wanted to see me face to face that one time to sound me out. Like a preliminary interview, to decide whether she could trust me enough to tell me more. She kept asking me if I thought I could help her. Offered to pay me whatever price I wanted, as long as it could be strictly secret. I replied that I didn't want money, and there was little I could do, without more information. She said she was sorry for being so secretive, and that when I knew the rest I'd understand why it had to be that way, and why she'd chosen me to confide in, and how much of a huge deal this was. We exchanged private email addresses, and then she was gone. We hadn't been together for thirty minutes. An hour later I was getting on a flight back home to London.'

Ben raised an eyebrow. 'What kind of a huge deal are we talking about?'

'What can I tell you?' McCauley said. 'But think about it. Why come to me? My job is to expose corruption in high places. That's what I'm known for, and it's fairly safe to assume that's why she chose me out of a thousand other guys. I could only assume this was something very big indeed, involving the kind of major high-profile players I have a record of chasing after. That's as much as I was able to glean, reading between the lines.'

'What about the emails?' Raul cut in.

'There was only one,' McCauley said. 'When I got back to London I found a message from Catalina in my inbox. She thanked me for my time, apologised once again for the strangeness and brevity of our meeting, and promised to be in touch soon. I didn't feel the need to reply to it, and I never heard from her again.'

Ben had the timeline firmly in his mind. In the three days between contacting the journalist and the meeting taking place, Catalina must have heard about Sinclair's death in the Greenland light aircraft crash, making whatever anxieties she already had even worse. Then, the day after their meeting, Lockhart had been murdered at home in New Zealand and Ellis had apparently gone on the run. That news must have been the tipping point, after which events had started rolling so fast that she hadn't had time to contact McCauley again. Within a week of the hotel room rendezvous, she'd disappeared herself.

'And that's all you know?' Ben said.

'That's all she told me,' McCauley replied. He paused a beat, seemed about to add more, then clammed up again.

'There's more, isn't there?' Ben said.

'She might have mentioned a couple of names to me,' McCauley said.

'Names?'

'Of people who were also involved. Three, to be more precise.'

'Names like Sinclair, Lockhart and Ellis?' Ben said.

McCauley went silent for the longest time. Like Catalina in the Munich hotel room, he looked as if he was trying to decide whether or not he could trust these strangers. Finally, he looked at Raul and said, 'You don't believe your sister committed suicide.'

'Of course I don't,' Raul said.

McCauley shook his head.

'Neither do I,' he said.

Chapter Thirty-Seven

'So you know about Sinclair,' McCauley said.

'Just that they had to scrape him and his science expedition colleagues off a glacier,' Ben said.

'And Lockhart? What happened in New Zealand?'

'What are the odds?' Ben said. 'Just two days apart.'

'My feelings exactly.' McCauley turned to Raul. 'Mr Fuentes, I can't tell you how shocked I was to hear the news about your sister. I only met her that one time, but she struck me as being a very sincere and decent person.'

'Thank you. I appreciate that,' Raul said.

'I've spent the last three months wondering what really happened. It's been bugging me. So much so, in fact, that I've been neglecting two other active investigations that I'd been working on, in order to try and delve a little deeper into this. I've managed to uncover a few facts that shocked me even more. Facts you most likely won't be aware of. Under the circumstances, Mr Fuentes, you might find what I'm about to say upsetting.'

Raul nodded. 'I understand. But nonetheless, I'd like to know.'

McCauley leaned his elbows on the table and knitted his fingers together with an air of concentration. 'Air crashes in Greenland are investigated by a Danish government agency, the Havarikommissionen for Civil Luftfart og Jernbane Langebjergvaenget, HCLJ for short, together with the Greenlandic police, who also operate under the auspices of Denmark. It wasn't easy to get hold of a copy of the official report, but I can generally get hold of anything I set my sights on. It states that flight GL-4306, chartered by the Reykjavik Ice Core Research expedition, departed from Ilulissat Airport at 10.37 hours on July eighth. It also describes how, at 08.06 hours that same morning, one of the mechanics responsible for final checks on the Piper before takeoff discovered a man inside the hangar, whom he believed to be acting suspiciously around the aircraft. When challenged, the man fled, whereupon the mechanic immediately reported the incident to his superiors. He described the man as being medium height, medium build, between twenty-five and forty-five years of age, brown hair. In other words, he could have been anybody. No other reported sightings of him around the scene that day. The same mechanic later told the police that before flight GL-4306 took off, he witnessed a discussion between Dr Sinclair and the pilot. It would seem that Sinclair was troubled by the incident and was highly reluctant to go up in the air.'

'He suspected something?' Ben said.

'Looks that way. Whether he'd already noticed anything odd prior to that, we'll never know. In any case, Sinclair insisted that the plane be checked once more from top to tail before takeoff, which it was. Nothing suspicious was found. But maybe it wasn't checked carefully enough.'

'Meaning what?'

'Meaning that on day thirteen of the twenty-two-day crash site examination carried out by HCLJ, forensic investigators discovered traces of cyclotrimethylene trinitramine among the wreckage of the aircraft's tail section.' McCauley pulled a grim smile at Ben. 'If my guess is right about you, that might sound familiar.'

'Chemical residue from RDX high explosive,' Ben said. His SAS team had used so much of the damned stuff to blow up everything from buildings to armoured troop carriers that he could still smell it.

'They bombed the plane?' Raul said.

'I don't think the expedition was packing it for blasting out ice core samples, do you?' McCauley replied. 'Now, isn't it interesting how that little detail was never reported anywhere else, and never found its way into the media? In fact, it was brushed over even in the official report. HCLJ seemed more interested in the weather conditions. The verdict: that "adverse crosswind conditions, gusting to forty knots, led to a flight course deviation and an accelerated rate of descent, causing the pilot to lose directional control".'

'Turbulence,' Ben said. 'That's their conclusion?'

'Neat little bit of bullshit, don't you think?' McCauley gave another cold smile. 'Now, let's turn to the James Lockhart murder in New Zealand, two days later. Again, I was able to pull a few strings, call in a couple of favours, and get hold of a copy of the Auckland City Police report. Or should I say, both of them. I'll explain that in a minute. It's not quite what you'll read in the news. Alerted by a neighbour who heard gunshots coming from the Lockharts' house in the middle of the night, detectives apprehended and arrested one Aidan Ruck at the scene of the crime. Ruck was armed with a nine-millimetre handgun that matched two bullets later recovered from Professor Lockhart's body. He was also carrying a hammer that forensically fitted the cranial wound suffered by Mrs Lockhart. Open and shut case? Think again, folks. Eight hours after his arrest, Ruck walked free. I'm not talking out on bail. He was *released without charge*. He hasn't been heard of since. Who was he working for? Ask all you like, you won't get any answers. There's not a single scrap of information on him anywhere, and if I can't find it, nobody can. Not only that, but if you got a hold of the official police report now, three months later, you'd see that it's been altered. The name Aidan Ruck was removed and the name of one Jess Cullen, a known Auckland drug addict and thief, inserted in its place.' McCauley spread his hands. 'So there you are, folks. Make of it what you will.'

Ben was silent. He glanced out of the window. Dusk was falling outside. It would be dark soon. He no longer knew where to go.

'It's bad,' Raul said.

McCauley shrugged. 'It's not good. A nebulous line exists somewhere between suspicious coincidence and clear evidence of a conspiracy. I'm afraid that line has been well and truly crossed. There's no doubt in my mind that we're dealing with a concerted and well-organised attempt to eliminate a list of targets. In particular, a group of scientists with some kind of very dangerous secret in common. The motivation isn't clear. But what is *very* clear to me is that whoever is behind these killings wields enormous and widespread influence. We're talking money and power, big time. These are not the kind of people you can escape from easily.'

McCauley looked seriously at Raul. 'I don't think your sister killed herself. I agree with you on that. However, when you tell me you're *looking* for her . . .'

Raul stiffened. 'Yes, so?'

'Mr Fuentes, whatever reason you have for believing you might find her still alive, and as much as I admire your obvious faith and persistence in searching for her, you need to face the facts.'

'You're not the first person to tell me this,' Raul said defensively. 'It doesn't change my mind.'

'I'm sorry,' McCauley said to him. 'I can only imagine how hard it must be for you, but you must accept the truth. I've seen cases like this before. Forgive me for being blunt, but I believe that whoever murdered Sinclair and Lockhart also murdered your sister. Some time between the tenth and fifteenth of July, they kidnapped her. They transported her, and her car, to Rügen Island. Then they drugged her, put her in the car and pushed it over the cliff. They may have removed the body afterwards, or not, there's no way to be sure about that part. But the rest is beyond doubt. These bastards mean business.'

'What about Ellis?' Ben asked.

'What about him? He's off the radar. If he's still alive, he's holed up somewhere crapping his pants.'

'A retired astronomer who builds telescopes in his garden shed in Brecon. How's someone like that a threat to anybody?'

'He didn't always keep such a low profile,' McCauley said. 'And he wasn't just an astronomer. He was a highly lauded and respected interdisciplinary scholar in his heyday. Geologist, geophysicist, astroglaciologist, cryospherologist. I had to look that one up. It's someone who specialises in the study of the cold parts of the Earth. Back in the late seventies, Ellis caused a stir when he claimed that glaciers were expanding at a phenomenal rate and the planet was entering a new ice age. Wrote a book about it, which sold pretty well.'

'That's hardly going to get him noticed now, though, is it?' Ben said. 'Times have moved on. Like the climate. So why him?'

'I have no idea.'

'I'd like to find out. You could help us track him.'

McCauley shook his head. 'Forget it. Sorry, I don't want to get any deeper into this than I have already. This shit's too dangerous for me.'

'Scared there won't be an award in it for you?'

'They don't give out awards for being dead,' McCauley said. 'Frankly, what with you people turning up here like this today and sneaking up on me so easily, I'm feeling vulnerable. I don't want to end up like . . .' His eyes met Raul's and his words trailed off.

Raul stared at him. 'Go on. Say it. Like Catalina.'

'Look, Mr Fuentes—'

Raul clenched his teeth and his fist, and hammered the table so hard with his knuckles that the coffee mugs jumped an inch in the air. 'Enough! I heard you the first time, *idiota*. We're done here. I'm going to go find my—'

Raul never finished the sentence.

Because two men had just appeared side by side in the kitchen doorway, pointing pistols at them.

Chapter Thirty-Eight

The two men stepped into the room and quickly spread apart to flank the doorway. They were both about the same age, late twenties, early thirties. Both had the dead-eye look and the well-practised moves of professionals. One had the build of a runner, stringy and spare, the other was heavily bulked out from the weight room. A greyhound and a Rottweiler. The guns in their gloved fists were Glock nine-millimetres fitted with long tubular suppressors. A useful apparatus. They didn't quite silence the high-pressure crack of a nine-millimetre to the soft *dooophh* you heard in movies, but they did mute the decibels conveniently enough for close-up execution work indoors. The two gunmen could empty their magazines into Ben, Raul and McCauley right here, right now, and not even the closest neighbour would hear a thing.

Raul and McCauley sat there speechless, locked rigid. Ben didn't move either, but his mind was calm as he lucidly assessed the possibilities. Kitchens were often favourable environments for an unexpected armed confrontation, being generally well equipped with readily improvisable weaponry, and a savagely violent and swift counterattack was nearly always the best means of defence. McCauley had a row of copper pans hanging from hooks over the kitchen counter.

Ben had once killed a man with a skillet, and had learned never to underestimate the combat value of high-quality cookware. Also prominent on the kitchen counter was the usual wooden knife block, housing the most effective lethal weapons that every household in Britain possesses, mostly without even realising it. The steel would be Sheffield, not Solingen this time. An academic distinction, under the circumstances.

But Ben knew it wouldn't do him much good either way. The kitchen counter was a whole ten feet distant, and he was further disadvantaged by the fact that he was sitting down with the table between him and his objective. Even if by some miracle he could leap across to the knives, rip one out and hurl it accurately and fast enough to pin one of the two guys against the wall like a butterfly to a board, all the other one had to do was twitch a finger and the fight would be over as quickly as it had begun.

Ben forgot about the knives and switched his thoughts instead to the coffee mug in front of him. A solid piece of kiln-fired clay, with a bit of heft to it. As good as a cricket ball. A solid impact, well aimed, could shatter a nose or a cheekbone and put one enemy out of commission long enough to focus on the other. But then the other guy would still have ample time to pump four, five, six rounds into Ben. Same result.

So Ben forgot about that too, and considered the possibilities of evasion rather than resistance. The sliding glass door looking out onto the dusky back garden was a metre from his elbow. It had a metal frame and a metal handle with a key in it. No time to open the latch. He wondered how solid the glass was. What kind of an impact it would take to get through it. How badly a person might get cut by the jagged edges of the pane before managing to escape into the falling darkness. And what the odds were of all three of them getting through it before a shot was fired. Not great, that was for certain.

But even before Ben had given up on that option as well, two more men appeared in the back garden and came striding up to the glass window, carrying two more pistols down at their sides. Same make, same silencers. One of them rapped on the glass with the muzzle of his gun.

The Greyhound said to McCauley, 'Open it.' He spoke with an American accent. His voice was calm, almost casual. You didn't need to be jumpy and tense when you were holding all the cards. McCauley stood up and stepped over to the window to turn the key in the metal handle. The gunman who had rapped on the glass opened the latch and slid the door brusquely open, and he and his companion stepped inside.

At which point, whatever ideas Ben might have had about resisting the invasion were reduced to less than zero. In a situation like this, four guns were considerably worse than twice as hard to fight against than two. It wouldn't even count as a heroic death. It would be about as clever as trying to stop a runaway train by throwing yourself under the locomotive.

'Sit down,' the Greyhound said to McCauley, wagging his pistol at the empty chair. McCauley sat, pale-faced. Raul stared at the guns. Ben was perfectly immobile, his hands resting loosely on the table.

'Stay exactly where you are,' the Greyhound said. 'Hands on the table where I can see them. Palms down. Nobody moves. Nobody speaks. Is that understood?'

Ben said nothing. Not because he'd been ordered to be silent, but because there just didn't seem to be a lot to say. He remained still, and watched, and waited for whatever was going to come next.

The Greyhound stepped up to Ben. For an instant, Ben thought he was going to shoot him and his leg and back muscles tensed, ready to come spinning up out of the chair and trap the gun and break whatever bones were necessary to get it from the man's hand. He might go down, but he wouldn't go down alone.

But the Greyhound didn't shoot. He bent quickly and picked up Ben's green bag. Carried it over to the kitchen counter, undid the straps and checked inside. He gave Catalina's science files and computer a cursory look-over, appeared satisfied that he had what he wanted, then strapped the bag shut and slung it over his shoulder.

'Be careful with that,' Ben said. 'It's a valuable antique.'

'Shut up,' one of the others said.

The Rottweiler had his phone out and had stepped back towards the hallway to make a call. All he said was, 'S'done.' He stood with his big shoulders hunched over the phone for a moment as he listened, then ended the call and stepped over to the Greyhound. They had a brief whispered conversation. The Rottweiler pointed at McCauley and shook his head. The Greyhound shrugged impassively, then turned back towards the table and wagged his gun first at Raul, then at Ben.

'You and you, on your feet. Let's go. Not you,' he added for McCauley, who was confusedly getting up from his chair. 'You stay put.'

'I'm not going anywhere,' Raul said. 'You sons of whores will just have to shoot me.' The one who'd told Ben to shut up made a grab for Raul's shoulder. Raul slapped his hand away. 'Get your fucking paws off me.'

The Greyhound walked up to Raul and pressed the business end of his Glock silencer against his temple. 'You'll do as we say, or you'll die. Your choice.'

Raul hesitated for a second, then glanced at Ben. Ben was ninety-nine percent certain that they wouldn't shoot Raul. They wanted him for something. But a one percent chance was still a one percent chance. He gave Raul a look that said 'Be cool'. Raul seemed to understand. He stood up.

'You,' the Greyhound warned McCauley. 'Stay in that chair for ten minutes without moving. Call the police at any time, breathe a word to anyone about what you have seen here today, we will know about it and will come back for you. Am I clear?'

The last Ben saw of McCauley was a blanched face staring at them in bewilderment from the kitchen table as he and Raul were marched out of the room with gun muzzles in their backs. Ben was wondering why they'd been singled out from McCauley. But more than that, he was wondering why he himself was still alive. In Germany, the strategy had been clear: Ben was the expendable one, to be taken down. Suddenly, it seemed that they wanted him, too. Something had changed, but Ben couldn't imagine what.

Two of the men brushed past them in the hallway. One opened the front door, the other stepped outside to check the coast was clear, then motioned for the rest to follow. Ben and Raul were walked outside. Night was falling and the air was cold and heavy with dampness that swirled and drifted in amber haloes around the street lights and the lit-up windows of the street. Outside McCauley's garden gate was parked a plain black Hyundai crew-cab van that hadn't been there earlier, with a fifth man waiting at the wheel and the engine running.

Ben hesitated when he saw the van. The Rottweiler's big hand pressed against his back and shoved him forwards. Ben could have twisted the hand and snapped the bones in the man's forearm quicker than it took to jerk a trigger. He let himself be pushed towards the gate. The Greyhound opened up the crew-cab side door and tossed Ben's green bag inside. The one with the German accent walked to the back of the van and opened the rear doors. 'Inside,' the Rottweiler said, and this time it was hard steel Ben felt pressing against his back.

The cargo area of the Hyundai was bare metal inside, with nowhere to sit but the two facing wheel arches. Ben had ridden in the back of plenty of vans before. He should be used to it by now. 'This is the worst limo service I've ever seen,' he said to the Rottweiler.

The man didn't seem amused as he waved them inside with his gun. Ben sat on the hard, cold wheel arch. Now might be the time to light up one of those Mayfairs. Have a smoke, wait for them to get moving, then start planning a way to break out of the van and make their escape while it was stopped at a red light. It wasn't much of a plan.

And it turned out to be even less of a plan a second later, when the Rottweiler and one of his buddies clambered into the back of the Hyundai with them and produced two black cloth hoods. Ben sat and let himself be hooded. He heard Raul mutter a curse in Spanish. Then a gun was pressed to his temple as his hands were grabbed and his wrists fastened quickly and expertly together with something thin and strong that felt like a plastic cable tie.

So much for escape. Ben felt the rear suspension lighten as their captors jumped out, leaving them alone in the back. The doors slammed shut with a resonating clang. More noises as the men all piled into the van, doors closed and then they were speeding away.

Chapter Thirty-Nine

For the first half hour of the journey, the van's stop-start motion, bouncing and jolting over potholes and swaying left and right through frequent twists and turns, told Ben they must be cutting through the city. Then their progress smoothed out, the jerking and lurching stopped, and the vehicle maintained a steady speed.

It was cold in the back. Ben and Raul couldn't talk to one another easily, their voices muffled by their hoods and drowned out by the road and transmission noise that resonated through the bare metal shell. Like hostages and prisoners always do sooner or later, each man lapsed into the silence of his own separate world. Ben could only imagine what Raul must be thinking. He had plenty to ponder himself.

Ben's head was buzzing with questions, and a lot of them involved Mike McCauley. Was it just a coincidence that the armed men had turned up at the house at that particular moment? Was it safe simply to assume they'd been watching the place, or was there more to this? What if the journalist set a trap for them? Had he known they were going to turn up in London, and if so, how could he have known that? Was he more deeply involved in this thing than he was letting on? These people could have got to him. Or he could have been one of them, from the start. That could explain why they'd let him go. Ben could think of no other reason; and yet none of it seemed to add up.

He was still trying to make sense of the situation when the van finally slowed and braked to a halt. The engine went silent. Everything seemed very still.

'We've stopped,' said Raul's indistinct voice, sounding far away.

Ben listened and heard doors opening, and voices, and the sound of footsteps. Boots on concrete. Gusts of wind were buffeting the side of the van.

'Where are we? What's happening?' Raul said. His muffled voice was tinged with panic.

The rear doors squeaked open, and the van's suspension juddered with the weight of men clambering into the back. Rough hands grabbed Ben's arms and jerked him upright, hurting his tethered wrists. He didn't resist them. The sharp night air swirled over him as he was hauled out of the van. Hard ground under his feet. Through the heavy material of the hood, he could make out bright lights and formless shapes. Some kind of building loomed up behind the van, large and square and squat. More light shone out from inside, but he couldn't tell whether it was a house, or an office block, or an agricultural building.

He'd been wondering why they hadn't shot him yet. Maybe the time for that was now. He steeled himself for it. Every man had to die some time. It was just a question of why, and how, and when. The truth was, he'd always been ready. But he wouldn't die alone. That was the silent, grim promise he made to his captors.

But still they didn't shoot him. He could sense Raul's presence close by as the two of them were led from the van.

And he could hear something. A distinctive high-pitched whistling whoosh that seemed to grow in volume and drowned out the voices around him and the sound of the wind. It filled his ears and became deafening as he was led closer to it.

It was the noise of jet turbines.

The wide open space Ben and Raul had been delivered to was some kind of private airfield. The building was a hangar.

The blinking nose-, wing- and taillights of the stationary aircraft were visible through Ben's hood, as well as the interior glow from its single line of windows and open fuselage door. He could see it wasn't a large plane. A medium-sized business jet, like a Gulfstream G200 or a Learjet 85. And it appeared to be waiting for them.

Ben was held back as the men led Raul ahead of him to the boarding steps. The roar of the engines was building steadily. Evidently, someone was in a hurry to get out of here. Someone grabbed Ben's hands and he felt something hard and slim pass between his wrists; a quick sawing motion and the knife had sliced through the plastic tie. His hands were free. He rubbed his wrists where the bonds had bitten into the flesh. Then someone shoved him onward, and he gripped the handrail of the boarding steps and climbed up into the warmth of the aircraft. The roar of the engines was muted to a softly vibrating thrum as the fuselage hatch was closed behind him.

'Sit here, please,' said a voice.

Please? A few moments earlier, Ben had been getting ready for a bullet in the back of the head. He wondered at the sudden courtesy as he felt his way to the seat he was being guided towards, and lowered himself into it. Next, his hood was removed and he blinked at the sudden dazzle of the plane's brightly lit interior. The private jet was plushly done out in tan leather and highly figured wood panels. Something of a contrast to the inside of the van. This kidnapping had taken a turn for the stylish.

Gazing around him, Ben recognised the figures of the four men who'd taken them from McCauley's house. The fifth man who'd been at the wheel of the van seemed to have vanished. As had the guns that had been pointing at Ben and Raul earlier. If the men were still armed, the weapons were concealed under their jackets. Raul was already seated across the narrow aisle, hoodless and blinking in confusion. He and Ben exchanged looks.

'If this is the magical mystery tour, which one of you is Ringo?' Ben asked the four men.

'I apologise for the roughness of your treatment,' the Greyhound said. 'Please try to see it from our point of view. I'm afraid it was the only possible way of carrying out our orders.'

'Who are you people?' Raul demanded.

'All will be explained to you, when we land,' the Greyhound said.

Raul stared at him. 'Where are we being taken, asshole?'

'Again, that's not for me to say. You'll see for yourselves, a few hours from now. In the meantime, I'm instructed to make your flight a pleasant one. Can I offer you some refreshments?'

Ben laughed at the absurdity of it. None of this was doing much to answer the questions that had been filling his head since leaving McCauley's house. Something had changed, all right. He was completely without a clue as to what was happening.

'Go to hell,' Raul said, still staring.

The Greyhound smiled thinly. 'Fine. Then can I please ask you to buckle your seatbelts, as we're due to take off at any moment.'

Chapter Forty

They flew deep into the night. The Greyhound brought them each a plate of mixed cheese and tuna sandwiches, and a bottle of San Pellegrino mineral water. Ice and a thin slice of lemon. It was without a doubt the classiest abduction Ben had ever been a party to.

While Raul barely touched his food out of protest, the military spirit of 'eat when you can, sleep when you can' was too deeply ingrained in Ben for him not to finish everything on his plate. The water was pretty good too, although he might have relished something a little stronger.

The two of them communicated nothing between them above the occasional glance, conscious of the presence of the four men sitting a little way behind them towards the rear of the plane. Some time around midnight, the Greyhound got up and dimmed the cabin lights. Knowing that they'd get no more information out of their escorts and not wasting energy on trying to understand that which couldn't be understood, Ben sat quiet and still and gazed out of the dark window, seeing nothing but his own shadowy reflection in the glass. There was no way of knowing what direction they were flying in, or where they might be headed.

Glancing across the aisle, he saw that Raul was slumped

over in a fitful sleep. He closed his own eyes and let himself drift. Some time during the night, he had a long dream that consisted of an involved conversation with his sister Ruth. When he awoke, the dream was gone like a burst bubble, but it had left a tinge of strange emotions in him. Faint light was filtering into the cabin, the first glimmer of dawn ahead of them on the horizon. Ben looked at his watch and saw that it was still only 4 a.m., London time. To have skipped ahead a couple of time zones meant they were travelling east, chasing the rising sun.

The plane was flying low over an ocean that looked from above to be as dark and smooth as a lake of wine, just the occasional ripple flecked with crimson reds and golds of the approaching sunrise. To the east, Ben could see a cluster of small islands in the distance, still untouched by the light and nothing more than a featureless mound against the glow on the horizon. The seascape looked Mediterranean. A rough calculation of flight duration, times estimated cruising speed, taking into account their approximate direction, could have put them anywhere in an arc stretching from the Libyan coast off Tripoli, to Malta, to somewhere just beyond the heel of Italy.

As Ben watched the beginnings of the sunrise spreading over the ocean, the plane gently banked as if heading for the smallest of the islands, which lay separated by a few kilometres of water from its larger neighbour. He wondered why they were flying towards it. There didn't seem to be anything there.

But as the dark mound grew closer and details began to come into view, Ben was able to make out the shape of a lighthouse perched on the cliffs that overhung the northern end of the island. It looked like a miniature model from above. A round white stone tower, its tiny windows glinting red in the early light. At its foot was a cluster of white stone buildings that were the only habitation he could see.

The aircraft swooped lower, and they overflew the island. It was humped like a gigantic turtle shell rising up out of the sea, sparsely covered here and there with woodland intercut with exposed ridges of rock and what looked like a tiny road winding lengthwise across it, to connect the lighthouse complex with whatever lay at the island's southern extremity, not yet visible from the air. As the plane descended lower still and passed over, now the rest of the island came into view: a long, flat prominence lying close to sea level. The first thing Ben saw there was the graceful twin-masted schooner lying at anchor within a short outboard ride of the shore, where a narrow wooden jetty stretched from a little boathouse. The sailing yacht was a striking enough sight on its own; but what made him blink was the long, perfectly straight tongue of concrete skirting the edge of the island that he realised at second glance was an airstrip.

Ben estimated that the landing distance of a jet this size was about nine hundred metres, which Ben's eye for measurements told him the airstrip exceeded by just a few plane lengths. A neat fit. Then whoever owned the jet presumably owned the schooner, and probably the island too. They'd reached their destination. Ben felt a tingle of adrenalin, knowing that confrontation was coming.

The unseen pilot brought the aircraft around in a loop, approaching the island from the south. The sea rushed past below them as they dropped altitude. Ben caught a glimpse of the sailing yacht flashing by the windows. Then he felt the soft jolt of landing, and their rapid deceleration on the airstrip. The aircraft taxied to a stop and the pilot began shutting down the engines. Moments later, Ben and Raul were escorted from the hatch and onto the concrete strip.

The pilot emerged from the cockpit. Ben recognised him as the driver of the van that had taken them from McCauley's place.

The October early morning chill wrapped itself around them after the warmth of the aircraft. Raul looked at Ben, as if to say, 'What now?'

Ben made no reply. He looked around him. The sunrise was slowly brightening the sky, its glow bathing the island blood red. Perhaps ten kilometres away to the west, Ben could make out the eastern side of the nearest neighbouring island and the tiny breakers rolling into the foot of its cliffs.

Hearing the sound of vehicles approaching, he turned to see two soft-top Jeep Wranglers bouncing along the little road towards them. The Jeeps pulled up in tandem a few yards from the aircraft. Motioning towards the lead vehicle, the Greyhound said, 'They're waiting for you up at the house.'

Ben looked at Raul, and Raul looked at Ben. No point in asking questions. They'd get answers soon enough. And perhaps more.

The driver barely glanced at them as they got into the lead Jeep. He gunned the engine and they went roaring back up the narrow road, twisting through the trees, snaking their way back up the hill in the direction of the lighthouse. Ben twisted round to look behind them, and saw the second Jeep following with the four men inside. Then, as they cleared the brow of the hill, the lighthouse came back into view and the ocean beyond it, the smooth horizon flooded with glittering crimson streaks by the rising orb of the sun.

The Jeep continued across the island until it reached the lighthouse. The driver stopped the car, still without a word or a glance. The tower that had seemed so tiny from the air loomed over them, shining white against the red sky. Both it and the cluster of neighbouring smaller buildings were erected at the highest point of the cliff, with a sloping path down to the road. The second Jeep pulled up behind them as Ben and Raul climbed out. Two more identical vehicles were parked up by the lighthouse.

The adrenalin was pumping faster through Ben's system now. In no way was he reassured by the change in demeanour of their captors. Just because he couldn't see the guns, it didn't mean they weren't there. And it didn't mean he wouldn't be seeing them again, at any moment. He and Raul had been brought here for a reason. Things could be about to turn very nasty. Which was fine by Ben. He was ready for whatever came next.

They're waiting for you, the Greyhound had said. The moment had arrived. Now for some answers, Ben thought. All his senses on alert, he turned towards the lighthouse.

And saw the figure walking slowly towards them down the slope.

It was the shape of a woman, her outline darkly silhouetted against the sunrise. The ocean breeze caught her shoulder-length hair.

Raul was about to say something to Ben when he suddenly saw the woman too, and froze. A strangled sound came from his mouth, halfway between a cry of pain and an unintelligible mutter. He stood staring at her for a moment that seemed to hang in time forever. Then tears welled up in his eyes, and he rushed towards her with his arms open wide.

'Catalina!'

Chapter Forty-One

Ben stared at Catalina Fuentes. She was wearing jeans and a navy jumper, a far cry from the photos he'd seen of her. She was also about six times more attractive in real life. Her hair was trimmed a few inches shorter and dyed a few shades lighter, as if she'd been trying to alter her appearance. Most noticeably of all, it appeared that she certainly wasn't dead. Raul had been right all along.

'You're alive!' Raul yelled in Spanish, his voice cracking with emotion. 'Oh my God you're alive!'

Ben watched him run up the path towards her. She'd stopped walking and was just looking at her brother. Instead of embracing him, she suddenly lashed out with the flat of her hand and slapped him hard across the cheek with a sound that reached Ben's ears like the crack of a whip.

'*Eres un estúpido!*' she shouted.

Raul drew back as if he'd touched a high-voltage fence. He touched his fingers to his cheek where she'd slapped him. 'Why did you do that?'

'You shouldn't have come looking for me!' Catalina yelled at him in Spanish, taking an angry step towards him. 'Now you've ruined everything, you fool!'

It wasn't exactly the welcome Raul had expected. He was speechless with shock. Ben was almost as taken aback as he was. Raul stood blinking at her for a few seconds, then his shock burned away into anger and he started shouting back.

'*I've* ruined everything?! What the hell is all of this about? Have you any idea what you've done to our family, to your parents? You broke their hearts. Are you crazy? Tell me!'

'I'm not crazy,' Catalina said, tight-lipped. 'If you knew, you'd understand.'

'Then tell me!' Raul yelled. 'To begin with, tell me what the hell you're doing here on this rock in the middle of the ocean!'

Catalina's gaze shifted away from Raul and landed on Ben. 'Who's this with you?' she demanded.

Ben walked towards them and was about to introduce himself, but Raul did it for him. 'His name is Ben. He's been helping me to find you. It's thanks to him that I'm here.'

'Then he's a stupid idiot as well,' Catalina said. 'Does he speak Spanish?'

'*Sí*,' Ben said.

She crossed her arms and gave Ben a hostile glower. She looked a million miles from the terrified, furtive victim Ben had observed on the pawnbroker's security video footage back in Munich.

At that moment, a second figure emerged from the lighthouse and started making his way down the path towards them. He was ten or a dozen years older than Catalina, slim and well-groomed with a thick head of hair going elegantly silver. He was dressed as if he'd been about to take in a leisurely nine holes before breakfast, in chinos and a silk shirt with a V-necked cardigan to keep out the morning chill.

Raul raised an accusing finger at him. 'Oh, no. Please tell me I'm dreaming. Keller? What's *he* doing here?'

'This is his island,' Catalina said. 'He owns it.'

'I should have known that slimy bastard was behind this,' Raul growled, clenching his fists.

'You don't understand,' Catalina said. 'You have absolutely no idea, Raul.'

Keller reached them. The four stood facing one another, Ben at Raul's shoulder, Keller at Catalina's. Up close, Keller's face was lined, but tanned and handsome. His eyes were cool blue. They passed over Raul and he looked at Ben. 'Austin J. Keller the Third,' he said confidently, putting out his hand. His accent was Canadian, softened by years in Europe. 'And you are?'

Ben ignored the hand. 'Interested in hearing some explanations,' he said.

Keller stiffened, and the confidence in his eyes wavered momentarily. Catalina and Raul were still bristling at one another. Raul was shaking his head in disbelief, his face dark. Catalina looked ready to slap him again. Behind them, Keller's crew had got out of the Jeeps and were clustered beside them, watching from a distance and ready to intervene if needed.

'You already met my guys,' Keller said. Pointing at the Greyhound, he added, 'That's Bauer. He's my chief of security.' Then he pointed at the pilot. 'Avery, he's my Top Gun. Then there's Spencer, Willis, Emmert, Fulton and Griggs. They're all good guys.'

'You can tell the Magnificent Seven not to get any closer,' Ben said.

Keller stared at him for a second, then waved a discreet signal to his men, telling them to stand down. 'I think we'd all better go inside.'

The interior of the lighthouse was adapted into one of the most luxurious homes that Ben had ever seen, a circular open-plan mansion on numerous floors that must have cost millions to convert. The art and antiques were worth probably as much again. But then, Ben realised, millions were clearly nothing to a man who owned private islands and jets and could sail the world in his magnificent twin-masted schooner. So this was Austin Keller. The man whose name Raul Fuentes couldn't utter without the prefix 'That bastard'. The man who'd broken Catalina's heart. And now, it appeared, the man Ben and Raul had to thank for bringing them here. Ben was beginning to realise how mistaken his assumptions had been – but the truth seemed even stranger.

'So this is where you've been all along, is that right?' Raul said, still speaking Spanish and looking around him as if he could spit on the priceless Persian carpet under his feet. 'How nice for you.' Eyeing Keller with open dislike, he then switched to English to snort, 'Are we allowed to know where we are, exactly?

'The island of Icthyios, west of the Southern Sporades,' Keller said with something of a flourish. 'Karpathos a little to the south of us, Rhodes a touch further to the east. Our own little private haven, right where the Aegean meets the Sea of Crete. Eight and a half square kilometres. Mentioned in Ovid's *Metamorphoses*.'

Ben realised his location estimate was off, but only by about five hundred or so miles. 'And nobody lives here?'

'Nobody but us,' Keller said, proudly sweeping his arm.

'Icthyios,' Raul said. 'Isn't that some kind of skin disease?'

Keller flushed a shade darker and cleared his throat. He glanced at Catalina, then smiled and in a breezy tone said, 'You must be hungry. Some breakfast, perhaps?'

'Let's go,' Raul said to Catalina. 'We're getting out of this place.'

'Go where?' Keller asked, eyes widening.

'I was talking to my sister, if you don't mind.'

'I'm sorry things are like this,' Catalina said to Raul. 'What more can I say to you?'

'You could tell me what happened. That would be a start.'

'I wasn't in the car,' Catalina said.

'Obviously. I gathered that.'

'I drove all the way to Rügen Island, making sure nobody followed me. I took the car up onto the cliff path and parked a little way from the edge with the gearbox in neutral. Then I got out, and reached back in and put it back in drive, took off the parking brake, and I stood back and watched it roll off the edge.'

Catalina's eyes clouded thickly with tears as she spoke. 'You want to know the last thing I said before I did it? I said, "Forgive me, Raul." Because I knew how badly I was going to hurt you, and everyone else that I love. I can hardly stand the guilt, living with what I did to you all. But I did it for a reason, Raul. You weren't supposed to come looking for me. This is all messed up. You've compromised my whole plan.'

Raul was crying, too, as mixed emotions of relief and anger finally got the better of his self-control. 'Your *plan*? What kind of plan is it to pretend to your family that you didn't even want to go on living? Was that your idea, or do we have this guy to thank for it?' Raul jabbed a finger towards Keller without looking at him. 'I mean, we all know he's this oddball recluse or whatever he's supposed to be, and he was always pressuring you to run off and hide away someplace in one of his retreats with him. I thought that was all over and done with, years ago. I thought you were stronger than this. How could you do it?'

'I am not an oddball recluse,' Keller said, indignant. 'I just value my privacy, is all.'

'You're getting this completely wrong, Raul,' Catalina said. 'Austin had nothing to do with it. Nothing at all. I'd never intended to involve him, but then I needed a safe place to go, and he offered to bring me here. Up until that moment I acted alone, just me, nobody else, and it was the hardest decision I've ever had to make. You have to believe that hurting you, hurting our parents, was the last thing on earth I would ever have chosen to do. But I had no choice.'

'You trusted *him*,' Raul said, throwing a look at Keller. 'But you couldn't trust me, your own brother?'

'I did what I had to do,' Catalina said.

'What have you got yourself into? Who are these people who are after you?'

Catalina turned a little pale. 'You know about them?'

'Of course I know about them.'

'How? Why?'

'Because they tried to kill me too,' Raul said. 'They had guns. They kill people, that's what they do.'

Catalina was too stunned to reply, so Ben spoke to her for the first time. 'Actually, that's not quite what happened,' he said. 'Whoever these people are, they were trying to kidnap your brother, to extract information from him that would help them find you. You're in a lot of trouble, Miss Fuentes.'

Catalina stared at Ben as if seeing him for the first time. 'They tried to kidnap Raul?' she asked in a shaky voice.

'They were professional gunmen,' Ben said. 'The best money can buy.'

'Then how—?'

'How did we get away?' Raul said. 'Because they weren't the best. Ben is the best. I would be dead now, if he hadn't been there.'

Catalina didn't take her tear-filled eyes off Ben. 'I'm sorry, but I don't understand. Who *are* you? How do you know my brother?'

'He's just a guy I met in a bar,' Ben said.

Catalina stared a little longer, then another thought hit her. 'Oh, God. And this happened—?'

'In Germany,' Raul said. 'At your observatory. We had some problems there.'

'Your friend Kazem is dead,' Ben told her. He couldn't think of a gentler way to break it. 'I'm sorry. He didn't suffer,' he added.

Whether Catalina believed his lie or not, the news left her winded. Suddenly looking years older, she staggered to the nearest armchair and fell into it. Keller hurried to her side and clutched her arm as she buried her face in her hands and didn't move for a long minute. Then she looked up, her eyes wet with tears and pain etched deeply into the beauty of her face. She looked at Raul, and in a steady voice she said, 'It's because of you that Kazem is dead. If you hadn't come looking for me, everything would have been all right. I had everything planned. That place was a *secret*, Raul, and you must have led them there.'

Raul's face fell. 'What was I supposed to do?' He muttered it a couple of times, then went quiet.

Catalina stood up and took his hands in hers. Squeezing them tightly, she kissed his cheek where she'd slapped him. 'You're my twin brother. I love you, and I forgive you, like I'd forgive you for anything. You weren't to know what would happen. It's as much my fault as it is yours.' Turning to Ben, she said, 'I thank you for protecting Raul, whoever you are. I can never repay you for that.'

'If it's money you want—' Keller began.

Ben silenced him with a look. He said to Catalina, 'I don't want your money. I want just one thing. I need you to tell me what this is about.'

Chapter Forty-Two

'It's my business,' said Catalina Fuentes. 'Not yours.'

Ben looked at her and could see the same stubborn streak in her that he'd seen often enough in her brother to realise now that it must be a family trait. It made him think of himself, and Ruth, and Jude. Maybe if you traced the ancestral lines back far enough, you'd find Hope and Fuentes DNA mixed up together in the most hardheaded, hotblooded part of the human gene pool.

'Not any more,' Ben said. 'More people are involved in this now. You can't undo that.'

'Ben helps people, Catalina,' Raul said. 'You need to let him help you.'

'He's quite an enigma, your friend,' Catalina snapped back at him. 'But I don't need anyone's help, thanks.'

'Sinclair is dead, and Lockhart,' Ben told her. 'Ellis ran. For all we know, they got him too. Whatever it is that you were all involved in, you're the last one of the group.'

'You wouldn't even understand.'

'About your solar research?' Ben said. 'About William Herschel and the price of wheat? You're right. Then how about enlightening us?'

Catalina narrowed her lustrous brown eyes at him. 'You know about Herschel?'

'And I know what kind of people are coming after you,' Ben said. 'The kind that won't stop until they get the job done. You think you can handle them all by yourself?'

'She isn't by herself,' Keller said, stepping close to Catalina and putting an arm around her shoulders. 'Not any more. I have people working right now on a whole new identity for her. She'll be safe here with me, forever.'

Ben noticed the way Catalina squirmed out of his grip. Austin Keller might have seen the situation as an opportunity to rekindle their relationship, but it seemed that, so far, things hadn't quite gone his way. From the hurt expression on Keller's face, Ben could tell his feelings were sincere.

'We talked about this, Austin,' she said. 'I'm not going to stay on this island for the rest of my life. This was a temporary measure, nothing more.'

Keller raised his hands. 'What, you think you can go back? How's that gonna work, when you're supposed to be dead? Jesus, I mean, the whole suicide thing was your idea. One-way ticket, remember?'

'I am aware of that,' Catalina replied, giving him an icy look. She sighed, then walked over to an antique sideboard, opened it and took out a bottle of scotch. Bowmore single malt, eighteen years old. Ben noticed that, too.

'Little early in the day, don't you think?' Keller said, frowning. 'How about coffee instead?'

'I need it,' she said.

'Me too,' Raul said. 'Ben?'

'I rarely touch the stuff before breakfast,' Ben said. 'But I'll make an exception.'

Catalina poured three measures into cut-crystal tumblers and sat back in the armchair, cradling her glass pensively. She took a sip, then looked up at Raul. 'You're right,' she said. 'I owe you an explanation. I've managed to let you become involved in this, and you must be wondering how you ended up here and what on earth this is all about. So I'll tell you.'

Raul perched on a chair opposite her. Ben leaned against the wall, took a swallow of the whisky. The Bowmore's rich, deep, smoky aroma filled his nose. Eighteen years spent maturing in oak casks. Definitely best enjoyed first thing in the morning on an empty stomach. He took another swallow and waited for what Catalina had to say.

'It all happened so suddenly,' she said. 'There was so little warning. The first inkling I got that something was wrong wasn't until early July, in London. I was there to meet with a publisher to talk about a new book. One that will never be written now, obviously.' She pulled a grim smile and took another sip of her drink. 'I arrived in London on July third, a day early, to spend some time with a girlfriend I hadn't seen for a while. I booked into the Dorchester, as usual when I'm in town. That evening, the two of us attended a private party that was being thrown by some people she knew at a club in Kensington. The normal kind of thing, everyone getting drunk on Pimm's and champagne and lots of annoying celebrities kissy-kissing and pretending they wouldn't cut each other's throats if they had the chance. Not long after we'd arrived, my friend went off with this guy she was flirting with, and left me hanging. I was kind of annoyed about it, and I would have gone straight back to the Dorchester then, if it hadn't been for the guitarist.'

'The guitarist?' Raul said.

'The musical entertainment for the evening. Just one guy on solo classical guitar, sitting on a stool in the corner, very good-looking, Hispanic, dark, long curly hair. And he could *play*. Great tone, excellent technique. You know how much I love the guitar. He had the whole repertoire down – Granados, Villa-Lobos, Rodrigo. I stood there for quite a while watching and listening. That was when this older man came up to me and introduced himself. I had never met him before, but he's quite well known in certain circles. His name is Maxwell Grant.'

'I've heard that name,' Raul said.

Keller let out a loud grunt. 'Yeah, I'll bet you have. That degenerate asshole.'

'Let me tell it, Austin,' Catalina said. She went on: 'Maxwell Grant is one of the biggest investors in Green energy in Europe. Billionaire, philanthropist, entrepreneur, champion for the environment, a leading force behind the development of alternative power technologies. I'd read a lot about him and it was interesting to meet him. He came across as charming, very cultivated and witty. A real English gentleman. At least, that's what I thought to begin with. We talked about all kinds of things: politics, and ecology, and renewable energy, and music, and travel. He told me how he loved all things Italian, and had a villa in Calabria. He was very friendly, even gave me his personal business card.'

She paused, frowning as if the memory was physically uncomfortable to recall. 'Then he said something very strange to me. I don't mean that he started hitting on me, or anything like that. I get that all the time and I can handle it. This was different. It was weird.'

'Strange how?' Raul asked.

'Well, while we were chatting, I was still half listening to the guitarist. At a certain point, he started playing a study by Tárrega, *Recuerdos de la Alhambra*. It's one I play myself, but I'd never heard it sound so good before. Hearing it distracted me from the conversation, and Grant noticed. That's when he said it to me.'

Raul blinked. 'Said what?'

'He said, "He plays it well, but you play it better. You have the tremolo technique mastered perfectly." Just like that. Looking me right in the eye.'

'And?'

Catalina raised her eyebrows impatiently at her brother. 'And, how could he have possibly known that?'

'I don't know,' Raul said dismissively. 'You're famous, you're in the media, people know things about you, all kinds of details about whatever you do.'

'That's the whole point, in a way,' Catalina replied. 'When you're famous, it's like living inside a glass cage. Every shred of your life is photographed, written about, analysed, dissected. As much as the vultures can get a hold of. So you always keep something back, just for yourself. Private things that nobody will ever intrude on. A little corner that's secret and sacred, that you never reveal to a soul. Not even to your blood. For me, part of that was always music. I've never played guitar in front of anybody. Never even told anyone about it. It was for me, and me alone. Where I go to unwind and forget everything. My retreat. My sanctuary.'

Keller said, 'I can relate to that.'

'Be quiet, Austin. What I'm saying is, there is absolutely no way that this Maxwell Grant could know I even play the guitar, let alone whether I ever tried to master *Recuerdos de la Alhambra*. Let alone again how good my tremolo technique is. I thought, "Is he confusing me with someone else? Is he drunk?" He'd certainly had a few glasses of champagne by then. But there was no doubt he knew what he was saying.'

Raul was frowning. 'Sister, I came a long way to find you, and you're talking to me about guitars.'

'Let her talk,' Ben said. He was listening hard and trying to anticipate where her story was leading. He liked her scientific-minded approach and the way she systematically laid out every piece of information. In Ben's experience, there was no such thing as trivial detail when people were trying to kill you.

Catalina flashed a look at Ben that said, 'Thank you'. But Raul wasn't satisfied. 'You didn't ask him what he meant by it?' Raul asked.

Catalina nodded. 'I said, "Excuse me?" He turned all red and started trying to talk his way out of it, saying, "Oh, I imagine you'd be much better, being so talented" and all this kind of bullshit. Then he tried to change the subject by talking about how much he loved classical guitar, tried to take it up when he was younger, this whole stupid story. He looked very embarrassed, and angry with himself, as if he'd let something slip out that he shouldn't have said. But it was too late to retract it. I was really unnerved, and so I very quickly made my excuses, and left. I went back to the hotel and spent the whole night wondering about it. The morning of the fourth, I had my scheduled meeting with the publishers, which I just kind of sleepwalked through because I hadn't shut my eyes all night, and then I flew back to Munich. Nothing more happened until the following day, when I was out getting some groceries. That's when I noticed the car.'

Chapter Forty-Three

'Car?' Raul said.

Catalina nodded. 'Following me, in the street.'

'What colour was it?' Ben asked her.

'Dark. Metallic grey, I think.'

'What make?'

'I don't really know cars that well. It might have been a BMW. It was a big saloon car. Why are you asking?'

'Go on,' Ben said.

'They weren't the usual photographers chasing me around. This was different, and I was scared. I ran down an alley that was too narrow for the car. Two men got out and started walking fast after me. I ran. My heart was thumping like crazy. I was certain they were coming after me. For what purpose, I didn't even want to imagine. Then, by a miracle, I spotted an empty taxicab coming by and I managed to wave it down, and got the driver to drive randomly around half of Munich before I finally let him bring me home. Even then, I kept thinking about what Maxwell had said. By now, I was absolutely sure that something sinister was going on, and somebody was bugging my apartment. How else could Grant have known all that about my guitar playing?'

'But why?' Raul said, bewildered. 'Why would anybody

bug your apartment? And what's this guy from the party, this Grant, got to do with it?'

Catalina held up a hand to shush him. 'Just listen, okay? I'll explain. I was so freaked out, I didn't know what to do. I kept thinking about Grant and what he'd said to me. Was it just a coincidence that he was at the party? Or was he there because I was? What could that mean, that I was being followed? Targeted? Had someone sneaked into my apartment when I wasn't there, and planted listening devices? Hidden cameras, even? I spent the whole day searching, but I couldn't find anything. I felt as if I was being watched all the time. It was so creepy, I couldn't bear to be there alone at night, so I packed a bag and slipped out. If anyone was following me, I had to give them the slip. I've never ridden in so many buses and taxicabs in my life. Place to place, all over the city, until I was sure nobody was behind me. Hours later, I turned up at the Mandarin Oriental wearing my blonde disguise, and took a room under the name Carmen Hernandez. They probably thought I was a high-class prostitute, looking like that. The next day I called a firm in Munich who specialise in surveillance detection, and arranged for one of their experts to sweep my apartment for bugs.'

'This was July sixth,' Ben said. He was counting off the days. There were only ten of them to go before Catalina's car dropped into the Baltic Sea.

She nodded. 'But the bug people said they didn't have anyone available until the eighth. Talk about German efficiency. The same day, I contacted Mike McCauley at his newspaper offices.'

'Posing as Carmen Hernandez again,' Raul said.

'I suppose he told you about our meeting three days later in Munich?'

'He told us everything.'

'It was a long time to wait. I kicked my heels the whole of the seventh in my hotel room. Then, late morning on the eighth, I was just about to set off to meet the bug people at my apartment when I got the call from Jim Lockhart, telling me . . .' Her words trailed off and she took another quick sip of whisky.

'Telling you that your mutual colleague, Dougal Sinclair, and his entire expedition team had just been killed in Greenland,' Ben said.

Catalina looked at him. 'You know a lot.'

'All except what this is about,' he replied.

'Does Mike McCauley have no idea?' she asked.

'If he does, he's the best liar I've ever come across.'

'I could have revealed everything to him that day in Munich, but I chose not to. By then I was beginning to understand what was going on. I knew we were in danger.'

'Then the next day, Lockhart was killed,' Ben said.

'And when I tried to call Steve Ellis, he wouldn't answer his phone. First I thought the worst had happened to him, then I saw the message on his website and realised that he'd run. That's when I knew I was going to have to do the same. They were hunting us down one by one. My only hope of cheating them was to disappear. So I started making my plans, working them out down to the finest detail. I had to be extremely careful, to make it work and not to get caught in the process. The first thing I did was leave my Porsche hidden in an underground car park, where nobody would find it.'

'Next you went to your doctor,' Ben said. 'You told him the old feelings of depression were coming back, and that you needed medication.'

Catalina cocked an eyebrow at him. 'You do know a lot,

mystery man. That's right. I put on quite a show for him, too. So many tears, he was almost weeping too. How could he resist filling out a nice prescription for the damsel in distress? Then I sneaked back to my apartment. That was the scariest part. I was terrified one of them would be there waiting to murder me. But nobody was. I slipped inside and planted the drugs, where I knew they would be found by the police. Of course, first I flushed a lot of pills down the toilet, to make it look as if I'd been taking them like there was no tomorrow, literally. What better way to lend credence to my suicide?'

'I can't believe you could plan it like this,' Raul said. 'It was so cold, so detached.'

'I'm a scientist,' Catalina replied. 'Cold and detached is what I do. But don't think this was easy for me. While I was trying so hard to be methodical, at the same time it ripped my heart out, knowing the step I was about to take. Next, I knew I was going to need money. But for my scheme to work, I couldn't afford to leave a glaring clue like a large bank withdrawal just days before my death. There had to be another way to raise some cash.'

'That's the easy part,' Keller cut in, grinning.

'Not for me, not in that moment,' she said, firing him a look. 'Coming to you for help wasn't part of my plan then. So,' she resumed, 'while I was in the apartment I gathered my most valuable pieces of jewellery. The following day, I slipped out of the hotel for the last time and took a very roundabout route to this pawnshop I remembered passing, where I got what pathetic sum of money that nasty little man would give me for my beautiful things. I couldn't even afford to pay the hotel bill. From the pawnshop, I took another roundabout route in more buses and taxis back to where my car was hidden, and drove away from Munich without anyone seeing me. Four days later, I was standing on the edge of a cliff on Rügen Island, watching the car fall into the sea with me supposedly inside it. And then I was alone. More alone than I'd ever been in my life before.'

'You didn't have to be,' Raul said. 'You could have come to me. Instead you went to him.' He pointed again at Keller.

'In case you hadn't noticed,' Keller said, 'I have the manpower and the resources to keep her safe.'

Raul glared at him. 'I'm her brother. Nobody would protect her like her own family. Not even you.'

'Oh, Raul,' Catalina said. 'You know I wanted to. But how could I bring danger to you? Austin's right. His men are all experienced security personnel.'

Ben could see Raul was getting angry. The last thing anyone needed was Keller laid out flat on the floor from one of the Spaniard's formidable punches. Keller, least of all. Putting a hand on Raul's shoulder he said, 'Go easy. She panicked, nothing more. Don't take it personally.'

Catalina threw up her hands. 'It's true, I admit it. Everything had happened so fast, I hadn't had time to even begin to imagine what it would feel like afterwards. It didn't hit me until I was walking away from the cliff. Suddenly here I was, except I wasn't me any more. I was completely cut off from everything I'd been, everything I had, everyone I knew. Heartbroken and frightened, a fugitive, having to hide my face from the world. I spent my first night in a cheap hotel, worrying whether anyone would recognise me through my disguise. I was even afraid to eat a proper meal, because I kept thinking about how long my money was going to have to last. I didn't sleep for a second that night, even though I was exhausted. I kept working all those questions over and over in my head. Would these people fall for my ploy? Had I missed anything? Had I made any mistakes, left any evidence? The tiniest error, and they might see right through it, and all this would have been for nothing. If they came after me, they'd catch me even more easily than before. I couldn't hide out in expensive hotels any longer. I didn't even have a car. I was still alive, but—'

'But you were beginning to regret your actions,' Ben said. 'You've been regretting them ever since.'

Catalina eyed Ben curiously, as if wondering how he could see inside her thoughts. 'Yes, I admit that too,' she answered after a beat. 'I rushed into it all too fast. I was too busy planning the details to see the bigger picture. In retrospect, it could have been a mistake.'

'No, babe, you did the right thing,' Keller said.

Ben saw the irritated flash in her eye at being called 'babe', and wondered about the relationship between the two. He considered Keller for a moment. The Canadian didn't seem like a bad guy. He was obviously highly protective of her. Then again, all this was working out nicely for him.

Ben turned to Keller and said, 'So – these expert security guys of yours. You had them watching McCauley's place in London in case the bad guys would turn up there, didn't you? He was the bait.'

Keller was about to reply, but Catalina did it for him. 'I didn't mean it to be that way. It was Austin's idea. He convinced me that it was the only sure way to tell if Grant's people believed I was dead or not. If they hadn't fallen for the deception, then sooner or later they'd come for him.'

Ben smiled. 'Then what, you'd have let them kill the guy?'

'My men are better than to let that happen,' Keller said.

'Don't count on it,' Ben replied.

'The idea was to try and gather some kind of incriminating evidence to use against Grant,' Catalina said. 'It was the only way to prove for certain he was involved, and why.'

'Flimsy,' Ben said. 'For a start, it's unlikely that hired hitters would even know who was paying them. Did you see that work in some third-rate movie you produced, Keller?'

'You have any better ideas?' Keller demanded.

'In the event, it turned out differently,' Catalina said. 'When they saw two men turn up at McCauley's place they photographed you on your way in, and emailed the images to us here. I couldn't believe it was Raul, searching for me and putting himself in danger. I had to do something to get you away from there.'

Raul gave Keller a dark grin. 'You're lucky you're not having to recruit another bunch of goons right now.' He pointed at Ben. 'This guy here, he could have taken them out, just like—'

'All right,' Ben interrupted him, then turned to Catalina, who was watching him with the same intense curiosity as before. 'So here we are in protective custody on Austin's cosy island retreat. Safe as houses. And you still haven't told us what this is all about, but I can guess.'

'Then guess,' she said.

'I think you already have a pretty clear idea why this Maxwell Grant is involved,' Ben said.

Catalina smiled. 'So do you, by the sound of it.'

'Two astronomers, one a solar physicist and one an astro-glaciologist, ganged up with a climatologist and an Antarctic oceanography expert. Just a little rag-tag team of maverick scientists, apparently under fire from one of the richest and most powerful players in the environmentalist lobby. That's what you're suggesting, if I'm not mistaken.'

'You don't have to be a genius to figure it out, do you? Did I forget to mention that Grant is also the founder and chairman of ISACC, the International Society for Action on

Climate Change, which attracts gigantic funding from governments all over the world?'

'The four of you must have stirred things up quite a bit.'

'That would be an understatement,' she said. 'When you consider what's at stake. Our future. The fate of our planet. Not to say the multi-billion-dollar industry run and promoted by the likes of Maxwell Grant. And the biggest scientific fraud of all time.'

Chapter Forty-Four

'Hold on a minute,' Raul burst out after a stunned pause, staring at Catalina as if he'd never seen her before. '*That's* what this over? Green politics? The environment? Seriously? You're *climate change deniers*?'

Again, Ben remembered the poster on Raul's wall back in Frigiliana. The polar bear cub stranded on the melting ice floe. He was looking at his sister as if she'd just finished bludgeoning it to death, the bloody club still in her hand.

'Don't call me that,' Catalina replied. 'It's the most idiotic and meaningless term. To deny the existence of climate change would be like denying basic principles of physics. Like denying Kepler's laws of planetary motion, or general relativity.'

Raul flung up his arms. 'Okay. I'm confused. What, then?'

'I'm saying, of course climate change exists,' Catalina explained. 'It always has; the climate has always changed. But I'm also saying that climate change, contrary to everything you've probably ever heard in the media, from politicians and even from scientists, categorically has nothing whatsoever to do with carbon emissions or any other kind of human involvement. And as for this global warming we're forever hearing about . . .' Catalina rolled her eyes. 'If you believe that, Raul, then I have a few thousand acres on the moon that I could sell you. The fact, which even government agencies like NASA and the National Oceanic and Atmospheric Administration have tacitly had to admit, is that there *is* no global warming. The Earth's climate hasn't warmed up for nearly twenty years. Even if it had, we're not the least bit responsible. You've been sold a lie, brother.'

'Catalina, are you crazy? Everybody knows this stuff. It's settled science.'

She shrugged. 'So they say. And like lots of people, I passively accepted it for a long time. While I got on with the business of helping advance our knowledge of helioseismology, I trusted my fellow scientists in their own specialised disciplines to get on with their bit. If the climatologists said we were getting warmer, then okay, we were getting warmer. If they said it was because we were pumping too much greenhouse gas into the atmosphere, fine. I accepted that too. Until, one day, I opened my eyes.'

'Thanks to Herschel?' Ben said.

A little smile tugged at the corner of her lips. 'Wow, maybe you *are* a genius. That's right, thanks to Herschel. Before I got the job on the TV series, he was just a name to me, one of a long, long list of historical astronomers. Discoverer of Uranus and its moons, along with moons of Saturn. The first to realise the existence of infrared radiation, and a lot more besides. As well as being rather a good classical composer. A very clever man. But I had no idea at the time how much he would influence me. That was my epiphany. Everything snowballed from that moment onwards.'

'Maybe not such a good thing, as it turned out,' Ben said.

Catalina shook her head fiercely. 'Knowledge is always worthwhile. Always. No matter what.'

'Even if it gets you killed?' ·

'But humans are destroying the world,' Raul said. 'Who

can deny that? Look at the pollution. The rivers, the oceans. Look at the deforestation. The heavy industry. Oil. Mining. Tearing fossil fuels out of the ground. Wrecking our environment everywhere you turn.'

'It's true,' Catalina replied. 'In so many ways, humans are extremely bad news for this planet. You don't have to persuade me of that. In fact, I'd consider myself just as much of an ecologist as anyone. Somewhere down the line, our species fell completely out of tune with nature. From prehistory to modern times we've gone from being just another animal species, to being the single greatest biological scourge of the Earth. We proliferate, we consume, we pollute, we destroy. No other living creature fouls its own environment in this reckless, insane way.'

'So what's the argument?' Raul said.

'The argument is one that people should actually be very thankful for,' Catalina told him. 'Because, for all our malignant destructiveness, human beings are simply too small and insignificant to be able to wreak the kind of fundamental planet-altering harm that could bring about a lasting and catastrophic effect on Earth's climate. The belief that our species is capable of wielding power on that scale is like some kind of Freudian God complex, a delusion of grandeur. It's like when they talk seriously about terraforming Mars for the human race to colonise, as if our technology gave us the divine means to wave our wand at another planet and create some kind of new Genesis.'

She shook her head. 'It's pure *Star Trek* fantasy. Even if we could figure out a way to convert the atmosphere of Mars to support human life, and then raise the temperature above an uninhabitable minus fifty-five degrees centigrade, you then have the minor challenge of developing a technology that could prevent Martian radiation from cooking the astronauts who tried to settle there. That's just for starters. And that's only our next-door neighbour in the solar system. Who do we think we are? Even more insane was the plan that a bunch of NASA engineers hatched a few years ago to use asteroids to shunt Earth into a different orbit, further from the sun, to stop the planet from over-heating. Simple science, they called it. No problem, boys, let's get out the cosmic tug boats and just tow her over here a few thousand miles where it's cooler. Oh, and possibly render the planet uninhabitable while we're at it.'

'Okay,' Raul said. 'But what about the CO_2?'

Catalina shrugged. 'What about it? It's the stuff humans breathe out and plants breathe in. It's not poison.'

'Well, according to everything I've read and heard, it's the greenhouse gas that creates global warming. And we're pumping it out like crazy.'

'CO_2 is *a* greenhouse gas,' Catalina said. 'It's not *the* greenhouse gas. In fact, its effects are pretty inconsequential compared to those of, say, water vapour, which is naturally given off by our oceans. CO_2 is really not a big deal. If it were such a warming influence, then how come Mars, whose atmosphere is almost entirely composed of CO_2, is such a freezing cold planet?'

'Because it's further from the sun?' Ben ventured.

Catalina cocked an eyebrow and pointed at him, clicking her tongue.

'Wait a minute,' Raul said, unconvinced. 'I thought all this had been proved. CO_2 emission levels are rising to unprecedented levels on Earth, along with our temperatures. That's a clear and obvious correlation. If we don't cut our output and change how we live, we'll continue to heat up the planet. Right?'

'Fine,' Catalina replied. 'By all means, let's change the

way we live. Let's all become less reliant on electricity and oil, for a start. That definitely gets my vote. God forbid that we should contemplate drastically cutting the birth rate as a means of curbing galloping overpopulation, while we're at it. The planet can only benefit from that, but not in the way everybody has been conned into thinking. Why? Because cutting CO_2 emissions won't change the climate one iota, due to one slight flaw in the theory.'

'Which is?'

'That it's the wrong way round,' she said. 'Back to front. Upside down, whichever way you look at it. Claiming that high atmospheric CO_2 levels lead to high temperatures is what's known, scientifically speaking, as confusing correlation with causation. Put simply, CO_2 levels rise *as a result* of heat, not the converse. When the planet is warmer, carbon dioxide is released from the oceans into the atmosphere, as an after-effect. Like when a bruise appears on your flesh a few days after a knock. Can we say that the bruise caused the knock?'

'Of course not,' Raul said irritably.

'There's another element of the equation that's been largely ignored, which is the time dimension. The process doesn't happen instantly. As we know from ice core research, it takes between about eight hundred to a thousand years for warmer temperatures to show up as raised CO_2 levels in the atmosphere. In other words, the levels we measure now are nothing more than a record of something that happened many centuries ago.'

'But—'

'I know it's not easy, hearing the truth,' Catalina said. 'Not when your head has been filled with lies from every direction.'

'You're saying it's *all* wrong?'

'Not all,' she said. 'Some of it is true. Nobody disputes that atmospheric CO_2 levels are currently quite elevated, for instance. Not that they're doing any harm. On the contrary, our plant friends are loving it, and pumping out lots of nice oxygen in response. But if we trace those high CO_2 levels back eight hundred or so years to see where they originated, what we find is a neat echo of the Medieval Warm Period.'

Raul looked at her. 'The what?'

'I'm not surprised you haven't heard of it,' Catalina said. 'There are people out there doing all they can to bury it, play it down, even erase it from the history books. You might say it's an inconvenient truth. But we have clear evidence that for five centuries, from around the year 800 to 1300, the world entered a cycle of climate warming that brought about tremendous positive change in Europe and elsewhere. After struggling through a long and bitter period of glacial climate, they suddenly found themselves enjoying a time of idyllic summers and largely mild winters that brought with them rich agricultural harvests, rocketing food production, booming trade, expanding populations and a new era of optimism that generated an explosion of arts and culture, from painting to architecture. It was so warm in England that vineyards flourished and merchants started exporting enormous amounts of wine to France, of such good quality that the French viniculture industry tried to have it legally blocked as it was undercutting their own product. Can you imagine that happening now? They were even producing wine in Norway, and in Prussia as far north as fifty-five degrees. The Black Forest had vineyards up to two thousand five hundred feet above sea level, much higher than today. Crops were growing in Alpine valleys that we wouldn't be able to grow there now.

'Did you ever wonder how Greenland got its name?'

Catalina went on. 'After all, the place is a vast freezer. That's why Dougal Sinclair was carrying out research there, because Greenland ice core samples are so dense that they offer even better resolution for analysis than samples from Antarctica. How could one of the coldest, iciest countries on Earth ever be called green? Is it some kind of a joke? Not at all. Greenland was so named by the Viking chief Erik the Red, for the fertile and lush valleys that his people were able to settle and farm for three hundred years during the Medieval Warm Period, as far north as Upernavik. It wasn't until after about the year 1300 that the climate changed again. The Vikings' crops began to fail and their livestock starved or froze, forcing them to subsist on fish and seal meat until even that became impossible because of growing sea ice. The Norse settlers soon died out completely, as Greenland reverted back to what it is today.

'So the big question is,' she went on, 'what caused the warming cycle? Where were all the cars back then? And where was all the industry, burning fossil fuels and churning out carbon emissions? How could such a thing possibly happen without humans causing it? Surely, it couldn't have been a natural cycle?' Catalina let out a humourless laugh.

'But it couldn't have been warmer than it is in modern times,' Raul protested. 'Right now is the warmest century on record. Isn't it? That's what we're always hearing.'

'Depends on which records you look at,' Catalina said. 'The accurate ones that don't reflect anything of the sort, or the ones that have been cherry-picked and distorted to fit with the lie of anthropogenic climate change. All kinds of tricks are used to manipulate the data to show warming trends where there simply aren't any. There have been plenty of exposed cases where deliberate "adjusting" – read "tampering" – of temperature figures from weather stations has produced an apparent rise, while the original readings show an actual decline. For instance in New Zealand, where unadjusted data showing no warming trend at all between 1850 and 1998 was fixed, suddenly giving a warming trend of 2.3 degrees for the same time period.'

'Oh, come on,' Raul said. 'They wouldn't do that.'

'Don't kid yourself,' Catalina replied. 'They do it all the time. Take the Arctic. It warmed up rapidly in the 1930s and '40s, before temperatures there dropped again in the '60s and '70s. The record has been "adjusted" by lowering past temperatures so that today's can look higher, giving the impression that it's warmer now. Whereas in fact it was warmer eighty years ago.'

'That's insane,' Raul said.

'Insane is one word for it. Blatant fraud might be a better description. In 1999, official records showed that the years 1921, 1931, 1934 and 1958 were all much warmer than 1998, when those figures were compiled. In the case of 1934, it was actually a whole degree Fahrenheit warmer. But if you consult those same records now, they'll tell you that 1934 was 0.1 degrees cooler than 1998, in line with the warming agenda. Which can only mean one thing. Somebody went in there and altered the figures to make them fit the theory. Does that sound like good science to you?'

'I can't believe it,' Raul said, staring at her.

'It gets even better,' she replied. 'What most people don't realise is that only about twenty percent of the world's surface is even monitored by weather stations. Around 1990, the number of stations worldwide was more than halved, with the remaining ones tending to be concentrated in built-up areas affected by the urban heat island effect.'

'And what's that?'

'The term refers to the fact that cities and other densely

inhabited places tend to be slightly warmer than less populated rural or wilderness areas. The difference can be considerable, up to two degrees Celsius even within just a few miles. In other words, by decommissioning the temperature monitoring stations in those more remote locations, the results were actively skewed in favour of the warming hypothesis. To make matters worse, many of the active stations are in places like airports, in close proximity to large areas of asphalt and concrete that soak up the sun's warmth and radiate it back upwards, further exaggerating the readings. Not to mention all those massive jet engines passing by every few minutes, giving off enormous heat. Don't tell me that can produce an unbiased temperature reading. Computer "infilling" is then used to plug the massive gaps in the data generated by so few thinly scattered stations, to give the false impression that the information has been thoroughly and authoritatively assimilated.'

Raul said nothing.

'The same cherry-picking of data happens with polar glacier research,' Catalina explained. 'You see, at any given time, some glaciers are always growing, while others are receding. If the studies and temperature readings all focus on the melt zones, you can easily see how that could be used to twist the data. Hence, "Hey folks, didn't you know the Arctic sea ice is all melting away to nothing and all the cute polar bears are drowning and it's all our fault?"'

'Watch it,' Raul warned her. 'That's a really shitty thing to say about the polar bears.'

Stepped on a nerve there, Ben thought.

'It would be, sure,' Catalina replied coolly. 'If it weren't for the fact that polar bears are doing nothing of the kind, and their numbers have actually increased by up to five thousand or more in the last fifteen years, the same time period we were told would see the total disappearance of the polar icecaps.'

Raul fell silent again.

Catalina raised her hands in a gesture of helplessness. 'Basically, a whole area of science has fallen prey to fraudulent practices. You see it everywhere. Rising sea levels? False data measured on coral atolls that are slowly sinking due to the increasing weight of expanding human habitation. Storms and hurricanes worsening because of climate change? Not according to the proper graphs from NOAA, which show that hurricanes were much stronger in the 1940s and '50s than they are today. It's largely human mismanagement and poor wealth distribution that lead to so much devastation and death as a result of severe storms. Global warming causing fires that destroy swathes of real estate in Australia? Only because someone went and built new housing estates in arid areas where bush fires have been known to occur for generations. And on and on it goes.'

'I can't believe it,' Raul said. 'I wouldn't even be listening to it, from anyone else but you.'

'If you prefer to believe in a pack of lies, I can't stop you.'

'But why would they be lying to us?'

'Not a very original reason,' she said. 'It's all about money. What else? Green taxes. Carbon credits. Electric cars. Solar power. Wind power. So-called "clean" nuclear energy, which they'll start pushing more and more as fossil fuel technologies are increasingly demonised.'

Raul snorted. 'You're beginning to sound like that guy Mike McCauley. I never realised you were so cynical.'

'Raul, you have no idea of the vast business interests behind all this. For instance, in 2008 General Electric, part of the giant multinational corporation NBC Universal and coincidentally America's biggest producer of wind turbines, purchased the Weather Channel, thereby neatly becoming the owner of the best-positioned purveyors of images of so-called climate-related disaster in order to persuade the public of how indispensable their products were. Climate change has become a gigantic industry that has generated fortunes for its leading proponents. Have you checked out the Forbes list of Green billionaires lately?'

'Fine, fine. That being the case, I can't understand why this isn't all out in the open. If the truth is as clear-cut as you say it is, then why aren't other scientists saying so?'

Catalina smiled darkly. 'I'm afraid that many of them buy into the global warming propaganda, just like everyone else. For some in the environmental branches of science, it's the revenge of the Greens. They're not marginalised hippies any more. After being disparaged and embattled for years, they see this as their big moment, and the political environment has given them the power to grow militant. And to attract enticing cash payouts for their research, of course. It's become virtually impossible to secure funding for any kind of project that doesn't support the prevailing political trend. You say you want to study the procreative behaviour of horseshoe bats? Forget it. You won't get a penny. Say you want to study the procreative behaviour of horseshoe bats *in the context of anthropogenic climate change*, and they'll shower you with gold. This thing has spread like a cancer through the education system as well. I've been hearing more and more reports of the better students of environmental sciences dropping out of their courses when they realise the degree of unscientific propagandising that's going on. Lesser students, or ones with less of a conscience, soon discover that going along with the lies is a convenient way to get good grades. As a result, many or most of tomorrow's climate scientists are likely to be the kind of second-rate academics who toe the line, ask no questions and are good little mouth-pieces for the new establishment.

'Then, as if all that weren't enough, there's the simple and sorry fact that a lot of scientists just don't know what's really going on. They don't talk to one another about their research, as often the degree of specialisation and jargon can make it hard for a specialist in one discipline to understand a scientific paper in the other discipline.'

'They don't *know*?' Raul echoed in astonishment.

'Some do,' Catalina replied. 'Some are fully aware of exactly what's happening. But who can blame them for being afraid to speak out?'

Listening in silence, Ben had been growing increasingly restless. 'Let's cut to the chase here,' he said. 'Are you saying that you and your colleagues have been marked as targets because you don't believe in man-made global warming? Who by, militant Greenies? Because call me obtuse, but I find that hard to swallow.'

Catalina shook her head. 'That's not what this is about. There's more.'

'What more?' Ben asked.

'Come with me, and I'll show you.'

Chapter Forty-Five

Catalina led Ben and Raul from the palatial ground floor of the converted lighthouse and up a galleried inset iron stairway that corkscrewed up the curving inner wall of the tower like the rifling cut into the inside of a gun barrel, passing from one floor to the next all the way to the top. Each successive level was as luxuriously furnished as the last, the circular rooms diminishing slightly in width as the lighthouse tapered towards its roof. Porthole windows followed the line of the stairway, offering an increasingly dizzying ocean vista the higher they went.

'I'm sorry for the climb,' she said as they made their way up the endless steps. 'Austin said installing a lift would have spoiled the all-around views. It's actually pretty good exercise, running up and down. All forty-nine metres of it.'

Ben had to agree. Stair-running was one of the best ways he knew to stay fit. Raul didn't seem so pleased. 'Where are we going?'

'To my quarters,' she said. 'I live right at the top.'

'And what is it you want to show us there?' Raul asked irritably. Maybe he was still fuming about the polar bears, Ben thought.

'You'll see,' she said. 'Oh, by the way, this level here is the guest floor you'll be quartered in, for as long as you want to stay here with us. It's divided into two separate bedroom apartments. Austin has the next floor up. The one above that is mine.'

As she trotted up the last few steps ahead of him, it was hard for Ben not to notice the athleticism of her slim figure, nor to be reminded of why the mainstream media had taken her so much to heart. Being sexy and beautiful probably didn't do much to make you a better scientist, but it certainly couldn't hurt when it came to fame and star power. 'Here we are,' she said, opening a door and showing them through it.

Catalina's quarters were bright and modern, an open-plan design that was essentially one large circular room with part of the circle closed off to make a bathroom area. The curved walls were lined on all sides by high windows, and topped by a glass dome that made it feel as if they were standing on top of a mountain, dwarfing the island below them. From up here, Keller's sailing yacht in the distance looked like a model ship.

'The lighthouse was decommissioned in 1908,' she explained. 'It was just a ruin before Austin salvaged it, so there was no need to replace the original parabolic reflector lamp. He installed the dome instead, and a little roof parapet where I climb up and look at the night sky. It used to be his room, but he moved out to let me have it.'

Ben wondered just how soon Austin was secretly planning on moving back in.

'And this is my new office. Not quite as well appointed as the old one, but I get by,' she said, motioning towards one end of the room where a small desk had been set up facing west. For the sunset, Ben imagined. There would be some spectacular ones to view from up here. He noticed the laptop and stack of notes that had been removed from his bag and were now sitting on her desk. He was noticing other things, too. Like the expensive-looking tan leather travel bag lying open at the foot of the bed, at the other end of the room. It was full of clothes, all neatly folded and packed. After all this time, Catalina still hadn't fully moved into her new environment. It looked as if she was living out of her suitcase, like a person ready to leave at any time. It was just a detail, but to Ben it stood out, and he wondered about it.

'It's very nice, Catalina,' Raul said, looking around the room. 'But you didn't bring us up here to admire the view, did you?'

'I told you I was going to show you what this is all about,' she said.

'And?'

'And there it is, right there.' She pointed upwards.

Raul followed the line of her finger towards the bright sun, whose light was pouring down on them through the rounded glass of the dome. He shielded his eyes from the glare and blinked at it, then looked at his sister in puzzlement.

'Beautiful, isn't it?' she said, gazing up through the dome.

For a moment, Ben was beginning to wonder if this was Catalina's idea of a joke, though she looked perfectly serious.

'It's just . . . *the sun*,' Raul said, frowning. 'We've seen it before. This is what you brought us up here for? How about you stop talking in riddles and tell us what the sun has to do with anything?'

'Don't be silly, Raul,' she replied. 'That's like saying "What do we need oxygen for, or food, or water?" The sun is everything. It's the basis of all we are, all we have. Why else do you think the ancients worshipped it in so many deity forms through the ages? Because without it, human life on Earth could never have existed. Of all the gods in the history of human culture, that big guy up there is still the most compelling and substantial, by a huge margin.' She sighed. 'All those years I spent studying it, thinking I understood. But I was just stuck in a box, too focused on one narrow field, just like all the other solar scientists. None of us were getting the bigger picture.'

'I see,' Raul said. 'So you brought us to the top of this ridiculous tower to give us a lecture on the sun. What is this, some kind of withdrawal symptom from having to give up teaching?'

'I'm trying to explain. You see, modern science has generally held that the solar irradiance – that is, the sun's energy, which averages 1,336 watts per metre squared, by the way – is too insignificant to have any kind of major effect on Earth's climate. Meaning, basically, that the sun is the sun and the Earth is the Earth, two separate independent systems, and our planet's climate is internally regulated. I was one of those scientists. To my shame, for years I simply accepted that prevailing orthodox view. It was William Herschel who made me see everything differently. That was where this all began.'

'With sunspots and the price of wheat in 1850s England?' Ben said.

'It seems so irrelevant, doesn't it? I dismissed it at first, thinking it was just some quirky historical curiosity. But it wouldn't go away. That tiny seed of an idea implanted itself into my mind, and grew, and grew. Two hundred years after William Herschel failed to convince the Fellows of the Royal Society of the links between sunspot activity and Earth's climate, I started becoming obsessed with whether he might actually have been right. Soon afterwards, I discovered that I wasn't the only scientist out there thinking along the same lines.'

'Sinclair, Lockhart and Ellis?' Ben said.

'Dougal and Jim had only slowly started coming to these conclusions in recent years, through their separate research. But Steve Ellis has been heavily involved in the whole thing for decades. Even though he retired officially back in the nineties, he still wrote a blog, The Weather Report, which has over two million followers. That was how I first contacted him. Over time, the four of us shared ideas by email, and eventually agreed to team up. Of course, this was never an official research programme. More a private journey of discovery that just kept going deeper and deeper, until we began to realise the full extent of what we were dealing with. Except Steve, who I think knew it all along.' She went quiet for a moment as she reflected on her lost colleagues, then looked up at Ben. 'What do you know about sunspots?'

'About as much as your brother here apparently knows about global warming,' Ben said, drawing a filthy look from Raul.

'They're those dark patches that you can see if you reflect the sun's light onto a sheet of paper,' she said. 'Of course, with a dedicated solar telescope we can see them much better. They're basically magnetic in nature, with a much greater field strength than the rest of the solar surface, and are formed when very intense magnetic flux tubes erupt from the sun's interior and keep cooled gas from circulating back inside. Simply speaking, the more sunspot activity there is on the sun, the more energy it radiates to Earth. The less activity, the less energy. Meanwhile, the sun goes through cycles of fluctuating energy output. At its peak, it's called the Solar Maximum. At its lowest, the Solar Minimum. With me so far?'

'I'm with you,' Raul said. 'I just don't see the point.'

'Be quiet and listen. Our research was to statistically collate any and all links, past and present, between sunspot activity and the Earth's climate. And our conclusion was that Herschel had been right after all. The initial findings confirmed that wheat prices in England during that period did indeed fluctuate in line with solar activity, being higher at Solar Minimum than at Solar Maximum, suggesting that the crop was more difficult to grow when sunspot activity was at its lowest. Then, when we broadened our research, we realised that the same pattern held true all through history. During the last thousand years or so, there were five important periods of Solar Minimum, which each came to be named after a different astronomer. The so-called Oort Minimum lasted from 1010 until 1050, and was followed by the Wolf Minimum, 1280 to 1350. After that came the Spörer Minimum, 1460 to 1550; then the Maunder Minimum from 1645 to 1715, and lastly the Dalton Minimum from 1790 to 1820.'

A memory was rekindled in Ben's mind at the mention of those dates. He'd come across them before, while trying to make sense of Catalina's notes back at the inn in Germany, and he'd thought about them several times since with no greater understanding. But now he recognised the sequence 1010 – 1280 – 1460 – 1645 – 1790 as the start year of each of these historic Solar Minimum periods, and he was able to start piecing other segments of the puzzle around them. 'So the Medieval Warm Period must have happened in between the Oort and the Wolf?' he said.

Catalina smiled at him. 'You're getting it. That's right.'

'So, if I understand what you're saying, these Solar Minimum phases must have been intervals of much colder weather?'

Catalina's eyes glowed. 'Exactly. When the sun is at a low ebb in terms of energy output, and sunspots are at their fewest, the Earth gets cold. We're talking about periods when the temperature dropped very rapidly and suddenly, maybe over the course of a few years, which in Earth terms is overnight. Soon after the start of the Wolf Minimum in 1280, three hundred years of balmy weather in Europe came to an abrupt end, bringing hard winters of snow and ice and summers of endless cold rain. Life became incredibly hard. In northern latitudes, some places became uninhabitable – like Greenland, which as we know the Vikings had to abandon. Further south and across Europe, crops were ruined, famine and disease followed and a quarter of the population died off. If anyone thinks that those gruesome old folk tales like Hansel and Gretel, about child abandonment and cannibalism, were just the result of a writer's warped imagination, they're not looking at the historical context. Parents actually abandoned or murdered their children at that time because there wasn't enough food to go round. And it wasn't just in Europe that the changing climate caused devastation. In China, millions of people drowned when the Yellow River flooded as a result of the extreme rainfall. There was nobody left to bury them, so the bodies were just left lying around. That caused a huge boom among the rat population, which was a major factor in the outbreak of bubonic plague. The contagion spread across China, and eventually came to Europe because the starving Europeans were being forced to import grain from any place they could get it.'

Catalina paused and walked over to the desk to turn on the computer. 'Let me show you. Okay. Here we are. Now look at this graph.'

Ben and Raul both stepped closer to peer at the screen. 'I hate graphs,' Raul said.

The chart Catalina was showing them was marked

horizontally with year dates spanning several centuries, and vertically with temperature gradations in degrees centigrade. From left to right, a jagged red line spiked up and down at intervals, tracing a zigzag like the serrations of a shark's teeth.

'The red line represents cycles of warming and cooling through history,' she explained, running her finger along it. 'See how it fluctuates? With the end of the Wolf Minimum in about 1350, the temperatures shot up again as the sun's energy output increased, but only for about a century until the start of the Spörer Minimum. Up, then down. Once again, many parts of the world were plunged into the deep freeze.' She ran her finger along the line on the screen, to the point where it began to rise towards its next peak. 'Then up we go again. See that sharp peak some time before the year 1600? Now look what happens next.'

'It drops all the way down,' Ben said. Where Catalina was indicating, the red zigzag dropped from its previous peak and plummeted straight down into a trough deeper than any of the others on the graph.

'This is where we hit the Maunder Minimum, marking the beginning of the Little Ice Age that lasted for three hundred years, from the middle of the sixteenth century until the middle of the nineteenth. This was the last great cooling event in our history to date. Within a decade, the temperatures dropped so low that birds fell from the sky, frozen solid. All over Europe, seas and rivers turned to solid ice. The coastlines of France, Britain and the Netherlands became almost unapproachable by ship because of the ice sheet that extended for miles out to sea. In London, it became traditional to hold fairs on the frozen River Thames, which for months at a time could support the weight of thousands of people, horses, carts, stands and side-shows. By 1690, northern Europe had got so cold that Eskimos were forced to move south to Scotland, while native Scots had to leave their homeland in search of warmer climates. While across the Atlantic, New York harbour froze so solid that people could walk over the ice to Staten Island.

'A hundred years later, all of Europe was still struggling with intense cold. France suffered its iciest winter of the eighteenth century in 1788, causing massive crop failure and starvation. The famines caused chaos and panic as hungry crowds flooded into Paris demanding affordable bread. Everyone knows Marie Antoinette's famous response to that, "Let them eat cake". But what most people don't know is that the crisis was climate-related. Just a year later, France exploded into violent revolution, and it wasn't long before about a dozen governments elsewhere in Europe collapsed. Only after 1850 did the sun finally start to make a real comeback, resulting in a period of relative warming that's lasted, with a few minor blips, right until the present day.'

Ben was remembering that there was one more date in the sequence in Catalina's research notes that hadn't been mentioned yet.

It was the year 2016.

'What about now?' he asked her.

'Nothing stops these natural cycles from turning,' she said. 'And remember that a thousand years, or ten thousand, or a million, are just the blink of an eye to the vast forces that govern us. What happened in history will continue to happen in modern times, now and into the future. For instance, we can link the extremely cold European winters of 2010 and 2011 to low solar activity affecting the North Atlantic Oscillation. We know that solar ultraviolet radiation influences the position of the jet streams on Earth, and hence controls much of the climate. Any small change in the intensity of the sun can have a major effect. It's got nothing, I repeat *nothing*, to do with CO_2. And at this point in history we can't say it has anything to do with global warming, either. Because the world isn't warming. It's getting colder. And it's going to continue getting colder for a very long time.'

Catalina paused. There was a solemn look in her eyes that made Ben narrow his. She hadn't finished yet. Something more was coming. Something worse.

'. . . How much colder?' Raul asked after a beat.

'You wouldn't believe me if I told you,' Catalina said.

Chapter Forty-Six

Nearly two thousand miles away, Steve Ellis awoke in what at first seemed like unfamiliar surroundings that, for just a few moments, left him disorientated and anxious. He sat up in the bed, blinking, and then let out a relieved sigh as sleep melted away and, with it, the already-fading dream that he now realised must have unsettled him.

A drowsy squint at his watch made him sigh again, but this time with irritation at himself for sleeping in so late. Jesus, it was almost eleven o'clock in the morning. Through the small window of his bedroom, the sun was already high in the sky, burning pale over the hills that surrounded the isolated cottage.

He forced himself out of bed, groaning and muttering at the stiffness in his back. What an old crock he'd become. And what a slob, too, malingering in bed all bloody morning. But that's what you got for sitting up half the night watching the stars. Some habits just wouldn't die. The lightweight astronomical binoculars were the only piece of kit he'd managed to bring with him in his rush to leave home, but – being of his own design and manufacture, naturally – they were more than up to the job.

Under the circumstances, nightly skywatching should have been the least of his preoccupations. But with each week he spent in this place, he was feeling more relaxed in the confidence that as long as he stayed put, he was safe here from the people who wished him harm. Of all the infinite number of places he could have gone to ground, how was anyone ever to guess he'd holed up more than two hundred miles north of home, in the middle of nowhere overlooking an empty valley deep in the heart of the Lake District? It didn't get much more remote than this within British shores. No landline phone or mobile reception, no TV, no neighbours, the nearest village almost an hour's walk away. Even the taxicab that had brought him here from the railway station had had trouble finding the damn place.

The cottage belonged to Rex, his former brother-in-law, with whom Steve had kept in contact all these years since his younger sister Sally had grown to be such a grouching, sullen old bitch that Rex had finally had the good sense to divorce her. Rex's knees had become too dodgy with age these days to allow him to negotiate the slope leading up to the cottage, so he very seldom used it any more and kept it on only as a financial investment. When Steve had called him up late that night at home in Preston, hiding his panic with a hastily made-up story about wanting to get away from it all for a while, Rex had said he could stay there as long as he wanted, gratis.

Good old Rex. He might be an awkward bugger at times, but Steve had raised a few glasses to him since that day.

Steve padded stiffly to the tiny bathroom. It was cold. He urinated, then peered in disapproval at the crumpled, white-bearded face in the mirror. He wasn't getting any prettier, but who gave a toss? Then he wandered into the low-beamed living room, which was cold as well.

Better get used to it, old boy, he thought. Just in case you live long enough to be around when it all starts to kick off.

One day, everyone was going to wish they had a good old-fashioned fire and lots of nice fossil fuels to keep themselves warm. The warmists were going to love it.

Once he'd got the wood burner in the living room going, Steve went to the kitchen to brew himself a pot of strong tea, then returned near the fire to drink it in the rocking chair by the window, idly scanning the sky in case he might spot an osprey or a goshawk or even, wonder of wonders, an eagle. There wasn't an awful lot to do here except enjoy the absolute peace and quiet. The only things he missed from home were his workshop and his internet connection, the latter partly because he would have liked to keep up with his blog, and partly because even a prehistoric old fart like him had finally had to cave in and admit that the web was the best research resource going. How had they ever managed to cope back in the sixties, seventies and eighties?

Seeing nothing except a couple of buzzards, he let his thoughts wander. He wished he could phone Catalina Fuentes and find out if the poor girl was all right. He felt very protective towards her, and couldn't bear to imagine the same dreadful thing happening to her as had befallen their colleagues. Dear God, what an awful bloody mess.

When he'd finished his tea he got up and wandered back into the kitchen, contemplating lunch. All these dark thoughts had depressed him a bit, and he decided he could do with a nice cold can of bitter, to wash down the rest of the corned beef hash left over from last night's dinner. One thing about being a single guy, at least he could cook and fend for himself. Fried bread, bacon and eggs, even omelettes. Yup, he was a regular master chef.

But when he opened the fridge, he saw to his dismay that there was no beer left. Must've polished the last one off yesterday. *Damn.* He patted his belly. Maybe staying off the beer for a day or two wouldn't be such a bad thing. But now the thought was in his head, it wouldn't go away. He struggled with it for a while, but then human frailty got the better of him. The village shop was only a cycle ride away, and the exercise would give him an appetite.

He shoved another log on the wood burner to keep it ticking over in his absence, then locked the cottage and went outside into the chill. In the shed was the old mountain bike that Rex hadn't used for years, which Steve had cleaned up and appropriated for his forays to the village shop, returning with carrier bags full of groceries and clanking beer tins dangling from the handlebars. He got his leg over the bike and pedalled off down the gravelly slope.

He'd explored most of the area during these past weeks, and knew his way around pretty well. As usual, he turned off the road to take a route along a bouncy, rocky lane that cut about half a mile off the normal route to the village. Drystone walls and tufty dead grass flanked its verges, and the rolling, craggy hills loomed up all around, breaking here and there for patches of golden autumnal woodland. There wasn't a living soul in sight. It was glorious.

The only problem with the shortcut was the steep hill he had to negotiate about a mile from the cottage. As he approached, he pedalled harder to gain momentum and changed down a few gears. These newfangled bicycles seemed to have about a thousand of them. He fixed his gaze on the brow of the hill ahead, gritted his teeth and kept on pumping. By the time he was halfway up the incline, he was sweating and his heart was thundering away, but he was determined that today he'd reach the top without having to get off and push.

Not bad for an old crock, he thought, and grinned to himself.

Sensing the soft engine purr and tyre patter of a vehicle coming up behind him, he glanced back over his shoulder and saw the black Land Rover Freelander following him slowly along the path, spitting little stones out from under its chunky tyres. You didn't meet a lot of traffic on these lanes. He tightened in closer to the verge to let the Land Rover pass, but it didn't. He waved his arm to say, *come on, overtake me.*

Again, the vehicle stayed back, slowly keeping pace with him up the hill. He could dimly make out a pair of figures in the front seats.

The vehicle's presence irritated Steve, because he didn't like being watched while he puffed and panted and generally showed his age and condition. What was the matter with this guy? Worried about scratching his paintwork on the drystone wall? There was plenty of room on the narrow lane to overtake a bloody bicycle, for heaven's sake.

That was when he was gripped by a sudden thought that made the bicycle wobble under him and turned the sweat on his brow to ice water. He twisted in the saddle to look again, panic rising now. The two figures seemed to look back at him, their faces obscured by the tint of the glass. Was there a third man with them in the vehicle, or was he just imagining it? He tried to pedal faster, but his legs were trembling and the muscles in his thighs seemed to have liquefied. His breath started wheezing. The brow of the hill suddenly seemed impossibly far away.

But the breach in the drystone wall was coming up on the left. Beyond it was a stand of trees, behind which stood a little stone bothy that Steve had often visited on his rambles. In his panic-stricken mind, the tumbledown old stone building suddenly seemed to him like an ideal refuge.

In a flurry of arms and legs he dismounted from the bike without stopping, letting it fall away under him and somehow managing to land on his feet without tripping over it and going flat on his face. The bike clattered to the ground in the path of the Land Rover and he heard it crunch to a halt as he bolted for the gap in the wall. His breath rasped shakily in his throat and his feet tore through the long grass. He thought he heard the sound of car doors opening, but he didn't dare to look back. He stumbled onwards until he reached the trees, and only then did he throw another feverish glance over his shoulder.

Three men had got out of the Land Rover. All of them were looking straight at him. As one, they reached inside their coats and pulled out stubby black objects that he realised were guns.

Steve let out a groan of terror as he went on running. He had no idea how they'd found him. But they'd found him, all right.

He thought of Rex.

Rex was family.

Family were traceable.

Which meant *he* was traceable.

God, how could he have been so stupid?

Keep going! screamed the voice in his head. *Keep running!* He was certain he could hear the crackle of twigs behind him as the three men pursued him into the trees. A branch whipped across the side of his face, but he hardly felt it.

The bothy lurched closer with every step. He could see its craggy wall through the autumnal foliage. It had no windows, and a single oak door that was old and flaking, but thick and solid. If he could somehow wedge it shut from inside—

Steve burst out of the trees. Now he was just a few breathless paces from the door. It was slightly ajar. He reached a hand out in front of him to shove it open—

But his hand met only empty air when the door swung open before he got to it.

A man stepped out of the shadows of the doorway to meet him. Tall, clean-shaven, wearing a long dark coat. Holding a gun.

'Hallo, Steve,' he said. And the gun came up to point at him.

All Steve Ellis could do then was close his eyes.

Chapter Forty-Seven

'Don't take my word for it,' Catalina said to Ben and Raul. 'Look at this.' Returning to the computer, she clicked out of the graph they'd been looking at, and in a few deft moves brought up another.

'Here we are.' She stepped away from the screen to let them move closer.

The graph showed an exaggerated wavelike pattern of wild spikes that had been smoothed out into a single swooping up-and-down curve that stretched across a range of year dates starting in 1985 and ending at the present day, a little over thirty years. Ben immediately noticed that the line formed three distinct peaks, diminishing in size from left to right. The first covered the years 1985 to 1996 and was by far the tallest, surging all the way to the top of the graph. The middle peak covered the period from 1996 to 2007 and was far less pronounced, perhaps two-thirds of the height of the first. The third peak, for the years 2008 to the present, was much smaller again, no more than a third of the size of the first. Ben could clearly make out an eleven-year cycle in the pattern, but the overall trend was very obviously one of radical decrease. Decrease in what, he had no idea.

But he had a feeling Catalina was about to enlighten him.

'This is a graph of sunspot numbers over the last three decades,' she explained. 'It's based on my own research, but it's virtually identical to what NASA have. You'd have to be blind not to see how the sunspots have declined dramatically during this period. Their numbers are falling through the floor. And now that you guys understand the connection between solar activity and climate, you should be able to tell what's going on here, yes?'

'You're telling us we're entering a new Solar Minimum,' Raul said between gritted teeth.

Catalina shook her head. '*I'm* not telling you anything. This is not a matter of opinion. The scientific facts are more than able to speak for themselves. But you don't have to study technical data to see what's happening. All you have to do is look around you with open eyes. The truth is out there, if you're prepared to find it.'

She turned towards the window and swept a slender arm westwards towards the horizon. 'Look at North America, for instance,' she said, gazing in that direction as if she had a commanding view for seven thousand miles from the top of the lighthouse, clear across the tail end of southern Europe and the whole of the Atlantic Ocean.

'Nobody who's lived through the last few winters in the USA would be hard to persuade that it's getting colder, year on year. Minus two degrees Celsius in Pensacola, Florida, last January, for God's sake. Land of emerald golf courses, palm trees and white-sand beaches. Cut up the Eastern Seaboard to Boston, and you've got the all-time snowfall recorded there in winter 2015. Meanwhile, waves froze solid off Cape Cod and mini-icebergs landed ashore. In the same winter, ice cover on the Great Lakes reached over eighty-eight percent higher than the previous year's already high figure. In April, fifteen cargo freighters became icebound on

Lake Superior and had to be rescued by icebreakers. That's a main commercial shipping route between the US and Canada. Unheard of, so late in the year. And for the first time ever in modern history, that month it was possible to walk for fifty miles across Lake Huron in Ontario. And it's not just North America. Sweden is having its coldest winters in over a century. Britain has recorded its lowest temperatures in a hundred and twenty years. All over the world, glacial ice fields have started to grow again, something that's been confirmed by NASA. Glaciers are growing on Mont Blanc. Signs of the same happening on Ben Nevis in Scotland. The Brüggen Glacier in Chile continuing to thicken. Antarctic sea ice expanding to record levels, despite our being told the icecap had reached a melting point of no return . . .'

'Those aren't exactly warm countries you just mentioned,' Raul said. 'Now who's cherry-picking the facts?'

'You want warm countries? Fine. How about South Korea? A subtropical climate that in 2011 saw record-breaking snowfall way beyond anything that they'd experienced for a century or more. The following year, snow fell in all nine provinces of South Africa on the same day, for the first time ever. Snow hadn't been seen in Pretoria since the sixties. Needless to say, that incident wasn't reported in much of the global media. Then the next year after that, snow fell in Cairo for the first time in, guess how long?'

'A century, I get it,' Raul said grudgingly.

'While in Lebanon, the army had to be called out to distribute emergency provisions and blankets to freezing Syrian refugees as snow covered much of the Middle East. Winter 2015 was even worse. Freezing temperatures, snow and ice from Turkey to Jordan. Blizzards in Jerusalem. Babies freezing to death in the Gaza Strip. You could go sledging in the Sahara, or build a snowman in the Libyan Desert.'

'All right, all right,' Raul said, holding up his hands in submission. 'You made your point. So it might get a bit colder for a while. Is it really such a big issue?'

'You only have to look at history to answer that. Human populations are alarmingly vulnerable to even small drops in temperature. It doesn't take much to seriously disrupt the fragile order of a society that's become heavily reliant on mild climates and has come to take them for granted. Even a few degrees' difference will expose all the weaknesses of our civilisation.'

'But you said yourself, these things are cyclical,' Raul said. 'It won't last forever. Pretty soon things will come back round to the way they were before. No?'

Catalina shrugged. 'Assuming we can rely on the cycles endlessly repeating themselves in the same old way, then maybe. Yes. But we can't. It's not that simple.'

Raul looked at her. 'It's not that simple?'

'No, because that would require that all the factors in the equation remain constant, forever. And that's simply not the case. There's a problem. Quite a big problem, for us.'

'What problem?'

'The sun,' Catalina said, pointing upwards. 'Events are happening up there that we've never seen before. I believe that's why we're seeing this disturbing decline in the solar cycles.'

'But you told us that it was normal for sunspot numbers to vary up and down,' Raul said.

'I know I did,' Catalina replied, going back to the computer. 'But that isn't the whole picture. Let me show you another graph.'

'Please, not another graph,' Raul groaned.

'Are you a moron?' she asked him.

'No,' he said, stung.

'Then you'll understand it just fine. It's really not that difficult. Now look.' She clicked a few more times, then waved them closer to show what had come up onscreen. The scientific graph was labelled 'Estimated Planetary K Index'. It was a black grid crisscrossed by broken white lines, with the last four days' dates along the bottom and the numbers one to nine vertically up the left side. Unlike the others, instead of zigzags or waves this one had only a row of bright green bars, like stunted high-rise buildings in a line, some higher than others but none reaching higher than the number 2 mark on the vertical axis.

Like the others, it was incomprehensible to Ben.

Catalina quickly explained, 'This is data compiled from the magnetometers at the National Oceanic and Atmospheric Administration's Space Weather Prediction Center in Boulder, Colorado. I preferred to compile my own data, back in the days when I still had the facilities . . .' She sighed. 'But these folks are close enough to the mark to provide good working figures. Anyway, as you can see, this is very fresh data. Don't worry too much about the readings, just look at these little green bars here. They should be way up the graph, but they're down here.' She shook her head, as if she was surveying the aftermath of some terrible disaster. 'It's been like this for a while now. We confirmed the findings with our own Zeeman Effect research. That's when you use a spectrometer to split up the spectral lines on the sun. The stronger the magnetic field, the wider the separation of the lines. All we could see were lines so close together they were almost touching.'

'Wow, that made sense,' Raul said.

'And you're saying all this is unusual?' Ben asked Catalina.

Catalina gave Ben the same solemn look she'd given them

before. 'That would be something of an understatement. It's unprecedented. And it's very, *very* bad news.'

'Elaborate,' Ben said. He had the feeling that, after having led them through the logical process step by step, Catalina was finally ready to get to the nub of the matter.

'Haven't we elaborated enough already?' Raul muttered.

Catalina ignored her brother. 'Let me boil this down for you. We have two processes happening at once, closely interlinked. One, as I've explained, is that sunspot numbers are declining. Which could be normal, as Raul pointed out. The second, which this graph and other research consistently show, is that while the sunspots are becoming much *fewer*, they're also becoming much *weaker*. Their average magnetic field strength is rapidly declining, by about fifty Gauss per year if you want to be specific about it. And with them, the entire magnetic field strength of the sun is dwindling. Which is definitely not something we've seen it do before, but is in keeping with its age. You see, our sun is a middle-aged star. Past its prime. It's gradually becoming weaker, losing its power.'

'Stars become senile now?' Raul said, half grinning.

'It's perfectly natural,' Catalina explained. 'When a star like our sun gets older, just like a living organism it begins to experience physical changes. For one, it begins to rotate more slowly. Some scientists believe that rotation and activity might decrease with the square root of a star's age, a theory I happen to agree with. If you think of it as a giant electromagnetic dynamo, you can imagine how a slowdown in its rotation would lead to a loss of energy. And when the process begins to happen, it can take a hold quite quickly. A lot of stars similar to our sun have suffered a significant loss of luminosity in just a few years. Tau Ceti and 54 Piscium are two examples of that happening.'

Ben recognised the names from her research notes. 'And that's what ours is doing, too?' he asked. He looked up at the sun, and had to shield his eyes with his hand. It looked pretty damn bright to him. But then, what did he know?

Catalina nodded. 'I'm afraid so, yes. Another way we can tell when the sun is entering a very quiet phase is when there's an increase in GCRs, or galactic cosmic rays, which come from faraway parts of our galaxy and perhaps from other galaxies as well. When the sun's energy dips, solar wind decreases—'

'Solar wind?' Raul interrupted, still in facetious mode. 'Wind from the sun? I never felt anything.'

Catalina shot him a look. 'It's not really a wind, that's just what we call it. It's a stream of electrically charged particles that make up something called the heliosphere, which we're right in the middle of and which interacts with Earth's magnetic field causing electrical phenomena like auroras. When it decreases in strength, it allows more of these galactic cosmic rays to enter our atmosphere, which causes all kinds of disruption. Screwing up satellites, for one. Right now, GCRs have reached the highest levels ever recorded. NASA has reported having more single-event satellite upsets than ever before. Then there's the data from the GSCB.'

'You people have more acronyms than the military,' Ben said.

'It stands for Great Solar Conveyor Belt. A huge circular current of very hot plasma within the sun. Consisting of two branches, one north and one south. Each of these takes about forty years to complete one circuit. It's thought that the turning of this belt controls the sunspot cycle. Normally, the belt should rotate at one metre per second. I could show you more graphs—'

'No,' Raul said.

'—Which illustrate how the belt's motion has decelerated by up to sixty-five percent. NASA data confirms that it's slowed to a record crawl. In fact, they've known about it for some time. They held an emergency conference in 2008 that confirmed it. Now, as the solar conveyor belt slows down, the solar wind will get weaker and weaker. One thing leads to another. More galactic cosmic rays will enter our atmosphere, and as well as damaging satellites they'll also produce more cloud cover, which in turn will make the climate colder. A vicious circle, in effect. The more our star slows and weakens, the less of its energy reaches Earth. Are you following this? I'm making it as simple as I can.'

'Go on,' Ben said.

'There's nothing we can do to stop the process. Like a battery running down. Once its energy is sapped, you just have to replace it. Except that we can't replace the sun's energy, and that's why we can't simply rely on the ages-old cycle coming round again. Like I said, this is an unprecedented event, with serious implications for us all. As serious as it gets.'

'You're saying the sun is dying?' Raul burst out.

'Everything has to die some time,' she replied.

'Okay, everyone knows it can't last forever. But that doesn't happen for billions of years.'

'One billion, give or take,' Catalina said. 'In its final stages the sun will give out one last great gasp of energy. It'll become brighter and bigger, scorching the Earth to a cinder and boiling the oceans away to nothing. Then as it swells up even more, becoming a Red Giant, its mass will swallow up Mercury, Venus, Earth and Mars, the nearer planets in the solar system, or what's left of them. Then its core will collapse as it finally dies. Ultimately it'll end up as a lifeless, cold lump of carbon that we call a Black Dwarf.'

'Right, so we still have a very, very long time,' Raul said, waving his arms around. 'You said yourself, millions and millions of years are just a blink of an eye in the big scheme of things. Who knows what amazing technology we could have by then, so we could escape this solar system and go and find another one that still has plenty of life left in it?'

Catalina gazed at him sadly. 'That's just a wishful fantasy, Raul. The sun will go through many, many stages of evolution before any of that happens. What may be about to happen will be just one of them. And if I'm right, that could be all it takes.'

He blinked. 'All it takes for what?'

'All it takes to finish us,' she said. 'To bring about the end.'

Raul's jaw dropped. 'The end? *The* end?'

'I'm not talking about the transient periods of cold climate that resulted from historical solar cycles. I'm not even talking about something like the last major Glacial Period, twelve thousand years ago. We came through that and survived. No. I'm talking about the very real possibility that the current solar cycle could be about to lead us into an ice age of the kind that hasn't happened for an extremely long time. It could be a repeat of the Cryogenian Glaciation eight hundred million years ago, when the whole planet was covered in a layer of ice up to two kilometres thick. Snowball Earth, we call it. A super ice age lasting perhaps thousands of years. Certainly spelling the demise of human civilisation as we know it. Very probably, the end of human life altogether.'

There was a silent lull in the room. Ben could hear the distant crashing of the breakers. Now he could understand why Catalina had built up to it so gradually. This kind of revelation wasn't something you could feed to the uniniti-ated in one bite.

Raul stared at his sister. 'Have you lost your mind? This is crazy talk.'

She shrugged. 'We wouldn't be the first species to become extinct as a result of catastrophic climate change.'

'When? How soon?'

'Projected timescale? I can't say for sure,' she replied. 'Based on the scientific facts, it could be as soon as a hundred years from now.'

'A *hundred*?' Ben said.

'Or even less,' Catalina replied, in absolute earnest. 'Of course, it wouldn't happen overnight. It's not as if we'd all waken up one day to find glaciers popped up in our front gardens, out of nowhere. The change will be gradual, taking over the planet bit by bit, degree by degree. Winters will start to get longer, summers shorter. There'll still be sunny days. But slowly, even those will disappear. That's when the bad times will really begin.'

Nobody spoke.

'Christ, you're really serious about this, aren't you?' Ben said after a long moment.

'And I'm not the only one who takes it seriously,' Catalina replied. 'Someone out there knows it's true and will do anything to stop it getting out. *That's* why they want to shut me up. *That's* why they want me dead.'

Chapter Forty-Eight

Later that day, Keller showed Ben and Raul to the guest accommodation on the fifth floor of the lighthouse. The guest floor was partitioned into two compact, self-contained, semi-circular units each consisting of a bedroom, a small living area and an even smaller bathroom. But what they lacked in size, they made up for in modern comforts. Left alone, Ben discovered that Keller's men had already brought up his bag and left it neatly on the bed. He wondered if all their abductees got such five-star service.

He tossed the bag aside, stretched out on the bed and closed his eyes for a few minutes. He had a bewildering amount of information to process after listening to Catalina talk. It was going to take some time to sink in fully.

After a long, cool shower, he returned downstairs. Raul, Catalina and Keller were nowhere about. Ben stepped outside into the afternoon sunshine. He shielded his eyes, squinted up at the sun and thought about what Catalina had said. It seemed strange to imagine its fires slowly dying. He could feel its warmth on his face. One day, people would stand looking at it the way he was now, and feel nothing from it at all. That was a sad, comfortless thought.

The island was very quiet, just the constant whisper of the surf breaking the silence. Keller's men were nowhere in sight either; he supposed they must be in their residential block, busy doing whatever they did to bide their time in their boss's paradise hideaway, or maybe preparing to head back to London to resume the surveillance vigil over Mike McCauley's home.

Ben walked over to the row of four Jeep Wranglers parked nearby. All four sets of keys were dangling from their ignitions. He didn't suppose that car crime was much of an issue on Icthyios. He didn't suppose anybody would miss one of the Jeeps for a few minutes, either. He climbed behind the wheel of the nearest one and fired up the engine. Nobody came rushing out to stop him, or demand to know where he was going. Perhaps that was just because there weren't many places he *could* go.

He followed the twisting, undulating road over the brow of the island and down towards the beach at its low-lying end. Where the road met the airstrip, he pulled up on the asphalt near the hangar in which Keller's plane was housed. The roll shutter had been left open; he could see the pearly-white nose of the aircraft inside, and the drums of kerosene and pumping system used for refuelling. Getting out of the Jeep, he looked across the little wooden jetty and saw a lone figure sitting facing away from him at its far end, gazing pensively out to sea.

Catalina.

He walked over the sand to the jetty, stepped onto the weathered planks and approached her. Hearing his footsteps, she turned and smiled.

'Hello again,' she said. 'Exploring the island?'

'Actually, I was thinking of going for a run on the beach,' he said.

'You look like a runner.'

'It relaxes me,' he said.

316

'Care to join me for a moment?' she asked.

'If I'm not disturbing you.'

'Be my guest,' she replied, and motioned at the empty space beside her.

He got the feeling she didn't want to speak about the things she'd talked about earlier. As he sat beside her, letting his legs dangle over the edge of the jetty the way hers were, he resolved not to mention any of it. The end of the world couldn't be a difficult conversational subject to skirt around.

Below their feet, the water swirled and slapped gently around the wooden support posts. 'Peaceful here,' he said.

'I come down here a lot,' Catalina said. 'I've covered every inch of this island on foot. This is my favourite spot, where I just sit and gaze out to sea. It's not as if I have a lot else to do these days,' she added.

Ben gazed across the Aegean. It was bright and blue, smooth and flat all the way to the horizon. He could see the slightly larger island a few kilometres away.

'That's Sárla,' she said, following his eye. 'Our only near neighbours.'

Ben nodded and spent a few more moments drinking in the view. 'I love the sea,' he said. 'I had a house in Galway, right on the Atlantic coast. Used to spend a lot of time there, just like this, looking out at the ocean.'

'I've never been to Ireland.'

'It's beautiful. Wilder than here. This place reminds me of it, even though it's so different. I had my own little bit of beach and a big old flat rock I used to sit on. I did an awful lot of thinking on that rock.'

'Sounds like you miss the place.'

'I do,' he said. 'I don't know why I ever left.'

She smiled again, sadly. 'I know the feeling.'

Ben looked at her, said nothing. Her hair stirred in the

317

breeze. She was pensive for a while, and Ben went back to gazing out to sea. In the distance, a tiny white dot against the blue water caught the sunlight as a vessel emerged from behind the island of Sárla, trailing an even tinier thread of white wake. He shaded his eyes from the sun to observe it.

'That's the closest I normally get these days to seeing a living soul apart from Austin and his men,' Catalina said, pointing. 'It's the ferry from Karpathos. It goes back and forth, carrying supplies, mail, the occasional party of tourists. We get nothing like that here, of course.'

Ben asked, 'How many people live on Sárla?'

'Only a few hundred,' she replied. 'Mostly fishermen and their families. So I'm told, that is. I've never been there, and I don't suppose I ever will. Sometimes I don't think I'll ever go anywhere again.'

She bowed her head, and a moment later Ben realised she was crying softly. 'I feel so alone,' she whispered. She sniffed, wiped her eyes and composed herself with a visible effort. 'Please forgive me. I must look awful.'

'You look fine,' Ben said. Which was an understatement. Even streaked with tears, the perfection of her face took his breath away.

'What must you think of me, crying like a little girl?'

'You should see me, sometimes. I get through whole boxes of tissues. That's before I even get onto the kilo tubs of chocolate ice cream. It's pathetic.'

She laughed, brightening up, and touched his arm. 'You're anything but pathetic.' She smiled. 'Thank you for being here, talking to me. I'm sorry for what I said before.'

'That we're all going to freeze to death?'

'No, I mean, when we first met. I called you an idiot.'

'You might have been right. First impressions, and all that.'

She chuckled, shook her head.

'What?' he said.

'I was just thinking that this is the first real conversation I've had with anybody in months.'

'You must have conversations with Austin.'

'We exchange points of view. It's hardly the same.' She looked at him, studying him with a deep gaze. 'It's funny; I feel I can really talk to you, even though I don't know anything about you.'

'I'm just Ben. That's all you need to know.'

'Because you won't say?'

'Because there really isn't all that much *to* say.'

'I don't believe that for a moment. Tell me, Just Ben. What kind of man would risk himself to help a perfect stranger find their lost relative?'

He shrugged. 'It's what I do, I suppose. Or used to do. Maybe old habits die hard.'

'Used to? You mean, professionally?'

'A lot of the time, there was no other option for people in that position.'

'How did you help them?' she asked.

'In whatever way was necessary,' he replied.

'Are you a detective? A cop? Or should I say, an ex-cop? I suppose you'd have arrested me otherwise. I must have broken a hundred laws in doing what I did.'

He had to laugh. 'A cop is the last thing I am.'

'I don't suppose you're the type,' she said, studying him. 'A soldier, maybe. I could see that.'

He gave a shrug. 'That's a little closer to the mark. Once upon a time, at least.'

'And what about now?'

'Retired.'

Her eyes twinkled with amusement. 'I understand, old

man. Lots of retired folks go to live in Frigiliana. For the peace and quiet. That's where you met Raul, isn't it?'

'That's not quite why I was there,' he replied. 'I like to travel around. It was just a chance thing.'

'I'm glad, whatever the reason. I need to thank you again for looking after him. He means the world to me.'

'Raul's a good guy,' Ben said. 'The best.'

'Yes, he is,' Catalina said, then she smiled. 'I remember how my mother used to get so worried about him when we were little. She always said that Raul had a devil on his shoulder. I was the quiet one, who never got into any trouble. Look at us now.'

'He kept on believing he'd find you, even when everything seemed to go against him. Even when everyone thought he was crazy. That kind of faith and devotion are rare.'

'What about you, Ben? Did you think he was crazy, too?'

'The thought occurred to me a few times,' Ben admitted. 'But I was wrong to think it. You're very lucky to have a brother like him.'

'I know I am. Where is he now?'

'Catching up on lost sleep,' Ben said, backpointing in the direction of the lighthouse with his thumb. 'I don't think he's had much peace of mind in the last three months.'

'My fault,' she said. 'A lot of things are my fault.'

'You were only trying to do the right thing.'

'And now it's over.'

He looked at her. 'What will you do?'

'Do?' She shrugged. 'What else is there for me to do but stay here? Like an exile. Stuck in a cage.'

'A gilded cage,' he said.

'Still a cage.'

'There are worse ways to spend your life,' he said. 'Napoleon lived in grand luxury when they exiled him on

320

Elba in 1814. Household staff, personal guard a thousand strong, fine wine, beautiful residence.'

'And then he escaped.'

'Yes, he did. It must have felt good, to be free again. But it only lasted for a hundred days, before they flattened him at Waterloo.'

'You're saying he should have stayed on Elba.'

'Better than where he ended up, made an example of and living in a crummy shack on St Helena, wishing they'd just put a musket ball in him and be done with it.'

She smiled. 'You know your history.'

'Some. What's that saying? Those who don't learn from history are doomed to repeat it.'

'Would you choose a cage?' she asked after a beat.

Ben shook his head. 'Not me. I would have done exactly what he did, busted out of house arrest and taken my chances at Waterloo.'

'Death or glory.'

'Then again, I'm not that smart.'

'I think you are,' she said. 'Among other things.'

'That just proves it. You don't know me.'

Catalina shook her head. 'I can tell a lot about people. You're a decent man. You risked yourself for my brother, and for me. You're obviously educated, sensitive. A little sad, maybe. Are you lonely? Is there anyone?'

He looked at her. 'You mean, as in, "anyone special"?'

She smiled. 'It's a very horrible expression, isn't it?'

'It certainly is,' he said, smiling too. 'No, there isn't anyone special. There was, but that was over a long time ago.'

'Nor me,' she said.

'What about Austin? He seems very fond of you.'

'Austin least of all,' she said. 'What did Raul tell you about that?'

'He told me that you broke up because Austin wanted you to live the same kind of life he does. I understand he's a very private person. This island says it all.'

'A little too private. No, I never wanted that life. And now I've been forced into it, by my own actions.' She sighed. 'Austin is a good person, he really is. I know he still loves me, or at least thinks he does. But things can't ever be that way again between us.'

She fell silent again for a while, and the two of them sat quietly, gazing out to sea for several minutes without either feeling the need to break the silence. Ben hadn't met many people in his life with whom he could share a moment like that, let alone a stranger.

But when he looked at her again, he could see that hers wasn't a tranquil quietness. A deep frown was corrugating the perfect smoothness of her forehead. Her eyes seemed to be moving from side to side without seeing, the way people sometimes unconsciously do when lost in internal reflections. Finally she said, 'When you were a soldier, did you kill people?'

The question took him aback. 'What kind of thing is that to ask?' he said.

'What's it like, to kill a person?'

The way she said it, she clearly wasn't getting any kind of thrill or ghoulish kick out of it. She was asking the question as though it were a matter of dispassionate, scholarly curiosity. Informing herself. The facts, and only the facts. It struck Ben as odd, but then he already knew very well that Catalina Fuentes was someone who was hungry for knowledge. All kinds of knowledge, the bad along with the good.

Ben didn't reply right away. 'It's the easiest thing in the world,' he said. 'It takes very little effort to end a life. Humans aren't hard to kill. We're soft-skinned, relatively defenceless, really quite vulnerable. That's why a predator like a tiger or leopard that's too old or sick to hunt its normal prey will often turn man-eater. Easy meat, literally.'

'I see,' she said. 'That's interesting.'

He paused, then added, 'And it's the hardest thing in the world. People weren't meant to kill one another. When you're forced to make that choice, it's something that stays with you forever. Something you always wish you could undo. No matter what the circumstances might have been that made you go down that road, you keep thinking there might have been another way.'

Catalina was watching his face very closely as he spoke. She digested his words, and nodded. 'What if there was no other way?' she asked.

'It doesn't make it right,' he answered. 'But maybe it makes it necessary.'

Something in her tone, and in her eyes, made him realise that her question went beyond mere academic curiosity. It made him uneasy.

'Nothing will ever be the same,' she said. Her voice was quiet but firm and determined.

'I think I'll go for that run,' Ben said.

Chapter Forty-Nine

Austin Keller had had the first floor of the lighthouse converted into a grand dining room, complete with cherrywood panelling, lapis lazuli fireplace and a vast antique table that might have come from the Palais de Versailles. All-around stained-glass windows gave a three-hundred-and-sixty-degree sweep of the island and the sea, and a magnificent view of the sunset as the four of them sat down that evening for dinner. Keller proudly told Ben and Raul that his resident cook, Melina, had been a celebrated chef at a top Athens restaurant, where he'd been so impressed with the food that he'd snapped her services up there and then, at double her old salary. She and her husband Andréas, who served as a butler and all-around maintenance man, lived in the residential block behind the one that housed Bauer and the rest of the crew.

Ben wasn't able to tell if Keller was putting on an extra-special show for his guests, or whether he always lived like this. Either way, the dinner was as grand as the room in which it was served. A filo pastry pie called Spanakopita filled with feta cheese and spinach to start, followed by a dish of slow-baked lamb marinated in garlic and lemon juice, which was the tenderest meat Ben had eaten in his life. The wine was a 1998 vintage Saint-Émilion, and there seemed to be no shortage of bottles.

Table conversation was awkward, marked with uncomfortable silences. Catalina seemed subdued, eating slowly and speaking little, taking frequent sips of wine. Raul was in a strange mood at first, glancing frequently at his sister, sometimes frowning in consternation, sometimes gazing at her with a dreamy, sentimental look in his eyes and smiling to himself, as if he couldn't quite make up his mind whether he was still angry with her for what she'd got herself involved in, or whether he was overcome with joy and relief at finding her alive and well after all he'd gone through to search for her. Maybe, Ben thought, it was a bit of both. But as the meal wore on, the relieved side seemed to win over. As Raul helped himself to glass after glass of the Saint-Émilion, the twinkle in his eye grew more starry and his grin spread all over his face.

'That's quite some schooner you have there, Austin,' Ben said, making conversation.

Keller looked pleased. '*Shanghai Lady*. I had her modelled on Errol Flynn's old *Zaca*. Hundred and eighteen feet, twenty-three across the beam. Looks like a handful, right? But don't let appearances fool you. She's a breeze to sail. All fully automated, with state-of-the-art electronics. Hell, I could take her round the world single-handed, and I'm not exactly Peter Blake, you know? Just fire up the motors, set your course and you can kick back with a cool drink and pretty much let her do it all for you. Are you a yachtsman yourself, Mr Hope?'

The last sailing yacht Ben had been aboard had been the *Isolde*, little more than half the size of Keller's vessel, belonging to a movie soundtrack composer called Chris Anderson. Ben had co-piloted her across the English Channel overnight in heavy weather, making an illegal landing on the Normandy coast with Leigh Llewellyn. Leigh had been someone Ben had once loved a great deal, and he didn't talk about that period of his life.

'I've done a little,' he said, and left it at that. Noticing that Catalina's glass was empty, he reached for the bottle and leaned across to refill it for her. Her downcast eyes flashed up at him, and a tiny smile twitched at the corners of her lips. Ben caught the warmth in her look. An unspoken entente seemed to have formed between them since their conversation on the beach earlier.

Keller noticed Ben's gesture and Catalina's response, and his expression clouded momentarily. As the conversation fell into another lull, he shot a nervy glance at her, then broke into a forced smile and said, 'Hey, you know, I really think Melina outdid herself tonight. Isn't this lamb something else?'

'Yes, it's very nice,' Catalina replied quietly.

Keller flushed as if he'd scored a point, and pressed on to score more of them. 'I'll bet you there isn't anyone living this well for two hundred miles. Five hundred. You'd have to go to Athens to find anything like it, and even then you'd have a hell of a job finding anything of this quality. What do you say, Mr Hope?'

Ben barely knew the man, but even he thought it was embarrassing to watch him trying so hard to impress Catalina. He said, 'We appreciate your hospitality, Austin.'

'I always look after my guests,' Keller said happily. He turned to Catalina. 'Isn't that right, babe?'

She laid down her knife and fork, a little abruptly, and replied, 'It's wonderful, Austin. The dinner is perfect, just like everything else. I can't express how grateful I am for your kindness, to all of us, and especially to me.'

'Ah, you don't have to thank—' Keller began, leaning back in his chair with a magnanimous wave.

'But you know I can't live the rest of my life like this,' she said, cutting him off. 'I'd go insane.'

Keller's face fell, then clouded again. 'Insane? Really? Oh, great. Most people would kill to be here, living like this. Lap of luxury, not a care in the world.'

She frowned at him. 'Is that really what you think, that I don't have a care in the world, as if I could just forget everything that's happened?'

'You went through a rough time. You were smart enough to get yourself out of it, and now it's over. Done. Time to move on.'

'My life,' she said. 'That's what's over. Everything I am, everything I've been working towards. I panicked, and I threw it all away. I was too frightened to think clearly, and I made a terrible mistake.'

'And now you're thinking clearly, I suppose?' Keller said, growing redder. 'Funny how a few glasses of Bordeaux will do that, hmm?'

'It's not the wine, Austin. Give me some credit.'

Keller shook his head, confused. 'Then what? I don't get it. What's the matter with you? Is it me? Did I do something wrong?'

'You didn't do anything wrong. And there are a million women who would love to be here, living this life. I'm just not one of them. There, now you've forced me to say it.'

Keller pursed his lips angrily, then turned to glare at Ben. 'Do we have you to thank for this dumbass idea? Or you?' he added, jabbing a finger in Raul's direction. 'It can't be a coincidence that she suddenly comes out with this shit after you turned up.'

Ben gave Keller a warning look. 'Let her speak,' he said quietly.

Catalina sighed, then reached over and touched Keller's

327

arm. 'Austin, please. This isn't just some impulse thought. I've had a lot of time to dwell on it. In case you hadn't noticed, there isn't a lot else for me to do around here.'

'And so what then?' he demanded, jerking his arm away from her touch. 'You're going to leave? And do what? Where will you run and hide this time?'

She shook her head resolutely. 'No more running and hiding. I have to finish this.'

Keller shoved his plate away from him, as if he was too disgusted to eat another bite. 'Finish this? What the hell does that mean, *finish this*?'

She said, 'Don't you see? All I'm doing here is hiding my head in the sand, hoping this whole nightmare will just go away of its own accord. Who am I trying to kid? It won't go away, not ever, not for any of us, unless I put a stop to it.'

Keller threw up his hands. 'Put a stop to it how?'

'For a start, by blowing the whole thing wide open on live television. I have more than enough connections.'

'Aren't you forgetting something? You're dead and buried. You no longer exist.'

'All the better publicity. Talk about the immediate attention I'd get, just by walking into any TV studio in the world right now.'

'And telling them what?'

'The truth,' she said.

'That you faked your own suicide? They'll crucify you. You'll blow up the biggest storm in the history of the world media.'

'That's exactly what I want,' she said. 'I'll be on every news channel on the planet. Giving me the perfect opportunity to bring the whole story out into the open. Murder. Conspiracy. Every last filthy little detail of what those bastards did. By the time I'm done, they won't be able to touch me. They'll be too busy hiding for their lives.'

'And your research? You planning on spilling the beans about that, too?'

'Of course. It's what this is all about. The people have a right to know.'

Keller snorted. 'My God, I can't believe you're really contemplating this. It's unbridled folly.'

'Why? Why is it folly?'

'I got two words for you. Hatchet job. Nobody's going to listen to a mentally unstable woman who popped a barrel load of antidepressants before punting her own car off a cliff. Especially when you start on the science bit. The end of the world? Sure, that'll work. Forget crucified – you'll be hung, drawn and quartered. And meanwhile, all this will have been for nothing. You'll be right back where you started. Except this time, you'll be an even easier target for these sons of bitches. They're not the kind of people you can get away from twice.'

'I hate to say it,' Raul told Catalina, wagging his fork at Keller. The wine was making him slur his words a little. 'And I never thought I'd ever find myself agreeing with this guy. But he's actually making sense.'

'There,' Keller said to her, pointing at Raul. 'If you won't hear it from me, then at least hear it from your brother.'

Catalina slumped in her seat, as if suddenly deflated. 'You really think so?' she asked Raul.

Raul nodded. 'I really do, yes. You can't go back. It's too late for that now. You'd be crazy to. As for all this stuff about an ice age, it's not exactly something your adoring fans are going to want to hear. They'll think you lost your mind. Even *I* think that, and I know you better than anyone.'

'Thanks a million, brother,' she said, but the resolution

in her voice had faltered. She looked imploringly at Ben for support.

'It could backfire,' was all Ben said.

Catalina gulped down half a glass of wine, then closed her eyes and fell silent for a lingering moment. Finally, she let out a heavy sigh, and nodded in resignation. 'You're right. All of you. What was I thinking?'

Keller was all smiles now that he'd won. 'Don't beat yourself up, Cat. We all understand how tough it's been for you. You're entitled to have a few doubts now and then. Just remember, you're in safe hands.'

'I must seem so ungrateful. You've done so much for me.'

'Not a bit of it,' Keller said, and leaned over to put his arm around her shoulder and give her a tender squeeze. 'It's my pleasure to do things for you, you know that, right? And the last thing I want is that you feel trapped here. Didn't I already set up your new ID, passport, driver's licence, the works?'

'Carmen Hernandez,' she said. 'I know you did, and I really, really appreciate it.'

Keller grinned a mile-wide grin. 'And before you know it, this whole thing will have blown over, and you and I will go travelling all over the world. Free as a couple of birds. Never have to worry about anything again. A totally fresh start. I'll even buy you a house. You can have a castle in Spain if you want. With the world's fanciest observatory built in, just for you. Now who gets that kind of an opportunity in their lives? Huh? Tell me that. We just need to hang on a little longer for the dust to settle, is all.'

Catalina spoke hardly another word through the rest of dinner, sinking back into the same subdued and reflective state as earlier. Ben watched her and wondered what she was thinking. After Andréas took away the main course dishes and served dessert, she picked at her food for only a minute before politely excusing herself, saying she was feeling tired and wanted to get an early night.

Not long after Catalina had left the dining room, Raul stood up, full of 1998 Saint-Émilion and nearly as unsteady on his feet as he'd been when Ben had first met him in Frigiliana, and announced he was ready to call it a night as well.

'Scotch?' Keller said to Ben when it was just the two of them.

'Bring it on,' Ben said.

'Rocks?'

'As it comes,' Ben said.

For another hour, they worked their way through the remainder of the eighteen-year-old Bowmore while Keller talked mostly about *Shanghai Lady*, her technical specifications, the money that had been lavished on her, the many ports she'd docked in all over the Mediterranean, the Caribbean, the Indian Ocean.

Ben wasn't really listening. He was thinking about Catalina Fuentes. Trying to puzzle out the questions that had been gnawing at him since that afternoon on the beach. Playing back in his mind the things she'd said, both then and during dinner, and wondering what the truth really was.

Because he was even more certain now that she was holding something back. He just didn't know what it was yet, and it was troubling him.

It wouldn't be very long before he discovered that the truth was something he couldn't even have imagined.

Chapter Fifty

Ben was the last to retire for the night, long after one in the morning. As he passed Raul's door he could hear the steady rasp of snoring from inside. Out for the count. He was careful not to make noise as he let himself into his own room, although probably nothing much short of a shotgun blast would have roused the Spaniard from his heavy sleep.

Ben took a shower and then climbed into bed, but he couldn't sleep. The idea forming in his mind was becoming more unsettling the more he thought about it.

He wanted to be wrong. But he was very much concerned that he was right. There was only one way to know, and he didn't much like that either. He was just going to have to wait and see what happened.

An hour went by. He couldn't sleep. He got up and paced his room, did some press-ups and went back to bed. Still couldn't sleep. Another hour passed. Then another – until, at last, he began to drift away into that otherworldly state somewhere between thinking and dreaming, where nothing seemed quite real—

Except for the sound that yanked him back to consciousness and made his eyes snap open and his body jack-knife up straight in the bed.

It was still dark in the room. He hadn't been dreaming.

What had woken him was the sound of an engine starting up down below. One of the Jeeps. He could hear it revving. Accelerating rapidly away from the lighthouse. Someone in a hurry.

By the time he was up out of bed and going over to the window, the Jeep was already taking off down the road, its taillights disappearing into the darkness.

'Shit,' he muttered.

The luminous dial of his watch read almost five thirty a.m. Whatever was happening down there, he didn't like it. He pulled on his jeans and ran barefoot and shirtless from his room, down the lighthouse staircase and out into the cold morning air. First light was still more than an hour away, and the moon was still glimmering over the smooth ocean. The buildings that housed the staff and Keller's men were all in darkness. So was the lighthouse, all except for the top floor: Catalina's floor, its encircling windows and glass dome all lit up as if she couldn't sleep either.

Or something else. He paused to listen, and thought he could hear the distant sound of the engine over the whisper of the ocean. The Jeep was right across the far side of the island.

Ben ran back inside the lighthouse and took the iron stairs all the way to the top, slowing as he passed Keller's quarters on the floor below Catalina's so as not to wake him. He entered her room without knocking, because his instincts told him she wouldn't be there.

And his instincts were correct. If she'd gone to bed at all, the sheets were now neatly made up. There was no sign of her.

Literally no sign of her. All her things were gone. The laptop and the pile of notes were gone. The tan leather travelling bag that had been lying at the foot of the bed was gone. The wardrobes and drawers were empty. The bath-room was stripped bare of any and all personal effects.

'Shit,' he said again.

He'd been right.

It was her who'd taken the Jeep. She'd driven to the low-lying end of the island because it was from the beach that she was intending to make her escape. Catalina Fuentes had no intention of remaining a prisoner in her gilded cage. Not for another day, not for another hour. She was getting off Icthyios. Making good her pledge to end this, once and for all. Her apparent change of mind at dinner had only been a feint to throw off any suspicions that Keller or Raul might have that she still meant business. Ben hadn't been so easily duped. But then, Keller and Raul hadn't been there on the beach earlier that day. Neither of them understood the depth of her frustration.

After thinking about it for so many hours, Ben was certain that her plan was to snatch one of the motor boats from the boathouse, and use it to cross over to neighbouring Sárla in order to catch the morning ferry to Karpathos. Where he was sure she intended to board a plane heading God knew where. She still had some money, and with her new identity papers she'd be able to travel freely as long as nobody recognised her face. She'd already become expert at disguising herself to give the paparazzi the slip. With her different hair and some judicious makeup, nobody need ever suppose that Carmen Hernandez was in fact the late, lamented Catalina Fuentes.

Ben hurried back down to the guest level. He could still hear Raul snoring behind the door. Ben had no intention of waking him up. He quickly buttoned on his shirt, hauled on his shoes and returned down below, taking care not to let his footsteps ring on the iron staircase. Outside, he raced to where the remaining Jeeps were parked, jumped into the nearest one, fired up the engine and the lights and took off into the darkness after Catalina.

At high speed, the drive from one end of the island to the other took no more than ninety seconds. He skidded off the road and went roaring over soft sand towards the jetty and boathouse. There was no sign of the other Jeep. He killed the engine and jumped out and ran along the clattering boards of the jetty.

Ben reached the steps that led down to the boathouse. He flung open the door and peered inside. At first he could see only shadows; then as his eyes adapted to the murk he was able to make out the swirling reflections of the water and the shapes of the three boats moored up there, bobbing gently, their sides clunking together with the swell. He could see no sign of any loose moorings. It didn't look as if Catalina had taken one of the boats, after all.

Then where was she? And where was her Jeep?

It was at that moment that Ben heard the sound of another engine starting up. It wasn't the Jeep, or anything remotely like it. It was the rush of twin turbofan jet turbines rapidly gaining pitch and power from a whooshing whine to an ear-splitting roar as Austin Keller's private aircraft prepared for takeoff.

Ben scrambled out of the boathouse and went sprinting back along the jetty, the noise of the plane filling his ears with every advancing step. He raced for the pebbly rise that blocked the view of the airstrip from the beach.

It was impossible. *Catalina was flying the plane? By herself?*

As he reached the top, the full blast of the noise hit his ears. The asphalt was all lit up like a motorway. The aircraft had taxied out of the hangar, past where the Jeep was parked with its doors hanging open and its headlamps burning. The runway lights gleamed on the sleek white fuselage. The jet turbines were still mounting in pitch, reaching a noise level that sent needles of pain lancing through Ben's eardrums. He ran down the other side of the rise towards the asphalt, waving his arms and yelling, 'Stop! Wait!' But his voice was so completely drowned by the enormous noise that even he couldn't hear a word he was shouting.

The aircraft began to roll. The howl of the turbofans grew even louder, breaking the limits of all possible noise. The nose and wing lights seared his eyeballs with their dazzling whiteness, making him blink. Some insane part of him wanted to chase after it, grab hold of it, pit his strength against its and force it to stop. He couldn't let her go.

But she was going, and nothing he could do could prevent that now. The engine blast drove him back. The immensity of the sound resonated through the ground under his feet like an earthquake tremor. He could feel his ribs vibrating. He clamped his palms tight over his ears, stopped running and came to a halt on the runway. Stood helplessly by and watched as the jet accelerated away from him. Faster – and faster – and faster still, scorching the air in a wake of super-heated exhaust gases from its nozzles.

Then it was up, and away, leaving him feeling tiny and powerless on the ground as it hurtled into the night sky.

And she was gone.

Ben's ears were still ringing wildly as he ran back to his Jeep. He fired up the motor, threw it into drive and spun it back towards the road.

Ninety seconds later, he was back at the lighthouse. The noise of the departing jet must have woken the household, or at least part of it. Keller's floor was all lit up, as was Andréas' and Melina's little building around the back of the residential block. As Ben skidded the Jeep to a halt, Keller emerged in his pyjamas from the lighthouse entrance, hair all awry, rubbing his eyes and gaping up at the sky in disbelief. A moment later, Andréas and Melina appeared from their doorway, wrapped in dressing gowns and looking startled and anxious. Keller saw Ben getting out of the Jeep and demanded, 'Hey! What the hell's going on?'

Ben said nothing. He glanced up at the lighthouse and saw that the guest-floor windows were dark. Raul must still be asleep, but then the quantity of wine he'd downed that evening would have knocked out a horse. Ben wondered if Bauer and the rest of Keller's crew had the same excuse. Because there was no sign of life coming from their block either. No movement, no lights.

'That was the plane,' Keller was saying in a stunned voice, jabbing a finger up at the empty, dark sky. '*My* plane.'

Ben ignored him and made for the crew block. He had a bad feeling, but he didn't yet know why.

When he threw open the door and found the light switch, he knew. And his bad feeling suddenly got worse by a factor of ten.

Bauer, Emmert, Spencer, Willis, Fulton and Griggs stared back at him, their eyes wide and blinking in the light. They were all facing the doorway, side by side, trussed helplessly to a row of chairs, struggling against the ropes that bound their arms and ankles and the gags tied tightly over their mouths. Each of them had a livid, fresh bruise on his forehead.

Six men. One was missing.

Avery, the pilot.

Ben walked around the back of Bauer's chair and yanked his gag free. Bauer spat bits of fibre and yelled, 'Untie us!'

'Talk to me, Bauer,' Ben said.

'She's out of her head,' Bauer said. 'I can't believe she did this to us.'

Keller stood in the doorway, eyes boggling at the sight of his men.

Ben got to work on the knots that held Bauer's wrists. They were pretty good ones. 'One woman, against six of you? She's a scientist, not a Royal Marines commando.'

'She made Avery tie us up,' Bauer jabbered. 'Got us one by one. Banged each us over the head in turn while we were sleeping. Dragged us in here and tied us up. Must've got the rope from the store shed.' His arms came free and he rubbed his wrists to get the circulation back into his hands. 'She's fucking insane!'

'Then she and Avery were working together?' Ben said.

Bauer shook his head. 'No chance. Pete Avery's one of us. She made him do it. Had that goddamned Glock pointed at him the whole time. I don't blame the guy. She'd have shot him. She had the look.'

'Where did she get a pistol?'

'It was his.' Bauer pointed at the red-faced Willis three chairs down the row, who garbled something incomprehensible through his gag. Ben stepped over to Willis and tore the gag away.

'I was cleaning it—' Willis began.

'In your sleep?'

'No, no. Before I hit the sack. I left it on the table—'

'With a full magazine in it?' Ben said.

Willis nodded. 'Gun can't work on an empty mag, man.'

'You left a loaded firearm unattended on the table while you went off to bed,' Ben said. 'That's the definition of an idiot.'

'Give us a break,' Bauer said, leaning down to untie his own ankles. 'We're living on an island. Nothing ever happens

338

around here. She took us by surprise. We were sleeping, for Christ's sake.'

Ben shook his head. 'You're all idiots. Where's the gun now?'

'She took it,' Bauer said.

'And Avery?'

Bauer nodded. 'Him too. Once he'd finished tying us up, she made him go with her. He didn't have a lot of choice. Like I said, she meant business. Next thing, they took off in the Jeep.' As he talked, Bauer managed to loosen the ropes around his ankles and flung them away. He stumbled unsteadily out of his chair to start untying the rest of his men.

Ben turned to Keller. 'So now we know what happened. Catalina made Avery fly the plane.'

Keller looked stricken, jaw dropping, pale with shock. 'Wait. Wait. What are you saying? She *took my pilot hostage* and *stole my Lear*?'

'Apparently so,' Ben said. 'Unless you have any better theories.'

'Where's she gone?'

'Away,' Ben said.

'I can't believe she'd do something like that,' Keller protested. 'It's impossible. It wasn't her idea. It was that lunatic brother of hers, right? You know there's something wrong with him, don't you? I always thought so. This was his plan.'

'That would be why he was still fast asleep and snoring like a bull after she and Avery had already left in the Jeep,' Ben said. 'It doesn't sound very plausible to me. But you can always go and ask him, when he wakes up. I'm sure he'll be happy to explain.'

Keller's mouth dropped open another inch. 'Holy crap.

You're right. Then it must be true. Has she lost her mind? What the hell does she think she's doing?'

'Getting off this island,' Ben said. 'The only way she thought she could. If you ask me, she's been planning it for a while.'

'And it's partly my fault,' Keller said with a deep frown. 'Because it was me who arranged to have those false papers made for her. I got the best guy in the business for the job. Cost me thirty thousand bucks, and I thought I was doing a good thing. She was planning on running out on me, all along.'

'What was the alternative, Keller? Would you rather have kept her prisoner here?'

'No, damn it!' Keller yelled. 'But why would she run? She had everything here! Everything she could possibly need!'

'Except the one thing she wanted,' Ben said. 'The one thing you couldn't offer her, Keller. Her freedom.'

'Freedom? Freedom to do what? Go and spill her guts out on TV? Go and make a fool of herself, and maybe get herself killed in the process? Is that what this is all about?'

Ben said nothing in reply, but the answer to the question was clear in his mind. And he now understood exactly what it was Catalina intended to do next. The uncomfortable thoughts nagging inside him were falling into place at last. The things she'd asked him on the beach made sense to him now. Asking him what it was like to kill a person. Telling him nothing would ever be the same.

He remembered the other things they'd talked about. Napoleon Bonaparte's historic escape from his gilded cage on the island of Elba. The exiled warrior going back to attend to unfinished business.

Death or glory.

Ben knew that Catalina hadn't forced Avery at gunpoint

to help her steal Keller's jet so that she could get to the nearest television studio and cause a major sensation. The whole thing at dinner had been a deliberate smokescreen, to distract them all from her real intentions.

She was going after Maxwell Grant in revenge.

Chapter Fifty-One

When Ben and Keller returned to the ground-floor light-house living area a few moments later they were met by a dishevelled and hungover Raul, who had finally been roused by all the commotion and come stumbling downstairs, clad in only his boxer shorts. The instant Ben saw his face, he knew something was wrong.

Raul was clutching a note. 'It's from her,' he muttered in a cracked voice. 'I found it on my pillow just now, when I woke up. It says, "*I'm sorry. For the second time, I ask that you try to understand that I had no choice, and forgive me. Love to you and our dear parents, Catalina*".'

'No choice?' Keller yelled, veins standing out all over his forehead. 'That's a joke. Do you know what your maniac sister just did? Oh, nothing serious, just a small matter of hijacking my damn plane. Gone. Whoosh. Out of here. Disappeared into the night. Her and my pilot, with a frigging gun to his head. Get the picture?'

Raul turned to Ben, speechless.

'It's true,' Ben said.

'What am I supposed to do now?' Keller said, pointing a finger upwards at the sky. 'That crazy fucking bitch has got my Learjet.'

Raul darkened a shade at the insult. 'Watch your mouth, Keller. You don't talk about my sister that way.'

'You people are all the same,' Keller went on loudly, jabbing the finger at Raul. 'Deep down, she's just another Spanish hothead like you are. Christ, what was I even thinking, getting mixed up with her?'

Raul clenched his jaw and showed Keller a balled-up fist, four white knuckles under his nose. 'You say one more word, *pendejo*, and you'll get this right in your teeth.'

'What did you call me?' Keller said, stiffening.

'You've had it coming for a long time,' Raul said. 'Don't push me, understand?'

'Oh, yeah?' Keller exploded. 'I'll push you, Fuentes. I'll push you right off my fucking island. All the way back to fucking Spain.' He shoved Raul in the chest.

By the time Ben had had time to think, *Here we go again*, it had already happened. Raul seemed to coil like a snake, and then his fist lashed out too fast for the eye to follow. It caught Keller square in the side of the jaw, with a sound like a cleaver chopping into a bony shoulder of mutton. Keller's head snapped back. He seemed to hang in space for an instant, unconscious on his feet. Then he collapsed into an armchair and lay slumped with his chin on his chest and his arms hanging limply by his sides.

'That was constructive,' Ben said. 'At least you didn't set him on fire.'

'To hell with him,' Raul said, with a gesture of contempt. 'Now let's go. We have to find her, and stop her.'

'No, Raul,' Ben said.

Raul looked at him.

'*I* have to find her and stop her,' Ben said. 'You're not

343

coming with me. I almost let you get yourself killed the first time. That's not an option any more.'

Raul blinked.

And in the instant that he blinked, Ben punched him. It had to be fast, because Raul had the reflexes of a panther. And it couldn't be a tickle, either, because the Spaniard could probably take the knocks as well as he could deliver them, and Ben wasn't much inclined to get into a protracted toe-to-toe fistfight with the guy. Then again, it had to be well judged. If there was one thing that separated someone of Raul's training from someone of Ben's, it was that not everyone was taught how to inflict a lethal single blow. And fewer people still had had occasion to practise it for real.

So Ben hit him as suddenly and as hard and as square as he could without killing him or doing lasting damage. Raul didn't see it coming. The punch knocked him out cold and he hit the floor at the feet of the unconscious Keller, still clutching his sister's note.

Ben felt bad about it, but he would have felt worse if it had been any other way. He hauled Raul's limp body into a facing armchair, wondering which of the two would wake up first.

'I won't let anything happen to her, Raul,' he said. 'That's a promise.'

Every second that counted down, the jet plane with Catalina on it was approximately sixteen kilometres further away. Ben ran up to his room and grabbed his jacket and bag, then raced back downstairs and outside to the Jeep.

The first light of dawn was approaching, a blood-red glow on the eastern horizon. Bauer and the other five of Keller's remaining crew were hanging around the buildings, looking variously sheepish and ready for war. Griggs and Spencer were nursing pistols, as though somehow the situation could be remedied with firepower. Ben suspected that Willis would have been clutching his, too, if Catalina hadn't got it now.

'Where's the chief?' Bauer asked Ben.

'Indisposed,' Ben said. 'I'd leave him to get over it, if I were you. That's if I wanted to hang onto my job.'

Without another word, Ben got back into the Jeep, roared it into life and accelerated away, leaving them all standing there watching him. For the third and last time, he did the ninety-second high-speed drive between the lighthouse and the beach, and skidded to a halt at the foot of the pebbly rise. The breaking dawn was bleeding through a morning mist that shrouded the coastline of Sárla in the distance.

Ben clambered out of his vehicle and took a few steps up the rise. The Jeep Catalina had used to make her escape was still exactly as it had been before, looking abandoned and forlorn with its doors hanging open and its headlights dimmed to an amber glow as the battery ran down. He turned away and ran for the jetty, heading for the boathouse. If Catalina had taken one of the boats, as he'd mistakenly anticipated, then he might have had a chance of catching up with her as she cut across to Sárla to catch the ferry to Karpathos. As things stood, there was simply no way he'd ever make up for the head start she had on him. He could maybe reckon on crossing the stretch of ocean in an hour, minimum. During which time a Learjet with a cruising speed of around Mach 0.8 would have covered a further nine hundred kilometres or more. And then he'd still have to waste yet more time waiting for the ferry to take him from Sárla to somewhere they had things like aeroplanes.

Not good.

Then a movement caught the corner of Ben's eye, and he paused in his step to turn to his left and look in that direction. What he'd seen were the mastheads of Keller's yacht, visible over the rise and drifting gently from side to side on the ocean's swell.

She's a breeze to sail, Keller had said. *Hell, I could take her around the world single-handed.*

'Hmm,' Ben said.

Five minutes later, the outboard motor boat was burbling away from the shore, across the shallows to where *Shanghai Lady* lay at anchor. Up close, the schooner's sides reflected the crimson dapples of the dawn sun off the water, and her elegant masts and immaculately furled sails towered overhead. Ben brought the motor boat in close to the hull, where a retractable boarding ladder extended down to meet him. He tossed his bag up onto the deck and mounted the ladder, letting the motor boat drift away.

The smooth hardwood deck, all hundred-and-twenty-odd feet of it, pitched and heeled gently under his feet. *Shanghai Lady* was a thing of beauty, a floating work of art – but Ben was more concerned about his practical ability to sail the thing single-handed. The moment he stepped inside the wheelhouse, he saw that Keller hadn't been kidding about the electronics. Amid all the expanses of magnificent varnished walnut, there was probably as much technology at his disposal as Avery had on board the Learjet. Multifunction displays boasted everything from smart-control autopilot to sonar fishfinder module, automated sail control, thermal marine cameras, radar and GPS navigation, voyage planner, chart plotting software and plenty more stuff that Ben wasn't going to need.

'Now let's see if we can't make up a little lost time,' he said to himself. It was already nearly quarter to seven and the sun was breaking free of the horizon. In minutes, the anchor had been winched aboard, the engines were thrusting at full throttle and *Shanghai Lady* was tracking away from Icthyios, cleaving through the water with a white bow wave and a foamy white wake curving away behind her. Ben set his course to bypass the island of Sárla and make sail for Karpathos, which his on-board trip computer told him would take just a few hours. He radioed ahead to inform the port harbour master of his arrival, and got his permission to land. Insurance and harbour fees were all magically taken care of, courtesy of Austin J. Keller III.

Keller been right about *Shanghai Lady*. The schooner could sail itself, and it was much faster than it looked. But not fast enough. Frustrated, Ben paced the deck and wished that he had his cigarettes. He hadn't smoked a Gauloise since leaving Germany. The way he was going, there was a real risk that he might lapse into a clean and healthy lifestyle.

The morning wore on. Sky and ocean lightened to a glittering azure blue as the sun climbed high overhead. Ben gazed up at the bright yellow ball in the sky, and wondered whether it was his imagination that it didn't feel particularly warm for the time of year. Catalina's climate predictions were hard to shake from his mind. He was still musing about them when he spied land on the horizon, dead ahead in the far distance. The wheelhouse instruments confirmed that he was approaching Karpathos.

Seven forty-five a.m. Just over two hours had already passed since Catalina's escape from Icthyios.

By eight fifteen, *Shanghai Lady* was sailing into the larger island's main port of Pigadia, filled with all manner of vessels from tiny fishing boats to giant superyachts, and overlooked by clusters of traditionally whitewashed Greek houses, apartment blocks and hotels. Ben found his allocated mooring point within the harbour, and soon afterwards the schooner was lashed securely into place among a forest of masts. Back on solid ground, Ben made his way through the port and immediately started hunting for a taxi.

An hour after that, he was buzzing from an overload of thick, dark Greek coffee and sitting twiddling his thumbs in the departure lounge at Karpathos Island National Airport, impatiently counting down the minutes before his flight was called, and still wishing he had his cigarettes.

He kept thinking about Catalina. No way to know what direction she'd flown off in. Impossible to tell where she was now. Not a chance in hell of following her.

That was, if it hadn't been for one lucky detail.

Ben reached into his pocket to check the phone one more time.

Chapter Fifty-Two

Three hours earlier

At around the same time that Ben was clambering on board *Shanghai Lady*, Austin Keller's Learjet was cruising at forty-three thousand feet over the Ionian Sea, approaching the coastline of what was sometimes described as the 'toe of Italy'. A very unhappy Pete Avery was at the controls. Catalina Fuentes was beside him in the co-pilot's chair, still holding the pistol she'd taken from Willis.

The argument had been going on since they'd taken off, though it was Avery who had done nearly all the talking. His voice was hoarse from shouting at her. 'I don't know how you think this is going to work,' he was saying now. 'If you had even the first, tiniest clue about aviation, you'd realise we can't drop in out of the sky just anywhere we please, unannounced, without permission. There are regulations.'

'I'm well aware of the regulations,' Catalina said calmly.

'That's wonderful,' Avery barked back at her. 'Then you must know that you have to give the Italian authorities at least seven days' notice before you can enter their airspace. You want a whole division of *carabinieri* waiting on the tarmac to arrest us the moment we touch down?'

'There's nothing to worry about,' she said.

'You're right! What do I care? I'm the victim here. *You're* the armed hijacker they'll shoot to pieces the moment they figure out what's going on!'

Catalina shook her head. 'Nobody's getting shot, and nobody's getting arrested. Not where we're landing. They won't even know we're there.' Still keeping him covered with the gun, she reached with her free hand into the leather travel bag at her feet and brought out a slip of paper, which she handed to him. 'Here's where you're going to set us down,' she said.

Catalina hadn't spent all her time on Icthyios exploring the island or engaged in solar science research. The coordinates written on the slip of paper were the location of an old, abandoned former airfield deep in the heart of rural Calabria in southern Italy, a few kilometres from Serra San Bruno. One of seventy-seven all-but-forgotten airfields in the country, it had been built in August 1943 by the US Army Corps of Engineers ahead of the Allied invasion of Italy in September of that year, and used as a temporary base by the US Air Force 86th Fighter Bomber Group. After their last combat operation was flown in April 1945 and the 86th pulled out, War Department plans to dismantle the base and airfield had never quite materialised and it remained to this day, semi-derelict amid disused farmland behind a rickety perimeter fence.

Catalina had zeroed in on it using Google Earth to ascertain its condition – which she'd concluded was quite usable despite some degradation of the concrete runway – and its dimensions, which provided more than adequate landing distance for a small jet. As usual, she had worked everything out to the last detail.

'You're nuts,' Avery growled at her when he'd finished entering the coordinates into the on-board navigation computer. 'There's nothing but empty farmland. How'm I supposed to bring this thing down there? Catch a rut, bounce over a rock, we'll flip and crash and burn and that'll end your little joyride pretty fast, won't it?'

'We'll see,' she said patiently.

Catalina owed her choice of landing site to the other, and more important, piece of research she'd been engaged in during the last three months. Keller had necessarily been involved in that one, because although she'd never allowed him to know how she was secretly planning on using the information, it was through the kinds of discreet inquiries that only money like Austin's could make possible that she'd been able to learn the precise location of Maxwell Grant's favourite of his three homes. The townhouse in Mayfair was generally only a stopover for when his business affairs took him to London, as was the forty-million-dollar Manhattan penthouse for his New York trips. The place Grant liked to spend most of his leisure time was the grand seventeenth-century Villa Callisto, set within a secluded fifty-acre estate an hour and a half's drive up the coast near the Gulf of Táranto. She had the exact coordinates for that, too.

Pete Avery might have been a deeply unhappy man that morning, but he was a skilled pilot, especially with a gun pointed at him. 'I'll be damned,' he breathed some time later when they swooped down out of the clouds and spied the old airfield in the distance, like a ghostly apparition bathed in the light of dawn. There was nothing but open countryside around it for kilometres. No sign of habitation, and certainly no sign of Italian Air Force fighters coming to intercept them.

Avery made two passes over the deserted airfield before he determined the best angle of approach. On the third pass, he brought the plane down in a steep descent. The Lear was as agile as an airborne Ferrari. They overshot the perimeter fence by fifty feet to make a bumpy but successful landing on the cracked, weed-strewn runway. Exactly as she'd calculated, they had been in the air for just under ninety minutes.

'I still think you're nuts,' he grumbled at her as he started powering down the engines.

'That was a very good landing,' she replied, getting out of the co-pilot's chair. 'Thank you for your help.'

Before he could reply, she hammered him over the head with the butt of the pistol, twice. Avery went out like a light and slumped in his chair.

'I'm sorry,' she said to the unconscious pilot. 'I hope you'll be all right.'

Catalina reached again into her bag, and brought out the last length of the rope she'd taken from the storage shed on Icthyios. She carefully looped it around Avery's chest and arms and tied him into the pilot's seat. His bonds weren't intended to hold him indefinitely, because she didn't want him to die of dehydration out here with nobody to rescue him. She just needed to hold him up for a while. By the time he got loose and called for help, she'd be far away.

She opened the exit hatch and hurried away from the aircraft carrying her travel bag. Once she was the other side of the hole she found in the perimeter fence, she started walking. The fields were rutted and hard going, but after a couple of kilometres she reached a road and checked the GPS app on her phone to make sure she was heading in the right direction.

Some kilometres further down the road a friendly old Calabrian farmer called Giuseppe pulled up in his battered pickup truck to offer a lift to the lone female hitchhiker. With her complexion she easily passed for southern Italian, and it also happened to be one of the languages Catalina spoke to perfection. She introduced herself as Lucia Verde, explaining that her car had broken down and that she absolutely needed to get to Serra San Bruno for her sister's wedding later that morning. Giuseppe was only too happy to oblige, and regaled her all the way there with stories about his seven grandchildren.

After Giuseppe dropped her off with a cheery goodbye in the town of San Bruno, she made her way to the bus station, via a coffee bar where she stopped for a light breakfast. Nobody recognised her, which was one of the few parts of her plan she'd had to leave to chance. Either the hairstyle was working, or her fame had never quite reached rural southern Italy. Either way, it was a relief.

By eight fifteen, Catalina had boarded a bus that was headed all the way up the coast to Táranto. It wasn't too crowded, and she sat alone near the back. As the bus wound its twisting way northwards up the Calabrian coast, she ignored the spectacular ocean views. She'd seen enough pretty beaches to last her the rest of her life. Instead she sat clutching her leather bag on her lap and gazed into space, working over and over her plan.

The desire to avenge the murders of Jim Lockhart and Dougal Sinclair had been burning inside her even before she'd arrived on Icthyios. So many times she'd visualised herself going after the man she was certain was responsible, picturing the whole thing in detail, working out exactly how it could be done. Then so many times she'd vacillated, thinking that she must be mad: that she was a scientist, not an assassin; that revenge was out of her grasp, and that she was going to drive herself mad if she didn't put all such notions out of her head and do her best to move on.

And she'd very nearly succeeded in dropping the whole insane idea, until Raul had found her and told her that Kazem was dead too. That had been the tipping point, making her realise that she had no choice. She had to cut the head off the snake. Kill it before it killed everyone she knew, everyone she loved.

Just two things bothered her. The first was the very real possibility that when she got to the Villa Callisto, Grant wouldn't be there. He led a hectic life and could easily be away on business, just about anywhere in the world. It was a concern, but only a minor and not insurmountable one.

The second thing that worried her, as much as it reassured her, was nestling inside her travel bag. But that, too, was a matter that could be addressed. Everything in its own time. *Stay calm*, she told herself. It was no different from a complex astronomical calculation. Method and attention to detail were everything. Once you knew your formula was sound, it was just a matter of following the logical steps through, clear-headed and systematically, until you achieved your result.

She didn't care what happened after that. If she didn't make it out alive, then so be it. At least then she would have met her end doing something good, instead of running and hiding like a coward. There couldn't be a better way to atone for the shame she felt.

And, anyway, Catalina Fuentes was already dead.

Chapter Fifty-Three

Around nine forty-five that morning, Catalina stepped off the bus in a small coastal town some way east of Rossano, on the southern edge of the Gulf of Táranto. Checking her bearings once more, she ascertained that she was exactly 17.2 kilometres from her destination. Now it was time to address the first of her two main concerns.

She was walking down a narrow street away from the bus stop when she spotted the group of teenagers hanging around on the corner. They were aged around fourteen or fifteen and should have been in school. Noisy and unruly, but they were exactly what she'd been looking for. She smiled as she walked up to them, and they all turned to stare at her. 'Hey, guys,' she said breezily in Italian, and plucked a banknote out of her purse. 'Any of you feel like making a quick hundred euros? Won't take you more than a minute.'

Which got them all clamouring to be the one who got the cash, even before they knew what the job entailed.

'You,' she said, picking out the tallest one of the bunch. He looked the most adult, with dark eyes that looked sharp and quick. 'What's your name?'

'Luca,' he said. His voice was mature enough to pass for an eighteen-year-old's, or even older. Perfect.

'Do you have a phone, Luca?'

Silly question. They all had phones, and eagerly whipped them out of their pockets to show her, nobody wanting to be out of the money. Catalina took out the private business card that she'd been carrying around in her purse ever since July third, the night of the party in Kensington. She showed the card to the tall kid. 'See this number here? Then I want you to call it and ask to speak to Signor Grant. That's his name on the card.'

'Grant,' Luca repeated. 'Okay. What do I say to him?'

'Say that you're calling from the offices of the Gruppo Poste Italiane, and that the satellite dish package he ordered is due for special delivery to Villa Callisto this afternoon. You're checking that the householder will be there to sign for it. Can you remember all that?'

'I think so.' Luca repeated it all back. 'A hundred euros? Are you sure?'

'Easy money,' she said. 'I want you to switch your mobile to speaker phone mode, so I can hear.'

'Fine,' Luca said with a laconic shrug. 'Who is this guy, anyway?'

'Just a friend,' she said. 'It's kind of a trick I'm playing on him. He's very suspicious, so you have to sound really grown-up and convincing. And he might answer in English, but don't let that put you off. Just say exactly what I told you. Can you handle it?'

'Sure, no problem,' Luca said. His friends were all clamouring round him. He cuffed a couple of them over the head, told them to shut the fuck up, then cleared his throat and dialled with his phone on speaker. Catalina moved close so she could hear. If Grant wasn't there, she'd already planned to find a cheap place to rent locally and keep trying until he was.

The teenagers fell into a hush, all grinning and loving the

356

prank. Loving the hundred euros even more. She pressed a finger to her lips to warn them to stay quiet.

Grant's dial tone rang five long, tense times before a man's voice answered. '*Pronto?*' His voice was rich and deep, sonorous and smooth. Unmistakably Maxwell Grant's. He spoke Italian with a strong British accent, but he wouldn't have been speaking it at all if he'd been in London or New York. Catalina felt her stomach tighten with excitement, mingled with fear.

Luca must have really wanted the hundred euros, because he played the part perfectly. Grant appeared genuinely flummoxed by the call. 'What are you talking about? I never ordered a satellite dish.'

'I'm afraid you still have to sign for it, even if you don't want it,' Luca said, sounding exactly like an infuriatingly anal-retentive low-level bureaucratic robot. Maybe he was related to one.

'Now listen to me. If you cretins have screwed up, and it's not the first time, it's none of my responsibility and I have no intention of signing for anything. I don't expect to receive any such delivery here today. Sort out your own bloody mess. Is that understood?' And Grant ended the call.

'Nice guy,' Luca said.

'Nice job.' Catalina handed over the hundred-euro note, and the rest of the teenagers all resumed their clamouring and clowning around.

'Is that it?' Luca said.

She smiled at Luca. 'That's it. Spend it wisely. *Ciao.*'

Luca was in love. '*Ciao,*' he replied, and stared at her as she walked away.

One less thing to worry about. Maxwell Grant was definitely where Catalina wanted him to be, seventeen short kilometres to the southwest. Now to attend to the other small concern on her mind – but that wasn't something she could do in the middle of town. A few streets away, she managed to flag down a passing taxi driver, who saw the dark-haired beauty waving from the kerb and almost crashed his Fiat stopping for her.

Men.

'Where to, Signorina?' He was unshaven and looked a little crass, but there probably weren't too many other taxis in town and it didn't pay to be fussy.

'Out of town. That way,' she said, pointing southwest.

'You don't know the name of the place?' he said, grinning.

'I'll know it when I see it.'

'Fine by me. Jump in.'

The taxi hadn't gone more than a kilometre past the town limits before the driver was trying to chat her up. Some people were just painfully predictable, she thought, as she listened to his patter. 'Are you from around here? Haven't seen you before, and I'd remember. I'm Roberto. What's your name? You don't talk much, do you? Come on, don't be like that. How about a smile?' Catalina didn't respond to any of it, and kept her eyes on the road. Roberto eventually got the hint, and drove on in moody silence, throwing her the occasional look that she pretended not to notice.

As they travelled inland, the terrain rose rapidly up into the hills and the scenery alternated between patches of thick autumnal forest and open farm country. They passed a couple of villages, and the ruins of an ancient church high on a hill. The mountains of Calabria loomed in the distance. At last, some fifteen kilometres inland, she pointed through the windscreen and said, 'This is fine. You can drop me off here.'

'You're kidding, right? It's miles from anywhere.'

'No, this is the place,' she insisted. 'My fiancé is coming to pick me up.'

Roberto made a face. 'Whatever you say, lady.' He pulled over to the side of the road, waited for her to get out, then took her money and drove off with a last wistful glance and a puff of burnt oil smoke.

It was just after ten thirty in the morning.

Catalina waited until the car was out of sight, then climbed up the grassy verge and over a rickety wooden fence that bounded the field next to the road. Whatever kind of crops had been planted were razed down into a brittle yellowed stubble that crackled underfoot as she made her way over the field perpendicular to the road. Beyond the far side was a patch of woodland that offered the right kind of cover for what she was about to do. There wasn't a house or a living soul anywhere to be seen, but all the same she preferred to avoid prying eyes.

Reaching the trees, she came across the stripped-out shell of an old car that had been abandoned there long ago. She laid her bag on the ground nearby and knelt down to unzip it and take out the gun. Now it was time to allay the other concern that had been nagging at her mind.

Catalina didn't care for guns, or weapons of any sort that could be used to inflict pain and death. She'd never handled one before, until that morning. Still less ever fired one. Even though she'd obviously made a convincing show of pointing it at Avery, she had little idea how it worked, and wished now that she'd paid more attention to all those stupid action films on TV. There was always something to be learned from anything.

The pistol was ugly and black. The part you held, and the part where the trigger was, were made of some kind of very tough plastic, rubberised in places for a better grip. The upper metal part, which to her untrained eye appeared to house the barrel, was square in profile and GLOCK 19 – AUSTRIA was stamped on its left side. Which meant very little to her, except that she supposed that anything manufactured in Austria must probably be well-made and reliable.

A sudden thought made her anxious. It had never occurred to her until now that she should check whether the weapon was loaded. What if it wasn't? How did you tell? She vaguely remembered that the part that held the bullets was separate to the gun and went inside the handle. She'd seen actors in films slamming the thing in there to reload the weapon. After some searching, she found the button that released it, and it dropped out of the handle into her hand: a simple oblong box made of black metal, containing some kind of spring-loaded mechanism that she could see held the bullets in place. There was a name for it – a *magazine*, that was it. It was heavy, and to her relief, it appeared to be fully loaded. Just to make sure, she prised the rounds out one at a time by sliding them forward with her thumb, and they popped out under spring pressure and dropped into her lap. Fifteen of them, each marked in tiny letters on its circular base WIN – 9mm LUGER. They looked small, and it perplexed her that something so tiny could hold enough energy to kill a person. She remembered what Ben had said to her on the island, about the fragility of human life.

Thinking of Ben distracted her for a moment. She sensed that she liked him, even though they'd only just met. He had depth, and intelligence, and an inner strength tempered by a warm tenderness none of the men in her life had shown. Under other circumstances, she'd have liked to have got to know him better. But that wasn't going to happen now. Like a lot of things.

She broke her thumbnail squashing the bullets back into the magazine against the stiff spring tension, then slotted the loaded magazine into the gun and felt it click into place.

Fifteen seemed like a lot of shots, and she reasoned that she should hold back twelve and use the remaining three for practice, to familiarise herself with how the gun worked. It took a minute or two before she figured out that to chamber a round from the magazine you needed to grip the handle in your right hand with your finger clear of the trigger, while using your left hand to rack back the metal slide, which had serrations to enable a firm hold. The weapon's cold, efficient Austrian functionality and ergonomic perfection were like something that had been designed in a lab, and appealed to her scientific mind. This was a precision instrument she could trust, however much she might have feared and loathed it in any other situation but the one she faced.

All she needed now was to fire it at something. Looking around, her eye landed on the wrecked old car, and she decided it would make a suitable practice target. She stood ten metres away from it and raised the gun two-handed more or less the way she'd seen it done in movies. There was no safety catch to click off. Everything was simple. The sights lined up intuitively and easily. She curled her finger around the trigger. Her heart thumped. Her hands were shaking.

She squeezed. The gun fired, jolting her hand. It was much louder than she'd expected, with a sharp report that hurt her ears. Lowering the gun, she saw the small, clean hole that had appeared in the door skin of the car, more or less where she'd been aiming. She raised the gun again and fired twice more, using the first bullet hole as an aiming mark.

After three shots, there was a high-pitched ringing in her ears. Taking her finger carefully off the trigger and keeping the gun pointed at the ground, she walked over to the car and discovered to her amazement that all three shots had hit inside a circle she could cover with her hand. She saw how cleanly the bullets had punched through the metal, a silver ring around each hole where the paintwork had been knocked away. Creaking the car door open on its rusty hinges, she found that the shots had gone right through the internal plastic and buried themselves deep in the front seats.

The gun's power and ease of use were a little alarming, but pleased her as well, on a scientific level. If it could tear through solid metal like that, it would have no problem penetrating the skull of the evil man who had murdered her friends.

Three rounds gone, twelve to go. Twelve would be plenty. Catalina replaced the gun inside her bag, and then took out her phone to check her GPS bearings one last time.

Maxwell Grant's villa was just a couple more kilometres away. She picked up her bag and started walking back towards the road.

Her heart was no longer thumping. Her hands had stopped shaking.

She was ready.

Chapter Fifty-Four

The road was quiet and lined with trees. The first fallen leaves of autumn littered the verges, and more drifted down from the branches as she walked, like snowflakes. Catalina felt strangely detached, emotionally numb. Empty of thought, as if she were a machine that existed only to carry out this single purpose. As if nothing existed beyond it. As if this moment was the definitive and final act of her whole life.

It was after eleven a.m. when she eventually came to the high, ivied stone wall that seemed to stretch forever along the roadside, and knew that it marked the boundary of Maxwell Grant's estate.

Several minutes later, she arrived at the main gate. Set between tall stone gateposts, the ornate black and gilt cast ironwork loomed over her like the forbidding entrance to a Gothic castle. Brushing aside the ivy that half-covered a plaque set into the wall, she saw the carved lettering that read VILLA CALLISTO. Beside the plaque was a small intercom unit for visitors to announce themselves at the gate. Catalina had no desire to be announced. She pushed at the gate. It was heavy. And locked.

She walked on another few metres, skirting the wall until it half-disappeared behind roadside foliage. She glanced to make sure no cars were coming, then squeezed herself in behind the trees where she couldn't be seen. She laid her bag on the ground at the foot of the wall, taking only the gun which she stuck firmly into the back of her jeans. The wall was at least twice her height, but its rough stonework offered plenty of handholds and footholds. Concealed from the road, she began to climb. It wasn't difficult.

Until she reached a grasping left hand over the top of the wall to haul herself up, and let out a cry of pain and shock as she felt something lacerate her fingers. Managing to heave herself a little higher, she saw that the entire length of the wall was topped with broken glass set into the mortar.

She gritted her teeth and clung on with her bleeding hand while she pulled the pistol out of her jeans and used its butt as a hammer to knock away as many of the jagged spikes as she could reach. It took a lot of hammering to clear an area wide enough to clamber over without disembowelling herself. She hated Maxwell Grant more than ever.

The climb down was much easier, even with just one good hand, and once back on solid ground she found herself at the edge of the villa's heavily wooded estate. Her gashed left hand was bleeding. She tore a strip from her blouse to bind it up, clenched her fist tight to stem the blood and set off through the trees.

The estate was as peaceful as a country park. Now she saw lawns beyond the trees; moments later she caught her first glimpse of the house itself. It was a fabulous place, regal and imposing.

Catalina reached the point where the woods thinned out to nothing and the gardens began, and paused. Leaving the cover of the trees made her feel naked and far too easily visible, but she had no choice but to walk straight up to the house. Her cut hand was throbbing badly. The shakes returned as she set out across the lawns, every muscle trembling and rigid. It was just adrenalin kicking in, she told herself. The body preparing itself for the coming fight. Nothing to worry about. She needed to embrace it, use it.

Closer. And closer still. The house growing larger and more ominous with every step, windows like eyes watching her. Her heart beating faster, her breath coming in short gasps.

The long driveway cut up between the formal lawns and terminated in a classically styled courtyard that ran the width of the villa's facade, surrounded on three sides by a low stone balustrade and tall decorative urns filled with the last of the season's flowers. There was a Rolls-Royce limousine parked in the courtyard, an old model with gleaming coachwork, all sweeping curves and as big as a barge. The house stood majestically at the end of a broad, stepped path that passed between perfectly trimmed ornamental hedges and through an archway flanked by a pair of carved lions on marble pedestals, bigger than life-size, that seemed to follow her with their eyes as she approached.

Catalina reached the villa. She leaned her back against the cool stone wall and closed her eyes.

'Forgive me, Raul,' she said, not for the first time.

Then she took out the gun.

She moved around the side of the house. Froze, hearing a voice.

His voice.

It was coming from inside the villa, and sounded as if he was talking on the phone. She couldn't make out the conversation, because his words were muffled through a window.

Closer. Closer again. Her injured hand had stopped hurting. It was the adrenalin response flooding the body with hormones like dopamine, one of the most effective natural painkillers known to science. But the shakes were worse, uncontrollable, as if she could no longer govern her own body. Her legs felt as if they were going to wash out under her. Panic was just a hair's breadth away. Every molecule of her wanted to take flight, run away and never stop running.

Oh, my God, I can't do this.

Then she saw him, and all her resolve came rushing back into tight, hard focus. He was standing with his back to the window, a broad, wide-shouldered figure in a well-cut silk shirt, talking on the phone inside a room that looked like a study.

She thought, I am going to kill you.

All Grant had to do was turn around, and he would see her standing there on the other side of the window, gun in hand. For a few anxious seconds that felt like minutes, she thought about finding a way inside the house. Then she thought, *No.* Easier just to shoot him from right here. One bullet to shatter the glass. Then the next one, two, three, four, five, whatever it took, for him.

Grant was still talking, apparently so absorbed in his conversation that he was completely unaware of her presence. Catalina willed herself to breathe calmly. She raised the pistol and took aim at him through the window. Her finger curled around the trigger. She lined up the sights, fighting to control the tremors in her hands.

Then a voice close behind her said, 'Drop the weapon.'

Catalina felt something hard and cold press against the side of her head.

Chapter Fifty-Five

Catalina felt her knees go weak and her stomach flip.

'Drop it. Or you die.'

She opened her fingers and the gun fell from her hand. One of the two armed guards who'd come up behind her quickly stooped to pick it up, while the other kept his weapon pointed against her temple.

She bowed her head in defeat and closed her eyes as they grabbed her and yanked her arms forcefully behind her back. Opening her eyes, the room Grant had been in was suddenly empty.

The guard who'd taken her weapon produced steel handcuffs and used them to fasten her wrists behind her. He squeezed the bracelets tight. 'Move it,' he commanded, shoving her. The whole time, the second guard's pistol was still trained right on her.

They marched her along the outside of the villa until they came to a side entrance. Catalina was shoved through it, and into the house. It was cool inside. The furnishings were of the same palatial ilk as those with which Austin Keller filled all his homes. The walls were lined with fine silk and hung everywhere with old oil paintings in grand gilt frames. Their footsteps echoed off mosaic floors of black and white marble. The guards yanked her roughly to a halt outside a door. The first guard rapped on it.

A voice – *the* voice – said from inside, 'Come in.'

The first guard opened the door. The second pressed a strong hand against her back and pushed her through it.

The room was a large, magnificent salon. Maxwell Grant was leaning nonchalantly against a tall fireplace. He broke into a generous smile as Catalina entered. 'Miss Fuentes. I must say, this was an unexpected pleasure.' He waved a discreet signal to the guard who'd handcuffed her. The guard unlocked and removed the cuffs, then he and his colleague turned and smartly left the room, shutting the door behind them.

Catalina glanced all around the room. Her eyes locked onto the wall-mounted display of crossed sabres that hung over the fireplace. For an instant, her imagination clouded over with the mental image of her making a rush for one of them, pulling it down and sticking it through Grant's guts before the guards came bursting in and gunned her down.

Grant greeted her like an old family friend. 'Welcome to my humble home. I'd ask to what I owe this surprise visit, but I think we already know the answer to that one, don't we?'

Catalina rubbed her wrists and said nothing. The blood was still seeping through the material wrapped around her injured hand.

'Satellite dish, indeed,' Grant chuckled. 'A worthy effort. Although I'm sorry to say I'm a little disappointed by your lack of knowledge of basic security. You don't imagine the villa would be so vulnerable to intruders, do you? I was watching you from the moment you climbed the wall. How's the hand? I can have it seen to, if you like.'

'Why, does the sight of a little blood bother you?' she fired back at him. 'I didn't realise murderers were so squeamish.'

He raised his eyebrows in mock surprise. 'Murderer? Says the intruder who invaded my property carrying a loaded pistol, with the obvious intention of shooting an unarmed man in the back.'

'Kinder treatment than you deserve. It would have been far too quick and easy a death for you.'

'Please,' he said, motioning to the luxurious armchairs and settees that filled the room. 'Won't you take a seat? You must be tired after your journey. I won't ask where it is you've been keeping yourself hidden away all this time.'

Catalina didn't budge from where she stood, looking him fiercely in the eye. 'Somewhere you and your paid scumbags would never have found me,' she said. 'Not in a hundred years of trying.'

'Then it would seem that you've saved me an awful lot of time and trouble, haven't you?' Smiling, Grant walked over to an antique sideboard and flipped open a lid to reveal a hi-fi system inside. 'Some music, I think,' he said, putting on a CD. 'Ana Vidovic performing Albéniz's *Asturias*. I listen to it often, and think of you. Although, as wonderful as she is, I don't think she's half the player you could have become, if you'd wanted to.' As the opening notes of the classical guitar piece sounded over hidden speakers, slow and melodious at first, Grant walked over to an armchair and stretched out in it with a contented sigh.

'You look more radiant than ever, by the way,' he said, gazing at her the way he might have gazed at one of the expensive oil paintings on his walls. 'You've evidently been taking good care of yourself. Or someone has. I admit it, I'm jealous. Who's the lucky man?'

369

'What makes you so sure there has to be a man involved?'

'A woman like you? Don't make me laugh. I can't have been your only secret admirer. Which I have to confess to having been for quite some time. In fact, if I hadn't been so foolishly bedazzled by your presence that evening we met, I might have watched my tongue, instead of blabbing like a schoolboy and letting you realise that I knew a little too much about you, and that our meeting was anything but a chance encounter. What can I say? I'm sure you have that effect on most men.'

'Please. You're making me sick.'

'We're all human. Even murderers have feelings.'

'So you're admitting it now,' she said.

'What I am is a businessman. A strategist, a pragmatist. Like you. We're not so different, you and I.'

'Now you're really going to upset me.'

'It's nothing to be ashamed of; far from it. We do whatever is necessary to achieve our goals. Mine is primarily to make money, while yours is to pursue scientific truth. But essentially, it's all much of a muchness. I don't take it at all personally that you came here today to kill me. You tried to do what you felt was required, under the circumstances. Just as you engineered that little piece of theatre of yours in July. Which was a neat bit of work, by the way. You certainly fooled the world at large, even if you didn't succeed in pulling the wool over everyone's eyes.' He paused. 'The problem with faking your own death is that nobody will notice when it happens for real.'

'If you're going to kill me, then do it now. If you've got the balls.'

'Perish the thought. I wouldn't dream of curtailing my chance to spend some time with such a beautiful and brilliant woman. It's just you and me, until our visitor arrives.'

He saw the flash of puzzlement in her expression, and looked pleased by it. 'That's who I was speaking to on the phone before, to inform them you were here,' he explained. 'He's en route from London even as we speak, and very much looking forward to meeting you in person.'

Catalina said nothing. She darted another glance at the crossed sabres over the fireplace. They suddenly seemed very far away and out of reach. Her hand began to throb painfully as the blood pulsed faster with the racing of her heart.

'You surely didn't think I was alone in this, did you?' Grant said with a grin. 'You and your friends drew the attention of far more powerful and influential people than I. I'm only the middleman, the errand boy, who simply does what he's told. The sanctions come from above.'

'Just obeying orders,' she said mockingly. 'Of course. I should have guessed that you didn't have the brains to do anything like this on your own.'

'Oh, I have my ways and means, and muddle along not too badly in general,' he said. 'They don't place their confidence in just anybody, you know. Though I'll admit, between you and me, that you had us all rattled there for a while. My associates were less than impressed with me for allowing you to slip through our fingers as carelessly as I did. Now you're back, you've done wonders to restore their faith in me. I should thank you. They're not the kind of people one wishes to make a habit of disappointing.'

'And naturally, you let them think it was you who found me, rather than the other way round.'

Grant shrugged. 'It doesn't always pay to tell the truth, the whole truth and nothing but. Sometimes it's wiser to keep your mouth shut. A lesson you and your friends would have benefited from.'

'We're scientists. We tell the truth. That's what we do, come what may.'

'What, you don't think there are plenty of your fellow scientists who keep the "truth" to themselves and say what they're paid to say? That's how it works in the real world, my dear girl. Even Galileo realised that, eventually. And I would be very, very surprised to think you didn't already know it perfectly well.'

'So what did these high-powered employers of yours pay you to kill my team, Maxwell?'

'Not a penny. Let's just say we came to an arrangement that serves our mutual business interests. But you shouldn't do yourself down, my dear. This wasn't about the others. *You* were always the star attraction, from the beginning. You were the one the world would have listened to, if we'd allowed that to happen. The others were just collateral damage. Their fates were sealed the moment you involved them. Moths to a candle.'

His words shook her deeply, but she refused to let him see it. 'That's where you're wrong, Maxwell,' she said in a strong voice. 'It's not just about me at all. Killing me won't end this. You're forgetting that Steve Ellis is still out there. *He's* the candle, still burning away where you can't hope to get to it to snuff it out. There isn't anyone who knows more about our research than Steve does. He was doing this ten years before I was even born. And when he broadcasts the truth to the millions of people who follow him, there won't be a hole in the ground you and your sick little associates will be able to hide in, or a rock that you can crawl under. He'll bury you all.'

Maxwell Grant listened pensively as she talked, and when she'd finished he gave a thoughtful nod. 'Funny you should have mentioned deliveries here to the villa,' he said.

'As it happens, I received one earlier this morning. Not a satellite dish,' he added with a chuckle. 'Something much more interesting, I think you'll agree. Here, let me show you.'

He stood, walked past her to the door and opened it. The two guards who had caught her were still standing outside in the corridor, along with two others. Grant had a quick, quiet word with them, and one of them hurried off. Catalina heard his footsteps ringing on the marble floor. The guard returned a few moments later, holding something square and brown. It was a cardboard box, cubic in dimensions, about eighteen inches tall and wide, wrapped with packaging tape that had been neatly slit along the top flaps. Grant took the box from him and carried it into the room, setting it down on a table.

'Come,' he said pleasantly to Catalina, beckoning her over. 'Go ahead. Take a look inside.'

She hesitantly approached the table, and he stepped back to let her get closer. She reached out her good hand and tentatively grasped the edge of one of the box's flaps and pulled it back so she could peer inside.

Inside the box was Steve Ellis's severed head. His eyes stared glassily into hers, like a dead mackerel's.

Catalina screamed.

Chapter Fifty-Six

After the Alitalia B737 touched down at Brindisi Airport at eighteen minutes past midday, Ben was one of the first passengers off the plane. Then, after the frustration of passport control, he collected his bag and left the airport at a run.

Outside, he took out the phone to check it once more. Not his own smartphone, but one of those he'd taken from the dead men at Catalina's observatory. Specifically, it was the one loaded with the software to mate up with the tracking device he'd found attached to the rental Kia, which had enabled the hired guns to tail them there from Munich.

The GPS tracker was a high-end professional piece of kit, capable of monitoring its target anywhere in the world. Ben was no hoarder, but nonetheless, handy gadgets like that weren't something you threw away. You never knew when you might find a use for them. Which was exactly what he had done after his conversation with Catalina on the beach on Icthyios. The things she'd said had troubled him so much that, later that afternoon, he'd slipped up to her quarters at the top of the lighthouse and hidden the homing device in the lining of her travel bag.

A gamble, based on pure instinctive guesswork, but it had paid off. He'd been following the moving red dot on his virtual map from the moment she'd escaped. Without it, he would have had no way of knowing she was heading for Italy. And without knowing that, he'd have had no proof of his suspicions that she was going after Maxwell Grant.

But it wasn't all good news. Even as he'd been sitting impatiently in the departure lounge on Karpathos waiting for the earliest flight he could get to Italy, he'd noticed that the little red dot had stopped moving. It was still in exactly the same place now.

It could mean that she'd found the tracker in her bag and ditched it. Or, as he feared, it could mean that she had reached her destination. And that worried him very much indeed, because the location of the dot was over two hundred kilometres southwest of his own.

Right country, wrong place. If southern Italy was shaped like a pointy high-heeled boot, he was right on the heel, and Catalina was near the ball of the foot, all the way down there in Calabria.

Calabria, where she'd said Maxwell Grant's villa was.

Where the signal had come to a standstill.

Well over an hour ago.

Ben didn't want to think about what could happen in that time.

From where he was standing outside the airport terminal, he could see part of the ubiquitous car rental offices poking out from behind the buildings. Even assuming he wasn't banned for life by every hire company on the planet, minutes spent signing forms and fussing over insurance agreements were minutes he should be spending closing the gap between himself and Catalina Fuentes, as fast as possible. Faster.

He needed speed. Public transport was out of the question. Following Catalina's example and hijacking a business jet from the private terminal wasn't a practical option.

But as Ben stood facing the airport car park, gazing around him for inspiration, suddenly, staring him right in the face, was the very next best thing. Its roof was so low off the ground that he almost missed it behind the other cars parked around it. The wide-bore twin exhausts pointed at him out of the bright yellow carbon-fibre bodywork like the barrels of a sawn-off shotgun. As he walked towards it, he could read the name LAMBORGHINI in curly chrome lettering between its wide-set taillights.

A petrol-head was one of the many things Ben was not. But even he couldn't fail to appreciate the nearest road-going equivalent of a Learjet. Especially when the road-going equivalent of a Learjet was the very thing he most needed at the moment – though the Lamborghini's open-roof cockpit looked more like something copied from a fighter aircraft.

The only problem was the one slouched behind the wheel, puffing on a cigarette with one gold-braceleted arm dangling over the sill. He could have been a drug dealer hanging around the airport to score a deal, or just a rich boy grabbing a quick smoke while waiting to pick up his girlfriend. Ben didn't much care either way.

'Nice car,' he said to the guy in Italian, walking over. 'Mind if I borrow it?'

The guy lolled his head to peer casually up at Ben through his wraparound shades. He puffed a cloud of smoke and said, 'Get the fuck out of here, *cazzone*.'

Ben was pleased to hear such vulgar profanity. The more offensive, the better. It made what he was about to do morally easier to bear. 'I'll take those cigarettes, too,' he said, pointing at the soft pack of Camels on the passenger seat, next to the guy's leather wallet. 'You can keep the shades, though. I don't need to look like a complete tool. That's your department.'

'Why would you want my car?' was all the response the guy could muster, gaping at Ben in open-mouthed stupefaction.

'Because my need is greater than yours, and because you're not going to stop me,' Ben said. 'Now, it's up to you how we do this. You can get out nicely, hand over the keys and promise not to report this to the boys in blue. Or we can do it less nicely. Which means you wake up some time tomorrow in the hospital and start the whole painful process of learning to walk again. What's it to be?'

The guy goggled mutely at Ben for a couple more seconds before he decided to go for the non-hospital option.

'Leave the wallet,' Ben said. 'Except for whatever cash is in it. That way I have your name and address, in case you forget the part about not calling the cops.'

The guy climbed shakily out of the car, and dropped the keys into Ben's palm. Ben almost felt sorry for him, but not quite. 'It's just stuff,' he said as he took his place behind the wheel.

Ben slid one of the Camels from the pack, lit it up with his Zippo and sucked hard on the smoke. It wasn't a Gauloise, but you couldn't have everything. Then he stabbed in the key, and fired up the engine with an exhaust blast that was only about half as loud as Austin Keller's jet taking off at close quarters, and all but drowned out the scream of the tyres as the Lamborghini did a reverse powerslide out of the parking space. Ben slipped the stubby gearstick into first, punched the gas and the car took off like a spurred horse, leaving its owner standing desolate and on the brink of tears, still clutching the cash from his wallet.

Two hundred kilometres to cover. No time to do it in.

Ben clutched the tiny racing wheel and got ready for the wildest drive of his life.

Chapter Fifty-Seven

Maxwell Grant had the box taken away by the same guard who'd brought it. 'Now you understand,' he told Catalina. 'You really are completely on your own.'

She was still shuddering from the horror of what she'd seen, and her stomach was cramping so badly she had to clutch at it. It was all she could do not to vomit. 'I should have killed you,' she whispered.

'Life is full of missed opportunities,' Grant replied with a smile. 'You had your chance. Fluffed it.'

'Don't start feeling too safe. If I don't come back, my brother won't rest until you get what's coming.'

'I'm well aware of Raul's fiery temperament,' Grant said. 'It seems to run in the family, doesn't it? It would have been so much easier for him if he'd simply accepted that his sister had committed suicide, as your parents and everyone else did. He could just have gone on living the same simple schoolteacher's life in that peaceful little town. Married a nice girl and raised a family, and lived to a ripe old age.'

Catalina stared at him with a boiling hatred she'd never thought herself capable of.

'You look at me as if I were the villain here,' Grant said, spreading his hands in earnestness. 'If we believed for a second your brother could be reasoned with, don't you think we'd do anything we possibly could to avert further grief to your family? Reckless behaviour like his just forces our hand. He's brought it all on himself. For heaven's sake, I'm running a business here. I can't have a wild man running loose and bringing on board mercenaries to decimate my employees.'

It took Catalina a moment to realise who Grant was referring to. 'Ben isn't a mercenary. He's Raul's friend.'

'Then God help Raul. Men like this Hope don't have friends. They're loyal only to the highest bidder. All it would take to turn him against your beloved brother would be a pocketful of money. And money's something we have no shortage of.'

'You don't know him,' she said. 'He wouldn't do that.'

'Actually, I think we have a rather better idea than you do. We know all there is to know about your Major Benedict Hope. And if you knew even half of the bloody little exploits he was involved in during his time on the dark side of Special Forces, things so ugly that the records don't even officially exist, then believe me, you'd be more afraid of him than you are of us. He's the kind of killer who gives killers a bad name.'

'Then you should be afraid too,' she said.

'Though, strangely, I'm not,' Grant replied. He looked at his watch. 'Now, as much as I'm enjoying your company, I have some calls to make before our visitor arrives. He'll be here in less than an hour. In the meantime, my men will show you to a guest room, where you can freshen up and prepare yourself for your journey later.'

The nonchalant way he said it chilled her through. 'Where are you taking me?' she asked.

He smiled. 'It's a surprise.'

The guards escorted Catalina through the sumptuous villa and up a marble staircase to a first-floor bedroom, where they pushed her inside and locked the door. Peeping through the keyhole, she could see one of them standing sentry outside. Moments later, a second stationed himself below the window, armed with a black rifle-like weapon and cutting off any chance she might have had of climbing down the ivied wall and escaping over the lawns.

Feeling hollow and too utterly exhausted even to cry, Catalina went into the adjoining ensuite bathroom and washed the blood from her wounded hand. A first aid kit had been left out for her, with the bandages pre-cut into strips and the scissors removed. She could see nothing else that might work as an improvised weapon. Not unless she smashed the mirror and turned a piece of broken glass into a knife. In which case, the best thing to do with it might just be to cut her own throat.

Catalina stood for a long time and stared at the mirror, and seriously thought about it.

No. Whatever happened, whatever awful thing they had in store for her, she had to preserve her dignity to the last.

She went back into the bedroom and slumped on the bed. 'I'm so sorry, Raul,' she said out loud. 'I tried. I really did.'

At that moment, the Lamborghini was hurtling along the autostrada like a bright yellow rocket fired from a launcher. Ben was frantically overtaking everything in front of him, his reflexes working right on the edge of sensory overload as the speedometer flirted with heights of over three hundred kilometres an hour. At that howling, screaming mad speed he couldn't snatch his eyes off the road to glance in the rearview mirror for more than a tiny fraction of a second. When he did, he kept expecting to see distant blue lights flashing in his wake. He must have triggered a thousand speed traps already, and it was just a question of time before the Polizia Stradale decided to hook and reel him in. Let them even try.

Speeding west from Brindisi, he'd sliced diagonally across the heel of Italy from coast to coast. Now he was curving southwards and skirting the Gulf of Táranto, which meant he was almost halfway to where he needed to be, and still not going fast enough, not even in a road-going missile that he'd learned from practical experience could accelerate from a standstill to two hundred kilometres an hour in under seven and a half seconds.

Two big articulated long-haul freight trucks were up ahead, coming up so quickly that they could have been standing still, or even reversing towards him. He swore as one of them pulled out lazily into the overtaking lane to lumber past the other, taking its time. Two abreast, they filled the road right in Ben's path, and he had neither the luxury nor the intention of slowing down for them.

A racing downshift of the six-speed box, and the all-wheel drive bit down even harder on the road and the mid-mounted V12 engine howled behind him as he stamped down on the pedal and aimed the nose of the car right for the gap. It felt like diving a fighter jet into a canyon tight enough to scrape his wingtips on both sides. For a terrifying moment, the looming sides of the trucks were like huge walls closing in on him and he didn't think he was going to make it. He gritted his teeth and kept his foot down hard, and then he was through and screaming out the other side and leaving them behind like two children's toys shrinking in his mirror.

Another life gone. It was a good way to keep the heart in shape.

The first rule of strategic planning was to have some kind of plan. Ben had none. None at all. He didn't know what he was going into. He didn't know what he was going to find when he got there. He didn't even know if he was going to get there in time. All he knew was that he had to keep moving like a rifle bullet. Nothing could be allowed to stop him. They could put up a roadblock, and it wouldn't even slow him down. They could call in an air strike, a tank division or a long-range massed artillery barrage to blow up the damn road under his wheels. And even then, he'd keep going.

'Hold on, Catalina,' he muttered. But the howl of the engine and the blast of the wind ripped the words out of his mouth.

He was going to find her again. And when he did find her, dead or alive, then somebody was going to have a very, very bad day.

Chapter Fifty-Eight

When Catalina heard the sound of the approaching helicopter, she rose from the bed and went over to the window. The guard was still on sentry duty down below, but now he was facing the grounds of the villa to watch the sleek silver chopper come in to land.

It came in over the trees and descended over the lawns, coming to rest at the centre of a circle of grass flattened by the downdraught of its rotors. As the skids touched down, the pilot slackened off the throttle. Moments later, Catalina saw the hatch open and the passenger step down. Maxwell Grant and two of his men she hadn't seen before came from the house to meet the visitor.

He was small, thin, and even at a distance he appeared much older than Grant. Old, but not bent. His white hair was blowing in the wind from the chopper. He was wearing a dark suit. Grant had put on a navy blazer and a tie, as a mark of respect for his superior. Watching, Catalina noticed that it wasn't returned. When Grant offered a handshake, the old man ignored it and instead started leading the way towards the house, as if he naturally assumed command of the situation.

She wondered who he was, and couldn't help but shudder.

Her door lock clicked open, and the guard who'd been

standing out in the corridor stepped into the room and motioned for her to come with him. Catalina followed him in silence, as composed as she could make herself act. It was the walk to the gallows. There was nothing else she could do. Run and hide somewhere in the villa?

The guard led her back downstairs to a different room, showed her inside without a word and closed the door behind her. Maxwell Grant was waiting for her there, together with the old man from the helicopter.

The visitor looked even older, close up. He was half Grant's width and stood no taller than his shoulder. His thinning white hair was slicked and patted back into place. He was gazing dispassionately, yet intently at her with pale eyes that never blinked. A bloodless little smile crinkled the corners of his mouth.

'So you're Maxwell's boss,' she said, forcing the tremor out of her voice. 'I was expecting someone a little more impressive. Less moribund.'

The old man stepped forward. He seemed to disregard Grant's presence completely, like an underling of such lowly status as to barely exist. 'My name is Braendlin,' he said, in a voice as dry as sand and devoid of any kind of accent. It wasn't English, and it wasn't American, and it wasn't European or South African or from anywhere else. As if the old man had no nationality at all, and belonged on some transcendent plane where those concepts were immaterial.

'I'm here on behalf of my group of associates,' he continued, 'the rest of whom weren't able to make it at such short notice. It's a pleasure to make your acquaintance at last, Cassandra. One that, regrettably, is destined to be short-lived.' A twinkle appeared in those pale eyes, but it wasn't one of warmth or charm.

Cassandra. For a moment, Catalina thought he was getting

her name wrong, and had the strange impression of being a small child again, meeting an elderly and slightly demented grandfather who had trouble remembering. But then she realised it was no mistake.

'What did you call me?'

The thin smile again. 'It's the name on your file. Rather apt. A little too apt, in fact, which was why I personally didn't give it my vote when it was first proposed. It's less than perfect intelligence tradecraft for a codename to reveal even a hint of the nature of an operation. But there it is. Times change.'

'Operation? Intelligence? Who the hell *are* you?'

'I'm afraid that's not for me to say. I'm here simply to verify that the person standing before me is indeed the individual known to us as Cassandra. Some things are too important to take anyone's word for.' Braendlin threw a brief glance back at Grant, acknowledging his presence for the first time since Catalina had entered the room. Grant shifted uncomfortably.

Catalina felt a surge of emotions rising up inside her that she couldn't stem. 'Why are you doing this to me?' she burst out. 'What harm did any of us ever do to you people?'

Braendlin looked at her coldly. 'Are you asking me for an explanation?' He considered for a moment, then made a small gesture and said, 'Very well. I'm a believer in granting the condemned man – or woman, as the case may be – a final wish before sentence is carried out. I can understand that as assiduous a seeker of knowledge as you wouldn't want to depart this earth without knowing why. So let me explain, and in the process perhaps help you to understand the necessity of these very unfortunate circumstances.'

He paused, the pale eyes unflinching, seeming to peer right through her. 'First, let me tell you a story. It's one you're no doubt already familiar with, being an educated woman. Cassandra was a princess of Troy. Daughter of King Priam and Queen Hecuba, sister of Paris. Blessed by the god Apollo with the gift of prophecy – or by mystical snakes, if you prefer to go with that version of the tale. Either way, the legend tells that Cassandra was able to foretell the future. This was a talent that she tried to put to good use when the besieging Greek army, defeated in their attempts to take the city of Troy, resorted to ruse and deception. When the Trojans woke up one morning to find the Greek forces gone and, left behind in their place outside their fortified gates, an enormous wooden horse, they took it as a peace offering from their enemies and wanted to bring it inside their walls. Cassandra, thanks to her gift, knew better. She realised what the Greeks were really up to, and that a unit of enemy soldiers was hiding inside the horse, waiting for the right moment to slip out and open the gates for the whole Greek army to storm the city. Naturally, she felt obliged to tell the people what she knew, and warned them that on no account should they bring the wooden horse inside.

'But in addition to being gifted, Cassandra was also cursed. After she fell out of favour with Apollo, he cast a spell on her that nothing she foretold would ever be believed. For that reason, many of the Trojan people considered her to be insane, and they refused to listen to her warning. She was ignored, ridiculed, prevented from exposing the truth. Ultimately she would go on to suffer abduction, rape and eventually murder. Not a very nice end for a princess. Things would have gone far better for her, had she kept her mouth shut.'

'But she was right,' Catalina said. 'She knew the truth. She had to say so.'

Braendlin nodded. 'She was indeed right, as the doubters soon found out when the Greeks' deception succeeded and the sack of Troy swiftly ensued. She should have been the heroine, the celebrated saviour of her people. But fortune isn't always kind to the hero. That's true of real life, as well as of mythology. Cassandra paid a heavy price for being the original whistleblower.'

'And I should have kept my mouth shut, too. Is that the point of this little story of yours?'

'Your gift was your devotion to your science. Your curse was that there's no longer any room in the world for idealistic seekers of knowledge. In fact there never really was. Because some kinds of knowledge just cannot be allowed to reach the ears of the ordinary people.'

'Then you're admitting that our climate predictions are right,' she said. 'You know it's going to get colder.'

'Of course we do,' Braendlin replied.

Chapter Fifty-Nine

Catalina just stared at him.

'We've known it all along,' Braendlin told her. 'And a very great amount of effort and resources are expended to keep that information from becoming general knowledge. Hence the great pains we take to persuade the public of the very opposite belief, namely that human activity is causing global warming to occur. It makes for a very effective smoke-screen, as well as being a highly profitable fiction in its own right, as Grant here can testify.'

Braendlin stepped closer to her. He wet his lips with his tongue. It was grey and pallid, like his eyes.

'Now, let me tell you another little story,' he said. 'This one, I doubt you'll be so familiar with, for the reason that only a tiny handful of people in the world have ever been made privy to it. The story goes like this:

'In 2003 the Pentagon commissioned a secret report that outlines the possible worst-case scenario in the event of a major new cooling event, using computer models to predict exactly what might happen and how nations might cope – or not cope. According to the projections, within a decade of the beginning of this new cold era, global food, water and energy resources are drained away. Massive shortages leave millions hungry and desperate. Panic and disorder are not restricted to the public, but extend to the level of government. Neighbouring European states, desperate to aid their populations, are forced to dispute access to shared rivers, oil reserves and whatever agricultural land is still capable of food production. As resources become increasingly restricted and precious, competition sparks off tense rivalry that inevitably escalates into war.

'At which point, the degenerating situation becomes the responsibility of the superpowers to take charge of. The USA radically steps up its role as the world's policeman, declaring a state of emergency across Europe, and mobilising peace-keeping forces to quell conflict and distribute aid to the struggling populations. Back on their own territory, the Americans suffer increasing problems as the US runs out of food and experiences mass migration from poorer countries south of the border. Meanwhile, China faces catastrophe as unprecedented famine begins to kill off the largest population on the planet by the tens of millions. The best efforts of the Chinese government to maintain control of the nation fall apart as civil war breaks out. Desperate, the ruling forces threaten to invade Russia to seize its rich natural gas resources. Chinese warships clash with the US navy in the Persian Gulf over Saudi oil reserves both sides badly need to keep their nations running. Neither the Russians nor the Saudis take kindly to these actions. In Asia meanwhile, both India and Pakistan join the fray, adding more weight to a volatile situation. As tensions continue to escalate, nuclear war between two or more of these rival nations becomes a real possibility, threatening to heighten the already catastrophic situation into an apocalyptic scenario of mutual destruction.'

Braendlin had related the whole account in a calm, matter-of-fact tone, like a science teacher describing some everyday chemical reaction to his class. He paused to gauge Catalina's reaction. She had none, because she was too horrified to speak.

Braendlin went on. 'Perhaps now, Miss Fuentes, you begin to understand? It goes without saying that the public at large is completely unaware that these future scenarios are being seriously discussed behind the scenes. And it's imperative that this situation be maintained for as long as we possibly can. If even a hint of what you and I both know to be the real climate science of the future were ever allowed to reach a significant audience through the mainstream media, we would very quickly find ourselves faced with a situation of widespread disruption, unrest, even panic. Surges in crime, social violence, looting, riots, would all inevitably result.'

He gave another dry, crackly smile. 'Human beings are capable of doing many things very well, but they're also very prone to irrational behaviour. Our psychological studies suggest that people would not respond well to the news that, within a century or less, humanity could be facing an unprecedented threat to its very survival. People believe in people. It's a human need. They want to believe we'll be here forever – or at least, for a billion years, which is close enough to forever in the minds of ordinary citizens. They don't want to think that their future children, or their children's children, might be doomed to witness, first-hand, such terrible pain and suffering as their world is destroyed around them. For billions of people across the globe, the burden of that knowledge will simply be too great.

'We are in the business of maintaining order,' Braendlin continued in an emphatic tone. 'Whatever the world's rulers – and I am not referring to democratically elected leaders, but the *actual* rulers – might be discussing behind closed doors, as far as the public are concerned, it's business as usual for the next billion years. The future must appear relatively stable and predictable, or else the very fabric of social order will unravel at the seams and we will descend into chaos, rapidly followed by the global economy. The effects at all levels could be catastrophic, the human cost untold. Do you really want to be responsible for that, Miss Fuentes?'

'But what about the truth? I don't care what you say. People have a right to know about their own future.'

'The truth,' he said, shaking his head. 'What was it Winston Churchill said? "In wartime, truth is so precious that she should always be attended by a bodyguard of lies." And we are at war, always. Truth is a virtue we can't afford, and seldom have done throughout history.'

'So you would murder innocent people in cold blood, just to keep that information quiet.'

Braendlin said, 'By the middle of this century there will be an estimated nine billion people on the planet. A handful of lives is a small price to pay for long-term global political and social stability. Our job is to protect the greater good, by whatever means necessary, in a practical and expeditious fashion. Don't take it personally.'

'You people are nothing more than vermin,' Catalina said.

For the first time in Braendlin's presence, Grant spoke up. 'For all your cleverness at sniffing out the truth, Catalina, you still haven't the first idea what's really going on. Kester Holdings, for instance. Not ringing any bells? Didn't think so.' He chuckled. 'I don't just make wind turbines, you know. And it's not only the so-called sustainable energy technologies that stand to do well out of the war on fossil fuels. Whether they're aware of it or not, our little Green friends are a great boon to the nuclear industry. As a matter of fact, what you and your kind would never cotton onto in a thousand years, because you're all so utterly clueless, is that the current Green fad was devised only as a long-term strategy to promote nuclear power to all the same people who kicked up a stink and thought they were being clever getting rid of it years ago. For now, let them think they're saving the world with their electric cars and their solar panels and their windmills. When we've milked that for all the billions we can get, we'll turn around and say, "Sorry, folks, this whole renewable energy idea isn't working, because we're going to need ten million more turbines to provide enough energy for Europe's population alone, and there isn't enough battery power available on the planet to store all the terawatts of juice. Still want to keep sucking up all that electricity? Fine, let's build you a bunch of nice new nuclear plants instead." By then, yours truly will have made a gigantic pile of money out of these fools. Then when we dismantle all the wind farms and go back to building power stations in their place, I'll *still* be making more money than ever before with Kester Holdings, because we've just spent the last twenty years becoming the go-to guys for companies with a mountain of radioactive waste to dispose of on the cheap, nice and easy, no red tape, no questions. The nuclear gold rush is a-coming, and we are waiting with open arms.'

It took a moment for Catalina to grasp the enormity of what Grant was saying, and understand the deeper game. 'All this time,' she said. 'You were working both sides. Playing the big environmentalist while you were filling the earth with poison.'

'It all has to go somewhere, doesn't it? It's the cost of doing business, and business is excellent.'

She shook her head in disbelief. 'You hypocritical bastard. Even you couldn't be this immoral.'

Grant laughed. 'A mere ninety grams of CO_2 per kilowatt

hour of electricity produced, immoral? What do you mean? Didn't you know that nuclear energy is the last great hope of mitigating man-made climate change? I'm a bloody hero. But enough about the rich, philanthropic Mr Grant,' he said, seriously. 'Let's talk about the late, lamented, and soon to be even more so, Miss Fuentes.' He looked at his watch. 'Four hours from now, there's a shipment of waste scheduled for disposal eighty kilometres off the Italian coast, north of Naples. Only a small cargo, bread and butter stuff, a little over five hundred barrels that will soon be sitting pretty on the ocean bed. And, as much as it pains me to say it, you, my lovely, will be sealed up inside one of them. Your final journey will be to the bottom of the Tyrrhenian Sea.'

'I hope you get cancer.'

'Dear me, what an ugly thing to say. I'm not offended, though. I'm still going to leave it up to you whether you want to take the last plunge dead, or alive. A quick bullet in the head before they stick you in the barrel like so much garbage? Or a slow, tortured asphyxiation alone in the darkness, in return for a little extra time in this world? Your choice. No need to decide this minute – you'll have a few hours to think about it on the road. Just tell my men which it's to be, when you get there, and they'll make sure that your final wish is honoured. You have my word on that.'

The meeting was over. They escorted her outside. Braendlin led the way, Grant walking behind Catalina with a heavy hand on her shoulder as they followed the path from the house, through the archway flanked by the stone lions and into the walled courtyard. A plain black panel van had pulled up to park beside the stately Rolls-Royce. The van's engine was running. Two of Grant's men were sitting in the front, and two more waited nearby, holding large automatic weapons. It looked as though they were set to accompany her on the drive north. At Grant's signal, the men opened the van's rear doors.

Catalina started to shake.

Seeing his employer emerge from the villa, Braendlin's pilot had started up the helicopter. The turbine was building up speed, its wind scattering the autumn leaves that had drifted over the lawn.

They paused in the courtyard. Braendlin turned to Catalina with a curt nod. 'Goodbye, Cassandra. I wish I could bid you farewell. But that would be inappropriate, under the circumstances.'

Catalina said nothing. She looked into the old man's eyes and wondered where that kind of cold evil came from.

And then, right in front of her, Braendlin's head burst apart.

Chapter Sixty

Ben left the hot, ticking Lamborghini at the roadside and checked the GPS one last time. The little red dot still hadn't moved. Its location was almost exactly the same as his own. Whatever else that meant, this was definitely the place.

Judging by the length of the perimeter wall, there was a very sizeable estate on the other side. Ben walked over to the tall iron gates. They were locked shut. He thought about getting back in the Lamborghini and using that to ram his way through. But lightweight mid-engined sports cars with flimsy carbon-fibre bodywork didn't make the best assault breacher vehicles. Plus, he couldn't think of a noisier, less unsubtle way to telegraph his arrival to the people inside.

He walked along the wall, inspecting it for ease of climbing. That wasn't the hard part. The hard part was not being seen. Which was what drew his eye to the trees a few metres the other side of the gates, screening part of the wall from the road. The perfect place to scale the wall. And Ben now realised that someone else had had the same idea. A leather travel bag was lying there in the grass. It looked expensive, and familiar. He unzipped it, felt in the lining and found the homing device still exactly where he'd hidden it.

Ben started climbing. When he reached the top of the

wall, he guessed that the same someone who'd left the bag had also used some kind of tool to chip away all the shards of broken glass set into the mortar. The butt of a pistol would do the job fine. There were specks of dried blood on the stonework. He could only hope nothing worse than a cut finger had happened to her since.

On the other side of the wall, Ben dropped down among the trees that lined the estate's perimeter. He stood very still, listening. He could hear the sound of a helicopter motor in the distance, the unmistakable rhythmic whoosh-whoosh of rotor blades beginning to spin and the rising note of the turbine powering up in preparation for takeoff.

Then Ben heard another sound, this time much closer by. The crack of a twig. He wasn't alone among the trees.

Ben saw the guard before the guard saw him. He was in his thirties, nondescript, dressed in dark clothes. His main feature of interest, as far as Ben was concerned, was the Colt M4 carbine dangling from his shoulder on a tactical sling. Ben wondered if Maxwell Grant always had armed men patrolling the perimeter, or whether this was a special security measure that might have something to do with Catalina being there. And the chopper, possibly.

Ben stepped out from behind a tree and said, 'Hey, have you got a light?'

Before the guard had time to react, Ben hit him a powerful snapping punch to the chin that knocked him instantly unconscious. Ben caught him as he fell, lowered him gently to the grass, then knelt beside him and compressed the veins and arteries in his neck to choke off all the blood to and from his brain. He held the blood choke for a full minute, counting off the seconds and listening to the chopper growing louder as the rotor neared takeoff speed.

When the guard was dead, Ben picked up his rifle.

Standard 5.56mm NATO chambering, thirty-round capacity, Trijicon ACOG optical sight with fixed 4x magnification. The kind of military combat rig not generally found in any old Italian country estate. He jacked a round into the chamber and crept through the trees until he could see the lawns and the house beyond.

The villa and its manicured gardens were all that Ben had expected them to be, given its owner's evident wealth. He took in the layout at a brief glance, and focused instead on what he could see between him and the house. In the foreground, the chopper was still resting on the grass, but not for much longer. Closer to the house, standing in a low-walled courtyard a few metres from a parked Rolls limousine and a black panel van with its back doors open, stood a group of figures. Ben dropped into a sniper's prone position at the edge of the trees and observed them through the rifle scope.

One of the figures was Catalina. There were two men with her. One was taller and broader and in his fifties, in beige slacks and a navy blazer. Ben was fairly certain he was Maxwell Grant. The other was small, wizened and white-haired, maybe late seventies, maybe older. He was standing nearest to the waiting chopper, and seemed to be saying a last word to Catalina before leaving by air. Whatever he was saying to her, she didn't look happy. It seemed safe to presume that the old man wasn't one of the good guys.

Behind them, it looked as though the two armed guards standing at the rear of the black van, and the two more sitting up front, were waiting for her to get in. It had all the makings of a situation in flux. Something was about to happen.

So Ben decided to move things along. He let the gunsights

centre on Grant, then changed his mind and altered the angle of the rifle a minute degree to take aim at the old man. He made the range about a hundred and seventy-five yards.

It wasn't going to be very subtle. And it was certainly going to be loud enough to get their attention.

Fuck it, he thought. And let off the shot.

The rifle went off with a high-decibel crack that punched his ears. The 5.56 bottlenecked round fires a comparatively light bullet at an extremely high velocity, producing very little recoil. Which meant that at virtually the same instant the shot left the barrel, the lack of muzzle flip enabled Ben to see the bullet impact blow the old man's head half away in a mist of pink spray.

Not too subtle at all. But they had to know he was here sooner or later.

The old man's body slumped to the ground. For a frozen moment that seemed to drag longer than it really lasted, both Maxwell Grant and Catalina stood and gaped at the headless corpse at their feet.

And then all hell broke loose.

The two guards in the van flung open their doors and burst out, while the other two shouldered their weapons, pointing left and right in full-on panic while retreating towards the cover of the balustrade wall. Grant made a grab for Catalina's arm and started dragging her, kicking and struggling, back towards the villa. Ben panned the rifle sights across and lined up on Grant, but Grant was a moving target at two hundred yards and Ben was worried about hitting Catalina, and his hesitation made him jerk the shot. Through the scope he saw the bullet hit Grant in the left shoulder, low and left from what should have been a perfect head shot.

Grant stumbled and nearly fell, and Catalina tore out of his grip and took off at a run. Ben lost sight of her as she disappeared behind the hedge. One of the guards made to run after her. Ben caught his intention, flipped the M4's fire selector to full-auto and drove him back with a rattle of gunfire that ricocheted off the balustrade wall and shattered one of the headlamps of the Rolls. The guards ducked behind the wall and the back of the van.

Ben leaped to his feet and started sprinting towards the villa, firing as he ran to keep them pinned down. The chopper pilot was gunning his throttle to the maximum and taking off in a panic. He was thirty feet in the air when Ben aimed upwards and squeezed off another burst. One second, fifteen high-velocity rounds, straight into the tail rotor. The blades shattered and the helicopter went into a spin as the pilot suffered an immediate and catastrophic loss of control. The wildly gyrating chopper managed to stay airborne for a few seconds; then it careered straight for the courtyard of the villa and crashed into the parked vehicles.

Both the van and the limo were instantly engulfed in flames as the helicopter's fuel tanks ruptured on impact and it exploded. Burning wreckage was hurled in all directions. Two of the guards, too slow to get away in time, were caught up in the incendiary blast. The force of the explosion threw one of them ten feet in the air and slammed him down over the bonnet of the blazing Rolls-Royce. The other bolted from behind the van, arms and torso and head ablaze, made it a few metres and then collapsed.

Ben still couldn't see Catalina. What worried him even more was that he couldn't see the other two guards, either. He sprinted past the burning vehicles, turning his face away from the scorching heat as he ran by. Smoke was pouring thick and black from the blaze. Ben kept running. Between the two lions and through the archway and up the stepped path to the house. There was a heavy blood trail on the ground, splashes and dribbles of bright red leading towards the entrance.

Ben was momentarily distracted by the blood trail when a loud shot blasted out to his left and a crater of masonry blew out of the wall just inches away, stinging him with stone chips. He spun round and saw the guard, face half-blackened, teeth bared in rage and fear, crunching the pump action of a combat shotgun to chamber another twelve-gauge round. Ben fired back from the hip, without aiming. The M4 stitched a ragged line of holes diagonally across the man's chest and sent him spinning and crashing back against the wall of the house, blood spotting the stonework like the flick of a paintbrush. The man slid down the wall, still clutching his shotgun. As his muscles began to twitch in terminal shock, the gun went off, pointing harmlessly into the air. Then it clattered from his hands and his eyes rolled over white, and he slumped over on his side.

Ben threw away his empty rifle, snatched up the dead man's shotgun. Pumped out the spent shell and chambered the next. It was a Mossberg Persuader with a cut-down barrel and a five-shot magazine. Two rounds gone.

Then he stepped around the corner of the villa and saw Catalina. And the other guard, too. He had an arm around her throat and was holding her tightly against his chest as she fought him and lashed back with her feet and tried to grapple his arm away from her. In his other hand was a pistol, pressed to her head.

Chapter Sixty-One

That would have been all the tactical advantage the guy ever needed. He could have yelled, 'Drop the shotgun!', and Ben would have had no choice but to do exactly that, and then the guy could have shot him, after which he could have shot Catalina if he'd wanted.

But the guy didn't do any of those things. Instead he whipped the pistol muzzle away from her head and straightened out his right arm at full stretch to aim it at Ben. Which slightly altered the angle of his body to hers. Not by much. But by enough.

In the black arts of combat shotgunning, something taught at the highest levels, to the most elite practitioners, was called the scalloping shot. It was used only in the most down-to-the-wire close quarter battle situations where bad guys using hostages as human shields had to be taken down in short order. It involved aiming off slightly to use the outer edge of a shotgun's conical spreading pellet pattern to chomp an incapacitating bite out of the visible portion of the bad guy without harming the innocent victim. It was one of the hardest and most high-pressure shots in CQB. Extremely easy to screw up with disastrous results, because if you misjudged the aim-off margin by even an inch or two, you risked destroying both bad guy and hostage in a single blast. Such finesse, coupled with extreme high-speed coordination under stress, was an art that very few people could master.

But Ben Hope was, always had been, one of those people. In the time it took for the pistol to swing his way, for the guy to square his sights up and for his finger to start compressing the trigger against the weight of the gun's mainspring, Ben pulled the shotgun in tightly to his shoulder, intuited the amount of aim-off, and fired. Even as he felt the backward kick of the recoil, he knew his shot had gone home.

The scalloping shot ripped the pistol out of the man's hand, and the man's fingers from their knuckle joints, and most of the flesh and muscle of his arm from the bone, all the way to the shoulder. A high-pitched keening burst from the man's open mouth. Catalina was pale and blinking, and the right side of her face was spattered with blood. Ben racked another round into the gun, moved in fast, pulled her away from the guy and shot him again, centre of mass. The close-range impact smashed him to the ground, dead before his back hit the flagstones.

'Ben!' Catalina opened her arms and slammed into him, embracing him so tightly that he couldn't breathe. He could feel her body shaking with shock and relief and terror and happiness, all mixed into one surging tumultuous emotional release.

'You're safe,' he said, patting her back. 'I've got you. You're going to be okay.' When she let go of him, her eyes were full of tears. He checked her quickly to make sure none of the blood on her was her own. The only damage he could see was the cut to her hand, from climbing the wall.

'Your mother was wrong about you,' he said. 'You're every bit as crazy as your brother is. What the hell possessed you to come here on your own?'

The tears had stopped as quickly as they'd started. She asked, 'Is Raul with you?'

'I left him behind on the island. Took a little persuading.'

'How did you find me?'

'Magic powers,' Ben said. 'Where's Grant?'

'I saw him run inside. He's wounded.'

'How many guards are there in this place?'

'I only counted four,' she said.

'I ran into number five back there in the woods. Then it's just him and us, by the look of it. Stay close. Anything happens to me, you run like hell, okay?'

Together, they doubled back to the doorway inside the villa. The blood trail seemed to thicken as it went, the splots and splashes increasing in size and frequency, smeared here and there as a badly injured man's running footsteps dragged along the floor. The ragged trail led from the entrance, through the formal lobby and up a marble-floored passage, where its uneven path veered right and disappeared under the bottom edge of a closed door.

'I know this room,' Catalina whispered.

Ben took a step back, then a step forward, and the sole of his shoe connected with the solid wood and crashed it inwards.

Maxwell Grant stood alone at the far side of the opulent salon, leaning against the fireplace in the middle of a spreading pool of blood that reflected little rectangles of light from the French window behind him. He was panting heavily, clutching his mangled shoulder.

Catalina stepped into the room. 'I told you, you should be afraid,' she said to Grant. Ben stood at her side, pointing the shotgun.

Grant coughed. 'Go on. Do it. Shoot me, if you dare.'

'Fine by me,' Ben said. He squeezed the trigger. The shotgun went *click*.

'You teach your guys to only load four rounds?' Ben said. He dropped the empty gun on the floor. 'Looks like we'll have to come up with something else for you, Grant.'

'Maybe we should let him choose,' Catalina said. 'He's very imaginative that way.'

'You think you can hand me over to the police?' Grant said in a hoarse rasp. There was blood on his lips. 'Just you try it. No court will ever convict me, not with my connections. I'll never see the inside of a jail. Hear me? I can guarantee it.'

'I know,' Ben said. 'But jail's not what we had in mind.' Stepping over to the fireplace, he reached up and lifted down one of the long, curved swords that were mounted crosswise in an X over the mantelpiece. It was lighter than it looked, beautifully balanced in his hand, and still sharp after so many years. 'Italian cavalry sabre,' he said, admiring it. Then he handed it to Catalina, hilt first.

'You must have read my thoughts,' she said to Ben. She clutched the sabre tightly and looked at Grant.

Ben said, 'Now do what you came here to do, and let's get out of here.'

Grant shrank away as Catalina walked slowly towards him. 'No! No!' he protested, his voice rising to a shrill cry as she kept coming. He staggered back until he was up against the wall and could go no further. 'Please!'

'This is for my friends,' Catalina said. What she did next, she did without hesitation. Grant screamed as she plunged the curved blade of the sabre deep into his gut. She used both hands to push and twist it in all the way, then let go of the hilt and stepped back. Grant's eyes were almost popping from their sockets. Red foam bubbled at the corners of his mouth. He staggered sideways a step, leaving a smear of blood down the silk wall covering. Then he fell to the marble floor, kicking and twitching and clutching at the steel with both hands and trying to pull it out.

Catalina spat on him. 'Rot in hell, you bastard.'

Grant opened his mouth to speak, but all that came out was a glut of dark blood and a gurgling croak. His eyes were already glazing over. His spasmodic movements became weaker and slower, until he went limp and lay still with the sword hilt pointing up like a flag planted on some conquered battleground.

'I think it's time we made our exit,' Ben said, touching her arm. She nodded. They turned away from the dead man and followed his blood trail out of the room, out of the villa.

The crashed chopper was still burning intensely, and the fire had spread all along the hedge. If the wind picked up in the right direction, it might reach the house. Ben walked over to the smoking, blackened body of one of the guards, picked up his fallen pistol and slipped it into his jeans pocket.

'Are we expecting more trouble?' Catalina said.

'Not from these guys,' Ben replied.

Crossing the courtyard, they paused at the corpse of the old man. 'Who was he anyway?' Ben asked.

'One of the secret rulers of the world,' Catalina answered.

Ben looked down at the twisted body. 'Why are these Masters of the Universe types always little blokes?'

She shrugged. 'I'm an astronomer, not a psychologist.'

'Come on, let's go. I have a car outside the gate.'

The two of them walked slowly, side by side, almost like lovers. To face danger and death together was to share the most intimate things. Ben found the Camel soft pack in his pocket, fished out a cigarette and lit up. Maybe he could get used to these.

'What will you do now?' he asked her.

405

'I have a lot of decisions to make,' she said, frowning. 'Like what to say to my family when I see them again. I lied to them and broke their hearts. It's not going to be easy. And I'll have to decide what on earth to do with the rest of my life. I have no job. I have very little money. I don't know what I'll do. Play guitar in the streets for coins, maybe. Actually, right now, that sounds pretty good to me.'

'What about TV stardom?' he said. 'The big revelation to the world?'

She smiled. 'We'll have to see about that. Maybe the world isn't yet ready for the return of Catalina Fuentes. Maybe I'm not, either. One day, perhaps. There's time.' She paused a beat, then asked him, 'Will you call Raul for me? I don't suppose Austin wants to hear my voice, after what I did to him.'

'Of course I will,' he said.

'I might go to stay with him in Frigiliana for a while.'

'I think that's a great idea,' he said. 'Raul will be happy.'

'What about you?' she asked.

'Me?' He shrugged. 'I gave up trying to make plans.'

'Maybe,' she said tentatively, 'maybe you'd like to come to Frigiliana with us. With me, I mean. I'd like that, too.'

He said nothing. They were reaching the gates at the end of the driveway.

'Ben? Did you hear what I said?'

'Cover your ears,' he said. He took out the pistol, shot out the lock and kicked the gates, and they swung heavily open on their iron hinges. The road was quiet and empty, apart from his car parked up on the verge. He walked out of the gate and went to fetch her leather bag from its hiding place at the foot of the wall.

Catalina was gazing at the bright yellow, slightly travel-stained, Lamborghini. 'This is yours?'

'It belongs to a friend,' he said, stowing her bag in the small luggage space in the nose. 'Hop in. Let's take you home.'

'You didn't answer my question,' she said, getting into the passenger side. 'You said you have no plans. I thought, maybe . . .'

Ben just smiled. He tossed away his cigarette, got behind the wheel and started the car.

Read on for an *exclusive*
extract from the new
Ben Hope adventure by

Scott Mariani

The Star of Africa

Prologue

Salalah, Oman

Hussein Al Bu Said stood at one of the tall, broad living room windows of his palatial residence and gazed out towards the sea front. The sunset was a mosaic of reds and purples and golds, cloaking its rich colours over the extended lawns and terraces of his property, reflecting gently off the surface of the pool behind the house, silhouetting the palm trees against the horizon. Beyond the landscaped gardens he could see the private marina where his yacht was moored, its sleek whiteness touched by the crimson of the setting sun.

Ice clinked in his crystal glass as he sipped from it. Pineapple juice, freshly pressed that day. Hussein was a loyal and devout Muslim who had never touched alcohol in his forty-four years. In other ways, he knew, he had not always proved himself to be such a virtuous man. But he tried. God knew he tried. Insha'Allah, he would always do the best thing for his family.

He smiled to himself as he listened to the sounds of his children playing in another room. Chakir had just turned twelve, his little sister Salma excitedly looking forward to her eighth birthday. He loved nothing more than to hear their happy voices echoing through the big house. They were his life, and he gave them everything that he had been blessed with.

'You look as if you're very deep in thought,' said another voice behind him. Hussein turned to see his wife Najila's smiling face.

'And you look very beautiful, my love,' Hussein said as she came to join him at the window. Najila was wearing a long white dress and her black hair was loose around her shoulders. She put her arms around his neck, and they spent a few moments watching the darkening colours wash over the ocean.

Nobody had to tell Najila she was beautiful. She was his treasure, soulmate, best friend. Hussein was a dozen years older, but he kept in good shape for her and was still as lean and fit as the day he'd spotted her and decided she was the one to share his life with. They'd been married just weeks later. Hussein was also about twice as wealthy as he'd been then, even though he'd already been high up in Oman's top twenty. Their home was filled with the exquisite things he loved to collect, but Najila was by far the most wonderful and precious.

Hussein set down his glass and held her tight. He kissed her. She laughed and squirmed gently out of his arms. 'Not in the window,' she said, glancing through the ten-foot pane in the direction of the cluster of buildings that were the staff residence where the security team lived. 'The men will be watching us.'

'I gave them the night off,' Hussein said. 'It's just you and me.' He drew her in and kissed her again.

With typical timing, their embrace was interrupted by the twelve-year old whirlwind that was Chakir blowing into the room, his sister tagging along in his wake. Chakir was clutching the handset for the remote controlled Ferrari, his favourite of the many toys he'd had as recent birthday presents. 'When can I get a real one, like yours?' he was always asking, to which his father always patiently replied, 'One day, Chakir, one day.'

'Please may we watch TV?' Chakir said.

Hussein knew Chakir was angling to see the latest Batman film on the Movie Channel. 'It's nearly time for dinner,' he replied. 'You can maybe watch it later, after your sister has gone to bed.' Chakir looked disappointed. Salma pulled a face, too, and it was obvious that her brother had got her all worked up about seeing the movie.

Najila bent down and clasped both her daughter's hands. 'Why don't you go and look at that nice picture book your father bought you?'

'I can't find it,' Salma said. She had the same beautiful big dark eyes as her mother, and the same irresistible smile when she wasn't pouting about not being allowed to watch TV.

Najila stroked her little heart-shaped face and was about to reply when a loud noise startled them all. It had come from inside the house.

Najila turned to Hussein with a frown. 'What was that?'

Hussein shook his head. 'I don't know.'

'Did something fall over?'

Hussein thought that maybe a picture or a mirror had dropped off the wall in one of the house's many other rooms. He didn't understand how that could happen. He started towards the living room door that opened through to the long passage leading the whole length of the house to the grand marble-floored entrance hall.

Then he stopped. And froze.

The door burst open. Three men he'd never seen before walked into the room. Europeans, from the look of them, or Americans. What was happening?

Najila let out a gasp. Her children ran to her, wide-eyed

with sudden fear. She wrapped her arms protectively around them. Little Salma buried her face in her mother's side.

Without a word, the three intruders walked deeper into the living room. Hussein stepped forward to place himself squarely between them and his family. 'Who are you?' he challenged them furiously, in English. 'What are you doing in our home? Get out, before I call the police. You hear me?'

The oldest of the three men was the one in the middle, solid, muscular, not tall, in crisp jeans and a US Air Force-style jacket over a dark T-shirt. His hair was cut very short, and greying. Probably prematurely. He probably wasn't much older than Hussein, but he had a lot of mileage on him. His features were rough and pockmarked and his nose had been broken more than once in the past. A very tough, very collected individual. He was giving Hussein a dead-eyed stare, unimpressed by all the angry bluster. He reached inside the jacket and his hand came out with a gun. The men either side of him did the same thing.

Najila screamed and hugged her terrified children close to her. Hussein stared at the guns.

'Now, Mister Al Bu Said, this doesn't have to be hard,' said the greying-haired man. So let's take it easy and do it right, and we'll be out of here before you know it.' He had an American accent. He was very clearly the boss out of the three.

'I -What do you want?' Hussein stammered.

'I want item 227586,' the man said calmly.

Hussein's mind wheeled and whirled. How could these men even know about that? Then his eyes narrowed as it hit him. Fiedelholz and Goldstein. This was an inside job. Had to be. He should never have trusted those dirty Swiss dogs with his business. Now that he'd changed his mind about selling, the bastards were betraying him. It was unbelievable.

'I don't know what you're talking about.'

414

The man sighed. 'Sure you don't. Oh well, I guess some people have to be difficult.' And he shot Hussein in the left leg, just above the knee.

The blast of the pistol shot sounded like a bomb exploding. Najila screamed again as she watched her husband fall writhing to the floor, clutching his leg. Blood pumped from the wound onto the white wool carpet.

The other two men stepped over Hussein. One of them put a pistol to Najila's head and the other grabbed hold of twelve-year-old Chakir and ripped him away from his mother. The boy kicked and struggled in the man's grip, until a gun muzzle pressed hard against his cheek and he went rigid with terror.

'Now, like I said,' the older man went on casually, gazing down at the injured and bleeding Hussein, 'this doesn't have to be any harder than it needs to be. You got a safe, right? Course you do. Then I guess that's where you'd be keeping it, huh?' He reached down and grasped Hussein by the hair. 'On your feet, Twinkletoes. Lead the way.'

'Take what you want,' Hussein gasped through clenched teeth as he struggled to his feet. The agony of his shattered leg had him in a cold sweat and his heart felt as if it was going to explode. 'But please don't hurt my family.'

'The safe,' the man said.

'Tell this bitch to quit howling,' said the one with the gun to Najila's head. 'Or I'm going to put one in her eye.'

Hussein looked at his wife. 'It's going to be all right,' he assured her. 'Just do as they say.' Najila's cries fell to a whimper. She closed her eyes, tears streaming down her face, and clutched her trembling daughter even more tightly to her.

Hussein limped and staggered across the room, leaving a thick blood trail over the carpet. The safe was concealed behind a $250,000 copy of a Jacques-Louis David oil painting on the living room wall, *The Death of Socrates*. It was a big wall, and it was a big painting, and it was a big safe too. Sweat was pouring into Hussein's eyes and he thought he was going to faint from the pain, but he managed to press the hidden catch that allowed the gilt frame to hinge away from the wall, revealing the steel door and digital keypad panel behind it. With a bloody finger he stabbed out the twelve-digit code and pressed ENTER, and the locks popped with a click. He swung the safe door open.

'Please,' he implored the leader of the three men. 'Take what's in there and leave us alone.'

'Oh, I'm going to take it, all right. Out of the way.' The grey-haired man shoved Hussein aside, and Hussein fell back to the floor with a cry of pain as the man started searching the shelves of the safe. Stacks of cash and gold watches, business documents and contracts, he wasn't interested in. Just the one item he was being paid to obtain.

He found it inside a leather-covered, velvet-lined box on the upper shelf. When he flipped the lid of the box and saw what was inside, his dead-eyed expression became one of amazement. You had to see it to believe it. 'Bingo,' he said. He took it out and weighed it in his hand for a second, keeping his back to the other two men so they couldn't see what he was holding. He slipped it into the leather pouch he'd brought with him, then slipped the pouch into his pocket. It would be transferred to the locked briefcase later that night, before they got the hell out of Oman never to return.

'Now you have it, go,' Hussein gasped. The agony was burning him up. He was losing blood so fast that he felt dizzy. The bullet must have clipped the artery. The white carpet all around where he lay was turning bright red.

The man stood over him, the gun dangling loose from his right hand. 'Pleasure doing business with you, Mister Al Bu

Said. We'll be out of here in just a moment. One thing, before we go. I need to ask – you wouldn't even dream of calling the cops and telling them all about this, now would you?'

'No! Never! Please! Just go! I promise, no police.'

The man nodded to himself, and a thin little smile creased his lips. 'Guess what? I don't believe you.'

The gunshot drowned Najila's scream of horror. Hussein Al Bu Said's head dropped lifelessly to the blood-soaked floor with a bullet hole in the centre of his forehead.

Then the living room of the palatial family home resonated to another gunshot. Then two more. Then silence.

The men left the bodies where they lay, and made their exit into the falling night.

Chapter 1

Paris

It should have been a simple affair. But in his world, things that started out simple often didn't end up that way. That was how it had always been for him, and he'd long ago stopped questioning why. Some people had a talent for music, others for business. Ben Hope had a talent for trouble. Both attracting it, and fixing it.

Which was the reason he was sitting here now on this chilly, damp November afternoon, parked under a grey sky on this unusually empty street in the middle of this bustling city he both loved and hated, at the wheel of an Alpina BMW twin-turbo coupé that had seen better days, smoking his way through a fresh pack of Gauloises, watching the world go by and the pigeons strutting over the Parisian pavements and the entrance of the little grocery shop across the road, and counting down the minutes before trouble was inevitably about to walk back into his life.

He wouldn't have to wait much longer. It was thirteen minutes past three o'clock, which meant the deadline for Abdel's phone call had been and gone exactly thirteen minutes ago. Precisely as Ben had instructed Abdel to allow to happen. If the Romanians anywhere near lived up to the image that was being painted of them, then such an act of open defiance would not be tolerated. They'd be here soon, ready to do business. And Ben would be ready to put the first phase of his plan into action. It might go smoothly, or then again it might not. That all depended entirely on how Dracul decided to play it. Either way, it wasn't exactly how Ben had planned on spending this brief return visit to Paris.

Naturally, things just couldn't be that simple.

When Abdel's broken deadline was twenty-one minutes old and Ben was two-thirds of the way through his next cigarette, the silver Mercedes-Benz turned sharply in out of the traffic and squealed up at the kerb outside the grocery shop, right across the street from where Ben was sitting. Both front doors opened at once. Two men got out, slammed their doors and converged on the pavement, glancing left and right.

Ben followed them with a watchful eye, and knew immediately that he was looking at the Romanians. They were both in their late twenties or early thirties. One was darker in hair and skin, with sharper features that hinted at gypsy ancestry. The other had more Slavic blood, or maybe Hungarian, with a long face and fairer hair. Ethnic variations aside, they could have been clones: big, heavy, hand-picked from the pages of the rent-a-thug catalogue, dressed to intimidate in leather jackets and big stompy boots and putting on a theatrical air of menace as they walked up to the shop entrance and pushed their way inside.

Dracul's enforcers, come to deliver on their promise of violence, bloodshed and broken bones. They looked more than up to the job. Little wonder they had Abdel and the rest of the neighbourhood spooked.

Ben took a last draw on his Gauloise, crushed the stub into the crowded dashboard ashtray, picked up his bag from the passenger seat and got out of the car. 'Here we go again,' he muttered to himself. Then he crossed the street and walked into the shop after them.